DON'T LOOK DOWN

ALSO BY JENNIFER CRUSIE

Bet Me

Faking It

Fast Women

Welcome to Temptation

Crazy for You

Tell Me Lies

ALSO BY BOB MAYER

The Novel Writer's Toolkit

WRITING AS ROBERT DOHERTY

Bodyguard of Lies

Lost Girls

Area 51

JENNIFER CRUSIE

DON'T LOOK DOWN

BOB MAYER

St. Martin's Press

New York

DON'T LOOK DOWN. Copyright © 2006 by Argh Ink and Robert J. Mayer.
All rights reserved. Printed in the United States of America. No part of this book may
be used or reproduced in any manner whatsoever without written permission except in the
case of brief quotations embodied in critical articles or reviews. For information,
address St. Martin's Press, 175 Fifth Avenue, New York, N.Y. 10010.

www.stmartins.com

Library of Congress Cataloging-in-Publication Data

Crusie, Jennifer.
Don't look down / Jennifer Crusie and Bob Mayer.—1st ed.
p. cm.
ISBN 0-312-34812-6
EAN 978-0-312-34812-0
1. Television advertising directors—Fiction.   2. Motion pictures—Production and
direction—Fiction.   I. Mayer, Bob, 1959–   II. Title.
PS3553.R7858D66 2006
813'.6—dc22   2005044803

First Edition: April 2006

10   9   8   7   6   5   4   3   2   1

For Bob & Jenny
who never gave up on us

Acknowledgments

We would like to thank:

Lisa Diamond, Henry Dunn, Angela Payne, and the cast and crew of *Third Watch* who let Jenny on the set to do research.

The Cherries, who read the forty different versions of the first scene of this book and improved it every time.

Kari Hayes, Corrina Lavitts, Robin LaFevre, Valerie Taylor, Judy Ivory, Deb Dixon, Pat Gaffney, and Heidi Cullinan, who read all or parts of this book in manuscript and gave us feedback, especially Heidi, who gave Pepper the binoculars.

Jen Maler, who put up with both of us for an entire day and took great photographs, and Charlie Verral, who let us use his brownstone as a studio in which Jen could work her magic.

Kari Hayes for running Bob's Web site and Mollie Smith for running Jenny's Web site and the Crusie/Mayer site.

Mollie, again, for running our business always and our lives most of the time.

Meg Ruley for rolling with the punches and representing us beyond the call of agenthood.

Jennifer Enderlin for rolling with the punches and doing an amazing job of editing us.

And everybody at the Jane Rotrosen Agency and St. Martin's Press for their enthusiastic and never-ending support.

Without these fine people, we'd never have made it through.

DON'T LOOK DOWN

1

Lucy Armstrong was standing on the Eugene Talmadge Memorial Bridge when she first spotted the black helicopter coming at her through the sunset.

Based on the rest of her day, that wasn't going to be good.

Twenty feet to her right, her assistant director, Gleason Bloom, ignored the chopper and worked the set like a depraved grasshopper, trying to organize what Lucy had already recognized as her career's most apathetic movie crew. Her gratitude to Gloom for his usual good work was only exceeded by her gratitude that he hadn't yet seen that the movie's stunt coordinator was Connor Nash, now half hidden behind his black stunt van, arguing with a sulky-looking brunette.

Of course, Gloom was bound to notice Connor sooner or later. *I'll just point out that it's only four days,* she thought. *Four lousy days for really good money, we check on Daisy and Pepper, we finish up somebody else's movie, we go home, no harm, no foul—*

Off to the west, the helicopter grew closer, flying very low, just above the winding Savannah River. All around were brush and trees, garnished with swamp and probably full of predators. "The low country," Connor had called it, as if that were a good thing instead of a euphemism for "soggy with a chance of alligator." And now a helicopter—

Lucy rocked back as fifty-some pounds of five-year-old niece smacked into her legs at top speed, knocking her off balance and almost off her feet.

"Aunt Lucy!"

"Pepper!" She went down to her knees, inhaling the Pepper smell of Twizzlers and Fritos and Johnson's baby shampoo as she hugged the little girl to her, trying to avoid the binoculars slung around Pepper's neck. "I am *so glad* to see you!" she said, rocking her back and forth.

Pepper pulled back, her blond Dutch Boy haircut swinging back from her round, beaming face. "We will have *such* a good time now that you're here. We will play Barbies and watch videos, and I will tell you about my Animal of the Month, and we will have a party!" Her plain little face was lit with ecstasy. "It will be so, so good!" She threw her arms around Lucy's neck again and strangled her with another hug, smashing the binoculars into Lucy's collarbone.

"Yes," Lucy said, trying to breathe and hug back, thinking, *Great, now I have to play with Barbies.* She pulled back to get some air and said, "Nice binoculars!" as she tried to keep from getting smacked with them again.

"Connor gave them to me," Pepper said. "I can see *everything* with them."

"Good for Connor." Over Pepper's head Lucy saw the helicopter cut across a bend in the river, zipping through an impossibly small opening between two looming oak trees. *It's heading right for us,* she thought, *and whoever is flying that thing is crazy.* Then Connor raised his voice and said, *"No,"* and she looked over to see the young brunette step up into his face, giving as nasty as she got.

Lucy thought, *Good for you, honey,* and stood up, smiling at Pepper. "But I have to work first, so—"

"I will help you work," Pepper said, clinging to her, her smile turning tense. "I will be your assistant and bring you apples and water."

Lucy nodded. "You will be a *huge* help." She took the little girl's hand and looked back at Connor. After kicking herself twelve years ago for having been so stupid as to marry him, looking at those broad shoulders and slim hips now reminded her why her brain had gone south when she was twenty-two. *Good thing I'm smarter now,* she thought, and looked again.

The way he was talking to the brunette, the way she leaned into his comfort zone, they were sleeping together. And she looked to be about twenty-two.

That must be his target age, she thought. *I should tell Gloom that, he'll laugh.*

Gloom. She looked back toward the set and didn't see him, but the helicopter was now zipping underneath one of the port cranes, then banking hard toward the bridge. Lucy shook her head, trying not to be impressed. The pilot probably had *Top Gun* in permanent rotation on his DVD player. *Whatever happened to the strong, silent type?*

"Aunt Lucy?" Pepper said, her smile gone, her face much too worried for a five-year-old.

"You'll be a *huge* help," Lucy said hastily. "*Huge.* Now, where is your mama—*Ouch!*"

Her head snapped back as Gloom yanked on her long black braid from behind. *"Connor Nash,"* he said, and she dropped Pepper's hand and grabbed the base of her braid to take the pressure off her skull.

"Yeah." Lucy tried to pry her braid out of his hand. "I was going to mention that."

"Really? *When?*"

"As late in the game as possible. Which appears to be now."

"What were you *thinking?*" Gloom glared at her, his gawky form looming beside her.

"Gloom?" Pepper said, and he looked down and let go of Lucy's braid.

"Peppermint!" He picked her up, swooshing her up to hug her, almost getting beaned by her binoculars as he smacked a kiss on her cheek.

Pepper giggled, happy again, and wrapped her arms around his neck.

"I'm *so glad* you're here," she said, strangling him. "We will have a party."

"You bet." Gloom peeled one of her arms away from his windpipe. "Tell you what, go get your mama and tell her we need to make plans. There will have to be a cake—"

"*Yes!*" Pepper said, and tried to wriggle her way to the ground. Gloom set her down, and she was off like a shot, blond hair flying and binoculars bouncing as she headed for the craft services table set up near Connor's van, the source of apples and candy and water bottles and, evidently, her mother.

Lucy frowned up at the sky. "We didn't order a helicopter today, did we?"

Gloom yanked her braid again.

"*Ouch. Stop* that."

"Now about that Aussie bastard," Gloom said.

Down the bridge, Connor looked up at them, distracted by the commotion, and saw Lucy for the first time. His face lit up—*God, he's beautiful,* she thought—and then he started up the bridge to her.

"Connor called and offered us an obscene amount of money to finish this thing and I said no," Lucy said, talking fast so that Gloom wouldn't say, "Hello, dickhead," when Connor reached them.

The brunette went after Connor, catching his arm, and he stopped and tried to shake her off.

Gloom's dark brows met over his nose. "If you said, no, why—"

"And then Daisy called and said to please come down because we hadn't seen her and Pepper in so long, and I said no, I'd send her the money to come visit us. . . ."

The brunette held on, but Connor yanked free, making her stumble back as he came up the bridge, oblivious to the chopper closing in on them. He kept his eyes on Lucy, everything in him focused completely on his objective.

And that's why I married you, Lucy thought.

"So why are we here?" Gloom said.

"Because Daisy put Pepper on the phone and I told her we weren't coming and she cried." Lucy switched her attention back to Gloom. "Pepper's not a crier, you know that, Gloom, but I understand that you hate Connor, so you go tell Pepper we're not staying. Take Kleenex. Meanwhile, I'll explain to Connor why he'll be directing these last four days himself instead of paying us a small fortune to do what we can do in our sleep."

"What?" Gloom said and turned to follow her eyes and saw Connor. "Oh, fuck."

"Be nice," Lucy said. "He—"

She broke off as the bubble-shaped helicopter suddenly gained altitude and swooped over the closest bridge tower, sharp against the red sun. Connor stopped and looked up at it and then got an odd look on his face, anger or surprise, she couldn't tell.

Gloom stepped closer to her as the chopper dived to the middle of the bridge and abruptly slowed, coming to a perfect hover just to the east, well out of the way of the cables that lined the roadway. Then it pirouetted smoothly, moved sideways down the bridge, and to the ground. Pepper came running back from craft services to say, *"Wow,"* as the chopper touched down lightly next to the roadway.

"There's no helicopter on the shooting schedule," Gloom said, frowning. "And that one has—is that a machine gun?"

Lucy peered at the ugly-looking contraption bolted to the right skid. "I think so." She bent to pick up Pepper. "I don't think it's on Connor's schedule either. Look at him."

Connor's shoulders were set as he reversed direction and headed for the chopper, walking past the brunette without even acknowledging she was there until she grabbed his arm again. *Honey, never interrupt him when he's on a mission,* Lucy thought and looked back at the helicopter.

A man got out, ignoring the blades whooping by just over his head, broad shouldered and slim hipped in Army camouflage, with none of Connor's electricity or glossy good looks, just tan and solid in the middle of the noise and wind. He walked forward out of rotor range and halted to look back at the chopper, his lantern jaw in profile, completely still in the storm, and Lucy lost her breath.

"Tell me that's my action star," she said.

Another man dressed in jeans, a black T-shirt, and flip-flops got out of the copter on the other side, tripping over the skid as he stumbled out from under the blades. Then he stood up and joined the quiet man on the edge of the road, swaggering as he went.

"*That's* your star," Gloom said. "Bryce McKay. Medium-famous comedian. Great at pratfalls. Action? Not so much."

"Right," Lucy said, but her eyes went back to the quiet man, so much like Bryce physically, so much his opposite in every other way. Anybody that still had to have his act together. None of that macho garbage that had driven her away from Connor after six months of marriage.

Connor shook off the brunette and moved down the bridge to the helicopter, his focus on the newcomer, his hands out at his sides. *Hell,* Lucy thought. *He's already gunning for this guy.*

The quiet man turned to face him. Connor stiffened, and the other man stared back, not moving.

"Oh, boy," Gloom said happily.

"Oh, great," Lucy said. "And they're both thinking, 'Mine's bigger than yours.'"

"I *love* this," Gloom said. "It's like *High Noon.* Maybe somebody will finally outdraw that son of a bitch."

"Yeah, that would be good except this is real life, not a Western," Lucy said, exasperated. "Why don't they just pull them out and show them to each other?"

"Pull out what?" Pepper said.

"Their binoculars." Lucy put the little girl down. "I have to go see what's going on, baby. You wait here with Gloom."

"I want to come," Pepper said, her smile gone.

"Oh, I do, too." Gloom picked up Pepper. "I think this is going to be *my* party."

"Try to control your joy," Lucy said and headed down the bridge to contain the disaster, trying not to admire the quiet man for remaining so still in the midst of the chaos.

Captain J. T. Wilder stood as still as possible in deference to his screaming hangover, looked around at what he'd figured was going to be a good deal, and thought, *Clusterfuck.*

Beside him, Bryce McKay, Wilder's cross to bear, shouted over the whine of the copter's engine and the whoop of the blades: "This is what a real movie set looks like. Well, usually there are more people."

A real movie set looked like a mess to Wilder as he looked down the bridge, although that was not something he was going to share with Bryce, since he wanted to keep his new temporary job. *Play nice,* he thought. *Do the man's stunts for him. Make lots of money. Then get the hell out of Dodge.* He heard the engine on the Little Bird start to shut down and winced, knowing that his second cross to bear was going to get out of the chopper and hang around, which had not been in the plan.

Wilder's attention focused on the pissed-off-looking ex-military guy heading their way, an angry brunette following him. The guy had a gun, a big one, resting on his hip in a quick-draw rig, something Wilder hadn't seen anywhere outside of, well, a movie. So he guessed that made sense, although Bryce hadn't said anything about this being a Western.

Wilder's buddy LaFavre came up after shutting down the chopper, surveyed the scene from behind his aviator sunglasses, and said, "Circle jerk."

Wilder said, "Pretty much."

"What, Major LaFavre?" Bryce said anxiously, and Wilder almost felt sorry for him. The poor guy had been trying to buy LaFavre's beat-up flight jacket for the past two hours on the flight from Fort Bragg and got nowhere, then he'd gotten airsick when LaFavre had played chicken with the crane, and now he wanted to bond. *Not going to happen.*

"Nice day," LaFavre said.

"Yeah." Bryce nodded.

"You can go now," Wilder said to LaFavre under his breath, regretting his drunken call the night before to have LaFavre fly up to Bragg and fetch them.

"Not yet. I came to see the actresses," LaFavre said, cheerful as ever. "Would that be one?" He nodded toward the pissed-off brunette, who'd caught the arm of the guy with the gun.

"No idea," Wilder said. The brunette looked like the kind of woman who was always unhappy, the kind of woman who sucked the life out of a man. *Angel of Death,* Wilder thought and almost felt sorry for the guy with the gun, who wasn't getting away from her anytime soon.

"Perhaps I should introduce myself," LaFavre said, and Wilder shook his head and then winced.

"No, you should not. Goodbye." His hangover was getting worse. If he could get rid of LaFavre, shut Bryce up, and defuse the dickhead with the fast-draw rig, he could find out what they needed him to do, do it, get paid, take some aspirin, and go to bed. "Who's the guy with the gun?" he asked Bryce.

"That's Connor Nash, our stunt coordinator. Connor planned all the stunts and picked the bridge. Isn't it great?" Bryce gestured to the steel suspension cables above them. "It's won awards and stuff. It's going to look awesome on film when the helicopter comes down."

"You're going to land a helicopter on this bridge?" Wilder looked up at the cables on either side and the light poles along the center and then glanced at LaFavre.

LaFavre shook his head. "Have to be a real hotshot pilot to get a chopper down on that roadway without doing a major crash and burn. If you fast rope in, you can't get back out unless you use STABO, and even that will be touch and go with the limited space between the cables. Hate to get a STABO line caught in one of those cables. Take out the man and the chopper."

Wilder knew LaFavre had lost Bryce even though the actor was nodding his head as if he completely understood.

"But they're not going to land it," Bryce said. "They're just going to bring it in low enough so that the bad guys can put the loot into the cargo net that hangs underneath it. Nash has it all storyboarded out."

"What kind of chopper are you using?" LaFavre asked, keeping one eye on the brunette, probably in case she took her sweater off.

"A Huey," Bryce said, clearly proud that he knew the name.

"Well, hell, boy, forget the net and just load it in the Huey. Damn things are big. Not that you're ever going to get it down on this bridge." LaFavre nodded at the cranky brunette, who was glaring after the guy with the gun—Nash—as he headed for them again, looking mad as hell. "She ever been in the movies?"

"No," Bryce said. "So they wouldn't have a cargo net?"

He sounded crushed, so Wilder tried for damage control. "They'd need one if they had a lot of people in the Huey. Five or six—" He stopped because Bryce was shaking his head.

"Only one. The head bad guy kills the others."

"Dumb bad guy," LaFavre said. "So you got any actresses around here?"

"I'll have to check with Nash on this cargo net thing," Bryce said in a low voice, sounding worried.

Yeah, Wilder thought. *Tell him the cargo net isn't right. That's going to make me popular.* He jerked his head, trying to signal LaFavre to leave, but the pilot missed it, staring down the bridge past Nash, who'd stopped a good ten feet away, his jaw set.

"What the hell is this?" Nash said, and Wilder almost winced when he heard the Australian accent. Made him think of beer commercials.

Bryce said, "Hey, Connor! Meet Captain J. T. Wilder and Major Rene LaFavre. Guys, this is Connor Nash, you know, I told you, he's our stunt coordinator?" He sounded like an anxious puppy, looking from Wilder to Nash and back again.

Wilder nodded, and Connor Nash's head twitched, not quite a nod, which Wilder took to mean that he wasn't happy to see him.

Bryce walked between them to clap Nash awkwardly on the shoulder, and Wilder thought, *Get out of the kill zone, you idiot.* Bryce, he'd learned in the past two days, had absolutely no survival instincts.

"My, my," LaFavre said, and Wilder followed his eyes as Nash turned and looked, too.

A tall woman, her hair in a long dark braid over her shoulder, was coming down the bridge toward them, her blue shirt blowing back in the wind to reveal a well-filled-out white T-shirt that made Wilder rethink white T-shirts. *Amazon,* Wilder thought. If Nash hadn't been standing there, he'd have looked longer and possibly smiled, but the stunt coordinator was a wild card, mad as hell about something and not to be ignored. *Mission first, women later.*

A tall, gangly man followed the Amazon, holding a little blond kid. He was grinning at Nash, but it wasn't a friendly grin. More a fuck-you grin. Wilder liked him.

"She an actress?" LaFavre asked Bryce, dropping his voice as he nodded toward the Amazon.

Bryce squinted and then dropped his voice, too. "No. I think that's the new director. Nash's ex-wife. She directs dog food commercials or something up in New York so he got her this gig. It's her big break."

"Healthy-lookin' woman," LaFavre said with appreciation, and Nash evidently heard, because he turned his stare on LaFavre.

Not so ex, then, Wilder thought and looked at the woman again as she came closer. She was tall, probably six foot, and she looked determined. Powerful. Hot. Yeah, she would be a hard woman to walk away from.

Maybe she was the one who'd walked. That sounded better.

Bryce added, still under his breath, "Nash'll still run things. It's mostly stunts this last four days. I think she's just here to make things look right."

She's got her work cut out for her, Wilder thought, and put his eyes back on Nash.

"Looks right to me," LaFavre said, still staring at the Amazon, and Nash's face darkened. "Does she like heroes? I could show her my medals. Women are usually real grateful to heroes."

"Go away," Wilder said, seeing disaster loom. LaFavre would hit on her, and then Nash would kill him. Or try to. LaFavre was remarkably hard to kill.

Right now he just looked wounded, or as wounded as anybody could look in aviator sunglasses. "What about my actresses?" he said.

"I'll get you one later."

"Let's go get a drink, then. Fly with me back to Hunter. There's a strip club—"

"No. Go away."

"Coin check."

"Screw you." Wilder fished his Special Forces coin out of his pocket and held it up. "Now *go away.*"

LaFavre grinned, tipped his World War II flight hat to Bryce and then belatedly to Nash, smiled warmly up the bridge at the Amazon, and ambled off toward the chopper.

"What's a coin check?" Bryce said, watching him go.

"Special Forces thing," Wilder said, keeping an eye on LaFavre to make sure he kept on going.

"Bunch of bullshit," Nash said.

Bryce nodded at the Amazon as she reached them. Her dark eyes swept them all and, Wilder was pretty sure, missed nothing.

"Lucy Armstrong?" Bryce said.

She smiled and held out her hand to Bryce, walking between Wilder and Nash to reach him. *Into the kill zone,* Wilder thought. These people wouldn't last five seconds in a gun battle.

"Bryce McKay." The Amazon shook his hand, her profile to Wilder. "Very pleased to meet you."

"Welcome aboard." Bryce nodded at her once, looking oddly serious.

"I cannot see," the little kid said, and Wilder looked down to see her holding up her binoculars, surrounded by adult legs, her face perturbed under its blond bowl-cut.

The Amazon—Armstrong, Bryce had called her—stepped back to let the kid out of the circle as Bryce said, "I want you to meet Captain J. T. Wilder, my new military consultant."

Armstrong turned those eyes on him and said, "Hello." She put her hand out and Wilder took it, still watching Nash, trying not to get distracted. Her grip was solid. And warm. He met her gaze and liked what he saw: Somebody was definitely at home in there. He'd been looking at Bryce for too long. Bryce's eyes said, "Back in a minute." Armstrong's eyes said, "Brace yourself, I'm coming at you."

"J.T. is a real Green Beret, just like Rambo," Bryce was saying to Armstrong, and Wilder flinched as Nash laughed.

Armstrong shot Nash a look that could have cut glass.

Rambo, Wilder thought. Fuck.

"Hey," the little kid said, but Armstrong had already turned back to Wilder.

"A Green Beret," she said. "Very impressive." She sounded as if she meant it, and Nash lost his sneer.

Wilder felt better.

"This is my assistant director, Gleason Bloom," she said, and the smile she directed to the lanky guy was affectionate. "Gloom, you know our star, Bryce McKay—"

Wilder watched while Bryce stood straighter when she said "star."

"—And this is Captain J. T. Wilder, his . . . friend."

"Military consultant," Bryce said, and Gloom shook first his hand and then Wilder's. *Good strong grip with nothing to prove,* Wilder thought. Armstrong had traded up if she'd gone from Nash to Gloom.

The little kid was staring out at the swamp through her binoculars, staying very still, leaning forward, and he followed her eyes but couldn't see anything. *"Hey,"* she said, looking up at Armstrong, reaching up to tug on her shirt.

"Military consultant," Nash said, a little too loudly. "We don't need one."

"Well, it's certainly something to talk about," Armstrong said cheerfully, with a note under her voice that made it clear that she'd be the one directing the conversation when it happened. She caught the little girl's hand and tried to hold it, but the kid pulled away.

"I want J.T.," Bryce said, getting that mule look that Wilder had learned to avoid in the two days they'd been together. "I'm paying for him, he's my hire, and I want him."

Armstrong nodded, still cheerful although her jaw was set now. "We will definitely discuss it. But now about your character . . ." She began to talk to Bryce about his role, which distracted him, and Wilder relaxed enough to let his eyes scan the set again. People standing or sitting, doing nothing, the lanky guy, Gloom, watching Connor with undisguised loathing, the little kid—

The little kid had climbed onto the bridge rail, wobbling as she tried to straddle it and hold the binoculars to her eyes, and it was a damn long way down to the Savannah River. Wilder was moving even before he realized it.

"Pepper!" Armstrong yelled a moment later and lunged for her, but Wilder was already scooping the kid off the rail and putting her on the ground. She looked up at him, blue-eyed and annoyed, and he said, "Please do not do that again," just as Nash reached them.

The kid frowned up at him. "Why?"

"*Because I said so!*" Nash exploded as Armstrong dropped to her knees and grabbed the little girl, hugging her close.

Wilder kept his eyes on the kid, trying to figure out what would make sense to her but not scare her. "Because it's too far up. When you fell, you would hit the water too fast for the molecules to part for you, and you would die." *Oh, that was good. Always smooth with the lines for women.*

Pepper blinked at him, squirming in Armstrong's arms. "Okay, but I was trying to tell you, I *saw* something." The little girl wriggled free and straightened her T-shirt. "Something in the swamp. Like a ghost. Or something." She sighed, exasperated, and looked up at Wilder. "So who are you?"

Wilder was taken aback for a minute, but then he figured the kid had a point. He'd just moved her out of a place she wanted to be without asking her. The least he could do was tell her his name. He went down on one knee so he could look her in the eye and extended his hand. "I'm J. T. Wilder."

"I'm P. L. Armstrong." The kid took his hand and shook it. Wilder almost smiled. *Smart kid.*

"Jesus Christ," Nash said from behind them.

Armstrong stood up. "Thank you very much, Captain Wilder." She met his eyes and held them for a moment too long, long enough to make Nash draw in his breath and Wilder straighten. "We're very grateful to you," she said.

How grateful? he thought, and then got a grip. *Get out of the kill zone,* he told himself, and then she smiled at him, nodded at Bryce and said, "We'll talk more later about your role," and took the kid's hand to lead her back to the monitors.

Wilder watched them walk away, trying to get his detachment back. *Mother and daughter.* They didn't look anything alike, and neither Nash or Gloom read right for the father, but Armstrong was definitely in mother mode. . . .

That was one hell of a woman.

Out of the kill zone, damn it.

He turned and looked out to the swamp. What had the kid seen out there? She might be little but she wasn't stupid. He stared out into the wilderness and then back at the human jungle on the bridge. Danger everywhere.

Clusterfuck, he thought and went back to scanning the swamp.

In the swamp north of the bridge, not far from the base camp where the trailers and trucks were circled, Tyler Branch sat cross-legged with his sniper rifle and laughed at the Stranger in military uniform standing on the bridge looking for him.

"Never gonna happen, asshole," he said and put the sight of his rifle on the guy's head. "Pow," he said, seeing the word in a big yellow comic-book star. "Pow. POW."

Jesus, he was bored. That's why he'd stood up and shown himself to that spoiled brat Kid, just to watch her freak out. It had been worth it, she'd almost fallen off the bridge trying to get a better look. That would have been cool. And nobody would believe her if she told, even if they did all fuss over her all the time. She was a kid. Nobody paid any attention to kids. Nobody sure as hell had ever paid attention to him, anyway.

Now they paid attention. Because when Tyler Branch moved, things died. He smiled to himself. Pretty damn cool, that's what he was.

And pretty damn bored. Four more days of this crap before he'd get to shoot anything. Even the Stranger showing up was boring. The Director, now, she wasn't bad. He found her and let the sight pan down her body. She was a big woman with a damn good ass. A J.Lo ass. Something there to grab on to.

"Oh, yeah, something there," he said out loud and startled himself.

Talking to himself. Bad sign. If he didn't do something soon, he'd start hitting on the gators, thinking, *Nice scales, I should get me some of that.* If it wasn't for the money, he'd have been gone by now, but money could buy a lot of good things. Like women. Women always wanted a piece of you, a piece of your wallet anyway. Guys with money, they had all the women they wanted cause they had lots of pieces. And that was gonna be him. Women paying attention to him all over the place. Women *dying* to pay attention to him. He put the sight back on the Director's ass, then moved it down the bridge to the Actress climbing up onto the hood of the little red convertible. Now there was a woman. Jesus, those tits—

A rustling sound to his right made him look. Less than six feet away, a nine-foot alligator was crawling up out of the dark water, trying to catch the late afternoon sun.

The reptile paused, half out of the water, and its massive head swung back and forth, nostrils flaring. The head came to a halt, one black eyeball secreted underneath scaly ridges staring straight at Tyler, the other missing, a thick scar marking the spot. The gator's mouth opened ever so slightly, revealing jagged teeth, and the single eye stared back, unblinking.

"You want a piece of me?" Tyler growled low, baring his teeth. He slowly got to his feet and took a couple of steps up the bank, water dripping off his body.

The gator lifted one large front leg to move forward, and Tyler hissed. *Back off, lizard breath.*

The clawed foot paused in midair. Then the gator pulled the leg back and slowly retreated, slithering into the dark water. The large tail swung, pulling it back twenty feet, where it stopped, eye and nostrils above the water, watching.

Believe it, buddy, I own this swamp. Holding the rifle above the water with one hand, Tyler reached into his vest pocket and pulled out a beer. It wasn't ice-cold, but a beer was a beer, especially when he was waist deep in a swamp staring down a gator. He popped the top and drained it in one steady gulp. He crushed the can and put it back in the same pocket. Pack it out if you pack it in.

He turned his attention back to the bridge. *Come on,* he thought. *Take off your clothes. Shoot somebody. Bleed. Die. SOMETHING!* Jesus.

The Kid was there, still with the binoculars. Staring right the fuck at him. Tyler blinked, sure his mind was playing tricks on him, but nope, there she was, little blond head just topping the concrete railing, the binoculars resting on it, and the two blacks lenses trained his way.

No fucking way she could see him now. For a second, Tyler's finger slid over the trigger, tempted to send a round straight through the left lens right into her beady little eyeball. Now that would be a shot. Too bad she hadn't fallen off the bridge. He could have hit her before she hit the water.

Of course, somebody would have noticed that, their precious baby with a big old hole in her. Well, fuck covert. He needed to shoot something.

He turned away from the bridge. There must be something out there that needed to die. He moved the gun, sweeping the sight along the shoreline of the Savannah River until he spotted something rooting through the brush. A wild hog. Searching for food near the old abandoned grain towers on the other side of the bridge.

Tyler adjusted for the slight elevation difference as the hog drew closer to the shore and his position. Distance was one hundred and sixty-two feet, according to the laser range finder. But there was something else, something in the river, close to the hog. Tyler looked back and saw that the gator was gone from its perch on the nearby bank. Out there in the river now. Stalking the hog.

"Not so fast, buddy-boy," Tyler whispered. He placed the sight's crosshairs on the hog, moving with it as it dug with its tusks. He noted that the gator was moving closer, very slowly, waiting to get within range. He imagined the hog getting caught in the gator's jaws, bone crunching, blood spraying.

"Outstanding," he said to himself.

Too bad for the gator that this was his kill.

Tyler adjusted ever so slightly for lateral movement, let out his breath, felt the rhythm of his blood, shut out everything but his heartbeat and the hog. In between beats, he squeezed the trigger.

The hog tumbled several feet and was still. Then the gator lunged out of the water, jaws snapping down on the dead body, and dragged it back into the river.

"Cool," Tyler said and pulled out another lukewarm beer. The gator disappeared underwater with the hog. Game over.

He looked up at the bridge and the Kid was there, looking for him again with her binoculars.

Fat chance you see me again, you little creep.

Fuck, he was bored. And hungry.

Gotta get me some Cheetos, he thought and put the sight back on the Kid.

2

"I'm really glad you're here," Pepper said, skipping along beside Lucy as they headed for the monitors.

"Me too," Lucy said, trying to get her heart out of her throat. "Don't climb on the rail again." She sat down in one of the four chairs at the monitors and helped Pepper up into the chair at the end of the row, thinking seriously about duct taping her to it. *My God,* she thought, *we almost lost her.* Somebody was going to have to watch her every minute. Somebody like her mother, maybe.

Where the hell was Daisy?

Gloom sat down on her other side. "I like the new guy." He smiled across her at Pepper. "Hello, trouble," he said, affection palpable in his voice. "Don't climb any more bridges, okay?"

Pepper beamed over at him. "Okay. Gloom, did you know there were Super Hero Barbies?"

"No," Gloom said, sounding honestly surprised. "Damn. Really?"

Pepper nodded, satisfied, and picked up her binoculars.

"As I was saying," Gloom said to Lucy. "The new guy is hot."

"So is Connor," Lucy said. "Look how gorgeous he is."

"It takes more than big broad shoulders to make a man," Gloom said.

Lucy closed her eyes. "Don't tell me. That's a movie quote from some macho—"

"*High Noon.* I'm just saying, the new guy? More than big broad shoulders."

"Great," Lucy said, trying not to look down the bridge at Wilder again. "Go for it. Have you seen Daisy?"

"He doesn't play for my team," Gloom said. "But I'm pretty sure he wants to play on yours."

"What team?" Pepper said, pulling away from her binoculars.

"My movie team," Lucy said brightly. "Like you and Gloom."

"Oh." Pepper sat back. "I think he should be on our team, too. I like him." She went back to scanning the swamp again.

"So, Daisy?" Lucy said to Gloom.

"Haven't seen her." Gloom nodded down the bridge. "About this new guy. I think you should pay attention there."

Lucy looked again. The three men stood in a loose semicircle, Wilder and Connor both looking solid and sure, Bryce doing his best with what he had to work with.

Gloom started to hum off-key, and Lucy tried to ignore him, but she finally gave up and said, "Okay, what is that?"

"Your theme song, babe," Gloom said. "Bonnie Tyler. 'Holding Out For A Hero.' It's got to be playing in your head whenever you look at that guy."

She turned back. "There are no heroes. And if I decide to go that macho route again, I'll go back to Connor. At least he's the devil I know."

Gloom shook his head. "I don't think this guy is Connor. I think maybe he's Will Kane."

"Who's Will Kane?" Pepper asked, looking away from her binoculars.

"The sheriff from *High Noon*," Gloom told her. "Noble, true, and brave."

"I *liked* that movie," Pepper said and then frowned. "Well, I liked the *ending* of that movie."

"Good," Gloom said. "Make your aunt watch it."

"Forget Will Kane," Lucy said. "Let's pretend we're professionals. Tell me about the set." She looked out at the aimless, milling people. "We've been here half an hour. I assume you're best friends with everybody by now."

Gloom sent one more speculative look down the bridge to Wilder and then said, "Well, if you must talk about this mess, we've got trouble right here in River City."

"Trouble?"

"The director died," Gloom said. "The first and second ADs both quit."

"I know this," Lucy said, distracted as Connor headed back to them. "Wait a minute, the second AD quit, too?"

"And the line producer went back to L.A.," Gloom said.

Lucy stopped. "There's no producer on set? What the—"

"Which is also when the DP quit," Gloom continued as Connor came up to the monitors.

"Hello, love," he said to Lucy, his grin lazy and inviting. "Not the way I'd planned our reunion, but—"

Lucy looked back at Gloom. "There's no *director of photography?*"

Gloom smiled at her, radiating *I told you so.*

Lucy looked over the monitors at Connor, whose smile was not quite as wide now. "Hello, Connor. Who's running the camera crew?"

"We've got three guys," Connor said. "That's plenty. And hello to you, too. I—"

"So forget running four cameras for the helicopter stunts on Wednesday and Thursday," Gloom said, and Connor lost his smile completely.

Lucy leaned closer to the monitors. "Connor, why is there not enough crew here?"

"It's a skeleton crew," Connor said, "but—"

"I'd say you're down to bone marrow," Gloom said.

Connor's face darkened, and Lucy braced herself for the explosion, but then he took a deep breath and shook his head. "We have what we need."

Lucy held on to her temper. "I'll let you know what I need. Which reminds me, you only faxed me the last pages of this script. Where's the rest?"

Connor shook his head and said, "You don't need—"

"I said I'd tell you what I needed," Lucy snapped. "And I need the whole damn script."

Connor set his jaw as the color rose in his face. He stared at her for a minute and then walked away.

"Well, at least he's learned how to keep his temper," Lucy said to Gloom.

"He hasn't changed, Lucy," Gloom said. "Trust me, I know this guy and he has not changed. Now about this Wilder—"

"No." Lucy refused to let her eyes stray down the bridge. "This is not a social visit, I'm finishing a movie here." Pepper looked up from her binoculars, and Lucy added, "And playing Barbies."

"Yes!" Pepper said, straightening in her joy.

"I suppose that's a plan," Gloom said, "but—"

"*Sorry* I'm late."

Lucy looked around to see the top of her sister's frizzy yellow head as she slid into the folding chair beside Pepper, looking like a demented dandelion as she clumsily balanced her notebook, her headphones, her bottle of water, her pen, her camera, and her wide-brimmed yellow straw hat. Then she tried to hug Lucy without losing any of it.

"Hey." Lucy hugged her back, careful not to dislodge anything, alarmed at how thin Daisy felt in her arms. "Look at you," she said, pulling back. "You look—"

Blond little Daisy gazed up at her, dull eyed, sunken cheeked, and ashen.

Lucy finished, "—*Great.* You look just . . . great." *Oh, God, what's happened to you?*

"I'm glad you're here," Daisy said. She sounded sincere but tired, almost groggy, and Lucy leaned down to see her better.

"I'm glad, too." *Your kid almost fell off a bridge.* Probably not the time to tell her that. "Are you okay?"

Daisy nodded, smiling weakly.

"Have you been sick, honey?" Lucy said, trying to see under her hat. "Are you getting enough sleep?"

"She sleeps all the time," Pepper said, her face solemn. "And I am very quiet."

"I'm *fine,*" Daisy said, ducking her head down.

"Lucy!"

Lucy looked up and saw Bryce standing on the other side of the monitors.

"I need to talk to Lucy before I go to makeup," he told Gloom and Daisy, sounding important. "Alone."

They got up to move away before Lucy could, Daisy juggling all her stuff, Gloom rolling his eyes. Even Pepper looked exasperated.

Bryce was oblivious.

Lucy watched Daisy move down the bridge, her little ex-cheerleader body slumped, five feet four inches of exhaustion. Pepper was the one who'd sounded unhappy on the phone, not Daisy, but maybe that was because Pepper knew something was wrong with her mother—

"There's something I need to tell you," Bryce said, leaning over the monitors, his voice low. "J.T. is not just my consultant, he's my new stunt double." He shot an uneasy glance down the bridge. "I thought you should be the one to tell Nash."

Stunt double. Lucy tried to bring her mind back from Daisy. Stunt double, that was bad, that was Connor's team, and Connor already didn't like Wilder. She glanced at Connor to see if he'd heard Bryce and saw him watching Wilder, who didn't seem to notice. She lowered her voice. "You know, Bryce, that would be really great. But it's the last week of shooting, you already have a stunt double, I don't think the production has any money left, and I know it's not insured for Captain Wilder—"

Bryce's face was eager to please. "No, no, he's replacing my double."

Lucy stiffened. "And where did your double go?"

"Away," Bryce said, not being funny. "He said he had to go away."

Sweet Jesus, Lucy thought. *What do all these people know that I don't?*

"And then I ran into J.T. at Bragg, and my agent heard I didn't have a stunt double and recommended him, and I thought, 'Well, he's the real deal, Special Forces,' so I hired him. It's okay, he's on leave and I'm paying him, and I'll take care of the insurance, too. So you're saving money." He nodded at her, sure of himself as he motioned Wilder over.

Wilder did not look happy at being summoned, but he came to stand beside Bryce, every bit as grim and efficient as when he'd saved Pepper. Lucy looked at him and thought, *Who knew grim and efficient could look so good?*

She took a deep breath, trying to get her detachment back. "Ever done stunt work before, Captain Wilder?"

"Only for real," he said without expression.

"Uh huh," Lucy said.

"So it's all settled." Bryce spread his hands and almost hit Connor, who'd come up behind him again. "It's a good deal for everybody. I know these last four days are your big break—"

"No, they're not," Lucy said, startled.

"—But J.T. will be a help, you'll see."

"What's up?" Connor said, clearly trying to sound cheerful and clearly failing.

"Well, *I'm* trying to shoot a movie," Lucy said, and then leaned back to yell, *"Gloom."*

Bryce turned back to his new best friend. "Now, J.T., I want you to meet Althea next—that's our lead actress, Althea Bergdorf—because she's nervous about the helicopter because it's gonna swoop down over her head, but you'll be in it so—"

"What?" Connor jerked his head up.

Oh, hell. "Bryce," Lucy began, but Bryce was all wrapped up in Wilder, oblivious to everyone else, talking on a mile a minute, telling Wilder all about the armored car robbery scene.

Pepper climbed up on the chair beside Lucy, an apple in her hand. "Stephanie is supposed to be your assistant but she's not very good. *I* will be a better assistant than her. *I* will get you apples and water. And I will stay with you *the whole time*."

She handed Lucy the apple, and Lucy said, "Yes, you will be a *very* good assistant. Thank you very much," and bit into it, looking around for Daisy, who had disappeared again. She was definitely going to have a long talk with her sister as soon as she got the hell off this bridge. She ate her apple and looked at the shot sheet and listened to the conversation going on in front of her, wondering which of the three men on the other side of the monitors was going to lose his temper first. Not Wilder, she decided, glancing at his impassive face. Probably didn't have a temper. *Probably doesn't have a pulse,* she told herself, trying for more distance.

Then he looked over and caught her looking at him and she looked away. *Very third-grade,* she thought. *Good thing I'm a successful advertising director or I'd feel like a loser geek.*

"Lucy." Connor leaned over the monitors. "Why the fuck is Bryce telling that asshole about the helicopter stunt?"

"Those are bad words, Pepper," Lucy said. "Do not use them."

"Yes, Aunt Lucy," Pepper said, craning her neck to look up at Connor.

"Sorry, honey," Connor said to Pepper, the edge in his voice disappearing. "I didn't see you there. Those are bad words." He came around the monitors to stand beside Lucy, lowering his voice. "I want that guy off my bridge."

Wilder was frowning at the cables overhead as Bryce finished his explanation. "Why use a helicopter at all? Why not use a car to cut off the armored truck?"

Bryce called back, "Why aren't we using a car, Nash?"

Connor jerked around, and Lucy nudged his ankle with the toe of her boot. "He's the star," she whispered to him. "Do not annoy the star."

"Unless this is a comedy—" Wilder was saying to Bryce.

"It's not a comedy," Bryce said, with more emotion than he'd ever shown on-screen. "I'm not doing comedies anymore. It's an action picture. I'm an action hero now."

Since Bryce had made his name slipping on banana peels, this piece of self-delusion was met by universal silence. Even Pepper looked up at him in disbelief.

"I'm playing an ex-Navy SEAL," Bryce said happily. "A real stud muffin."

Wilder frowned. "I told you at Bragg, SEALs are different from Special Forces. They work mostly in the water, so this robbery thing doesn't make sense—"

"Wait a minute," Connor said, and Lucy nudged him harder, more of a kick this time. He ignored her and said to Wilder, "Have you even read the script?"

"No," Wilder said.

"Well then, *mate*—"

Lucy kicked Connor so hard he flinched.

Pepper tugged on Lucy's shirt.

"Go find your mama, baby," Lucy said. "Tell her we're almost ready to shoot." *And take these dickheads with you.*

Connor leaned in close, his jaw rigid. "That asshole is not working on my set."

"Bad word again, Pepper," Lucy said as she put her headphones on.

Pepper nodded and slid off her chair to go.

Bryce tapped on the monitor in front of Lucy, and she pulled her headphones back to listen to him.

"J.T. says we'll have to change the helicopter, Lucy."

"The hell we will," Connor said, and Bryce frowned.

"Let me set up this shot first, Bryce, and then we'll talk about it." Lucy looked at the monitor again. They were doing a sequence of shots that would culminate in Althea, the actress playing Annie the Heroine, climbing over the bridge rail with Rick, the actor playing Rip the Bad Guy, trying to stop her since she was his hostage. Annie evidently had the survival instincts of a lemming. The view on the monitor looked good so if Althea and Rick could struggle through several scenes without falling into the river . . . "All right, people," she said. "Let's go."

"Lucy," Connor said quietly, and she looked up to see him on the other side of the monitors. "Wilder has to go."

"Lucy," Bryce said from behind him. "J.T. has to stay."

Lucy looked back at the rail where Wilder was standing, staring up at the bridge cables with all the expression of a G.I. Joe action figure. Not charming. Barely human. The Army couldn't possibly have recruited him. They must have carved him out of granite.

Wilder caught her staring at him and nodded and then looked away.

Really attractive granite that obviously wasn't impressed with her. *You have no idea what you're missing, buddy.*

But he was the one who'd pulled Pepper off the rail. And Gloom approved of him and Gloom was no dummy. And Bryce wanted him and Bryce was the star. And she was tired of Connor doing the Dick Thing. It was her shoot, damn it.

"He stays," she said and put her headphones back on.

"I have to go down to makeup," Bryce had told Wilder once Armstrong had okayed him. He'd winked as he said it, as if that were code for something else, and there had been a good half hour while he was gone to the base camp down under the bridge that Wilder had used to scope the place.

The bridge itself was beautifully engineered, high in the middle to allow for the container ships that sailed slowly along the Savannah to the port just on the upriver side. It was the people on the bridge that made him shake his head. As far as he could see, the movie crew consisted of people milling around doing nothing in front of other people sitting in chairs doing nothing. One grenade and they'd all be goners. Bryce had tried to explain the chain of command to him before he'd gone, saying, "Well, the first AD runs the shoot while the director directs the filming through the monitors. The second AD does all the paperwork, while the director's assistant assists the director who directs the filming while the first assistant director . . . uh, the first AD is the one who really runs things." That hadn't helped. What was clear was that Armstrong and Gloom were the ones in charge, sitting in chairs in front of a rolling cart with two TV sets on it—"That's video village," Bryce had said before he'd gone—talking with their heads close together in the middle of lots of lights and poles and booms and cameras on hand trucks, and several cars and a black van, all of them unattended. The sulky-looking brunette Nash had been shrugging off was arguing with him again, the kid was still watching the swamp with her binoculars, and in general the place looked like, well, a clusterfuck.

And then there was the swamp. People had ignored the kid when she'd said there was somebody out there, but he'd been watching her and she was pretty serious about what she was doing. Just because she was five didn't mean she didn't have good eyes.

Wilder would have bet there was something out there. Some*one* out there. She'd said a ghost, and she wouldn't have said that if she'd seen an animal. Could be just a hunter, some good old boy wading through the swamp, but then why hadn't she seen him again?

Probably nothing to worry about, he told himself, and looked out into the swamp again.

Then Bryce came back in tiger-stripe camouflage fatigues with a combat vest whose most prominent feature was a massive upside-down knife on his left shoulder, so big it covered half his chest. Wilder refrained from shaking his head because he'd learned the weekend before at Fort Bragg that Bryce was quick to pick up any negative cues and wrap his mind around them so tight, it took an hour to unwrap it, and with his hangover still throbbing, Wilder didn't feel like unwrapping anything other than some aspirin.

Behind Bryce was a little woman with a pouty face that had too much makeup on it. Bryce pretty much ignored her as he said, "So what do you think?" squaring his shoulders to show off his knife.

"I think people here talk a lot." Wilder watched Armstrong lean closer to Gloom at the monitors. *Not her lover after all,* he thought. Wrong body language. He thought, *Good,* and then shook his head. Not good. This was the kind of job you did and got out fast. No staying behind to hit on the boss.

Bryce followed his eyes. "What? Lucy and Gloom? They're just trying to get up to speed, coming in at the end of everything like this, last four days of shooting. It's tough. The old director had a heart attack, really bad, right on the set at the end of shooting Friday." Bryce shook his head at the brevity of life and the unpredictability of death and then looked down the bridge and brightened. "Look, there's Althea. Come on. You have to meet Althea."

Wilder nodded and followed Bryce down the bridge, while the actor babbled on, saying, "If you're hungry, we can stop by Crafty, that's craft services, the table over there with all kinds of food. I like the Ding Dongs. . . ."

Behind them, the little woman with the makeup pouted harder and then took out her cell phone.

"Who's that?" Wilder said, jerking his head back toward her.

"Huh? Oh, Mary Vanity," Bryce said. "Makeup girl." He winked at Wilder. "Hot." Then he leered. "Sorry it took me so long."

Wilder's head throbbed harder. Good to know that while he was on a bridge with an armed stunt coordinator and a hostile Amazon, Bryce was having a quickie in the makeup trailer.

"That coin thing, is it some kind of secret thing?" Bryce asked.

"What?"

"The coin check thing. With LaFavre."

If it were a secret, why would I tell you? "Every Special Forces unit has a coin," Wilder said. "Your name gets inscribed on yours when you arrive at the unit, you carry it everywhere, and if challenged, and you don't have it, you have to buy the challenger a drink."

"Can I get one?" Bryce said. "One of those coins? For the movie?"

"Your character's a SEAL," Wilder said. "I don't have any SEAL challenge coins handy and they might not take too kindly to someone outside the unit carrying one."

Bryce looked hurt and Wilder tried to think of something to say to make him feel better but then Bryce said, "Althea!" and Wilder looked up to see the blonde Bryce was leading him toward and forgot his hangover.

It was a damn good thing he'd gotten rid of LaFavre.

She was sitting on the hood of the red convertible they were going to use in the stunts, and she was a little thing, but she had impossible breasts that stretched her tight red T-shirt to the breaking point, and her short white shorts were just as tight.

"Althea," Bryce said when they reached her. "You have to meet J. T. Wilder. J.T. is a real Green Beret."

Althea looked at J.T. and smiled.

Wilder hated to admit it, but he liked Bryce sometimes.

"So you're like Rambo?" Althea ran her hand through her blond curls.

Not exactly, Wilder thought as he tried to focus on her eyes.

Althea smiled even more warmly at Wilder and made him swallow as she held out her hand. "I'm *very* pleased to meet you, J.T."

Wilder took her hand—slender and cool in his—and nodded, at a loss for words, which was not Bryce's problem. The actor prattled on about how they'd trained together at Bragg—that was a joke right there—while Althea looked at Wilder from under her lashes, biting her lip.

Bryce kept talking as Nash came up behind Althea and checked the harness hidden under her skimpy top, which looked even skimpier under the strain her breasts were putting on it. Wilder shifted his gaze as Nash tugged on Althea's harness and made everything jiggle. Then he looked up to catch Nash shooting more looks his way, looks he ignored this time. There were more important things than pissing contests, such as the amount of Althea-skin being shown as Nash pulled up the back of her T-shirt and checked the harness.

Bryce was still talking, but Wilder's eyes stayed on Althea. He'd seen her in some movie, but he couldn't remember what, something to do with the Navy, he thought. LaFavre would remember; he never forgot a great pair of breasts. And now here she was, flesh and blood. If Wilder remembered the movie rightly, she had shown quite a bit of flesh, more than was currently being displayed. She smiled at him again, dimples this time, and he was pretty sure it was an invitation. He dropped his eyes to her long, thin legs and decided that as soon as he remembered the title of whatever she'd been in, he'd go to Savannah and get the DVD.

"And we've got a real helicopter pilot," Bryce was saying to him. "Karen Roeburn. She's Althea's stunt double, but she's a real pilot, too. She thought the helicopter stunt was okay." He finally ran down, uncertain. "But you said you don't like it because of the bridge cables, right?"

Wilder looked away from Althea's legs as Bryce's buzz penetrated. Female chopper pilot. His second ex-wife had been a chopper pilot.

Before he could say anything, Nash faced him. "I know what I'm doing. We can get the chopper down on the roadway with enough safety clearance."

Not if there's a wind, Wilder thought. The guy was a pro so he had to know that trying to land a helicopter on this bridge was dumb. What was up with him?

"Connor," Bryce said. "You should listen to J.T. He's my consultant."

Nash snorted. "He the one that got you that knife?"

"No, no, I got it." Bryce unsnapped the leather stay and pulled the huge pig-sticker out of the leather sheath. "I had the props department order it special after I saw how my role was rewritten. I told them my character, Brad, would have a big knife. They got it custom made by this guy in Alabama. Same one who did Rambo's knife in *First Blood*."

Wilder truly believed he was going to have to get a rifle, climb a tower somewhere, and start shooting if one more person here said "Rambo." The blade was at least a foot long, the front edge honed razor-sharp, the back side serrated for—well, Wilder had no clue what Bryce would use that for other than cutting down a tree. If Bryce had shown that thing at Fort Bragg, the howls would have been heard all the way to Smoke Bomb Hill, where Special Forces had been founded long ago by manly men doing manly things with other men in a manly way. Wilder's first team sergeant had told him that line. He'd have told Bryce, but then he'd have had to listen to it for the rest of the shoot.

Bryce slashed the knife awkwardly through the air, making Althea step back.

"Careful," Wilder said automatically. "You never draw a weapon unless you mean to use it."

Bryce slashed again, almost nicking Althea, and Wilder slipped his hand under Bryce's extended arm, caught it at the wrist, twisted, and applied just a little pressure. Bryce screamed and dropped the weapon.

Wilder let go, feeling guilty, especially when Bryce turned those big puppy eyes on him. "What did you do that for?"

People were watching, including Althea, who was staring at the two of them as if making a decision. Wilder bent over and picked up the monstrosity. He felt the balance. Actually pretty good; he was sure the guy in Alabama knew what the hell he was doing. It was Bryce who didn't have a clue.

"Sorry." Wilder flipped the knife and caught it by the blade, extending the handle to Bryce, who eyed the proffered knife warily. He snatched it, almost slicing Wilder's palm open, slid it back in the sheath, and fastened the leather stay to keep it from falling out and impaling his foot.

"I don't get it." Bryce sounded like a kid whose mother had just questioned the drawing he'd done in school that day. "What don't you like about the knife? I got one for you, too, because you're going to be my stunt double."

"Thank you," Wilder said, trying to mean it.

"He's not doubling for you," Nash said, quiet but firm. "I heard your double left, but Doc can cover you." He nodded toward the round-faced stuntman in glasses hitting the craft services table. "He's an ex–Green Beret, just like your pal here."

"Doc doesn't look anything like me," Bryce said.

Wilder smiled, not his forte. "Please, coach, put me in?"

Nash smiled back at Wilder, and he was much better at it than Wilder was, even though the smile didn't reach his eyes. Perfect teeth. Tanned skin. Probably never had hangovers.

Nash shook his head. "He hasn't even read the script," he said to Bryce.

So you had to be a reader to make Nash's team? Yeah, that was tough. What the hell did these people know about being on a team anyway? There was only one kind of team for Wilder, a Special Forces A-Team, the eleven great guys he'd—

Althea shifted into Wilder's field of vision, and he lost his train of thought. He noticed that she wasn't wearing a bra under her thin, tight T-shirt. And the April evening was evidently a little chilly for her. *Got to get that DVD.*

"We about ready here?" he heard from behind him and turned. Armstrong stood there, the anti-Althea, tall and strong and in charge, not flirting with anybody, which was too bad. That would be something to see, Armstrong smiling, giving somebody the come-on. Probably that asshole Nash. Jesus.

"J.T. doesn't like my knife," Bryce said, and Armstrong turned those dark, steady eyes on Wilder.

Tough woman, he thought, his pulse picking up. Nothing like soft, bouncy Althea. Then he remembered the wind blowing her shirt back. Maybe a little bouncy—

"So I guess we'll have to change it," Bryce went on, close to whining. "I really want the knife, but once I saw the new ending, I went all the way to Fort Bragg and hired J.T. to help me make this real, so we should listen to him. For the movie."

Good for you, Wilder thought.

"And I would have been with you on that," Armstrong said, "if only you'd brought him in at the beginning. But it's the last four days of shooting and we can't afford to reshoot without the knife. I agree that authentic is good, but you filmed with the knife all last week, so that ship has sailed. Now let's get—"

"J.T.?" Bryce said.

Oh, fuck, here we go. Wilder felt bad for saying anything more, but Bryce was paying him to keep things authentic. "It's just not what Bryce's guy would wear. I know this Brad character is supposed to be an ex-Navy SEAL, and they are studs, no doubt about it."

Bryce stood slightly taller, trying to look the description. Wilder tried not to look at him.

"But they spend a lot of time in the water. That knife would tip a canoe over, never mind a swimmer. They carry dive knives. On their calves. And even if his character is only operating on land, you want something that can kill quickly. Your SEAL isn't going to get in a sword fight with a Roman gladiator and that's about all that knife is good for. He's going to sneak up behind someone late at night and slice his throat wide open or, just as good, but more difficult unless you're a pro, jam the blade up into the jaw to the brain so it's a quick and silent kill."

Armstrong winced, and Wilder ignored her.

"So, optimally, you want something slender, pointed, and double-edged. About six to eight inches long. And he's wearing it wrong." Wilder tapped the upside-down sheath that Bryce had the pig-sticker locked into. He stepped behind the actor, grabbed the handle, jerked it down and clear of the sheath, the leather stay giving way easily, then brought it up, the point a quarter inch from Bryce's jugular before Bryce could turn his head. "You want it in a place where you can easily access it, but the bad guy can't. And hell, if you got to use a knife, the shit has hit the fan anyway. I prefer a gun. Ten millimeter at ten feet. Double-tap in the forehead. Lights out."

They were all staring at him. Armstrong. Bryce. Althea. Even Nash had stopped scowling. Perhaps too much detail.

He lowered the weapon and slid it back into the sheath, giving Bryce a comforting pat on the shoulder with one hand as he locked it down with the other.

Armstrong smiled at them all, the kind of smile that said, *I'm cheerful but don't fuck with me.* "Thank you. The knife stays. Let's get this show on the road."

She walked off and Wilder watched her long, strong legs crossing concrete again, her red cowboy boots clicking on the pavement. Yep, she was in charge. He turned to Bryce. "Hey, no big deal. Stallone will have knife envy for sure when he sees you with that thing." He looked Bryce over and felt a wave of sadness. "I guess dumping the tiger stripes is a no go, eh?"

"What's wrong with the tiger stripes?"

Nash stifled a laugh, and Wilder looked out at the surrounding forest and swamp that looked nothing like tiger stripes and thought of John Wayne wearing the same type of camouflage in that terrible movie *The Green Berets,* detested by all the manly men on Smoke Bomb Hill. *Four days of this,* he thought. Of course, that was also four days of looking at Althea. And Armstrong.

"J.T.? What's wrong with the tiger stripes?"

Wilder gave up. "Not a thing, Bryce."

Screw the hangover; he really needed a drink.

3

By the time they were ready to shoot, Lucy had spoken to most of the cast and crew and was ready to ditch them all and go back to dog food commercials. The dogs were so much better behaved.

Daisy was refusing to talk about what was wrong with her, Pepper was being manic about some ghost in the swamp, Althea was distracted, Connor was fuming, Bryce wouldn't shut up, and Gloom kept humming "Holding Out For A Hero" whenever Wilder got close. Even the makeup department was getting on her nerves. A woman had come up to Lucy asking for him, her false eyelashes fluttering and her lipsticked mouth working nervously. "I need to see Bryce," she'd said, and Lucy had thought, *Why? A makeup emergency?* and sent her back to base camp.

But the worst was Wilder. If she'd had to choose only one of them to drop off the bridge, it would have been him. He wasn't doing anything wrong, but he was the one screwing up her concentration the most.

Shoving him firmly out of her mind, she headed for the rail where Althea Bergdorf, her lead actress, was cabled in under the bright set lights. Pepper followed, and Lucy thought about sending her back to the monitors at video village and then relented. Pepper's mom was having a very bad time. Pepper could stick close until Lucy found out whatever was wrong with Daisy and fixed it.

Lucy slowed. Maybe the problem was more complicated than just Daisy being tired. Maybe Pepper's climb on the rail had been a bid for attention. Maybe she needed somebody to ask what was wrong, somebody to listen to her.

"Is there anything you want to talk about, Pepper?" Lucy said, looking down into her niece's round little face.

Pepper nodded. "There's a ghost in the swamp."

"No, baby, I meant is there anything you're worried about? Anything you want? Anything you need?"

Pepper looked startled, then thoughtful, but before she could answer, Lucy heard Althea call, "Lucy?" and thought, *Oh, hell.* "We'll talk in a minute, okay?" she said to Pepper, and the little girl nodded, looking relieved.

When they reached her, Althea was leaning over the bridge rail looking at a gator parked on the riverbank below. *Meeting of minds,* Lucy thought, having heard about Althea in action with men. "Anybody you know?" she said.

Althea smiled, a perfect Hollywood smile. "He kinda reminds me of some of the guys I've dated. Listen, I—"

From behind them a woman said, "We're ready," and Pepper slid neatly between Lucy and the rail, folding herself out of sight.

Lucy turned to see a slender brunette gazing at her with what looked like contempt. *I don't even* know *you,* Lucy thought. *What's your problem?*

"I'm Stephanie, your assistant," the brunette said. "I'm sorry I wasn't here earlier." She didn't sound sorry. "I was helping Connor. He said to tell you Althea's cable is good to go." Her voice gave the slightest emphasis to *Connor,* as if she were talking about a celebrity, and she lifted her chin a little and met Lucy's eyes as if daring her to challenge any of that, especially the Connor part. "I realize you don't work much with stunt cables on dog food commercials, so I'd just take his word for it if I were you."

Would you now? Lucy thought, now recognizing her as the woman who'd been arguing with Connor. "Lovely to meet you, Stephanie. Get me a script, please. A full script, one with *all* the pages. Thanks." *Now go be snotty to somebody who cares.* She turned back to Althea. "You ready for the scene? Terror on tap?"

Althea looked over the rail at the dark river. "There's a *gator* down there," she said, her face distorted as she faked fear. "They're *dangerous.*"

"Yes, there's an alligator," Stephanie said to Althea, in a voice she'd use to talk to a small child she didn't like. "But since he's not going to be climbing up on the bridge, he's moot."

Watch it, Lucy thought, prepared to drop-kick her off the bridge if Althea took offense, but Althea just smoothed out her face and said, "Moot. That's a funny name for a gator."

"Moot?" Pepper said, forgetting to lie low. She looked over the rail and trained her binoculars down on the gator, floating in the moonlight now.

Stephanie curled her lip. "Yes, it is a funny name. Are you ready?"

"Just about," Althea said.

"You can go now," Lucy said to Stephanie. *And later we will talk about not patronizing the talent.*

Stephanie walked off into the darkness, and Althea dropped her chin and watched her from under lowered brows, no smile at all.

Mistake, Stephanie, Lucy thought.

"I think Moot only has one eye," Pepper said, still staring through her binoculars.

Althea met Lucy's eyes. "Maybe I'll get a chicken to throw to old Moot tomorrow."

"That would be better than throwing Stephanie."

Althea grinned, a real smile this time.

"It's *bad* to feed the alligators," Pepper said, looking up at them. "If you feed them, they lose their fear of humans and *attack*."

Lucy looked down at Moot, sneering at them from the river. "Too late. Moot already thinks we're worthless."

"Bryce throws Ding Dongs from Crafty to him," Pepper said sadly.

Althea rolled her eyes and then leaned a little closer to Lucy. "Listen, can we talk? After this take, I mean? About Bryce. And some other things."

I miss the dogs, Lucy thought. *They never want to talk.* "Absolutely. You ready to go here?"

Althea nodded, and Lucy smiled encouragingly at her and headed back to video village with Pepper in her wake, thinking, *It's going to be a really long four days.*

"How's it going?" Gloom said when she got there.

Lucy settled into her chair. "My assistant is an elitist snot who thinks Connor's God, my lead actress wants to chat about the lead actor, and there's a gator underneath the bridge who's gonna call for a wine list if anybody falls off."

"So we're good then."

"Oh, yeah," Lucy said as Pepper climbed up onto the chair to her far right, leaving empty the seat between them where her mother was supposed to be. *No script supervisor again,* Lucy thought. *That's not like Daisy.*

"You okay?" Gloom said.

"I'm beginning to sense a distinct lack of enthusiasm on the part of the crew," Lucy said, nodding at Daisy's vacant seat.

"I know how they feel," Gloom said and called, "Stand by," as people melted off the set. Then he called, "Roll sound," and someone echoed, "Rolling," and a cameraman shoved a clapper in front of Althea's face, yelled, "Take one," and smacked it shut.

Lucy called, "Camera," and then, "Action," and Althea slung her leg over the rail and boosted herself up and then screamed halfheartedly as Rick dragged her back down and called her an idiot with much the same force that he'd use to ask for a latte. Althea said, "What do you care?" as if she didn't, and then let him drag her back to the car.

Lucy yelled, "Cut," and looked at Gloom.

"Distinct Lack of Enthusiasm," he said. "Part Two: The Cast."

Lucy took off her headphones and walked over to Althea. "You feeling okay?"

"Yes." Althea blinked at her. "Why?"

"Because you're a better actress than that." *My dogs are better actors than that.* "Is there something wrong?"

Althea nodded. "Well, yeah. About Bryce. He—"

"Bryce isn't in this scene," Lucy said. "We're going to try it again and—"

"Again?" Althea seemed dumbfounded.

Connor came up. "What's wrong? You got the shot."

Lucy turned to him, glad to have somebody she could snap at. *"Go away."*

"What?" he asked, as dumbfounded as Althea had been.

"You're the stunt coordinator," Lucy said. "If you're worried about her cable, *check it,* but do not now or *ever* tell me when I've got the shot. *Understand?*" Connor jerked back, and Lucy turned to Althea. "You ready to do this for real?"

"Yeah." Althea straightened. "Yes, I am."

"Go to one," Lucy called to the set, and Althea went back to the rail while Rick took his position beside the car. Lucy stopped to talk to him on her way back to the monitors. "I don't know what's going on here, but we're going to shoot this sucker until we get a good take. That okay with you?"

"Yep," Rick said, also surprised. "More than okay."

"All right, then." Lucy went back to the monitors to sit down and found Daisy back in her chair. "There's something weird about this shoot," she said to Daisy.

"No idea what you're talking about," Daisy said, staring at the set, her notebook in her lap, as the set echoed with "Stand by," "Roll sound," "Rolling," "Take two," and the sound of the clapper.

Lucy watched the monitor and this time Althea flung herself over the bridge rail with such force that Rick really had to catch her and bring her back, and his "You little idiot!" sounded real, as did Althea's sobbed scream, "What do you care?" Rick yelled back, "Dead hostage? I care a lot," and dragged her toward the car while she fought him tooth and nail.

"Cut!" Lucy called, feeling much better. "That was *excellent*. Really great, guys. Let's go again and then we'll do the close-ups."

Althea beamed at her and motioned her over.

Oh, hell, Lucy thought and went.

Althea leaned close to her. "I need to ask you something. You know, girl to girl."

"Uh," Lucy said, thinking, *Kill me now.*

"I mean, I know you're really busy because this is your big break—"

"Not so much," Lucy said. *Where are they getting this big break stuff?*

"—But what do you think of Bryce?"

"Fine actor," Lucy said automatically.

"No, I mean, you know." Althea began to look impatient. "As a man."

Lucy tried again. "He seems like a really nice guy."

Gloom called, "Let's go," and Lucy smiled at Althea.

"Okay, that last take was a great one, so let's do another one to make sure."

Althea nodded. "Could you come back while they're doing the next camera setup?"

"Sure. You bet."

Lucy went back to the monitors and watched while Althea and Rick nailed another take and thought, *This could work.* "Fantastic," she called to them. "Reset, please."

Pepper climbed into the seat beside her. "I brought you an apple."

Lucy said, "Thank you," thinking, *I'm going to die of an apple overdose,* and then glanced at Daisy.

She looked like leftover death, her eyes red, her eyelids drooping as if she were struggling to stay conscious.

"You sure you're getting enough sleep?" Lucy bit into her apple, trying to act unconcerned.

"Uh huh." Daisy kept her head bent over her notebook.

So much for acting. "Daisy, what the hell—"

"Working here," Daisy said and kept her head down.

"Lucy!" Althea called, and Lucy went back to her, looking back over her shoulder at Daisy as she went.

When she reached Althea, she said, "That was great, Al," but she kept an eye on Daisy, slumped in her chair at the monitors.

"Thank you," Althea said. "Listen, anybody who can make Connor do what she wants knows what she's doing."

"What?" Lucy said, distracted from Daisy.

"I need your advice," Althea said. "About men. I want security, that's why I'm with Bryce right now, because he's good for my career. But I want something permanent, too, you know?"

"Oh," Lucy said, as Pepper came up to join them. "Well, Bryce is probably rich. He's done pretty well for himself—"

Althea frowned at her. "I don't mean for him to support me, I'm going to get my own money, I've got a line on that, but I don't want to be alone. I want security, you know? Somebody I can depend on?"

"Oh." Lucy nodded. "Emotional security." *And you're sleeping with an actor?*

Connor came up to the rail about ten feet from them to direct the camera basket in, and Althea turned her hip so that he could see her concave stomach and the bulge of her breasts in her tank top. Pepper watched her and then tried to do the same, her little potbelly sticking out where Althea's abdomen collapsed toward her backbone.

Connor looked over at them, much too offhand, and nodded, but Lucy saw his eyes connect with Althea's.

Althea met his stare and held it until he nodded again.

Oh, God, don't let Althea be cheating on Bryce with Connor, Lucy thought. Bryce did not look like a man who would take well to being dumped for a stunt coordinator. And if he found out and sulked, goodbye shooting schedule.

Althea turned back to Lucy. "Not just emotional security. I want physical security, too. I want it all."

"Physical security. Like bodyguards?" Lucy said.

"No, like . . ." Althea's eyes went to Pepper. "Uh, satisfaction security. You know."

"Oh," Lucy said, caught off guard. "Well. The best way to be, uh, secure—" she glanced down at Pepper, who was listening with great interest, "is to know things yourself." Althea looked confused, so Lucy added, "I think you have to know what you need and tell Bryce. Show him if you have to."

"Huh?" Althea said. "I mean *in bed*."

"Pepper, go get me an apple, please," Lucy said.

"Okay." Pepper ran for the craft services table.

"Because sex is *really* important." Althea didn't frown, but she was clearly thinking hard. "And I'm running out of time. I want seventy-four to be somebody who knows what he's doing and who will stand by me."

"Seventy-four?"

Althea nodded. "Stephanie told me about this article by this math woman that said that if you slept with seventy-five people, the person you were supposed to be with would show up."

"I see," Lucy said, thinking, *I must have a long talk with my assistant.* Then the meaning sunk in. "Seventy-four?"

Althea nodded again. "Bryce is seventy-three. After Stephanie said that, I counted."

"Uh huh." Lucy tried to sound supportive.

"And Bryce isn't . . . working out," Althea said, "so then I thought about Nash because . . ." she shot another look at the stunt coordinator, "he is hot. No wonder you're back together."

"We're not. Now—"

"I'd like somebody like him," Althea said, looking past her. "Somebody tough like him who would stick by me. I bet somebody like him would be good in bed." She blinked up at Lucy. "Is he good in bed?"

"Not very," Lucy lied, shafting Connor without guilt. "But I'm sure Bryce . . ." She let her voice trail off because Althea was now smiling past her.

Lucy turned and saw Bryce, looking perfectly normal next to his new buddy, J. T. Wilder, who looked pretty damn good if you liked deadpan, tight-assed, monosyllabic military men. She turned back to Althea.

Althea appeared to like deadpan, tight-assed, monosyllabic military men.

Damn it, Lucy thought. "Bryce is really a good guy. And he's a *star,* Althea. Big security."

"Comedies," Althea said, still staring at Wilder. "He acts goofy and falls down. Big deal."

Lucy gave up. "Althea, there are only four days left in this shoot. Please don't upset him until Friday or the shot schedule will go to hell."

"He wouldn't be upset." Althea looked back at Wilder. "He's doing one of the makeup girls. Mary somebody. Do you think J.T. likes me?"

"Everybody likes you," Lucy said grimly, as Pepper came running back with the apple.

"I had to look for a Gala," she said, presenting it to Lucy. "They were mostly Red Delicious. That's not as good, right?"

"Right." Lucy took the apple while watching Althea, who was still zeroed in on Wilder. "Thank you, Pepper, you did exactly right." *And now I have to eat another apple.*

"So," Althea said, "J.T.'s, like, in the Army?"

"You're welcome," Pepper said, frowning at Althea.

"Evidently," Lucy said. "Bryce seems to have found him at Fort Bragg."

Althea licked her upper lip. "What do you know about him?"

"Absolutely nothing." Lucy bit hard into her apple.

"He looks like a guy you could count on, you know?"

Lucy swallowed. "Althea, if you're looking for dependability, don't go to men. If you've—" she looked down at Pepper, who was listening intently, "*dated* seventy-three of them, you must have noticed that they often leave."

Althea transferred her interest back to Lucy. "You think Nash is going to leave? Is that what happened the last time? When you were young?"

Lucy looked at the twenty-something actress with distaste. "No. When I was *young,* he lied to me and I left."

"J.T. doesn't look like a liar," Althea said, going back to her first interest. "But I don't think he's really warmed up to me yet."

"J.T. is not a liar," Pepper said.

Lucy followed Althea's eyes to Wilder, standing alert and still in the middle of chaos, watching everybody with those flat, cold eyes. "I don't think Captain Wilder warms up to anybody." *Although it certainly would be interesting to make him try.*

"I can make a man warm up," Althea said, and Lucy felt a spurt of irritation that was as legitimate as it was hypocritical. "And he looks dependable. He might be marriage material."

"J. T. Wilder does not strike me as the marrying type," Lucy said with complete sincerity. "Now, about this next scene—"

Althea turned obediently back to her mark. "Do women count?"

"What women?"

"The women I've . . . known," Althea said, keeping an eye on Pepper. "Because if they don't, I'm only at seventy-one."

"They count," Lucy said.

Althea nodded, and Lucy looked back at Bryce and his new buddy and felt like kicking them both. She didn't want to fight for Bryce— the dumbass was doing the makeup girl, she'd have left him, too— but she only needed four more days. And she'd have them if J.T. Wilder would stop dazzling Althea, damn it.

"Gators do not eat apples," Pepper said.

Althea smiled down at her, probably recognizing a kindred spirit in somebody who would say anything to get attention. "You know a lot about gators."

Pepper nodded. "They're my Animal of the Month."

"Oh," Althea said, and Lucy thought, *And now she'll want an Animal of the Month, too,* and thought of Wilder.

"Tell me something scary about them," Althea said to Pepper, evidently gearing up for more terror.

"They can outrun a horse," Pepper said solemnly. "Although not for very long. You couldn't race them or anything."

"And they have sharp teeth," Althea said.

"No," Pepper said sternly. "They have dull teeth. They don't bite, they clamp down. And then they *thrash their victims to pieces.*"

Althea's eyes widened.

"Okay," Lucy said cheerfully. "Enough gator lore. Why don't you go wait for me at the monitors?"

"Okay," Pepper said without moving. "I know what I need. You know, what you asked me? I need a Wonder Woman Barbie. I have all the Super Hero Barbies except that one and I should have them all so that when I have friends, we can play with them."

When I have friends? Lucy looked at her, appalled. Pepper didn't have friends. Well, she wasn't in school, Daisy tutored her, so how could she have friends? *That's got to change.*

Meanwhile, Pepper had stopped, perplexed. "You know, SuperGirl has white mittens. I don't get that."

Lucy smiled at Pepper. *Get her into school later, make her happy now.*

"A Wonder Woman Barbie. I'll look into that. But for right now, go back to video village, baby. Tell Gloom I'll be right there."

Pepper nodded and walked away, her little shoulders slumping.

"Sorry about the gator lecture." Lucy peered at Althea. "You okay?"

"Well, I don't like Moot so much anymore," Althea said, but then she stopped, her eye caught by something behind Lucy.

Lucy turned and saw J. T. Wilder, looking stone-faced and dangerous.

Althea wiggled her fingers at Wilder.

Wilder looked at Althea as if she were Moot.

You'll never outrun her, Lucy thought, *she's faster than she looks.*

"I'm ready for my close-up now," Althea said, still staring at Wilder.

"I'll tell Mr. DeMille," Lucy said and went back to the monitors, more annoyed than she should have been.

Wilder watched Armstrong head back to video village under the lights of the set, attacking another apple as she went, and thought, *Apples and women.* Not a good history there.

The night wind picked up and blew back her shirt, exposing her curves in that white T-shirt again.

Course, he'd never been any good at history.

His satellite phone vibrated in his pocket and startled him out of staring. He turned and walked away from the set into the darkness as he pulled the phone out. Nobody had his number except Group and an ex-girlfriend who was so ex she was probably married with four kids by now and who wasn't supposed to have the number anyway since it was an Army-issue phone. Which meant this was an alert.

Fuck, Wilder thought. Alerting him on leave meant a real mission. He glanced at the display before answering: BLOCKED.

"Captain Wilder," he snapped into the phone, and Bryce looked up from playing with the clasp on the knife sheath, impressed.

The voice on the phone said, "Captain Wilder."

What the hell? He'd just said that. He waited and there was nothing but static for several moments, which Wilder recognized as a scrambler being used by whoever was calling him. That, combined with the fact that the call was bouncing through secure military satellites, confirmed that whatever was coming was going to be bad news.

"Captain Wilder, you have been seconded to the CIA and you need to make a meet. One hour. A diner in a small shopping mall in South Carolina right after you come off the Talmadge Bridge. Eddy's."

The static ended and Wilder pulled the phone away from his ear and stared at it. *What the hell?*

He put the phone away and caught sight of Bryce, looking serious, mouthing, "Captain Wilder," with different expressions, evidently trying to get the same look Wilder had just had.

If I really look like that, Wilder thought, *I'm going to stop answering the phone.*

Bryce caught him watching and flushed.

"Okay if I take a break?" Wilder said. *If he says no, I have to quit. Fucking CIA.*

Bryce grinned at him and nodded at the phone in his hand. "Girlfriend?"

"Uh, yeah," Wilder said. *Me and the CIA. We're close.*

"Take all the time you want." Bryce winked.

Wilder nodded back toward the set. "What about Armstrong?"

"I'll take care of her, buddy." Bryce winked again.

"Thanks." Wilder walked away before he got a third wink, almost grateful for the call.

He headed for his Jeep and then caught Armstrong watching him with a look he couldn't quite make out. *Not my day,* he thought. She hadn't wanted him, and Bryce had forced the issue. Might be a smart idea to take a couple of minutes, try to mend things. Hell, he could practically see where the meeting was to be, just north of the bridge. He had an hour to get there. He could check out with the boss lady, make her feel like she was in charge, scope out the T-shirt. Plus, he was in no rush to make this meeting. Anything, even being on this screwed-up set, was preferable to a meeting with the CIA.

He changed course and headed for Armstrong.

"I'm on leave, but I just got a call," he told her when he reached her. "Bryce said it was okay if I left for a couple of hours."

She shrugged, which did nice things for the T-shirt. "If Bryce is fine with it, just come back tomorrow afternoon. The set call is for one."

"Right." He shifted his feet, trying to think of a way to make peace. "Is your daughter okay? I didn't mean to scare her when I grabbed her."

She looked startled. "Pepper? She's not my daughter and you didn't scare her. She's my niece and she's fine. Thanks to you."

Okay, that was good, she was grateful and Pepper wasn't her daughter. "Uh, my appointment's in this shopping mall over . . . Do you need anything?"

"A Wonder Woman Barbie," she said and then caught sight of something over his shoulder. "Thank you again for Pepper, Captain Wilder," she said and moved around him, toward whatever problem she'd just spotted, and he could smell her scent, not perfume, something softer, soap maybe.

"Right," he said, as she walked away from him. "Wonder Woman." He shook his head, took a deep breath of fresh air, and escaped to his Jeep.

The CIA was starting to look better.

Wilder found Eddy's Diner in a dark, seedy, little strip mall, half the stores empty under a rusting sign that said CHERRY HILL PLAZA. It was flanked on one end by Eddy's and on the other by Maraschino's, A Gentlemen's Club, which sounded familiar. One of the guys had talked about it, Wilder thought. Probably LaFavre. He had a thing for strippers.

The other occupied storefronts were a florist, a sewing machine shop, a place painted black with JAX COMIX in Day-Glo pink letters painted on its dingy window, and an insurance agency. No toy stores, but there was a poster of Wonder Woman in the comic-store window, the only store open this late. Wilder imagined Armstrong's face if he showed up with a Wonder Woman doll. Then he remembered her walking up the bridge and the wind blowing her shirt back.

The CIA could wait. Forever, if Wilder had his druthers.

The shop was dim inside, lots of black shelves full of videos and DVDs and bins full of comics in clean plastic sleeves. Behind the counter, a skinny twenty-something with a shadow of a mustache leaned over a comic book, his hands planted protectively on each side of it while he argued with a kid of about twelve, up past his bedtime. The guy behind the counter stopped arguing when he saw Wilder. "Can I help you?"

"A Wonder Woman doll?" Wilder said, ignoring the twelve-year-old's snicker. He looked past the guy to see a mannequin on a shelf, one of those with the head and arms and legs cut off so the whole thing stood on its thighs. Stretched over its chipped flesh was a thin red T-shirt with skinny straps that had a double yellow W printed across the bustline and beneath that tight blue shorts with white stars on them.

"WonderWear," the guy said, following Wilder's eyes. "Wonder Woman cami and panty set. One hundred percent cotton. Very popular. Twenty-five bucks. For sixty bucks we got the whole costume including the cape, the bracelets, and the Lasso of Truth."

Lasso of Truth?

The guy looked Wilder up and down. "We got the Superman boxer with the Super Size shield, too. Twelve bucks."

"Just the doll." Wilder turned away to see a full-size stand-up cutout of a woman wearing the same outfit, more or less, her long dark hair curling thickly around her face while she stretched a yellow rope between her hands. She did not look like his vague recollections of Wonder Woman as a shiny, happy camper; she looked like a strong-jawed, patriotic dominatrix. Worse than that, she looked like Armstrong.

Yeah, I needed that *picture in my head,* he thought, trying not to dwell on the rope. Lasso of Truth. Made sense. If Armstrong wore that outfit and tied him up, he'd tell her anything she wanted to know. Everyone talked under the right pressure. They did teach that at Bragg. He looked at the cutout again. Yeah, Armstrong in that outfit would be the right pressure. He caught the twelve-year-old looking at him and stared the kid down.

The guy put a large blue box on the counter. "Wonder Woman doll, Masterpiece Edition. Comes with the hardcover history and a reprint of the first comic. Very hard to find, seventy bucks."

The woman pictured on the box also did not look like his memory of Wonder Woman. She looked like a picture of his Great-Great-Aunt Maude. In a hurry.

"But for you today," the guy said, "sixty."

Behind him, the WonderWear throbbed. Armstrong could do a lot for that underwear. He wondered what her hair looked like when not in that braid.

"Okay, okay," the guy said. "I can tell you're a collector and the box is a little worn. Fifty."

Wilder tried to picture Althea in the WonderWear, which should have been easy since she'd been wearing the same kind of red T-shirt with little straps, but she was just not . . . strong enough. He looked back at the life-size cutout. He could picture Althea with the bracelets, it was the lasso that didn't work.

"I know," the guy said, sounding resigned. "You looked on eBay, you know I'm selling them there for about forty, so okay, forty. But that's my final offer."

Armstrong, on the other hand, he could easily see snapping that rope—

"And I'll throw in the Wonder Woman Ultimate Sticker Book!" the guy said, desperation in his voice.

"Fine," Wilder said, trying to come back from Armstrong and the rope. So much for comics as kid stuff.

The guy nodded, relieved. "Great buy," he said as he went to ring it up. "Wonder Woman's hot."

The twelve-year-old snickered again.

"Come back when you're thirteen," Wilder told the kid and paid the guy.

4

When Gloom called second meal, Lucy went with everybody else on the shuttle down to the dirt lot under the bridge, but when Connor looked like he was heading her way, she veered off from the crowd around the catering tent to cross the dark lot to her camper. The battered Roadtrak was cramped inside, but it was quiet and it didn't have Daisy looking defeated, or Stephanie being snotty, or Connor bitching about Wilder, or Althea trolling for security, so it was good.

Lucy stepped up inside and pulled the white waffle curtains closed to shut out the darkness. Then she edged her way around the little blue Formica-topped table behind the swiveling driver's seat and into the short cabinet-lined space that separated the front of the van from the double bed that filled the back. There were apples in the little sink, but Lucy opened the undercounter refrigerator instead and got out IBC Diet Root Beer and cheese sticks. Comfort food.

She put her iPod in the speaker dock on the counter and dialed up Kirsty MacColl. "In These Shoes." That's what she wanted to hear, a woman in control, calling the shots. Forget "Holding Out For A Hero," there were no heroes—

The door to the camper opened and Daisy came in, looking worse than ever, and collapsed on one of the plush swivel chairs. "My God, what a night."

"It was filled with excitement," Lucy agreed. "And it's not over yet. Root beer?"

"I just heard about Pepper on the bridge," Daisy said, swallowing. "I could have lost her. If you hadn't been there—"

"Not me, Captain Wilder." Lucy surveyed her, trying to see past the exhaustion. Daisy was more than tired, she was beaten down, as if somebody had kicked all the sass out of her.

"I should have been there," Daisy said, her voice catching.

Yeah, you should have been. Lucy sat down across from her. "Are you going to tell me what's wrong anytime soon? Don't even think you're going to get away with 'I'm fine.' You're not fine. You're exhausted and depressed and you can't go on like this."

Daisy shook her head, and then the camper door opened again and Stephanie said, "I need to see you." She frowned at the iPod, where Kirsty was singing about not making love on a mountaintop.

Lucy frowned back at her. "We're talking here."

"It's okay." Daisy smiled weakly at Stephanie. "What's up?"

Stephanie climbed into the camper. "There's a problem."

I know and I was solving it before you barged in here. Lucy smiled at her tightly. "Really? What a surprise." She looked at Daisy. "Cheese stick? Root beer?" *Hemlock?*

Stephanie ignored Daisy to scowl at Lucy, her body rigid with dislike. "It's that knife of Bryce's. Friday's dailies came back. He keeps buckling it on different sides."

In spite of everything, Lucy grinned. The knife was a real problem for continuity—that would be Daisy, who should have caught it that the knife was wrong—but Lucy couldn't think about it without laughing. A fight with a gladiator, Wilder had said. A tight-ass with a sense of humor. There couldn't be a lot of those.

"And now he wants to strap it on his calf."

"His calf." Lucy couldn't help herself, she laughed out loud, picturing Bryce hobbling across the set, the knife splinted to his leg.

Stephanie was disgusted. "Because of what his *consultant* said."

"Ah. His consultant." *Thank you, Captain Wilder, for your inspiring lecture on jaw-jamming Navy SEALs and their handy-dandy calf knives.* Lucy looked over at Daisy. "How many shots do we have of the knife on the wrong side, Daisy?"

"Four. None on the calf." Daisy stopped smiling. "I missed it at first, but then I made sure that it stayed on that side for the rest of that scene. I don't think anybody will notice."

"Okay, then," Lucy said to Stephanie. "For the stuff we've already shot, left, right, even Bryce doesn't know. Let the microminds find it and post it on the Internet, I don't care."

"That's obvious," Stephanie snapped.

Lucy met Daisy's eyes. "Go check on Pepper. We'll talk tonight after the shoot's over."

Daisy nodded and escaped, edging around Stephanie to get out the door.

"Sit," Lucy said, and Stephanie looked mutinous, but she sat down in one of the swivel chairs. "We appear to have some problems."

Stephanie's chin went up. "Problems?"

Lucy leaned forward. "I know it's been rough, losing your director the way you did, but there are only four days left on the shoot, so if you could hold it together until Friday—"

"I am holding it together," Stephanie said sharply. "What did I do?"

"Well, to begin with, you're gone chasing Connor most of the time, so as an assistant you're not much help."

Stephanie jerked back but Lucy kept going.

"Then you patronized Althea on the set today, and she's not stupid, Stephanie. She plays dumb but she knew what you were doing and she didn't like it. That's no way to treat your actors. If you want a career in film, you should know that already."

Stephanie flushed. "But—"

"Also, you told Althea that if she slept with seventy-five people, she'd find the right man."

"What?" Stephanie looked outraged for a moment, and then her face cleared. "Oh, for the love of God. That woman is a moron."

Lucy repressed a spurt of irritation. "No, she's not. She's just confused. What did you tell her?"

Stephanie sighed. "She was flirting with Nash." Her jaw hardened. "She's been chasing him, really blatantly."

Lucy thought, *Hello, hypocrite.*

"I think maybe she wanted to make Bryce jealous, use Connor as a backup plan. I heard her talking to Connor about her future, about wanting security, like she thought he was going to give it to her."

"Right," Lucy said. "Now, about the seventy-five bed partners . . ."

Stephanie kept on as if she hadn't spoken. "And she's mad at Bryce because he's spending a lot of time with Mary Vanity so—"

"Mary Vanity?"

"One of the makeup girls. We always call hair and makeup the Vanities, and the one Bryce is paying attention to is Mary, so she's Mary Vanity."

"Right," Lucy said. "So how did you get from Bryce doing Mary Vanity to seventy-five men for Althea?"

"I *didn't*. I was trying to get her away from Nash, and I told her about this study I'd read that said once you'd slept with twelve people, you should pick the next best one because you'd have a seventy-five percent chance of being happy with him."

Lucy blinked at her. "And you told her this because . . ."

"I thought she had to be past twelve men by now," Stephanie said, her nostrils flaring. "And given where she probably came from, Bryce has to be the best one."

"Seventy-one men," Lucy said. "And two women."

"And she confused the seventy-five percent with the twelve." Stephanie rolled her eyes. "What an idiot."

"I don't think she ever claimed to be good at math. But from now on, don't give her dating advice. Just kneecap her if she tries to sleep with anybody but our star."

Stephanie nodded, and Lucy added, "Kidding."

"Of course," Stephanie said, her voice as flat as Wilder's.

"And I need the full script," Lucy said.

Stephanie reached into her bag and handed one over.

"Excellent," Lucy said. "Thank you very much."

"You're welcome," Stephanie said, in a voice that telegraphed, *Drop dead.*

Pepper opened the door to the camper. "Aunt Lucy, we are saving you a seat. There's *lasagna!*"

"Excellent, Pepper," Lucy said. "I'll be right out."

Pepper sat down on the step, and Lucy stood up. "We'll talk tomorrow," she said to Stephanie. "After I've read the script. I have some questions—"

"Fine." Stephanie stood, too. "One more thing." She looked stern. "About Wilder. He's upsetting Nash. He has to go."

"He stays," Lucy said.

Stephanie shook her head, disgusted, and went down the steps, almost trampling Pepper.

Pepper stood up. "I think we should have lasagna with J.T."

"J.T., huh?" Lucy said. "Well, J.T. had an appointment so he's gone. But I will have lasagna with you."

"Is he coming back?" Pepper said, looking alarmed.

"Tomorrow."

"Good." She took Lucy's hand.

"That remains to be seen," Lucy said and let Pepper pull her over to the catering tables, pretty sure the lasagna was going to be the high point of her night.

Forty-seven bucks lighter, Wilder pushed open the door to Eddy's, his Jax Comix bag in hand, and looked around. The only person in the steamy little diner who looked remotely official was a kid who couldn't have been more than twenty, tops, sitting at a corner table, watching the door.

Wilder's eyes flickered about the room, cataloging the other occupants in the dim light before coming back to rest on the kid. He had to be the contact. Pathetic. Armstrong would have bitten him in half. After she tied him up.

Wilder shook his head to get rid of the Lasso of Truth. *Damn women.* He figured this was why they didn't let women into Special Forces. Messed with a man's thinking ability.

Wilder walked up to him. "Who the hell are you?"

The kid slid awkwardly out of his chair. "Crawford." He extended his hand.

Wilder ignored it. "You called me?"

"Yes." Crawford lowered his hand, wiping it on his sport coat as he sat back down. "I'm your handler."

First the clusterfuck, now this. There was a reason Special Ops said that CIA stood for Clowns in Action.

The kid was in his seat. Wilder pointed to the other side of the scarred Formica table. "You sit there."

Crawford shrugged and moved, his back to the rest of the diner. Wilder took the chair across from him, dropping the Comix bag on the floor. "Why do I need a handler? I'm on leave."

The kid ducked his head. "Uh, not exactly."

Resignation settled in. He'd known it was too good to be true. "Then what exactly?"

Crawford's face scrunched up in confusion. "What?"

Wilder wondered if the kid was old enough to shave. He sure as hell wasn't old enough to handle Wilder. He rubbed his left temple, which was beginning to throb. "Beer," he said to the waitress who appeared behind Crawford.

Crawford jerked his head up. "What?"

Wilder arched an eyebrow and the kid looked over his shoulder. The waitress nodded and walked away.

Wilder waited for the kid to tell him what hellhole he was going to be flying off to now.

"*Don't Look Down,*" the kid said.

Wilder blinked, staying the natural impulse to look down. "Say again?"

"That's the name of the movie. It's also the name of the company that was set up to assist in financing the movie. Don't Look Down Incorporated. Let's call it DLDI."

Let's not.

"So far DLDI has invested four million dollars in the production of *Don't Look Down,*" Crawford continued. "That's a lot of money."

No shit. Wilder was still waiting for the really bad part, but he was relieved that Crawford hadn't mentioned places like Iraq or Afghanistan. Yet.

"The money is coming through DLDI from a man named James Finnegan," Crawford said. "We have Finnegan on our terrorist watch list. We believe he's putting dirty money into the movie in order to pull out at least a percentage of it clean when the movie is released and funnel it into funding for various organizations that we are opposed to."

Wonderful, Wilder thought. An international terrorist. That was all this mess needed.

Crawford shifted in his chair. "We want you to watch the movie set for Finnegan. Get us a lead on where he is, a phone number, anything." Wilder sat back. He should have known the easy movie work was too much of a good deal not to go wrong. "And you just got lucky that Bryce needed a consultant and put me on the set."

"Uh, no, not exactly," Crawford said. "We convinced his stunt double to leave. And then it was suggested to him via his agent, who has some issues with the IRS, that you might be a good replacement. He is highly suggestible."

No shit. "It was not suggested to me."

"We didn't know for certain he'd ask you. Now he has. Now you know. And now you can find us a lead to Finnegan."

Fuck, Wilder thought, but it was still better than Iraq. "Was it by chance that I was picked to be Bryce's guide when he was at Fort Bragg?"

"Uh, no. In fact, if you want the truth, Bryce's agent was the one who told Bryce to go to Bragg to get some help on being an action star. And we kind of told his agent to do that, too. And we got the Army to agree to it."

Wilder nodded, resigned to the situation. "If Finnegan's behind the movie, there have to be a shitload of legitimate contacts he's made. Why not just follow those?"

"Dead ends," Crawford said. "He's not dumb."

Nobody connected with that movie has any brains, Wilder wanted to say, but the jury was still out on Armstrong. And Nash wasn't stupid. "Tell me about Finnegan."

Crawford nodded. "James Finnegan. Seventy-three years old. His mother worked in the art museum in Dublin until she was killed in a cross fire. That's when he joined the IRA. Before 9/11, the IRA was getting a lot of cash in from the United States, and Finnegan helped them wash it by investing it in art. After that, Finnegan began freelancing, working for whoever paid him the most."

Wilder sighed. "A capitalistic terrorist. Great."

Crawford went on. "Finnegan disappeared off the intelligence radar until the Mexican authorities caught him in Cabo four months ago trying to take out some very rare and expensive stolen pre-Columbian artifacts from Costa Rica. Pornographic stuff. A bunch of jade dicks." He snickered, and when Wilder didn't join in, he cleared his throat and said, "Jade phallic symbols. Supposed to cure impotence and increase, uh, staying power."

Wilder resisted the urge to make wisecracks since Crawford was being juvenile enough for both of them. "It's a smart play. Use the dirty money to buy the art, then sell it on the black market and get clean money from the collectors in return. How much was the stuff worth?"

"The entire shipment would have been worth about five million without the Viagra factor. But if you believe the stuff will help you get it up, it's worth about fifty million. Finnegan's in his seventies. Maybe he believes." Crawford snickered again.

Just what I needed, Wilder thought. *Beavis as my CIA handler.* "But the Mexicans caught him."

Crawford nodded. "He paid them off and got away, but without the jade. Which leads us to DLDI."

Wilder shook his head. "He lost the art so now he's financing a movie? How does that help him?"

Crawford tried to look mysterious and just looked confused. "That's on a need-to-know basis."

Right. "Do you have a photo of him? For all I know he's already on the set, I just didn't get introduced to him."

"I'll get you a photo, but the odds are slim that Finnegan will ever set foot inside the country."

"Then why are you bothering me?"

"I told you. We need you to keep an eye on things. See if you can get a line on where Finnegan is."

Wilder sighed again. "What kind of backup do you have on call?"

The kid looked confused once more. " 'Backup'?"

Fuck, this was like talking to Bryce. "You know, if the bad guy shows up. Do I call you to send in the troops? Or am I supposed to handle him? And how? Tie him up? Club him? Tell him he has nice eyes and buy him a drink?"

Crawford tried to look disapproving and just looked grumpy. "You call me if Finnegan shows."

"And?"

"And I'll handle it."

Right. Wilder took a deep breath and let it out. The odds of this kid handling anything were about the same as Finnegan showing up on the movie set, so it really wasn't an issue.

"I said, I'll handle it," Crawford said, a little louder, disconcerted by Wilder's silence when he really should have been happy about it.

"This is a pretty vague mission. You could have told me this crap on the phone in five minutes. Why'd you drag my ass here?" Wilder raised a finger as Crawford's mouth flapped open to answer.

The waitress glided in and put a mug of whatever local brew was on tap in front of Wilder. She glanced at the kid. "You need a refill on that Coke?"

Crawford shook his head and she departed. Wilder was willing to bet it was Diet Coke.

"I wanted to meet you," Crawford said.

"Okay. Done it. Feel better? Bye."

Crawford placed both hands on the scarred table. Wilder could see the veins pulse as the kid pressed down, trying to regain control. "There's no need to be antagonistic. We're working together."

"What you mean 'we,' kemosabe?" Wilder picked up the mug and drained half of it in one smooth gulp.

"What?"

The kid liked that word, Wilder thought as he put the mug on the table. And he was too young to have seen *The Lone Ranger,* so the kemosabe crack was wasted. This was one shitty day. "Okay, we're working together. Work. Tell me about the people on the set who are most likely to be hooked up with Finnegan. The director—Lucy Armstrong." He felt a twinge of guilt asking about her, but she was the one in charge. "She just got on the set, but she's running things. What's her story?"

"I don't know."

Wilder spoke slowly. "That's your part of the 'we,' okay? Apparently, I'm the guy in the field whose ass is in a sling when things go to shit. You're the handler. You pump me for intel to report back to your boss, I pump you for intel so I can do my job. *Dah? Nyet? Mosybyet?*"

The Russian was lost on the kid. Wilder had seen the type before. The CIA sent a lot of their people down to Bragg to learn the abbreviated version of being a commando. Just enough info so they could justify carrying automatic weapons overseas and run hellholes like Abu Gharib. And let the military guys take the fall for it. He finished his beer and set the mug down on the table with a solid thump.

"I'll see what we have on Armstrong," the kid said, pulling out a pad and pencil from inside his jacket and exposing a shoulder holster with a small revolver in it.

Who the hell carries that kind of revolver? Wilder thought. From here it looked like a .38, a peashooter, not a Dirty Harry blow-a-limb-off-with-a-near-miss revolver like Nash had in his quick-draw rig. Jesus. "Find out about the first director, too, the one who died."

Crawford licked the end of his pencil and put it on the pad.

"Don't write it down," Wilder suggested. "Let's make believe we're running a covert operation here and we have to like, you know, keep secrets?"

"Right." Crawford scooped the pad off the table and jammed it back in his jacket.

That was better than "what," at least. Wilder held up the empty mug, his eyes going past Crawford's shoulder.

The kid frowned as the waitress came over with a fresh brew. "Do you think you should be drinking on duty?"

Had the kid just said what he had? Wilder rewound his brain, replayed it, and yes, the kid had. "First, I didn't know I was on duty until a couple of minutes ago. I was on leave and I am assuming I am *not* going to get charged leave time now." Wilder did not want to bring up the money Bryce was paying him. Screw the CIA.

"Second, I'm undercover. This is part of my cover." Wilder smiled, trying to be nice, but this nice shit was getting old. This kid was doing things as wrong as they were doing them on the movie, except this stuff was real. "Cover for action. You know, like they taught you at Langley."

"What, being a drunk?"

Was it the "what" or the sentence that pissed him off—or that he knew he'd been drinking too much since his last tour in Iraq? Wilder wasn't sure but his smile was gone.

The kid pushed his chair back slightly, looking wary. "Listen, I got thrown into this job just—"

"I don't give a fuck about your sob story," Wilder said, his voice flat. "You get me the intelligence I need to do my job. I want that picture of Finnegan and the files on Armstrong and the old director, along with anything else you have that ties anyone on that movie to Finnegan in any way. Yesterday."

He got up and walked out, leaving the beer and the kid behind, and then remembered that in two days he'd be hanging out of a helicopter and pretending to be Bryce while Althea screamed in a car below and pretended to care. Iraq or not, this was no time to give up drinking.

Should have finished that beer, he thought and headed back to the set to drop off the comic stuff at Armstrong's camper.

And then he was going back to the hotel to get a real gun.

The shoot wrapped at two A.M., and Lucy went down to base camp, exhausted by the chaos and worried sick about Daisy, who had sleep-walked through the rest of the night. An hour before, listening to Daisy slur her words, she'd thought, *If it were anybody else but my sister, I'd think she was on something.* Then she'd watched Daisy fumble with her notebook and stumble when she got off her chair.

Hell, she thought now as she opened the door to the camper. *She's on something.*

A big brown paper bag stamped JAX COMIX was sitting on her table next to the script Stephanie had given her, with a Post-it note on the bag: "Captain Wilder left this for you." She sat down in one of the swivel chairs and pulled a big blue box from the bag and looked at the cartoon of a forties Wonder Woman on the front, something else inexplicable in her life, right up there with Daisy and Connor.

Then she remembered.

"Barbie," she said out loud and looked at the small print at the bottom of the box: EXCLUSIVE WONDER WOMAN CIRCA 1941 ACTION FIGURE. She'd told him Barbie and he'd thought "doll." And then he'd hunted this down. Poor guy.

Nice guy.

"I brought candy from Crafty," Pepper said, climbing up into the camper behind her, her hands full of Twizzlers and Hershey bars.

"I thought your mom said you weren't allowed to eat sugar between meals," Lucy said. "And shouldn't you be asleep?"

"I took a nap." Pepper dumped her loot on the dinette. "What's that?"

"I told Captain Wilder you wanted a Wonder Woman Barbie and he got you this." Lucy pulled open the Velcro tab. Inside was a lurid comic book, a hardcover book with a picture of Wonder Woman in her pretty-baby phase, and a plastic doll.

"That's not a Barbie." Pepper climbed into Lucy's lap, pried the plastic cover off, and took out the doll while Lucy snuggled her close and thought, *Poor baby*. What had it been like watching Daisy get vaguer and vaguer? "I am very quiet," she'd said. *I'm sorry, honey*, Lucy thought and kissed the top of her little blond head. *I'll make it better, I swear*.

"What do you think?" Pepper said, sounding so much like Daisy had when she was little, superserious and asking for advice, that Lucy smiled as she looked at the doll. It had tightly curled plastic hair and an inscrutable expression, but it also had a brass eagle bustier and a blue skirt with stars.

"I think she's . . . interesting," Lucy said.

"Cool boots," Pepper said, doubt still in her voice, and turned the doll to look at the spike heeled red boots with the white stripes up the front.

"She runs in those?"

"She's Wonder Woman, she can do anything." Pepper put the doll on the table. "But she's too short to play with my Barbies."

"Oh, please, even short, Wonder Woman can kick Barbie's butt," Lucy said, and then realized Pepper wasn't old enough to know why legions of women wanted Barbie's butt kicked.

The door to the camper opened and Daisy climbed in. "Hey, guys." Her droopy eyes fell on the table and she shook her head, looking half asleep. "Pepper, no candy."

"It's for tomorrow," Pepper said, still staring at the doll. "You can't change her outfit. It's like glued on."

"It's an action figure," Lucy told her, keeping an eye on Daisy. "Not designed to play with, although I think you should anyway."

"Love the rope." Daisy slid into the swivel chair across from Lucy and smiled at her, her eyes unfocused.

Damn it, Lucy thought.

Daisy nodded to the Wonder Woman box. "Spoiling your niece?"

"Captain Wilder is spoiling my niece," Lucy said.

"Captain Wilder?" Daisy blinked.

"J.T. and me are friends," Pepper said. "Do we got any root beer?"

Lucy leaned back, took three bottles of root beer from the tiny fridge under the kitchenette counter, and opened them while Pepper put the doll back in the box and hauled the whole deal across the table to a chair of her own, leaving the script Stephanie had dropped off exposed in the middle of the table.

"Cheese sticks?" Lucy asked and took those out, too, while Pepper pulled the hardcover book out of the box and began to page through it.

"What's this?" Daisy picked up the script with more energy than Lucy had seen in her since she'd come on set. "Why do you have this?"

Lucy held out her hand for it, perplexed. "Why wouldn't I have that?"

"You're just shooting the last scenes." Daisy held on to it. "You don't need to read all of it."

Lucy reached over and took it from her. "Actually, since I'm the director, I do. In fact—"

"I can't read this yet," Pepper said, closing the book. "It's too hard. What else is there?"

Lucy dropped the script on the table. "Uh, a reproduction of the first Wonder Woman comic." Lucy handed her an opened root beer and then took the comic out of the box for her, watching Daisy to see if she'd try to take back the script.

Daisy looked at it, but she kept her hands to herself.

Pepper looked at the comic and sighed. "I can probably read this." She pushed the hardcover book back across the table and settled in with her root beer and cheese sticks to read.

Lucy opened the hardcover as Daisy said, "Thank Captain Wilder tomorrow, Pepper. *Without* telling him it wasn't a Barbie." She picked up the figure.

"Her clothes don't come off," Pepper said, frowning at the comic book.

"Like your Aunt Lucy," Daisy said, picking up a cheese stick.

"Hey." Lucy stared at the endpapers in the hardcover book where Wonder Woman was fighting with some guy in a black suit while a large fish watched. *Sort of like my day.* "I've been dating. Don't rush me." She smiled across the book at Daisy, trying to think of the most tactful, supportive way to say, *What are you on?*

"I'm just saying," Daisy said. "It's been twelve years. Connor never married again. You haven't been with anybody you've been serious about. What are you holding out for?"

The next page in the book had Wonder Woman laying down the law to some guy in uniform. *I like her,* Lucy thought.

"I know Connor can be domineering," Daisy said. "But you can trust him. I trust him."

Lucy stared at the book and thought, *Uh oh.* Gloom would say it was a sure bet that trusting Connor had gotten Daisy into whatever mess she was in. Not an affair—if she'd been with him, she wouldn't be trying to get them back together—but something . . . she looked up. "You remember how he used to get us into all those harebrained schemes?"

Daisy picked up the action figure. "At least her body is sort of probable. Those Barbies are awful."

"What?" Pepper said, looking up from her book.

"Barbies are too skinny to be real," Lucy told her.

"I know," Pepper said and went back to her book.

So now Daisy didn't want to talk about Connor. Which meant that he was definitely behind whatever was bothering her. Not good. Lucy turned another page and saw Wonder Woman tied to an electrified iron post—*Hello, phallic symbol*—while a woman with a foreign accent threatened to turn on the juice. "So a guy wrote Wonder Woman, right?"

"Probably." Daisy held up the action figure. "Look at this outfit."

"She has an invisible plane," Lucy said, looking at the next page.

"And she's wearing a skirt," Daisy said. "Definitely a guy wrote it."

Lucy kept an eye on Pepper as she turned the next page. "So what's wrong?"

"With the skirt?"

"No," Lucy said, giving up on subtlety. "With you."

"I'm fine," Daisy said, staring at the action figure.

"Pepper, why don't you take your book and your stash back to the bed?" Lucy nodded toward the end of the camper that was filled with the sideways double bed. "Curl up, get cozy." She smiled at Daisy, her jaw set. "And your mama and I can talk about . . . things."

Daisy looked at the door and started to get up.

"Nope," Lucy said. "Don't even think about it. We're going to talk."

5

Pepper looked from Lucy to her mother and back again. "Okay," she said and picked up the comic, her root beer, four cheese sticks, and two Hershey bars, which she neatly slid into the comic before Daisy noticed. Then she staggered down the three-foot passage to the bed, balancing everything, and climbed up onto the mattress.

"Good picture," Daisy said, nodding at the book, and Lucy looked down to see Wonder Woman gazing soulfully into the eyes of the guy in uniform.

Betrayed by an icon, Lucy thought and shut the book. "So I have some questions."

Daisy leaned back in her chair and drank from her root beer bottle, the combination of the bottle and her hat blocking her face. "Me too. Like what about this Green Beret who's bringing you presents?"

"So I get to the set today," Lucy said, pushing the book away, "and I don't have the full script, I'm missing three-quarters of my personnel, the people I do have are moving at half speed, and everybody seems surprised when I ask them to do more than one take. Plus they all keep saying this is my big break."

"It *is*." Daisy leaned forward clumsily, almost knocking over her root beer bottle. "This will get people's attention. No more dog food commercials. Maybe you and Connor—"

Lucy moved the bottle out of her way. "Okay, first, shooting four days of stunts is not going to get anybody's attention. This is just cleanup work, which I am doing for the money. Second, I do a lot of different kinds of commercials, not just dog food." Lucy picked up her root beer, trying not to sound annoyed. "Third, I'm good at working with animals, I'm famous for it, and I make a damn good living at it. Fourth, *I like what I do*. Feature work is insane, you're always away from home, the shoots are long, and they're a logistical nightmare." She stopped, realizing her voice had risen. She looked back over her shoulder and saw Pepper watching her from the bed. "It's not a real life, Daisy. You can't have a home and do that."

"It's real," Daisy said, her face flushed. "It's—"

"And it's particularly not real for a five-year-old," Lucy said, dropping her voice so Pepper couldn't hear. "I know you're doing a great job of homeschooling her, she's smart as a whip, but she needs to be with other kids. She's lonely. Come back to New York with me, get a steady job, put her in kindergarten there, and we'll both take care of her. Dragging her with you was fine when she was a baby, but she's five now—"

Daisy's chin went up. "She's fine. The shoot is fine. Everything's fine. I can take care of myself and her."

"No," Lucy said, in too far to stop. "Pepper's unhappy and you're dull and miserable and you're making mistakes—you who never missed a detail." She waited for Daisy to say, *Oh, that's the allergy meds I'm taking*, but Daisy just slid her eyes away. "And it's not just you, this set is a mess. There's something bad going on here, and I'm betting you know what it is. And I'm betting it's the same thing that's making you miserable."

Daisy chugged the rest of her root beer, still not meeting Lucy's eyes.

"You think I'm not going to find out what's going on?" Lucy said, holding on to her temper. "I know we haven't seen each other much in the past couple of years, but you can't have forgotten me that much."

"I haven't forgotten you at all," Daisy said, and Lucy couldn't read her voice.

"I'm going to be here another three days, I've got Gloom with me, how long do you think it's going to be before we know everything? Do you want me to find out from somebody else?"

Daisy shifted in her chair. "It's not a big deal. They were running out of money and Connor brought in a backer named Finnegan who wanted all this stunt stuff added to the end of the movie. So we're a little disorganized because it was all put in at the last minute." Daisy pulled the Wonder Woman book over to her side of the table. "So does Wonder Woman have a boyfriend?"

"That wouldn't make you sick and miserable." Lucy leaned forward. "That wouldn't put you on drugs." Daisy jerked her eyes up.

"I'm not . . . I don't do that stuff, Lucy."

"What stuff? You're on something, I can see it in your eyes, in the way you move."

"It's not coke or anything," Daisy said, her voice tired.

"Prescription meds count," Lucy said, exasperated. "Who are you kidding? Come on, Daisy, let me help you. You know I can. I always have. I can get you out of whatever trouble you're in, off whatever stuff you're on. *Tell me.*"

Daisy shook her head. "I'm fi—"

"*Stop saying that,*" Lucy snapped. "This isn't just about you; you've got Pepper so worried she's crying to me on the phone."

Daisy shook her head, her eyes blurring with tears.

"Wonder Woman is in love with Captain Steve Trevor," Pepper said from behind Lucy's shoulder, and Lucy jumped.

"Hey, baby," she said, and Daisy straightened, too, pasting on a smile. "Did you finish the comic book?"

"I looked through it." Pepper put the comic on the table. "There was some good stuff. But she always gets tied up. She gets tied up a *lot.*"

"She does?" Daisy reached for the book.

"She still wins in the end." Pepper sat down in her chair again and kicked the Jax Comix bag. "Sorry." She leaned over it. "There's something else in there." She reached in and pulled out a shiny white folder. "Oh, cool. *Stickers*."

Lucy leaned to see but kept Daisy in the corner of her eye. She looked like hell, worse than when she'd come in. *Damn it,* Lucy thought, and then Pepper thrust the folder under her nose, saying, "Look!"

The cover said WONDER WOMAN ULTIMATE STICKER BOOK over a picture of a beefy Wonder Woman with Angelina Jolie lips, standing with her legs spread and her hands on her hips, looking very snotty.

"This must be the eighties version," Lucy said, still keeping an eye on Daisy. "I think she was a cupcake in the sixties."

"She could crack walnuts with those thighs." Daisy leaned over to look, ignoring Lucy.

"Walnuts?" Pepper said, looking up from her book.

"Nice bracelets," Daisy said hastily.

"She catches bullets on them." Pepper went back to the book. "And the magic lasso makes people tell her the truth. She lassos them and they say, 'I am strangely compelled to tell you the truth.' That means they have to."

"That would be handy," Lucy said, looking at Daisy.

"Well, sometimes it's bad," Pepper said, "because they tie her up with it. But she always wins."

"My kind of woman." Lucy watched Pepper's serious little face pore over the sticker book. Pepper knew something was wrong, she was too serious, too intent on the book. So no more talking to Daisy with Pepper in earshot. *Dumb,* she told herself. *You should have waited.* Except there were no times with Daisy that were without Pepper. And she was already afraid she'd waited too long.

"I bet Wonder Woman could even beat Moot," Pepper said.

Lucy looked at her, surprised. "Don't you like Moot?"

Pepper looked up. "Moot is an alligator. He's dangerous. Alligators are not pets, they are very big and very fast."

"This is true." Lucy looked at Daisy. "Meant to ask. Animal of the Month?"

Daisy relaxed a little. "She picks an animal every month to learn about." She sighed. "Some are better than others. The Month of the Platypus wasn't pretty."

"People should not feed gators," Pepper said, still looking at her book. "Bryce should not feed Ding Dongs to him. Moot will attack."

Lucy was distracted by the image of Moot dragging Bryce away under the bridge. It was strangely plausible; Bryce was exactly the kind of guy who'd get eaten by an alligator while feeding it snack cakes.

"Let me see the sticker book," Daisy said, reaching across the table.

"It has cool stuff," Pepper said as Daisy took it. "There are all these stickers and then pages to stick them onto."

"Sounds excellent," Lucy said. *Good job, Wilder.* Who knew a Green Beret would know about stickers? Now, if he only knew how to rescue depressed, drug-addled sisters . . .

"Like it says she has winged sandals," Pepper said over her root beer, "but I like the boots better. They're like your boots, Aunt Lucy. Sort of. You should paint a white stripe up the front."

Lucy looked down at her snakeskin boots. "No. No white paint on snakeskin."

"I have red rubber rain boots," Pepper said. "Can I paint a white stripe on those?"

"Yes," Daisy said.

"So," Lucy said to Pepper, "why don't you go back and take a nap while your mom and I—"

"Time to go," Daisy said and stood up, sliding the sticker book back to Pepper.

"We just *got* here," Pepper said, outraged, but Lucy took one look at Daisy's stubborn, drowsy face and gave up for the night.

"It's hours past your bedtime," Daisy said to Pepper. "You can play in Aunt Lucy's camper all afternoon tomorrow if you want."

"No," Pepper said. "I have to be on the set. To bring Aunt Lucy apples. Because Stephanie is *worthless*."

"Pepper!" Daisy said.

"Okay," Pepper said with a dramatic sigh. "Can I take the Wonder Woman stuff with me?"

"Yes," Daisy said, not meeting Lucy's eyes. "Hurry up."

Pepper packed all her stuff back in the Jax Comix bag, checking first to see that there wasn't anything else in there.

"What are you looking for?" Lucy asked.

"I thought there might be another comic book," Pepper said. "I can read those."

Well, if she couldn't save Daisy tonight, she could at least give Pepper something to look forward to. She took the bag from her and read the stamped address. "I think this place is pretty close. Captain Wilder said he had an appointment someplace nearby, so he must have found it on his way there. How about tomorrow morning, we go look at this place and get you some comics?"

"Just you and me?" Pepper's face lit up.

"Just you and me, baby," Lucy said, relieved to be doing something right. "If that's all right with your mom."

"Yep." Daisy yawned. "First call isn't until one, so I'm sleeping in."

"*Thank you,* Aunt Lucy," Pepper said, her voice thrilled. "And then I can show Crafty and Estelle in wardrobe and Mary Vanity what I got."

I have to get this kid into school so she can play with somebody under twenty, Lucy thought and then looked at Daisy's strained face. *And I'm going to save you, too, you dumb-butt.* "I'll pick you up at eleven," she told Pepper, who hugged her and then climbed out of the trailer, the Jax bag clutched to her chest.

Daisy paused in the doorway. "Luce—I'm sorry I asked Connor to call you."

Lucy went very still. "You asked Connor to call me? I thought he'd sicced you on me when I told him no."

Daisy swallowed. "Connor wanted to just finish the shoot. Do it himself. But I told him he'd run into big-time union trouble, what with everyone bailing out after the director died; that he needed a real director. I told him he should call you."

Lucy frowned at her. "Why would you tell him that? You don't care about this movie, nobody here does."

Pepper's voice floated through the night air. "Come on, Mom!"

"I just wanted to see you," Daisy said, trying to smile. "And he did, too. He's never stopped loving you, Lucy."

"That would explain the ten thousand women he has undoubtedly slept with since I left," Lucy said.

"Come *on,* Mom," Pepper said.

Daisy shook her head and went out the door, and Lucy watched her take Pepper's hand and cross the parking lot to her car.

You told him to call me because you wanted me to save you, she thought. *Big sister to the rescue again. So why won't you tell me what's wrong?* She slumped back in her chair.

It was her fault. She should have kept a closer watch on Daisy, checked in more often with Pepper. She'd been all caught up in her own life, her career, and hadn't thought—

Well, that was then, this is now. Tomorrow, she'd talk to Gloom, find out what he'd learned talking to the crew, find out what Daisy was taking, solve whatever mess was driving her to take it, talk her into getting Pepper into school . . .

And she'd have to thank Captain Wilder for the Wonder Woman doll, too. *Big day,* she thought.

Then she got another root beer and sat down to read the script.

By the time Wilder recrossed the bridge, his hangover had turned into exhaustion despite the hair-of-the-dog beers in the diner. Or perhaps it was just Crawford and the fucking CIA suddenly showing up that had drained all his energy. Whatever the cause, he went back to the Westin to the room Bryce had gotten for him adjacent to his own, grateful to be away from both the CIA and the movie set. Those people were crazy.

But at the door he paused, his hand halfway to the knob that still had the DO NOT DISTURB tag hanging from it. Someone had been in the room. The telltale piece of clear tape he'd left on the lower-left corner of the door had been broken. Either someone had fucked up and entered by mistake or someone was waiting in there to fuck him up or someone had gone through his stuff, which would just plain be fucked up. His left hand snaked behind his back and he pulled out his Glock automatic pistol, making the decision to fight not flee.

He twisted the knob and entered low and fast, duckwalking, back pressed against the wall, moving to the right, weapon extended, sweeping with the eyes, finger on the trigger. The room was dark, shades pulled tight, but there was someone in there, he could smell . . . fuck, perfume. Who? He'd caught that scent before. On the set.

"Is that a gun?"

Althea. Wilder slowly rose out of his crouch, as his eyes became accustomed to the dark, the weapon suddenly feeling very heavy as he dropped his hand to his side. "Uh. Yeah." That sounded lame, so he told himself, *You're in control. You're the one with the gun, for Christ's sake.*

He turned on the light.

She was in his bed, the sheet up to her neck. Had she looked under the bed and found his backpack? He hoped not. She shifted and he smelled perfume again. Perfume had not been in his plans, either.

She smiled at him and ran the tip of her tongue over her lower lip.

Well, plans were made to be changed. They'd taught him that in Ranger School. "Improvise, Ranger," the Ranger instructors had screamed at the starving, sleep-deprived students. But they hadn't covered this kind of ambush.

Still, Wilder thought as he returned the gun to the holster in the middle of his back, an ambush was an ambush. And the U.S. Army Ranger School–approved solution was to assault right into the enemy force with overwhelming power and take control of the situation. Anything else meant being stuck in the kill zone.

Althea half sat up, and the sheet slid, catching on her breasts. "What kind of gun is it?"

Wilder swallowed, frozen. He was in the fucking kill zone. The RIs would have flunked him.

"A Glock." Had that come out wrong? He tried to replay what he'd said, but his brain wouldn't back up, it was going fast-forward.

"A what?" Althea placed a long, thin hand over her chest as she leaned forward, exposing her side and confirming that she wasn't wearing anything.

"A Glock Model 20."

"Can I"—Althea's voice went an octave lower—"touch it?"

Oh, fuck. They might as well get his body bag now. He drew the gun. Some semblance of sanity made him eject the magazine and then pull back the slide, ejecting the round in the chamber and pocketing it before he extended the weapon to her.

She reached with the hand that had been holding the sheet, and—he was so screwed—it dropped to her waist, exposing her breasts. She took the gun from his frozen hand, cradling it with both of hers.

"Tell me about it." She brought the gun closer to her. "I saw you and Bryce talking all night. Talk to me."

"Uh," Wilder said, trying to think of something besides breasts.

"What he did with the knife today. That was stupid, wasn't it?"

"Bryce. Well." *Breasts. Right here.* "You know. No harm, no foul."

"He could have cut someone."

"But, hey, he didn't." Wilder was starting to sweat.

"Tell me about the gun." Althea cradled it in her slender hands, the muzzle pointing, well, damn, toward her face, her mouth. He'd just handed his gun to someone. Fuck. His buddies at the Special

Warfare Center would be kicking his ass up and down Bragg Boulevard if they knew.

Althea now had one hand cradled around the pistol grip and the other one on the barrel. Stroking it. Not subtle, but Wilder didn't care.

Maybe his buddies wouldn't give him shit. Not if he told them who he'd given the gun to and under what circumstances. LaFavre would be buying him beers. And wanting to hear about it. Not that he would ever tell. There were some things you just didn't talk about. Wilder hated guys who talked. Which was just as well because right now, he was having a hard time forming words.

Althea brought the gun closer to her body, between her breasts, still stroking it, and Wilder made no pretense of not staring. Everything he wanted to see was now in one tight shot.

"Tell me about your gun," Althea said again.

Wilder swallowed. "It holds fifteen rounds of ten millimeter. That's the diameter of the bullet."

"Is that a big bullet?"

Just throw a knife in my throat and have it over with. "It's a good-sized round. Most people carry nine millimeter." He was still staring at her breasts and the gun. "So I went one larger. Like Spinal Tap. You know, the amp turns up to eleven."

Shit, he was showing his age. *Get out of the fucking kill zone.*

"It's got an integrated laser sight built into the recoil spring guide assembly, uh, there—" He pointed, his hand less than six inches from the gun and her breasts. He was definitely sweating. "—Just below the barrel."

"Oh, you mean the red dotty thing you see in the movies?"

"Yeah. Touching the trigger activates the laser."

"Can I do that?"

Touch the trigger? "Sure. It's safe. I've taken the bullets out." He forced his mind to focus. Had he cleared the chamber?

Althea turned the gun in her hands. She put her finger on the trigger. A red dot appeared on the far wall. She pointed the gun at Wilder. The dot was on his chest. "Neat."

Never point a weapon at anyone unless you're going to shoot him. Wilder bit back the words. It would be bad timing. And he had told her it was safe. And he had taken the round out of the chamber, right? Shit. He tapped his pocket and felt the magazine and extra round and resumed breathing.

"What was that double-tap thing you talked about?"

Wilder put two fingers to his forehead. "When you shoot someone, you always fire twice. You want them to go down permanently. So this is the spot."

She nodded.

"You know, the gun is only half the equation." He reached out and retrieved it from her. She looked slightly disappointed and he got a much better look at her breasts. He knew they weren't real, but so what? They were here. In his bed.

He took the magazine and round out of his pocket. He pulled the slide back and put the round in the chamber, letting the slide go forward. Then he put the magazine in. A round in the chamber, not approved for police departments or gun clubs, but Wilder had never been a cop or a member of a gun club.

"I load the rounds myself," he said as he put the gun back in the holster.

"Why?"

"They're hot loads."

Althea laughed and he was mesmerized by the way that made her breasts jiggle. "And what's a hot load, Captain Wilder?"

The way she said his name reminded him of Armstrong. Well, why the hell should he give a shit what Armstrong would think? Bryce said she was doing that asshole Nash. Bryce was doing the makeup girl. Nobody had any morals in this place. When in Rome . . .

Althea leaned back on the pillows, her nipples pointing up at an impossible angle, straight at Wilder, her version of designating a target. She had him, he was resigned to it. She might even know something about Finnegan.

She smiled at him.

Although now was not the time to ask. Well, if he had to take one for the team, so be it. He'd been worse places and in worse situations. Plenty of them.

"J.T.?" she said. "Hot load?"

"Hot loads. They're, um, designed for max muzzle velocity, able to punch through body armor, and then disintegrate inside the body for maximum damage." Geez, he sounded like some lame-dick instructor on the range at Bragg.

"Oooh."

Was that a coo? He'd heard the term; he wasn't sure he'd ever heard the reality.

"Maximum damage." Althea leaned forward. Her breasts jiggled but they didn't droop. It wasn't natural but at the moment Wilder didn't give a shit. "Where did you learn that?"

"Uh, Fort Bragg. Special Forces training."

She touched her lip with her tongue. "I bet you've seen a lot of action."

Wilder swallowed. "Some."

She shivered a little and that looked good, too. "Where?"

"Iraq," Wilder said, trying to remember. "Afghanistan." *Here.*

"Oh." She blinked at him. "Dangerous places. Are you working now?"

"I'm on leave," he said.

She smiled. "So what else do you have? I liked the gun."

Damn. Wilder mentally ran through the weapons he had strapped to his body, trying to figure out how he could get his clothes off without revealing them all.

"J.T.?"

"A man has to have some secrets," he told her, and turned out the light.

Lucy was halfway through the script and completely confused when Connor knocked on the door of the camper and opened it. She dropped the script and it slid off the table as he came in, smiling at her, his bulk filling the camper.

"We're good to go tomorrow," he told her, collapsing into one of the chairs. He looked beat, lines around his eyes, gray smudges under them, his five o'clock shadow making him look like a Hollywood bandit. "Late start, easy day. Nothing to worry about."

"Good," Lucy said, trying to stay businesslike. It was too much like old times, both of them bone tired way past midnight and Connor smiling at her.

Except that there was something wrong with the shoot. And something wrong with Daisy.

"Why aren't you back at the hotel?" he asked. "No reason for you to still be here."

"I was reading." *A script that makes no sense.* "Connor, what's going on here?"

He sighed. "We're trying to finish a movie, love. By contract it has to be done by six A.M. Friday, so we're pedal to the metal."

"No, we're not," Lucy said. "I've seen the shooting schedules. We're not even doing full days. And this stuff that we're shooting doesn't make sense. The crew is uninvolved, the actors don't care, and my sister . . . there's something wrong with Daisy, Connor. She's taking something, some prescription—"

"You're overreacting," Connor said, sounding as tired as Daisy. "As far as the movie goes, name me an action movie made in the past twenty years that's made sense. Don't worry about it, just finish shooting it. It doesn't have to be good, it just has to be done."

"Then why'd you get me to finish it?" Lucy said, exasperated. "You know I don't do 'good enough for government work.' If you just wanted it finished, you could have gotten any hack."

He smiled at her. "I wanted to see you." He leaned forward. "Look, I know we got off to a bad start today, but it doesn't have to stay that way. I really wanted you here, Luce. I want you back."

"Oh, Connor," Lucy said, shaking her head, but he held up his hand.

"Just hear me out, babe. I didn't appreciate you when I had you, I was young and stupid and not ready to settle down, you should never have married me. But now I'm older and I'm tired and I just want to sit on a deck someplace with a good woman and watch the sun set over the ocean. This is my last job, I'm retiring after this, finding one place to stay, one woman to stay there with."

Oceanfront property? *Expensive fantasy,* Lucy thought, but that didn't mean it was a bad one. Except that he must have been making a hell of a lot of money if he thought he could pay for it. Or he was working one of his schemes. Was that what was dragging Daisy down?

"And you've always been the best woman I've ever known," he went on. "Daisy said you weren't with anybody. She said you hadn't really had anybody serious since me. And I thought that maybe you still—" He swallowed hard. "I was better when I was with you. Things went better. You made my life better. You were the best time I ever had, Lucy. And I think maybe I've been looking for you ever since." He stretched his hand across the table and took hers, and she fought a sudden urge to pull it away.

"Connor. Listen—"

"I know." Connor let go of her hand. "Too much too soon." He grinned at her. "That's your specialty, rushing in too fast to fix things, and now here I'm doing it. But I have four days, well, three now, to show you that I've changed."

She bit her lip. "Look, I drove down from New York today, and then shot all night, and I'm worried sick about Daisy, so this is not the time—"

"I know, I know." He stood up and held out his hand. "Come on.

I'll take you back to the hotel and you can sleep on it and then we'll talk tomorrow."

She took his hand and let him pull her up. "I'll drive the camper. I need it to take Pepper to the comics store tomorrow."

He smiled again, his face softer than she'd ever seen it. "You're great with her. You should have kids of your own. Maybe that's something we should talk about, too."

"Kids?" Lucy said, dumbfounded.

"I want it all, Luce," Connor said. "It's time. And you're the woman I want to have it with. You make it all make sense." He leaned forward, so handsome, smiling at her, and kissed her, and she kissed him back to see what it felt like.

Nothing. Out of nowhere she thought of J. T. Wilder and shivered.

"There's a king-size bed in my hotel room," he whispered to her. "Gets awful lonely in there."

Right. Lucy thought of Stephanie and her excuse: *I was helping Connor.* And then there was Althea. "I find that very hard to believe," she said, and he grinned.

"Well, I'm going to be lonely in there now that you're back. There's nobody else for me from now on, Luce."

She pulled away. "Go back to the hotel. I'll follow you."

He nodded, not pushing. "Tomorrow we talk, okay?"

"I'm not going to be any less distracted tomorrow." She met his eyes. "Connor, what's wrong with Daisy?"

The light went out of his eyes. "There's nothing wrong with Daisy."

"She's taking something—"

"She's a single mother working long hours and trying to homeschool her kid," Connor said. "She's just tired."

"No," Lucy said, "she's taking something."

"You know what? This is none of my business." He opened the door and looked back at her. "You shouldn't be talking about your sister with anybody, Luce. You want to know something, ask her."

"*Hey,*" Lucy said and then he was gone. *You bastard,* she thought. Making taking care of Daisy sound like a betrayal. Anything to get her off his back. *Yeah, we'll talk tomorrow. And not about you and me getting together, either. The last thing I need in this mess is a man to deal with, too.*

J. T. Wilder came back to mind, and she tried to shove him away, thinking, *How pathetic is that?* If ever a man had shown no interest in her, it was Wilder. Forget him, forget all men until she finished the damn shoot and fixed her sister's life.

She began to clear off the table and saw the script where she'd dropped it. She picked it up and remembered why she'd been confused; she was sixty pages in and there was nothing in there but a basic romance plot. Where were the helicopters going to come from? The armored car? And that damn SEAL. In this script, Bryce's character was a stockbroker.

Out in the parking lot, Connor honked the horn of his van, and Lucy shoved the script into her bag. She could finish it tonight in bed, she would finish it so she'd know exactly how screwed up this shoot was. And then she'd fix it. And Daisy. And Pepper.

And Wilder, she thought and stopped, surprised. There was nothing about J. T. Wilder that needed fixing. Well, he could use a little warmth. She could do that.

No, she couldn't. He probably had a wife or a girlfriend keeping him warm. She did not need to add him to her To Do list.

She slid in behind the wheel and turned the ignition, trying to concentrate on her problems but her mind keep skewing back to Wilder and whoever was keeping him warm.

Lucky her, she thought and followed Connor's van out of the parking lot.

Lucy was still yawning when she and Pepper headed for Jax Comix at eleven the next morning with Kirsty MacColl singing "Us Amazonians" on the stereo, one of Pepper's favorites. A late night with the script hadn't made Lucy feel any better about the movie, but sunshine and Pepper beside her belting out "Us Amazonians make out all right" at the top of her lungs were going a long way toward cheering her up.

"You're not wearing your hair braided," Pepper said when the song was done.

"I'm not working." Lucy stifled another yawn.

"It looks pretty when you leave it down." Pepper leaned back against the seat. "I bet J.T. would like it down."

Lucy grinned at her. "You and J.T. are pals now, I guess."

Pepper nodded. "He got me that Wonder Woman stuff, so that means he likes me."

"Men who give you things usually like you," Lucy agreed.

"He got me very good stuff."

"Yes, he did. Are you going to get him anything?"

"Should I?" Pepper said.

"It would be polite. At least a thank-you note."

Pepper nodded solemnly and sat silent, evidently planning her thank-you, and Lucy sat equally silent, thinking about Pepper's J.T. Maybe she should get him a thank-you, too. Her mind veered off course and she thought of Pepper's song, MacColl singing that Amazonians just wanted somebody to hold in the forest at night. *That would be good,* she thought. Connor was volunteering, but for some reason, J. T. Wilder had more appeal. And no interest in her. The least he could have done was stared at her breasts or something, although with Althea on the bridge, she really wasn't a contender there.

They reached the strip mall, and Lucy parked in front of the comics store.

"What's a gentlemen's club?" Pepper said as they got out, staring at the sign that said MARASCHINO'S.

"A misnomer," Lucy said.

"What's a misnomer?" Pepper said.

"It means the wrong name," Lucy said. "That's not a club and there are no gentlemen in it. The comic-book store is over here." She pointed in the direction of Jax, trying not to be annoyed by the fact that Wilder's big appointment the night before had probably been with a stripper. There was a lot to be said about a man who scheduled time to see naked women, but none of it could be said in front of a five-year-old.

The inside of Jax was not impressive, including the twenty-something clerk with the limp mustache who looked half asleep, but Pepper was oblivious. She went up to the counter, lifted her chin to see over it, and said, "We want Wonder Woman comic books, please."

"You want the latest stuff or collect—" The clerk's voice trailed off as he caught sight of Lucy.

"Whatever she wants," Lucy said, figuring *somebody* should get what she wanted.

The clerk nodded, staring. "You know, you look a lot like—"

"New comics," Pepper told him. "And a Wonder Woman Barbie."

"We don't carry Barbies, kid," the counter guy said, and Lucy frowned at him. "But we have other action figures. Like . . ."

Lucy's cell phone rang and she took it out and looked at the caller ID. Blocked. "Can I take this, Pepper? It might be about the movie."

Pepper nodded, absorbed in her shopping.

The counter guy had backed up to the shelves behind him. "The action figure from the Kingdom Come comic, that's a good one. Looks a lot like your mom." He gave Lucy a smile that said, *Hello, I'm kind to kids and good with women,* and Lucy gave him a smile back that said, *Fat chance.* Her cell phone rang again, and she answered it.

"Hello?"

"Ms. Armstrong?"

"Yes?" Lucy said, trying to place the voice. An Irish brogue? She didn't know anybody Irish.

"This is James Finnegan."

Finnegan, the backer. "Hello, Mr. Finnegan." Lucy shot a glance at

Pepper, who was staring past the counter guy, up on her tiptoes now to see better.

"What's that?" Pepper pointed at a mannequin on the shelf behind him.

He turned around. "Wonder Woman WonderWear. One hundred percent cotton. Cami and—"

"Does it come in my size?" Pepper said.

No, no, Lucy thought as Finnegan said, "I wanted to thank you for finishing my movie for me."

"You're welcome, Mr. Finnegan," Lucy said, watching Pepper watch the WonderWear.

"The extra-small might sort of fit you," the counter guy said to Pepper, putting the package on the counter. He looked at Lucy. "Your mom would look good in the extra-large."

"My mom wears a small," Pepper said, following his eyes to Lucy. "That's my aunt."

"I know it was short notice," Finnegan was saying, "and I appreciate your help."

"My pleasure," Lucy said, giving up on Pepper for the moment. "Mr. Finnegan, about the script—"

"May I call you Lucy?" Finnegan said. "Such a sweet name."

"Sure," Lucy said, thinking, *I have a choice?*

"What's your aunt's name?" the counter guy said.

"Lucy," Pepper said. "I'm Pepper."

The counter guy stuck out his hand. "I'm Jax. Your aunt married or anything?"

"No," Pepper said. "I want the underwear."

Lucy tried to block them out to concentrate on Finnegan. "About the script, I think there's a problem—"

"So that's an extra-small, a small, and an extra-large in the Wonder-Wear?" Jax said to Pepper.

"A problem?" Finnegan said.

"Yes," Pepper said to Jax. "And I want to see the King doll."

"Kingdom Come," Jax said. "It's from the Kingdom Come comic. Looks just like your aunt."

Finnegan said, "The script is very simple."

"Well," Lucy said. "I've only read through it once, but basically it doesn't make sense. Brad isn't even a Navy SEAL until the last half hour, and Rip is a stockbroker, not a thief. Then all of a sudden there's a helicopter chase and then another helicopter with a cargo net and an armored car exploding."

"Most movies don't make sense," Finnegan said. "You do understand that when you agreed to take over the movie, you agreed to the terms of the contract I had with Mr. Lawton."

"Who?" Lucy said.

"The former director," Finnegan said.

"Contract?"

"In exchange for my investment of four million dollars, you agreed to film the movie as scripted, following the schedule as stated. Should you not keep this agreement, Ms. Armstrong, I'll be asking you personally for my four million back."

"Huh?" Lucy said, feeling the ground shift beneath her feet.

"I gather your boy Connor did not mention that when he called you in," Finnegan said. "Just let him handle everything."

"Connor is not my boy," Lucy said, thinking, *Oh, hell, twelve years apart and he's still scamming me.* She glanced back at Pepper, who was staring wide-eyed through the cellophane on a box labeled KINGDOM COME WONDER WOMAN.

"Wow," Pepper said.

"Connor will take care of everything," Finnegan said. "You listen to him and you'll be fine. Your role as director is just a formality."

Jax put three packages of underwear on the counter next to the box. "We got the comic that figure's from. All the superheroes fight the bad guys in this really big last battle."

"Cool," Pepper said.

"Mr. Finnegan," Lucy said. "Connor is the stunt coordinator, I'm the director."

"Well, it's the stunts you're shooting now, isn't it?" Finnegan said. "And one more thing, Lucy. That fine Green Beret you have on my set? He's not in the budget and he must go."

"Bryce is paying for him," Lucy said and then stopped to frown at the phone. "How did you know there was a Green Beret on the set? Did Connor call—"

"Connor did not call," Finnegan said. "I have my ways of knowing things. Get rid of him."

"I can't," Lucy said. "Bryce hired him, Bryce is paying him, and Bryce insists on keeping him. I've already tried, it's a no go. If I cross him, he'll sulk and your schedule will go to hell. If Connor didn't call, who was it?"

"Let's just say I have somebody keeping an eye on things."

"What?" Lucy said. "You have a mole on my set?" She looked over to see Pepper and Jax listening. She put her hand over the receiver and asked, "Done shopping, Pepper?"

Pepper shook her head and turned back to Jax, who was already grabbing another book.

Lucy uncovered the phone. "Why are you doing this? If you want to send an observer, send an observer, I have no problem with that. Why all the secrecy?"

"Only three more days, Lucy," Finnegan said. "All you have to do is follow the schedule."

"I'll meet your schedule," Lucy snapped. "But Wilder stays on the set because Bryce wants him. And the mole goes. Send all the observers you want, but no spies."

The silence on the phone stretched out while, behind her, the counter guy said, "How about the Masterpiece Doll? Comes with a hardcover book and a reproduction of the first—"

"I got that last night," Pepper said. "J.T. gave it to me."

"Tough-looking guy?" Jax said. "Doesn't say much?"

That's him, Lucy thought and wondered if catching moles was in his job description.

"You're really not in a position to dictate to me, Lucy my girl," Finnegan was saying.

"Yep," Pepper said to the counter guy. "That's J.T. He's a Green Beret. I should get him something, too."

"How about the Superman boxers with the Super Size shield?"

"No," Lucy said.

"I beg your pardon," Finnegan said, his voice icy.

"Sorry," Lucy said into the phone. "I was talking to someone else. But the mole—"

"Forget that," Finnegan said. "The schedule's the important thing. I want you to follow it exactly."

"I don't like any of this, Mr. Finnegan."

"It's my money, Lucy."

"I understand that, but—"

"You do a good job for me," Finnegan said, "and perhaps there'll be a bonus for you."

"I don't want a bonus. I want that mole off the set and—" She stopped as she heard a click and the phone went dead. *Bastard.*

"Sticker book?" Jax said to Pepper, putting it on the counter in front of her.

"Got it," Pepper said.

"Pez dispenser?" He put one on the counter and Pepper frowned.

"Maybe."

"Wonder Woman bobble-head doll?" He put one in front of her and Pepper rolled her eyes as the head bobbed up and down. "Yeah, that's what I think, too. Can you write? I got a Wonder Woman diary."

"I can write," Pepper said. "Some."

"How about *The Ultimate Guide to Wonder Woman*? It's where all the sticker pictures came from."

"Ooh, ooh, that one."

Lucy shut off the phone and looked at the pile on the counter.

"They don't have Barbies," Pepper said to her, "but they have all this cool stuff."

Lucy looked at Jax, who shrugged. Then she looked at Pepper. "Can you read the books?"

"Yes. I checked. Well, I didn't check the last one." She pulled the slender white book off the stack and opened it. "Yep, I can read it. Most of it."

"And the clothes?" Lucy said, picking up one of the packages.

"Wonder Woman underwear," Pepper said.

"WonderWear," Jax said.

"I thought we could have a party," Pepper said, in her best abandoned-child voice. "You and me and Mom because I have *nobody* to play with. And we could all wear the underwear."

She was putting it on, Lucy knew, but underneath the put-on, there was something true. Pepper was worried about her mom, but underneath that, she was achingly lonely. She really did need somebody to play with.

Hell, so do I.

There was a spy on her set. That was just creepy.

Lucy picked up the box that said KINGDOM COME. Inside was an eight-inch action figure that was the closest thing she'd seen to art in a cardboard box: a semibelievably proportioned woman with muscles and a gold rope, looking pissed as hell. "Wow."

"That's what *I* said," Pepper said. "Isn't she beautiful? But I don't really need her. I'd rather have the Barbie."

"Maybe I need her," Lucy said, looking at the tough lines of the figure. This was a bitch who could kick some Irish ass. And maybe some Australian butt—*he knew he was suckering me into that liability*—and find a mole, too. *Who?* She thought. Forty-odd people. It could be any of them. Althea saving for bigger boobs if that was possible, Bryce investing in a Ding Dongs factory, Mary Vanity putting out a hit on Althea . . .

"So can I have it all?" Pepper asked.

Lucy looked at the swag on the counter. She'd missed some things while she was on the phone. Magnets, a mug, a lunch box, a Superman key chain . . .

"Superman?"

"For J.T. To say thank you."

"Well," Lucy said. "I don't know."

Pepper looked up at her with huge eyes. "If I can have this stuff, I'll help you find the mole."

"What?"

"The mole you were talking about, on the phone, I'll help you find it and that way I can *earn* this stuff."

Big ears, Lucy thought. "You don't have to earn it. I'll find the mole. But thank you very much for offering."

"Okay." Pepper turned back to the counter. "Maybe I'll make moles my next Animal of the Month."

"Moles," Jax said, shaking his head. "They ruined my mom's garden."

I'm betting this one's not good for my movie set, Lucy thought. "Ring it all up," she said, putting the Kingdom Come box back on the counter.

"That, too?" Jax said.

"Especially that," Lucy said.

"I think Wonder Woman is very cool," Pepper said, watching her loot disappear into several bags. "I bet she could find the mole. I bet she could find a hundred moles."

"She's going to do her damnedest," Lucy said, and got out her wallet.

6

A little after noon, Wilder walked to the edge of the trailers and trucks parked in the base camp underneath the bridge. He reached into his back pocket and pulled out the shot schedule for the last three days of shooting. He scanned it and relaxed. Bryce was off, which meant that he was off. Wilder read on and winced as he saw the next day's schedule. The first helicopter stunt and Bryce was going to be shooting a gun. Blanks, but still. He already knew the gun was going to be all wrong, but he made a mental note not to make too big a deal of anything unless it had the potential to kill someone. When he'd pointed out what was wrong with the knife, he'd ended up with Althea in his bed. Which had been great. Well, good. And strangely enough, cold. Althea was the kind of woman who could heat you up and freeze you out at the same time.

Well, hell, he hadn't died. Even if he had given up his gun.

Guns. Bryce. Wilder checked his watch. Bryce was supposed to be picking him up but he was nowhere around, probably some-where with Mary Vanity, the makeup girl. Everyone was doing everyone here—he and Althea, Bryce and Mary Vanity, Armstrong and Nash. . . .

That wasn't good. The last thing he needed was Armstrong and Nash together against him. He thought of Armstrong in that blue shirt. *Should split them up,* he thought. Divide and conquer. Disarm the enemy. That's what had happened to him.

Guns, damn it. He hefted the backpack he'd hauled with him from the hotel room. It had been hidden under the bed, the reason he had gone to the damn room and been ambushed. Time to get a cache established since his room obviously wasn't the place to run to in an emergency. He strode away into the thick vegetation of the woods on the far side of the road and locked down his brain into mission mode. Pace count. Every time his right foot hit the ground he added. He glanced at his left wrist. The compass strapped on it gave him the bearing: 266 degrees, almost due west.

When he was 112 feet into the woods, out of sight of the road and base camp, Wilder paused and did a slow 360. There had been an old drawbridge whose roadway had been torn down after the new one was put up, and one of the concrete supports was less than fifteen feet from where he was, an old palm tree collapsed against it.

Wilder went over to it and removed the MP-5 submachine gun from his backpack. It and five spare magazines were tightly wrapped in plastic. He slid it under the log, and then covered it with leaves.

He stood up and checked his handiwork. Unless someone knew the gun was there, it wouldn't be found. He turned to leave, and then without conscious thought his hand went to his back and he slid the Glock out from underneath his shirt. *Something wrong.* He searched the immediate area in quarters, scan close, then out, then shift. There was the bridge overhead. The old supports. The forest. The swamp. He could see the top of a set of old abandoned grain silos to the east, on the other side of the bridge, and beyond that the hotel where Althea had ambushed him. Across the river and to the west were the cranes that loaded and off-loaded the cargo ships. It took over a minute, but he checked out everything.

Nothing.

Fucking Althea. She was making him jumpy.

Unless Pepper was right and there was a ghost.

He watched for a minute more and then was putting the pistol away when he heard something moving in the brush. He went to one knee, bringing the pistol up, and waited, perfectly still.

The noise came again and he saw a palmetto frond move about thirty feet to his left front, very close to the swamp. Wilder moved now, fast, toward the target, zigzagging, the pistol leading. Five feet short of the frond he came to an abrupt halt as he saw the cause of the noise and movement.

A nine-foot alligator had also come to a complete halt, hearing his approach. Its large left paw was frozen in midair, its nose toward the swamp, but the large head slowly swung toward Wilder and fixed him with its black eyes—check that—eye. The gator's left eye was missing, a scar running through thick scales above and below where it was supposed to be. The mouth was half open, revealing the large teeth.

Wilder nodded and took a tentative step backward. Then another. The gator still hadn't moved. Another step.

The gator moved fast, surprisingly fast, straight for the swamp. It disappeared in the foliage, and then seconds later Wilder heard it hit the water. He shook his head and headed back to the camp. Just before exiting the woods, he slid the Glock back into the holster and covered it with his shirt. Last thing he needed was Althea seeing him with a gun again—

He heard a car take the corner too fast and then Bryce zoomed up in a black Porsche Carrera and skidded to a halt in front of him.

"My man," Bryce said as he got out of the car and slapped the hood. "Like it?"

Wilder nodded, not sure what proper car etiquette was. He was used to guys for whom a mean ride was a sixty-ton Abrams tank with a 120-millimeter main gun that was ride-stabilized and could put a round on target over two miles away while moving at sixty miles an hour.

"I'm heading into town," Bryce continued. "Want to come? Between me and the car, we *will* get laid."

Right, Wilder thought. One of his ex-wives had told him that cars like Bryce's always made her want to yell, "Sorry about your penis." He'd thought it was mean, but she might have had a point.

Still, getting away from the set seemed like a good idea; it was too damn full of unknowns, worse than the swamp, which just had one-eyed gators. He looked over at the parking lot and spotted Stephanie the assistant coming out of Armstrong's beat-up camper looking bitchy again. Which meant Armstrong probably wasn't happy, either.

"J.T.?"

Good time for a retreat. "Sure. Let's go now."

Bryce smiled. "Cool. Let me just touch base with Althea, and we'll be out of here. Last free night before we get into the big stunts."

"Althea?"

Bryce rolled his eyes. "You know how girlfriends are, always wanting to know where you are. You gotta keep them happy."

"Girlfriends?" *Oh, shit.* "I thought you and the makeup girl, Mary—"

"Well, yeah," Bryce said with his trademark cocky grin. "But *Althea* doesn't know about that."

"Right." *Wrong.* This was not good. Not good at all.

"I always say, what people don't know can't hurt them," Bryce said cheerfully.

"Good point." Wilder considered backing into the swamp so Althea wouldn't see him and say, "Great lay last night." Plus there was Armstrong, who probably would not be happy if he was upsetting her star. Not good at all. It'd be a lot safer to run into the gator again. It had shown better sense than anyone he'd met here.

"You ready?" Bryce said, jerking his head toward the camp.

"Uh, sure." Well, how bad could it be? He'd been shot at by experts. What were a couple of angry women?

He thought of Armstrong biting into that apple and hesitated.

"J.T.? You sure you want to go?" Bryce sounded uncertain, as if afraid his new best friend didn't want to play.

Imagine how he'd sound if he found out his new best friend had screwed his girl. *Fuck.*

"Right behind you," Wilder said. *Way behind you. Cover me, I'm going in.*

Then he followed Bryce into the camp, wishing he were back at Bragg, where there were damn few women and no movie people.

Lucy had driven back to base camp with Pepper singing "Us Amazonians" again, riding shotgun with her loot. She'd parked the camper in the lot and Stephanie had opened the side door, stuck her head in, and said, "We're at the Wildlife Refuge today, starting with Rip and Annie driving and then arguing in the car."

"Good." Lucy unlocked the driver's seat and swiveled it around so that it faced the dinette. "Now come in here and explain to me why this movie was a Harry-Met-Sally romantic comedy about a stockbroker and a bank teller and then suddenly at the end Brad is a former Navy SEAL and there are helicopters and exploding armored cars."

Stephanie looked around and then climbed into the camper, narrowly missing a collision with Pepper, who was heading for the bed in the back to spread out her stuff. Stephanie sat down and lowered her voice. "Finnegan paid Lawton, the old director, to tack on the rewrite and the extra stunts even though they have nothing to do with the real movie." She leaned forward. "It's so wrong, Lucy. It was an honest love story when I wrote it. Then Lawton let Finnegan change the perfect movie into a guns-and-bombs mess."

Lucy blinked at her. "You wrote it? I thought Lawton wrote it."

Stephanie swallowed. "I met him when he taught a screenwriting course in my film school. He said he could get my script made if he put his name on it—"

"Oh, hell," Lucy said, feeling sorry for her for the first time.

Stephanie shrugged. "It worked. It was getting made." Her face grew dark again. "And then he hooked up with Finnegan and did this to it."

Lucy almost reached out and patted her hand. "Well, you did a good job," she said instead. "Except for all this stunt stuff at the end, it's really well written."

Stephanie flushed. "Thank you. But that's not the point. The point is that the characters are *violated* by that change." She looked at Lucy, her heart in her eyes. "Don't shoot the stunts, Lucy, they'll ruin my film."

Lucy blinked her surprise. "I have to. There's a contract, Stephanie. I have no choice."

"But they're *awful*," Stephanie said, her voice rising in a wail. "They're *ruining* my *script*."

"I know," Lucy said, patiently. "But I have this contract . . ."

Stephanie's face grew hard again. "I hoped you had principles. Connor thinks you're the best, he says so all the time." She shook her head. "I should have known better. You make *dog food commercials*. Of *course* you'd sell out."

"Actually, I was sold out," Lucy said, but Stephanie was already getting up to go, her chair swiveling behind her.

She stopped in the doorway. "Daisy said this was your big break, but you don't care at all."

"It's *not my big break*," Lucy said. "I like working with animals. *I like dog food commercials.*"

"Sure you do," Stephanie said and went out, slamming the camper door behind her.

Oh, hell. Lucy called to Pepper, "I'm going to go check on Althea, but I'll come get you when the shuttle's here."

"I'm going to stay in base camp today," Pepper called back. "I want to see if Estelle in wardrobe can make my WonderWear fit better. Do you need me to bring you apples?"

"No, no, I'll be fine," Lucy said, thinking, *Thank God, a day without apples.* She went back and kissed Pepper goodbye, getting a hug for her pains, and then left the camper and headed for Althea's trailer.

Halfway across the lot, she ran into Gloom.

"Tell me something good," she said, and he slung his arm around her shoulders and gestured to the lot.

"You are now the mistress of all you survey," he said expansively.

Lucy looked at the beat-up trailers and dingy foliage. "How is that good?"

"The crew has decided you're the real deal," Gloom said. "Morale is improving. Bryce thinks you're terrific."

"And what does Captain Wilder think?" Lucy said before she could stop herself.

Gloom grinned. "If he has any brains, he's thinking, 'That Armstrong chick is hot, I'm gonna hit on her.'"

"Forget I said that," Lucy said, thinking, *That would be good.* "I am not interested in Captain Wilder. What's going on with these dumb stunts? And what's up with Daisy?"

Gloom let his arm drop from her shoulders.

"Oh, God, that bad?" Lucy said, feeling a chill even in the sun.

"I don't know," Gloom said. "The best I can get is that she'd been tense ever since this Finnegan guy came in with the extra money, very nervous, crying a lot."

"Oh, hell," Lucy said and thought, *Connor.* It had to be Connor. Connor and Finnegan.

"Then about a week ago, she changed," Gloom said. "I didn't get any details, but the gist is that she got calmer, but she started screwing up, not paying attention."

"Oh, just hell," Lucy said, not wanting her suspicions confirmed.

"Yesterday when we got to the set, she wasn't there because she'd fallen asleep in the stunt van. My guess? Somebody's giving her something to keep her calm, Valium, Xanax, I don't know, but whatever it is, she's taking a lot of it."

Lucy closed her eyes. *My baby sister.* "I'll talk to her. I'll get the pills away from her."

"The best thing we can do is get her out of here," Gloom said. "Whatever it is that's making her crazy is here. You can take away all the pills you want, but she can get more. We need to get her happy again so she doesn't need them."

"She won't leave," Lucy said. "I don't know why—"

"Hello, Lucy," Althea said as she walked by, practically singing the words.

Lucy smiled at her mechanically. "Hello, Al. Good day?"

"Good *night,*" Althea said, swinging back to face her, looking smug and satisfied.

Well, good for Bryce, Lucy thought, and then remembered. Bryce. Althea was thinking of cheating on Bryce. "That's great, Al. Hey, before I forget, that dating thing Stephanie told you? It was twelve partners, not seventy-five, so you can stop at seventy-three." She tried to smile at her, in spite of her misery over Daisy. "I think you've found your guy in Bryce."

"Seventy-four," Althea said, beaming.

"Seventy-four," Lucy said, and then it registered. "Seventy-four?"

But Althea was now smiling past her, and when Lucy turned she saw Bryce heading for them, looking clueless as usual, and far behind him his best pal Wilder, broad shouldered and narrow hipped, looking anywhere but at Althea.

Lucy straightened. *Son of a bitch.*

"I think Stephanie's right," Althea chirped. "Seventy-four was pretty damn good. I can't wait for seventy-five."

"The first-team shuttle is here, Al," Gloom said, not unkindly, and Althea went, practically bouncing on her little round heels, while Wilder looked up at the empty blue sky.

Goddamn it, Lucy thought. *Holding out for a hero is not an option. I just want somebody who doesn't follow his dick through life. Is that so much to ask?*

Gloom was watching her. "I don't know what's going on here—"

"I do," Lucy said grimly, ignoring her disappointment to concentrate on her rage.

"—but don't do anything stupid."

"You going to catch this shuttle?" Stephanie called to Lucy.

"No, I have to speak to somebody," Lucy said between her teeth, knowing that would be more evidence for Stephanie that she was a lousy director. Well, screw her. Assuming J. T. Wilder hadn't already.

"Lucy," Gloom said, his voice heavy with warning. "They're free agents."

"Althea isn't. Bryce thinks she's with him," Lucy said and crossed the set, prepared to kill a Green Beret.

Finnegan would be so pleased.

"Hi, Lucy," Bryce said when she reached them.

"Hello, babe," Lucy said, trying to keep her voice light as she took in the macho betrayer beside him, cool-eyed as ever. "You're off today."

"I know. Just came for my man, J.T." He slapped Wilder on the back.

Wilder flinched, which was something, Lucy thought. Well, he was going to flinch some more before she was done with him.

"We're going over to Savannah," Bryce said. "Do some research." He shot her his famous loopy smile.

Wilder was looking at nothing over her shoulder.

"Why don't you go say hey to Althea before she goes?" Lucy suggested to Bryce. "Help her relax for her scene?"

Bryce nodded. "Good idea. J.T.—"

"J.T.'s gonna stay with me," Lucy said, pinning the jerk down with her eyes. "We have some things to discuss."

"Okay." Bryce wandered off toward Althea.

Wilder met her glare without blinking. "Problem?"

"Yes," Lucy said. "You fucked your boss's girlfriend."

His eyes flickered when she said "fucked," but she couldn't tell if he was insulted or turned on. Neither, probably. Emotionless bastard. Althea must have been dreaming if she thought this robot was energetic.

Maybe she inspired him.

She took a deep breath. "I thought there was some kind of code that said you didn't sleep with a buddy's girl."

"It's really more of a guideline," Wilder said, straight-faced, and Lucy wanted to kill him.

"No. Movie quotes do not make you funny. Or even marginally human. That was low, Wilder. Bryce isn't a genius, but he hired you and he thinks you're the best thing since sliced bread, he thinks you're his *buddy,* that the two of you are a *team,* and then you—"

He nodded, suddenly looking very human, almost shame-faced. "Look, I didn't know she was his girlfriend, and she was in my bed when I got back to my room."

"And you were incapable of saying, 'Get out of my bed'?"

"Are you kidding?"

She felt her temper spurt. He was worse than Connor. At least Connor didn't make jokes when he hurt people. "It's not funny. Bryce thinks this is his big chance to be an action hero, but you'll jeopardize all of that because you can't say no."

"I can say no. I just didn't want to."

Lucy jerked back. "Boy, you really don't care about anybody but yourself, do you?"

He drew back, too, his face shutting down, and she thought, *Got you. Good.*

"Look, it's just a movie," he said, and she lost it, getting into his face, poking her finger into his rock-hard chest.

"Listen to me, you bastard, this is not just a movie, this is people's paychecks on the line, this is *my financial future* on the line. But you don't care about any of that."

"Wait a minute," he said, his flat voice finally showing some heat.

"I have three days left to get this movie finished. I cannot afford to have Bryce sulking in his trailer because you screwed his girlfriend—"

Wilder frowned at her. "He was with the makeup—"

"I don't care," Lucy said, beyond logic. "I don't care who he's doing, I don't care who you're doing as long as he's on this set, thinking he's God's gift to women when I need him to be a hero."

"And you call me immoral," Wilder said. "What do you do, pimp for him?"

Lucy's hand jerked, and his hand moved a fraction of a second later, not much, just enough to let her know he'd have stopped her, his eyes on hers.

She drew in her breath and felt herself flush, and he must have seen it because he didn't move away.

"Come on, Armstrong, I didn't know she was with him," he said and smiled at her, apologetic, and the impact of the first smile she'd ever seen from him made her dizzy.

With rage. Dizzy with overwhelming *rage,* damn it. Fucking Army asshole.

"And anyway," Wilder continued, "it won't happen again."

Lucy took another deep breath. "Here's the thing. I need Bryce happy and working until we're done early Friday morning. Our backer has made his support of this movie contingent on our finishing by early Friday morning."

"Friday morning?" he said, the smile gone from his eyes.

"If we don't get this done on time, the shooting stops and we're in breach of contract and I'm liable for four million dollars. Which I don't have. And I don't want to lose everything because we get behind because Bryce can't work because he's unhappy because *you screwed his girlfriend.*"

She stopped because he hadn't said anything, no expression at all in those flat blue eyes, but he was listening, more alert now than when she'd begun talking.

"What?" she asked.

"Nothing."

"Right. Okay." She took a deep breath. "Please don't sleep with Althea again."

His face was wooden, but he nodded. "Already told you, I won't."

"Even if she's in your bed," she pushed.

"It won't matter. I won't be there."

Where will you be? She didn't care where he'd be. "Thank you."

He nodded again.

Show some expression, damn it. Then her treacherous mind added, *I bet you showed some with Althea.*

She squared her shoulders. "I apologize for . . . before. I wouldn't have hit you."

"I wouldn't have let you."

Lucy looked up at the night sky, trying to keep her temper. "You're an arrogant son of a bitch, Rambo."

"Not always," he said, and turned away to go with Bryce, and Lucy looked past him and realized they'd had an audience.

Across the lot, Connor watched Wilder, his face like stone. Beside him, a strange woman dressed in a flight suit, brunette but thicker and tougher than Stephanie, stared at Wilder, too, her face as hard as Connor's. *Karen, the pilot,* Lucy thought. Caught between them, Doc, the little ex–Green Beret with the glasses, looked way out of his league.

And they were all probably in cahoots with Finnegan.

"Oh, hell," Lucy said, and called after him. "Wilder? Be careful."

He looked back, surprised. "Careful about what?"

She walked closer to him. "The backer, Finnegan, called me this morning and told me he knew you were here. He wanted me to fire you."

"He called you?" Wilder said.

"Okay, the interesting part of that sentence was that he wanted me to *fire you,*" Lucy said, exasperated. "And I never told him you were here, so how did he know that?"

"Nash—"

"Nope."

Wilder went very still. "You got a spy on the set."

"Yes." Lucy took a deep breath. "Look, it's not just Finnegan. Connor and Stephanie want you gone, too. And Doc and Karen, the helicopter pilot, are staring at you right now. You've pretty much pissed everybody off, so watch your back."

He glanced over and nodded. "How about you?"

"Me?" Lucy blinked at him, surprised.

"Do you want me g—" He looked down, and she followed his eyes to see Pepper tugging on his pant leg. "Hello, P.L."

"Hello, J.T.," Pepper said, beaming at him. "Thank you very much for the Wonder Woman stuff. I got you this as a thank-you." She held up the Superman key chain, which he took soberly.

"Thank you very much," he said. "It's just what I needed."

Pepper nodded. "It's okay that the doll wasn't a Barbie. Aunt Lucy says Wonder Woman can kick Barbie's ass."

"I said 'butt,' " Lucy said.

"Wrong doll, huh?" Wilder said to Lucy.

"It's all right," she told him. "Pepper loves it."

"A Wonder Woman Barbie would be good, though," Pepper said, not looking at anybody in particular.

"Pepper!"

Bryce called, "J.T!" across the lot, and Wilder said, "I have to go." He nodded at Pepper. "I'll be careful, but she's the one to watch out for. She's little and there's a big old one-eyed gator in the water that comes up on land every once in a while. I don't think he's much afraid of people."

"Moot?" Lucy said.

"Moot?" Wilder said.

"That's what Althea called the one-eyed alligator she saw under the bridge yesterday. There can't be a lot of one-eyed gators around."

Wilder smiled. "Moot. I like that."

He almost seemed human, Lucy thought. But then he said, "You have a good afternoon," nodded to Pepper, and walked away to go be a hotshot and get laid with his actor buddy in Savannah.

Well, she'd warned him off Althea and tipped him to his unpopularity. She'd done all she could. The bastard.

"I really like J.T.," Pepper said.

Lucy watched him climb into the car, torn between wanting to kill him and just wanting him. "Yeah," she said, "he's a peach."

Gloom came to stand beside her. "You okay?"

"Why wouldn't I be okay?" Lucy snapped.

Gloom sighed. "Well, at least this time you fell for a good one."

"I have not fallen for anybody," Lucy said and walked away before she betrayed herself again.

The sun was setting as Wilder leaned his head against the leather rest and Bryce took a corner a little too fast. The day so far had been a bust. Bryce had driven around in circles—literally—as Savannah seemed filled with parks right in the middle of where the road was supposed to go. Plus, traffic was a bitch, and not for the first time Wilder felt slightly better about having a job where a commute meant a C-130 Hercules cargo-plane ride that ended in a parachute drop, even if the landings were always a bit dicey.

They weren't the only ones lost; a gray Ford sedan had been behind them off and on all afternoon. If Bryce had been a master spy, Wilder would have worried, but as it was, he figured the sedan was just as confused by Savannah as Bryce was.

The bar Bryce finally picked was a dive two blocks away from the waterfront, a place Wilder would never have gone into. But he was tired of driving around in circles and feeling bad about Althea. The right thing to do would have been to come clean: *Hey, buddy, your girl was in my bed when I got there, so I screwed her brains out, but I didn't know she was yours, so no harm, no foul, right?* Yeah, that would make things better.

He went into the bar with Bryce.

It wasn't a biker dive or he wouldn't have let Bryce go through the door. More a locals-only dive, since everyone in the place gave them the once-over as they walked in. He steered Bryce toward a booth, but Bryce had his mind set differently, and one thing Wilder had learned was that it was hard to redirect Bryce's train of thought once the tracks were laid.

"Let's sit at the bar."

Bad idea, Wilder thought, but kept his mouth shut. Everyone was giving him shit for saying things were wrong, and then there was Althea. Bryce parked himself in the middle of the U-shaped bar, loudly pulling out one of the bar stools and straddling it. Wilder slid around the stool to Bryce's left, careful not to jostle the fat man on the next perch. He didn't like the position, but anyplace at the bar put his back to some part of the room. He wished they could go someplace a little more upscale and better populated with women, since he wouldn't be seeing Althea naked again. After all, what was the point of being out with a moderately famous actor with a toy car if you couldn't be his wingman?

Or we could go back to the set, he thought, although the only thing there was Armstrong bitching at him, so what was the point? Although she'd been worried about him, too—

"Hey," Bryce said.

The bartender had been ignoring them to let them know they weren't accorded the same status as the regulars. Wilder expected this, but Bryce was apparently from a different place. Pluto, maybe, Wilder thought as Bryce slapped his hand on the bar.

"Barkeep."

Who the hell uses that word? Wilder wondered as everyone in hearing distance turned and looked once more.

The bartender was a big guy with white hair and didn't look very happy to be on his feet. He slowly shuffled the short distance from where had been lounging, reading a newspaper.

"Yeah?"

Bryce straightened. "Can I see your wine list?"

He did not fucking say that. Wilder was already pretending he didn't know the guy he'd walked in with. His wingman was flying solo.

"Red and white," the bartender growled. "That's the list." He shifted his attention to Wilder. "What do you want to see?"

"Bud. Draft. For both of us." He couldn't leave Bryce that open without some covering fire.

The bartender seemed mollified but Wilder noticed he filled the dirty mugs half full of foam.

"Thank you," Wilder said quickly as Bryce prepared to complain, undoubtedly about the dirty mugs, the foam, and the lack of a medium-priced merlot.

"Eight bucks."

Now Wilder was getting ticked. Four bucks for a crappy draft of Bud, there damn well better be naked women dancing on the bar. He was tired of getting fucked with. Plus, he had a headache, and he still hadn't sorted out the mess Crawford had handed him last night. And then there was Althea, whose effect was more powerful than any hangover and, for some reason, almost as bad. And Armstrong, mad at him and sleeping with Nash.

Fuck it. Wilder reached into his pocket and pulled out his combat pay roll, and said, "Sprinkle the infield."

"What are you doing?" Bryce asked.

Wilder peeled off a hundred-dollar bill and laid it on the bar. Considering there were only eight people at the bar, Wilder figured that would cover it and there'd better be change or a handful of naked women suddenly appearing. He'd be damned if he'd do the outfield, especially the three guys who had just walked in and taken a booth.

The bartender stared at the bill, but the pressure from the others at the bar was too much. He got everyone another round, including himself, which was on the slippery edge of bar manners in Wilder's opinion, considering they weren't regulars. Then he took the cash, rang up the bill, counted out the change, and slapped it back down in front of Wilder.

Bryce had watched all this with wide eyes. Wilder had no doubt that whatever movie Bryce was in next, there would be a bar scene and he would be sprinkling the infield.

Bryce held up his dirty mug and turned to Wilder for a toast. "To my buddy, J.T., for teaching me all he knows."

You know nothing I know, Wilder thought. He didn't want to, but he held up his mug and lightly clanked it against Bryce's. "To my man, Bryce. Anytime."

Bryce smiled and Wilder saw why he was on film. He was awkward-looking, but he had a goofy charm, something that made it impossible to stay mad at him.

"The whole movie set thing is pretty wild, isn't it?" Bryce asked as he took a sip of the tepid beer.

Fucked up was what it was. But Wilder was pretty far on his learning curve with Bryce so he didn't say that. "Yeah."

"Nash isn't too keen on you." Bryce tried to sound like a man of the world, but it wasn't coming in clearly.

"He's worried I'll interfere with his job." Wilder looked over Bryce's shoulder at the three guys in the booth. Something wrong there. Two of them looked dumb as dirt, but the third one . . .

"That isn't all," Bryce said.

"What do you mean?"

The guys in the booth were glaring at the bar. No drinks yet. *Well, there's no waitress, dipshits.*

"Lucy," Bryce said.

"What?" Fuck, he sounded like Crawford now.

"Nash and Lucy. They were married like twelve years ago, but he's still pretty possessive."

The three in the booth were still sitting there, getting steamed over not getting served. Which meant they definitely weren't locals. Of course, they'd looked pretty stoked walking in.

Bryce leaned closer. "I think Nash is mad because Lucy kind of likes you."

What are we, in grammar school? Wilder wondered. Maybe he should give Bryce a note to pass to Lucy: *Meet me at the swings after school.* Actually, not a bad idea. They could go down to the river together and feed Moot something. Like Nash.

He looked over Bryce's shoulder. One of the three guys was coming over to the bar. Doofus One. Stocky. Weight-lifter muscles. Definitely on 'roids. Tattoos covering his arms. Probably had FUCK YOU on his knuckles.

The weight lifter shoved his way to the bar between the two of them, jostling Bryce's arm and splattering beer all over him. He missed Wilder because Wilder moved.

There were seventeen people total in the bar, and the way he was sitting, Wilder could account for fifteen of them; the other two directly behind him in a booth were too old to be a threat, considering their walkers were parked next to their table. Of the remaining fifteen, Wilder estimated that besides the three he'd already tagged, only the bartender and one young guy three stools to the left could be trouble, but not likely. Not good odds, considering his wingman was Bryce. He did have the Glock but he didn't want to cause a massacre and the rule was never draw unless you plan to shoot.

"Hey." Bryce had waited a couple of seconds too long to protest, probably searching his mind for the proper reply. *"Excuse me!"*

Doofus One turned to Bryce, his back to Wilder, which meant he was stupid, which was good. "You're excused," he said loudly. His partners at the table guffawed, though Wilder thought it was not exactly the wittiest repartee he'd ever heard. He wasn't even sure it qualified as repartee.

The partners were getting up. One looked to be an ex-high-school football player—a lineman—whose gut was now threatening to match his height. Doofus Two. The other was short and thin, the smallest of the bunch, but the most dangerous because Wilder could see it in his eyes. They were not dull and vacant like the eyes on Doofus One and Doofus Two. Thin Man, Wilder tagged him. Bad news.

"The least you could do is replace my beer," Bryce whined, and Wilder's shoulders sagged because that was such an obvious opening that even Doofus One would jump on it.

"Sure," Doofus One said. "Bartender, get me another for our friend."

The bartender looked as resigned as Wilder to what was coming. He hit the tap as Wilder considered a quick retreat, but a military axiom is never retreat while still in contact with the enemy. The sad thing was that Bryce had no idea they were in a battle.

Doofus One took the mug from the bartender and emptied it on Bryce's head, and Wilder stood up.

7

Bryce surprised everybody and jerked his knee up hard, right into the weight lifter's balls, making him scream. Wilder reached out with his left hand and snatched the mug from Doofus One, at the same time striking hard with his right, three short quick jabs into the kidneys. The combination of smashed balls and pummeled kidneys caused Doofus One to go to his knees, then collapse forward. Down and done.

Wilder was already looking at the second wave coming in, Doofus Two, the Football Player, reliving his glory days, rushing the quarterback. Wilder dropped the mug and stepped forward to get in the open, but Bryce fucked it up by sliding in front, running interference like a real wingman.

"Get out—" Wilder didn't finish because Bryce disappeared inside Football Player's grasp. There was a muffled squeak.

Wilder felt bad for Bryce but he had his eyes on the third guy, Thin Man, whose hand was hovering over his right hip where the shirt was untucked. Wilder hoped he had a knife there, because if it was a gun, the place was going to be a mess very quickly.

Knife it was. One of those that required Thin Man to flick his hand back and forth to open it with flair. Wilder had seen that in movies but never in real life because a real soldier was as likely to carry that as he was Bryce's sword. Still, it was metal and it had a sharp edge.

Technically, he could double-tap Thin Man with his Glock considering things had now escalated to assault with a deadly weapon, but he thought of how Crawford would hang him out to dry, and then there was Armstrong—

Bryce was making strange, squeaking noises in Doofus Two's grasp. Was Two trying to hug Bryce to death?

Wilder moved forward, short controlled steps, and Thin Man slashed the blade across his front, more a threatening preparation for attack than an attempt to actually cut, which meant Thin Man knew nothing about real fighting. Wilder went low, his left arm blocking the knife arm up and out of the way as he side kicked right into the front of Thin Man's closest knee.

The sound of the knee snapping backward froze everyone in the bar. Thin Man's scream cut through the silence as he collapsed, but Wilder had already turned. He hit Doofus Two, who had not yet registered that he was now the Lone Ranger, a bare-knuckle shot in the temple.

Wilder had to give Doofus Two credit: He let go of Bryce, who staggered back to the bar, but he didn't collapse. He slowly turned toward Wilder, rage competing with near unconsciousness on his face.

Drop, Wilder thought.

Doofus Two raised his huge arms and took a step toward Wilder. Was that the only move he knew? Wilder wondered. He backed up a step and Doofus Two came forward a step.

Drop, asshole.

He didn't.

Bryce jumped on Doofus Two's back, his arm snaking around his shoulders, trying to get a chokehold, except his arms were too short and Doofus Two was too wide. Bryce was doing it all wrong, but damn, he was doing it.

Wilder went in for his wingman. He hit Doofus Two with the

knife edge of his left hand right across the throat, holding back the blow so he wouldn't crush the larynx and make him drown in his own blood, but hard enough to cause extreme pain and make him think about other things for a while.

Doofus Two went to his knees, his gasping mixed with the muted screams coming from Thin Man, who was curled in a ball, hands wrapped around his destroyed knee. Bryce let go and staggered back, as shocked as everyone else.

Wilder checked out the bar, now stunned into silence. The bartender had not moved. He had not brought a weapon out from under the bar. He was watching, eyes dead. Wilder nodded at him and tilted his head toward the door. The bartender nodded in return and tilted his head also. Wilder peeled another hundred off his roll and slapped it on the bar.

"Let's go." Wilder didn't wait for Bryce to acknowledge, just grabbed his arm and hustled him out the door, grateful the Glock was still in its holster and all its bullets were still in the magazine, including the one in the chamber. Men. Fucking assholes. Over nothing. *Nothing.*

"That was un-freaking-believable," Bryce gushed on an adrenaline high as Wilder pushed him toward the Porsche. "Did you see that guy go down?"

I put him down, Wilder thought as he unlocked the car doors. *Of course I saw him.*

"I mean, what was the move you did?" Bryce asked. "Could you—"

"Shut up." Wilder held a hand up to emphasize the two words while he put the other on the car roof to steady himself.

Even Bryce could see that the hand in front of his face was shaking. "You all right?"

No. Wilder closed his eyes and took a deep breath. "Yeah."

"You don't look okay. I didn't even see you get hit."

"I didn't get hit. I maimed a guy for life."

"But he—"

"I know he was an asshole, and I know they started it, but it doesn't change what I did." Wilder opened his eyes, took his hand off the car roof, and handed the keys to Bryce. "You drive. And don't tell anyone what happened."

"I'm going to have to tell Lucy," Bryce said, raising a hand to his face.

"No, you are not—" Wilder broke off as he saw Bryce's face, the entire right side red from being mashed into Doofus Two's chest.

"I'm sorry," Bryce said.

"Get in the car," Wilder said. "Just get in the car."

When they stopped shooting for second meal that night, Lucy took the shuttle back to her camper and collapsed into one of the blue swivel chairs, exhausted from wrangling people into shooting stupid scenes while keeping an eye on Daisy so she wouldn't pop any pills. Pepper's Wonder Woman loot was spread out on the table, the Kingdom Come action figure standing in the middle of it all, looking determined, rope in hand. Lasso of Truth. That would be good. She could think of several people she'd like to tie up and ask a few pointed questions. Connor. Daisy. Finnegan.

Wilder.

Captain Wilder, did you have a good time with Althea last night? Ha. Of course, he'd had a good time. Althea practically had GOOD TIME tattooed on her forehead.

Okay, that was just depressing. She punched the iPod on and hit Kirsty again, looking for anything cheery, and ended up with "Treachery." Not a good time for songs about wanting someone at night, she decided. And definitely no Bonnie Tyler.

Kirsty sang, "Treachery made a monster out of me," and Lucy thought, *Maybe I overreacted.* Wilder didn't owe her anything. He was, as Gloom said, a free agent. Jealousy was ridiculous in this situation. Completely inappropriate. He could do whatever he wanted. He could do *whomever* he wanted.

The son of a bitch.

Two more days and he's gone out of your life, she thought, and then the camper door opened and Pepper said, "Aunt Lucy, *look!*" and Lucy swiveled her chair to see Pepper in her WonderWear, now modified by the wardrobe department to fit her: red cami and blue-and-white-starred shorts topped with a piece of blue material safety-pinned to the straps of the cami as a cape. She'd painted white stripes on her red rain boots, picked up some gold-painted rope somewhere, and wrapped aluminum foil around her wrists, now secured with silver duct tape.

"Wow," Lucy said.

"Connor gave me the rope and put the duct tape on for me," Pepper said, her fists on her hips. "I don't have a crown though."

"That was good of Connor," Lucy said. "You look great, baby."

Pepper sat down in the swivel chair across from Lucy. "So can we have a Wonder Woman party now?"

"Now?" Lucy said and then remembered her promise in the comics store. "Oh, Pepper, I forgot." Pepper's face fell and Lucy added hastily, "Tell you what, let's do it tomorrow night, and we'll get a Wonder Woman cake and ice cream, too. How about that?"

Pepper nodded, woebegone.

"And maybe a video," Lucy said, desperate. "Do they have Wonder Woman videos?"

Pepper shrugged.

"Oh, baby, I'm sorry." Lucy opened her arms and Pepper climbed onto her lap. "I really am," she said into Pepper's hair as she held her close. "It was a bad day and I was really busy, it just slipped my mind. But it will be a better party tomorrow, I swear. Hey, we should have root beer and cheese sticks. Let's—"

Pepper pulled back to look into her face. "Did you find the mole?"

"The mole." Lucy blinked. "No, I haven't had a chance to look, sweetie. He's probably run off by now. Don't worry about him."

"Did he go into the forest?" Pepper said.

"Yes," Lucy said. "And he's very happy there. Moles love forests. Forget about him. So how about some root—"

"Will you have to look for him tomorrow?"

"Pepper, I swear, we will have the party tomorrow night, mole or no mole. And I'll wear my WonderWear, too. I promise."

"And Mom?"

"She'll wear hers, too," Lucy said, condemning Daisy to Wonder-Wear whether she liked it or not. Hell, looking that ridiculous might cheer her up. "And there'll be a cake, I'll find a Wonder Woman cake." *Gloom will find a Wonder Woman cake.* "And maybe I can find a crown."

"A *crown,*" Pepper said, perking up. "That would be *so cool.*"

"A crown it is," Lucy said, praying that Estelle in wardrobe would be able to make a crown. "It'll be fun. You'll see."

"I can't *wait.* We can *all* have crowns!" Pepper squinted at the Kingdom Come action figure. "She doesn't look like she has a crown. She looks like she has a gold headband."

Easier to make, Lucy thought. "Well, headbands are better. They'll hold our hair back for us. You can take the action figure with you to wardrobe tomorrow and show them." *I'm going to have to wear a Wonder Woman headband.*

"Headbands are better because they hold our hair back when we're fighting crime," Pepper said.

"Exactly," Lucy said, thinking of Finnegan. "So about that root beer—"

Stephanie opened the door of the camper and said, "You'd better see this."

What now? Lucy thought and stood up, letting Pepper slide off her lap before she went to the door.

Bryce and Wilder were standing there under the base-camp lights, Bryce looking like a kid who was waiting to get grounded and Wilder looking like hell. "What?"

Stephanie jerked her head toward Bryce, and Lucy looked at him closer.

The side of his face was red and starting to swell.

"What the . . ." Lucy came down the step to look at him more closely, Pepper right behind her.

"It was my fault," Bryce said. "I went into the bar, I—"

"This was a bar fight?" Lucy said, incredulous.

"We didn't start it," Bryce said. "This guy spilled—"

"We?" Lucy looked at Wilder. "Bryce generally doesn't get into *bar fights.*"

"Lucy," Bryce said.

"Could I see you in my camper, Captain Wilder?" Lucy said, and Wilder turned and went up the step without a word.

"Lucy." Bryce grabbed her arm as she started to follow him, and she turned and glared at him, but he didn't let go. "No, it was my fault. I took him there. I picked out the bar. I wanted a tough place. For the movie."

"There's no bar in the movie."

"No, but Brad would go into that kind of bar. It was research."

Lucy shook her head, too mad to argue. "Stephanie, take Bryce to makeup and have them put arnica on his face, and then take Pepper back to Daisy, please."

"No," Pepper moaned. "I want to stay with you and J.T."

"Bryce, find out from them what you have to do to look decent tomorrow. We'll have to shoot you from the left tomorrow if it's noticeable."

"That's not my good side," Bryce said.

"It is now," Lucy said and went back into the camper.

Wilder was sitting at the table when she went in, his hands pressed flat against the surface.

Lucy cut Kirsty off on the iPod and stood in front of him with her arms folded. "Captain Wilder, are you *trying* to kill this movie?"

Wilder shook his head once, not meeting her eyes, his rugged face in profile to her.

Lucy stared at him, willing him to look at her. "Why in the name of God did you let him go into that bar?"

"His choice," Wilder said.

Lucy bent over the table, determined to get his attention. "Look at me, Wilder. Take some responsibility here. Bryce wouldn't know a dangerous bar if it had a DANGEROUS BAR sign out front. You would. Why did you let him go in there?" When he didn't answer, she said, *"Look at me, damn it."*

He turned his head and she looked into his eyes and saw misery, bone deep.

She straightened, thinking, *What the hell happened?* His eyes went back to the table, and she went over to the cupboard and got out her emergency kit: a bottle of eighteen-year-old Glenlivet and two glasses. She put the glasses on the table, poured a shot into each, and sat down, sliding one across to him.

He picked up the glass and she saw his hand shake, not much but not steady.

He's vulnerable, she thought. *Who knew?*

He tossed back the scotch and put the glass on the table again, and she poured another shot. The third time seemed to do it; the rigidity went out of his shoulders and the hand that held the glass stopped trembling.

When Wilder spoke, his voice was low. "It wasn't a dangerous bar when we went in. Three guys came in after. They were the dangerous part."

"What happened?"

He swallowed. "I crippled a man."

Lucy drew back, knowing from the way he said it that "crippled" wasn't a figure of speech.

"One of the three," Wilder said. "He pulled a knife. It wasn't a good knife, but it had a sharp edge."

Lucy thought about what a knife could have done to him and crossed her arms in front of her.

"He never got near Bryce," Wilder said.

Lucy shook her head. "It's not—"

"I'm sorry about screwing things up for tomorrow," Wilder said, and Lucy thought, *The hell with tomorrow.*

She picked up her glass to drink and then on second thought offered it to Wilder, and his hand covered hers as he took it, warm, still a little shaky. She waited a moment to let go of the glass, looking into his eyes. "It's all right. I get it now." She smiled at him. "Thank you for saving Bryce's butt."

He nodded and took the drink.

"So how did the fight happen?" she said. "Did somebody recognize Bryce?"

"No." Wilder tossed back the shot and then leaned back, looking more thoughtful than bleak now, relaxing by millimeters. "Those three guys just started it."

"Why?" Lucy said. "Did Bryce say something?"

"Well, he didn't fit in real well," Wilder said. "But they were looking for trouble."

"And Bryce looked like trouble to them?"

Wilder shook his head.

"They were looking for you," Lucy said, her heart sinking. "Finnegan said he wanted you gone. I didn't think he meant permanently."

"Maybe, but that's a stretch," Wilder said. "It's all right."

"It's not all right, there was a knife, they could be waiting in your room for you right now—" She stopped when Wilder shook his head.

"I won't be in the room anymore."

That was the second time he'd said that. Was he leaving? Lucy nodded, going for nonchalant. "Where will you be? In case we need you for a stunt. Or something."

"Around. Don't worry about it. I'll be close." He relaxed into the plush chair, evidently in no hurry to get to his mysterious place, his eyes almost warm now, and she was treacherously glad he'd be close.

Don't be stupid. She poured herself a drink and sipped it. "You know," she said, as the warm glow of the scotch spread, "this shoot was already a mess, and now I've got Finnegan, and you had this bar fight. I thought it was just a management screwup, but now I think there's something very wrong here." *Daisy wouldn't be upset about bad management. It has to be more than that.*

"Maybe," Wilder was saying. "What do you think it is?"

"I don't know," Lucy said. "But my sister is involved in it, and I like her a lot, so I'm going to have to stop it."

Wilder straightened a little. "Pepper's mother is involved?"

Lucy nodded.

"Tell me about it," he said, completely focused on her now.

The temptation was great. She sipped her scotch and watched him, alert and still across from her. He looked powerful, certain. If things went very wrong, he'd be a very good person to have on her side. "I think Connor roped Daisy into whatever it is that's going on. I don't know how. Stephanie says the old director was behind the deal with Finnegan, but I think it was Connor. And Daisy follows Connor without question; he's been looking out for her since Pepper was born." Lucy met his eyes and flushed. "I know, I should have been the one taking care of her, but—"

He looked confused. "I didn't say that."

"Well, I should have been there for her." Lucy drank more of her scotch, relaxing as it sank into her bones. "I should have gotten her away from Connor, I knew that. I just didn't want to fight with her. It was her life. But I swear I had no idea Connor would do something that would hurt her. Connor cares about her and Pepper; Daisy's always been like his little sister and I'd have sworn he wouldn't hurt them."

Wilder still looked confused. "I thought you lived in New York."

Lucy stopped, jarred out of her rationalization. "I do, but that's not the other side of the planet. I chose to go to New York, I could have gone to L.A. with them—"

"You like L.A.?"

"I hate L.A."

Wilder nodded. "Did Daisy ask for help?"

"No," Lucy said, getting annoyed. "But she's my little sister—"

"When did you know she was in trouble?"

Well, aren't you chatty all of a sudden, Lucy thought. "She called on Saturday, three days ago, and asked me to come down to direct this mess. She said it would be a good opportunity."

"And you said yes."

"No," Lucy said. "I said no. I don't like doing full-length features. But then Pepper got on the phone and cried, and she's not a crier, so I said yes."

"So, as soon as you knew something was wrong, you came." Wilder shrugged.

Lucy shifted in her chair. "Look, I knew Connor had a lot of influence on her and I never got her away from him."

"How old is Daisy?" he said.

"Thirty." Lucy shook her head. "Yeah, I know, that's a grown-up. But that doesn't mean I haven't let her down. I should have invited her to come stay with me before this, told her I'd put Pepper in school, help her take care of her, and I didn't. I was selfish." She sat back, suddenly tired. "We have kind of a rocky history. When she was eighteen, she told me to get lost. Actually, I divorced Connor, and she chose him instead of me. She wanted a big brother more than she wanted a big sister." She stopped. "That's not fair. She chose to stay and work on her own career in feature films rather than come to New York and be part of mine in advertising. Which makes sense, she had a job, and why follow your big sister around, especially if you think she's going to the dogs." Lucy tried to smile. "Family joke. My specialty is working with animals. I like dogs."

Wilder nodded, relaxed in his chair.

"I'm sorry," Lucy said. "I'm babbling. The point is, Daisy's in trouble now, and it's my responsibility to save her and her kid, and given that whatever is going on here involves Finnegan, and that he wanted you off the set, and that right after I said no, you had a knife pulled on you . . ." Lucy swallowed and then tried to look chipper. "Well, I guess that means now I have to save you, too."

Wilder jerked his head up.

"Well, I'm the director," Lucy said. "You're my responsibility now."

"No, I'm not," Wilder said. "The bar fight could be just dumb-ass good old boys. Probably nothing to worry about. Forget about me. Your sister's different. What's wrong with the movie?"

"Oh, God, where do I start?" Lucy poured herself another drink and offered him the bottle. When he shook his head, she went on. "Well, everybody with any responsibility quit when the old director died, and I think they all left so they'd be far away when whatever it is hits the fan. Which should be shortly."

"*High Noon,*" Wilder said. "The townspeople clearing out."

"Not you, too," Lucy said. "Has everybody seen that damn movie?" She took another sip and went on. "Then we're working with almost no crew and I'm betting that's because whoever's behind this wants to keep most of the four million for himself."

"Four million?" he repeated, looking very interested.

"According to Stephanie, this Finnegan, the guy who wants you gone, paid four million dollars for the extra week of stunt shooting."

"So the old director made the deal?"

Lucy shook her head. "I'm betting Connor made it and cut the old director in on it. This whole mess has Connor written all over it." She realized she sounded bitter and looked up to see if he'd noticed.

If he had, it wasn't bothering him much. In fact, he looked almost cheerful. "I thought you and Nash were . . ."

"Were what?"

"Together." He looked uncomfortable even as he said it.

"Uh, no," Lucy said. "That ended twelve years ago."

"He thinks you're together."

"He's wrong. I've got Daisy in trouble and a shoot that makes no sense, and if Connor's behind any of it, I'm going to want him dropped off the damn bridge." She stopped, surprised to realize how angry she was.

"I can do that," Wilder said, and she grinned at him, feeling less of an idiot. "What else is wrong?"

She leaned back in her chair, the combination of the scotch and Wilder making her feel better than she had since she'd arrived. "Well, the change in the script is ridiculous. The movie was a romantic comedy, but now it turns out Brad's a Navy SEAL and Rip's a thief. It's like going to see *Sleepless in Seattle* and finding out Bill Pullman is a terrorist and they blow up the Empire State Building."

Wilder looked lost. Must not have seen *Sleepless in Seattle*. "The Empire State Building is in New York. How do—"

"Okay, forget that. Try Brad jumps out of a helicopter and lands on a car trying to save Annie, not breaking every bone in his body. Whoever wrote these new pages didn't care about it making sense." She stopped. "Finnegan pays them all this money to shoot the stunts and they make them stupid. I don't get it."

Wilder shrugged. "If they're going slow enough and low enough, it'd be possible to jump and land on the car without getting hurt. Personally, I'd double-tap the bad guy, but then the movie would be over."

"Right," Lucy said. "Then there's the helicopter stunt on Thursday night which does not make sense. So why are they doing it? Because I think Connor really expects Karen to bring that copter down low enough on the bridge so that the actors can fill that cargo net. And there's something else. Connor just handed me another script change today. Rip, the bad guy, handcuffs Annie to the armored car and then puts a bomb on it. Only Brad runs up and puts a gun on the chain between the cuffs and shoots it out. Wouldn't that blow off Annie's hand?"

"Maybe not if she stretched her hand out. Depends on the caliber of the gun." He shrugged. "But it's a movie. Why—"

"Because I'm wondering if it's all a movie," Lucy said. "The whole helicopter thing is stupid. Why not take the money, jump into the car, and go off. Why a helicopter?"

"It's easy to follow people on roads," Wilder said. "Hard as hell to track through the low country, especially if the copter drops them on a boat. They'd be pretty much free at that point—"

The camper door banged open and Daisy looked in, her face drawn and tense. "Is Pepper here?"

"No," Lucy said. "I told Stephanie to take her to you."

"She did," Daisy said, breathing harder. "And I told her to wait for me until I finished my notes, but she said she had to find somebody so we could have a party tomorrow, and I told her to come right back. When she didn't, I looked for Connor because she likes to be with him, but he's gone, rehearsing with Karen."

"Who'd she have to find?" Lucy said, watching Daisy vibrate. If she'd been shaking like this, it was easy to see why somebody had prescribed something for her.

"Somebody named Mole?" Daisy said, her voice shaking.

"Oh, God, no." Lucy stood up, her heart in her throat. "The mole. She thinks it's in the woods."

Wilder was out the door before Lucy could say anything else, not moving particularly fast but moving just the same.

"The *woods*?" Daisy said, her voice rising.

"You stay here and search base camp," Lucy said, pushing past her. "Tell everybody to look for her. Look *everywhere*."

Then she ran to catch up with Wilder.

Tyler was about to crush the beer can when he heard something moving through the swamp to the east, between his position and the movie camp. He slipped the empty back into the ammunition pocket and stared at the open bag of Cheetos, knowing he couldn't touch it for fear of making too much noise. It was still half full. A damn waste.

He slid onto his belly and crawled, moving away from his hide site, staying in the thick undergrowth, slithering in the mud, and then paused as he heard rustling to his right. Without moving his body or the sniper rifle, he turned his head and peered across the swamp. Peering back was the one-eyed gator, less than twenty feet away in the water, its head raised, the body almost completely submerged, next to a mound about three feet high. As he watched, it opened its mouth, revealing teeth and fangs.

Looking past it, he could see several eggs near the top of the mound and realized the gator was not a buddy but a chick. *Well, that puts a whole new light on the situation,* Tyler thought. Mothers and their kids—bad news there. He remained still, staring, until the alligator finally lowered her head back into the water.

Won that one pretty easy, he thought.

The sound of a branch snapping echoed through the swamp. The gator shifted its attention to the latest visitor.

Tyler slid the sniper rifle up along his body into the ready position. He peered through the scope, getting only narrow snatches of clear vision through the leaves and branches. Something yellow, about three and a half feet above the ground.

Then through an opening in the leaves he saw the damn Kid from the movie set in her mom's straw hat, taking tentative steps through the swamp along the almost overgrown dirt road.

Nobody with you now, Kid, Tyler thought. *Welcome to my world.*

Tyler watched her for several seconds, and then smiled as he pulled a small-caliber silenced pistol out of his backpack.

Finally, something fun to do.

8

Wilder was standing in the dark at the edge of the forest when Armstrong caught up to him, tripping on a root just as she reached him so that he had to catch her, the first time he'd ever touched her. "Slow down," he told her, keeping his mind on the mission.

"Slow down?" She grabbed on to him. "*Moot's* in there."

She was shaking under his hands, and he held on to her a moment too long, trying to make her calm. "I'm thinking." *Trying to think like a five-year-old girl.* "Moot's in the swamp, not the forest. As long as Pepper stays on dry ground, she'll be okay."

For the first time since he'd met her, Armstrong lost her cool, clutching him tighter. "We have to get *in there, she could be in danger—*"

"Wait."

"*No.*"

"Stop it," he said, his voice sharp, and her head jerked up. "You're panicking."

"But . . ." She drew in a deep breath. "Okay. Okay. No panicking. What do we do?"

Wilder wanted to say, *You go back to base camp and I'll go into the forest,* but he knew that she wouldn't. "If you're coming with me, you're coming as part of the team, not as a crazy aunt, understand?"

"Yes," Armstrong said, meeting his eyes, and he saw raw fear there, barely under control, and tightened his grip on her.

"You stay behind me," he said quietly, trying to calm her down. "You watch my back, and if you see Pepper, you do not go rushing to her until I tell you to."

She swallowed and nodded. "All right. Yes."

Her voice was steadier, low again, and he let go of her and turned back to the road, figuring there was a fifty-fifty chance she'd follow orders.

Okay, Pepper was looking for a mole and she'd gone into the forest. Probably looking on the ground, in the bushes . . .

He walked into the woods, moving low, trying to see what she had seen, circling the base camp in a clockwise direction, searching in the dusky light for clues. He could feel Armstrong, silent behind him, staying close, and that was good. He came to an old dirt trail that headed deeper into the forest and paused. A kill zone—that's what a road like this would be taught as in Ranger School. But what would the pathway underneath the overhanging oak trees and the Spanish moss be to a five-year-old?

An invitation to a mole hunt.

Wilder went to his knees and crawled out onto the road, searching as much with his hands as his eyes in the dim reflected light from the camp. He felt Pepper's track, the faintest imprint. He lightly ran the tip of his forefinger along the dirt, getting the impression. Then he felt another. She had been heading down the road, away from the camp.

Wilder got to his feet. "She went this way."

"I'll get a flashlight," Armstrong said.

"No. Ruins your night vision. I know this road. I parked my Jeep down there, off to the left away from the swamp. If we're lucky, that's where she went, to the left, into the forest."

"Why—" Lucy started to say, but then she stopped. "You're sleeping out here instead of the hotel."

Wilder nodded and began to move down the trail, eyes shifting left and right, trying to see if there was a point at which the little girl had left the trail, which he sincerely hoped she had not since there was swamp—and Moot-like creatures—to the right. Left would be better. Forest. Safer.

Mole hunting, jeez. Wilder guessed that kids Pepper's age took things literally, something he'd have to take into account in the future.

"Let me call for her," Armstrong whispered from behind him. "She'll come if I call."

"No. I'm listening. Sound is more important at night than seeing." *And you don't know what else is out there.*

He moved forward once more, taking short steps, eyes shifting, looking off-center of his pupils where the night vision was better. A small flash of orange caught his eye and he stepped closer to it. A Fritos wrapper hung on a palmetto branch. On the right side of the trail, of course. "What was that fairy tale where someone left a trail of bread crumbs?"

"Hansel and Gretel."

Wilder pointed at the wrapper. "I assume Pepper knows it."

Armstrong reached out for the wrapper, but Wilder grabbed her hand, stopping her. "Best leave it if Pepper put it there."

Wilder shifted his focus to what was ahead. He pushed into the undergrowth and then he heard a soft popping sound, wrong for the forest, wrong for the swamp. "Stay ten yards behind me," he whispered to Armstrong and moved ahead, and as soon as he was clear of her vision, he drew the Glock. The ground went down ever so slightly and soon he was in a mixture of trees and swamp—*hell, swamp*—decorated every few yards with a Fritos or Cheetos bag. He kept the Glock extended in front of him with his gun hand and placed his off arm, bent at the elbow, in front of his face to protect his eyes from branches and leaves. It was getting dark. *Damn dark,* Wilder thought. But the popping sound had not come again. Was that good?

He thought of Pepper alone in this place. What the hell had she been thinking? Did five-year-olds think? Wilder was in uncharted territory as far as the nature of his mission objective. He moved his feet carefully, stepping over the soggy ground without making a noise, in hunter mode.

He heard another popping sound and then something large and heavy splashed through the water for several seconds before silence ruled once again.

The damn gator.

But not Pepper. No way the gator got her. She would have screamed. But he still felt the adrenaline pumping and something else—fear. Not for himself, but for Pepper, and it was a disturbing feeling because he had never experienced fear for another person.

Damn kid.

He took another cautious step and saw Moot, the upper half of her body out of the swamp, resting on a spit of dry land, her head going back and forth as if looking for something. Wilder took a step closer and stumbled on something soft, hitting the ground and rolling to avoid falling on Pepper.

Moot swung her head in their direction and Wilder froze. If she went for them, would the Glock stop her? He was aiming it when something hit the water in the swamp and Moot swung her head around, back in the direction he'd come from. Something else splashed, and then Wilder saw a good-sized rock bounce off Moot's back. He followed the trajectory and saw a shadowy figure about fifteen feet away and realized what was going on.

Lucy was distracting the gator from him and Pepper. She was risking her fool neck, but by God, she had his back. She had a damn good arm, too, he saw as she pitched another rock at Moot.

Hell of a woman, he thought, and crawled back to Pepper, keeping an eye on Moot and his hand on his Glock in case the gator decided to head for Lucy. When Moot stayed where she was, he put his hand gently on Pepper's back, on top of her Wonder Woman cape. "Hey. P.L., you okay?" he whispered.

"Shh," Pepper whispered, staring into the swamp. "M-moot."

"I see her." And she was too damn close, Wilder thought. Less than fifteen feet away, just some thick underbrush between her and their location, probably the same distance from Armstrong. Wilder felt Pepper shivering under his hand. He had to get them both out of there fast.

"She's protecting her nest." Pepper pointed, her finger shaking, her foil-and-duct-tape bracelets reflecting the little moonlight that filtered through the trees.

Wilder peered into the dark. Through the brush and palmetto bushes he saw a mound, about three feet high, about ten feet behind Moot.

"She's dangerous when she's protecting her eggs," Pepper whispered in a wavering voice.

Wilder put his hand once more on her back, taken off guard at how small and fragile she felt. "That's okay. I'm dangerous when I'm protecting you."

Pepper looked up at him. "Really?"

Ah shit, Wilder thought and then froze.

There was something else out there, moving just once, not natural, wrong, something bad, something worse than Moot. Nothing Wilder could pin down to confirm that feeling, but he was absolutely sure of it. *Pepper's ghost*, he thought. And if Pepper hadn't been lying next to him, he'd have gone and tracked down whoever or whatever it was. But she was right next to him, and she was scared. And that gator was too close and too on edge.

And Armstrong was out there alone.

"Let's go," Wilder said quietly. "Your aunt is worried."

He got to his feet and saw Armstrong standing ten feet away now, as ordered, absolutely still. He knew she must have wanted to run to Pepper, but she hadn't. Teamwork.

Pepper got up, and he shepherded her behind him as he backed away, blocking her from Moot. When they reached Armstrong, she snatched up Pepper, wrapping her arms around the little girl, and he pulled her close with one arm, keeping Pepper between them as he whispered in her ear. "Moot is right *there*. Take her. I'll be a little while."

"No," she whispered back. "I'm not leaving you alone in here."

"Get her out *now*," Wilder said, his voice flat, and Armstrong hesitated and then turned for the road.

Wilder shifted his attention back to the swamp as he heard the strange, light popping noise again. Another pop and then all hell broke loose as Moot surged out of the water in their direction. Wilder brought up the Glock, but then he heard a third pop, and Moot slammed to a halt, swinging around to look in the other direction.

Armstrong was moving for the road, Pepper in her arms. Wilder stayed, gun at the ready, watching Moot watch something behind her. Minutes passed and yet the sounds of the low-country night did not return to normal.

There was a sudden splash and Wilder saw Moot turn and dive into the water heading back to her nest.

Time to go.

He backtracked toward base camp, not sure what was going on in the swamp but damn sure he didn't like any of it, and even more sure that whatever it was, it was not going to touch Pepper or Lucy Armstrong.

Lucy walked down the center of the road as fast as she could, Pepper's foil bracelets scratching her neck and Wilder a silent, comforting presence behind them.

"I'm sorry," Pepper whispered into her neck.

"Not your fault," Lucy whispered back, not knowing if gators attacked people for talking and not wanting to find out. "It was my fault, I forgot your party."

"I just wanted everybody to be happy," Pepper said miserably. "Mom and you were fighting, and I thought a party would make you happy—"

"Oh, God, Pepper, we're so sorry." She held the little girl tighter. There was light ahead, the glow from the base-camp lights, and the green darkness of the swamp and woods ending, and Lucy picked up speed, almost running.

"—And I wanted more Wonder Woman stuff," Pepper said and sobbed once before she caught herself.

"I'll get you more," Lucy said, stricken with guilt. "I will fix *everything*."

Pepper sniffed. "Really?"

"Yes."

Pepper sniffed again. "That's what J.T. said."

"He did?" They reached the edge of the woods and Lucy glanced back at Wilder, who was watching the dark forest.

"He said he was dangerous when he was protecting me, just like Moot was dangerous when she was protecting her eggs."

"Does that make you J.T.'s egg?" Lucy said, and Pepper giggled and then sniffed. *She's okay,* Lucy thought. *Thank you, thank you, she's okay.*

Then they came out into the open, and Gloom yelled, "Lucy's got her!" and people began to converge on them, makeup and wardrobe and grips and camera people, Althea and Bryce, everybody crowding around under the lights.

"Wow," Pepper said, cheering up at all the attention.

Gloom took her out of Lucy's arms and hugged her, getting tangled in her blue cape in the process. "Don't you ever do that again, young lady."

"I won't," Pepper said, and then Estelle from wardrobe grabbed her and hugged her, too, as Daisy pushed through the crowd and saw Pepper and burst into tears.

"Okay," Lucy said, cheerfully. "Into the camper."

Estelle put Pepper into Daisy's arms while Lucy turned back to the crowd.

"We are so grateful for your help," she said, putting as much feeling as she could into her voice. "It means so very much. Thank you very, very much."

"Is she okay?" Mary Vanity asked, her heavily outlined eyes avid, trying to see Pepper as Daisy carried her toward the camper, hugging her the whole time.

"She got a little scared," Lucy said. "There was a gator."

"Moot?" Althea said from behind Mary. "Oh, no." She looked after Pepper with real sympathy on her face. "She must have been terrified."

"She's a tough little kid," Lucy said. "Everything is fine now." *Or it's going to be,* she thought grimly and headed for the camper.

"Hey," Gloom said to her and she stopped. "Real story?"

Lucy spoke low. "She was scared because all the adults were acting like idiots so she wanted to make sure there was a party tomorrow night and everybody would be happy."

Gloom shook his head. "We have to get her out of here."

"Working on it," Lucy said.

"Can I assume Captain Wilder was a big help?"

"Captain Wilder is a fucking hero," Lucy said, looking over at the edge of the trees, where Wilder stood still as a shadow, looking back into the woods, still protecting them. *Oh, God,* she thought as her heart thumped, *do not get suckered into another one of those guys. You learned your lesson with Connor.*

Gloom nodded. "He sounds like Will Kane."

"Give it a rest," Lucy said and turned toward the camper, only to stop when Gloom grabbed her braid and tugged on it. "Ouch?"

"Tell the nice hero thank you," Gloom said, and Lucy pulled her braid from his hand, took a deep breath, nodded, and went toward Wilder, determined to be grateful but businesslike.

"Thank you," she said when she reached Wilder, and he turned, looking surprised.

"Is she okay?"

"Yes, thank you very much." Lucy tried to say more and then realized she was shaking. "Look at me," she said, appalled. "I'm a mess."

"Delayed reaction," Wilder said. "You were tough when you needed to be. That was a good thing you did with the rocks."

His matter-of-factness undid her. Lucy held out her hands, trembling. "That alligator was *right there*."

"Shhhh," he said, moving closer, broad and solid in the darkness, and without meaning to she leaned against him, her forehead on his shoulder, her hands on his chest, so grateful he was there, she didn't care that she was shaking. He put his arms around her without hesitation, and she was grateful for that, too, more than grateful; it seemed like forever, maybe never, since anybody had held her and made her feel taken care of. He patted her awkwardly on the back, clumsy but sincere, and it felt so good that she sniffed into his collar.

"I'm sorry," she said, not really sorry at all as long as his arms were around her. "I'm not a wimp, I'm really not." *But I could learn to be if it gets me this.*

"No, you aren't," he said, "you were great in there," and she felt tears well up and relaxed against him until she remembered Pepper saying she'd just wanted them all to stop fighting.

She pulled away. "Don't be nice to me," she said, as he dropped his arms. "It's my fault she went in there. I was so caught up in all this movie mess that I didn't see her go—"

"None of us saw," Wilder said. "Jeez, lighten up."

Lucy started to laugh, blinking back tears. " 'Jeez'?"

"You did good in there," Wilder said, clearly ill at ease. "You backed me up, you were there when we needed you, you completed your mission."

"Oh." Lucy smeared tears away with her fingertips, hating that she was making him uncomfortable. "I'm a good soldier." Well, that was something.

"No," Wilder said, looking flustered. "I didn't mean . . . I meant you're a good wingman."

"Oh." She sniffed and nodded, trying to be chipper. "Wingman. That's great. Thank you." *Get away from the poor guy before he hates you for being so wet.* She took a step back, not wanting to go, wanting to know she'd see him again off the set. "Uh, listen, we're having a Wonder Woman party for Pepper tomorrow night. Pepper would really love it if you'd come." *I'd really love it if you'd come and I swear I won't cry.*

"I'll be there," Wilder said.

Lucy nodded until she felt like that stupid Wonder Woman bobblehead. Then she jerked her thumb toward the camper. "I have to go. You know. Pepper."

"Right." Wilder nodded to the woods. "Me too."

"Right." Lucy took another step back and tripped, and Wilder lunged forward and caught her, steadying her with his hands again, which she liked a lot more than she should have. "Jeez," she said, her voice bright as he let go. "Tree roots."

"Well, it is a forest," Wilder said.

"Yes, it is," Lucy said and thought, *Kill me now.* "So, uh . . ."

"Party tomorrow," Wilder said.

"And stunts," Lucy said, brightly. "You know, you, falling out of a helicopter on a cable."

"No problem." He was fading back into the trees as he spoke, almost disappearing, and Lucy felt twelve again, digging her toe in the dirt and watching some sixth-grade boy go home, wishing he would stay.

"Yeah," she said, almost to herself. "No problem."

She turned and went back to Gloom feeling worn out and stupid and happy, which made no sense whatsoever. Her life was a *mess,* for crying out loud.

"Hey," Gloom said when she joined him. "What do you need me to get for this party tomorrow?"

"A Wonder Woman cake," Lucy said, looking back at the woods. "And a Wonder Woman Barbie." She faced him. "You got time to get that?"

"I'll make time," Gloom said, determination on his long face. "That kid gets her party."

"Why aren't you straight?" Lucy said, putting her arms around his waist. "I could live happily with you for the rest of my life."

"No, you couldn't," Gloom said into her hair as he held her close. "You need somebody who'll fight back and have sex with you. Which brings us to Captain Wilder the fucking hero. I think you should stop holding out."

Lucy let go of him before she betrayed herself. "We have to get back to work. But extend second meal for another half an hour. We've got the time and I need it right now."

"Daisy?" Gloom said.

"Yeah," Lucy said.

"Okay, family first," Gloom said. "But don't forget the hero, will you?"

"Not a chance," Lucy said and headed for the camper.

In the forest, Wilder was searching his brain. He'd heard that popping noise before, in some other place at some other time, but his mind couldn't process it. Too many females around, muddling his brain. Pepper and Lucy Armstrong. What a pair.

Especially Armstrong, coming unglued there at the end. Never thought he'd be patting her on the back while she sniffed into his collar. That had been, well, pretty damn good, actually. She'd felt great against him. And Pepper, trusting him like that in the swamp, that was—

Something moved in the trees and Wilder froze. A bird flew out of the brush and he relaxed again.

It hadn't been a bird in the swamp with Pepper.

Nash? The stuntman hadn't been in the base camp, but Wilder saw no reason the Australian would be messing with the alligator, especially with Pepper close by. He really seemed to care about Pepper. As he pondered it, Wilder saw no reason for *anyone* to be out in the swamp. Except that Pepper had seen a ghost.

Someone moved outside the trees. "Wilder?" Gloom called out.

"Right here." Wilder moved out of the woods and nodded toward the camper. "They okay?"

"Lucy's in charge, they'll be okay," Gloom said. "Thanks. For Pepper."

Wilder nodded, surprised. All these people, thanking him. What did they think, that he'd go out for a beer while they searched?

"Yeah, I know, you'd have done it for anybody," Gloom said. "Listen, about Lucy . . . "

"Yeah?" Wilder said cautiously.

"She's really special."

Wilder nodded.

Gloom shook his head. "No, really special. You know how some people see the glass as half full and some see it as half empty?"

What the hell?

"Well, Lucy looks at it and says, 'Somebody forgot to fill the damn glass,' and then makes sure it's filled up for everybody else." He looked back toward the camper. "But this time she's out of her league. You know?"

"Yeah," Wilder said, feeling sorry for him. The poor guy had no idea how far out. If he knew about the CIA, he'd probably have Armstrong's butt back in New York with the dogs by now.

"She's going to try to fix it all on her own," Gloom was saying. "Lucy's not good at asking for help."

"Okay," Wilder said, not following.

"But she thinks you're great," Gloom said. "Says you're a fucking hero."

Wilder didn't know how to react to that. "She was pretty good in there herself." *A fucking hero?* Damn.

Gloom nodded. "I love her a lot. Take care of my girl, will you?" Then he walked away.

Wilder watched him go, perplexed. That had been strange. Still, she thought he was a hero. That was pretty good. Wilder remembered LaFavre, talking the previous afternoon, saying, "Women are usually real grateful to heroes." Lucy Armstrong, grateful. That would be something.

Then he shook himself. Like Althea hadn't been enough trouble. Of course, she had acted like he ought to be grateful, like she'd done him a big favor and he owed her, which made him glad he was camping out in the woods. *Mind back on the mission.*

It hadn't been Nash in the swamp playing ghost, it hadn't been anybody from the movie; they'd all have rescued Pepper. Which left the only other players in the game.

Wilder got out his cell phone as he made his way to his Jeep, punching in the numbers. When Crawford answered, he said, "Meet me at the diner in fifteen."

"I can't—"

"The fuck you can't," Wilder said and turned off the phone.

When Lucy got into the camper, Daisy was sobbing and Pepper was breathing hard, her eyes wide with fear.

"I'm *so sorry*," Pepper said, her little chest heaving as she clutched at her mother, "I'm really *sorry*," and Daisy cried harder, sobs shaking her thin frame, her pale face blotchy under her blond frizz.

"Okay, that's it," Lucy said sharply as Daisy began to hyperventilate. Her cries got louder, and Pepper's eyes got wider and she began to whimper.

Lucy got a glass from her cupboard, filled it with water, and threw it in Daisy's face.

Daisy jerked back and stared at her, eyes wide as the water matted her hair and dripped off her face, drawing in sharp breaths but not sobbing anymore.

"You are scaring your daughter," Lucy said gently, and Daisy turned to look at Pepper, now almost rigid with fear and guilt.

"Oh, baby, I'm sorry." Daisy hugged her close, breathing hard but holding back the cries.

"It's all my fault," Pepper wailed into her chest.

"No," Lucy said. "It was nobody's fault, it was a misunderstanding because we didn't talk to each other." She stared at her sister until Daisy met her eyes. "So from now on, we're *talking.*"

They sat in silence, Daisy rocking Pepper in the swivel chair until the little girl's breathing slowed and her body relaxed. When Lucy was sure Pepper was asleep, she stood up and held out her arms.

"Give her to me, I'll put her on the bed," she told Daisy, and Daisy stood up, staggering a little under Pepper's weight, and handed her over.

Lucy put Pepper on the bed and covered her with her blue-checkered quilt and then stood looking at her for a moment. She could have been gone in an instant, so little. It was a miracle they'd found her in time. No, not a miracle. *Thank God for J. T. Wilder,* she thought, and held on to her feelings with both hands. He was a good guy, a great guy, but that was all.

Then she got two root beers out of the fridge and sat down across from Daisy.

Daisy looked like hell.

"Here." Lucy handed her a root beer. "Now, you're going to tell me everything. I was being patient and tactful, but that's over. You're in trouble and Pepper knows it and you can't take much more and neither can she. You tell me everything now."

"I can't," Daisy said, her voice a whisper.

"I won't go to the police," Lucy said, and Daisy looked up sharply. "That's what you're worried about, isn't it? That whatever Connor's gotten you into is illegal—" Daisy started to protest and Lucy held up her hand. "Forget it, I know it's Connor. He's suckered you into something and you're afraid you'll end up in jail. Well, it's not gonna happen. Not on my shoot. Gloom wouldn't stand for it."

Daisy smiled weakly and Lucy said, "Tell me."

Daisy sighed. "The backer, Finnegan. He's using the movie as a front for something. Connor won't tell me what, but it's about that helicopter. He paid me to keep my mouth shut about the changes, about how there's no continuity in the script."

"Helicopter," Lucy said, thinking back to the script. "Explosions. Armored car. Are they planning to really rob an armored car?"

"I don't know." Daisy slumped back in her chair, misery personified. "According to the script it's happening on the bridge. And there's a speedboat, it's supposed to be under the bridge for safety, but Doc slipped and said he's supposed to take it into the swamp." She swallowed hard. "Connor gave me fifty thousand dollars to keep quiet, Lucy."

"Oh," Lucy said, knowing exactly what that kind of money would mean to Daisy, to any single mother.

"And he said there'd be another fifty thousand after it's over. I want that money," Daisy said, the old stubborn look in her eye. Then her face softened and her lips quivered again. "But there's something wrong, I knew it was going to go wrong, I knew whatever it was, was so big that it had to be illegal. And then Lawton died and everybody quit, but I can't, I need the rest of the money, and . . ." She held out her shaking hand. "I was like this. So Connor got me something to calm me down."

"I'm going to kill him," Lucy said, grateful to have a concrete goal.

"No, no, he was *good to me,*" Daisy said, her eyes pleading. "He helped me. Don't say anything to him, I really need the money." She leaned forward. "Lucy, a hundred thousand would be enough to support me and Pepper for a long while. Years. I can go to school and be a teacher, I'm a good teacher, Pepper's learned a lot."

"I know," Lucy said, thinking, *Jesus, all she wants is a teaching degree?* "Look, I can help you get that—"

"I want to do it on my own," Daisy said. "No more getting bailed out by my big sister. All that money you've sent me over the years, I'll *never* be able to pay it back—"

"Those weren't loans," Lucy said, appalled. "I don't want you to—"

"I *want to*," Daisy said, her voice rising. "I want to be strong, I want Pepper to look at me the way she looks at you. She thinks you really are Wonder Woman."

Lucy waved that away. "That's just an aunt thing. She doesn't see me enough to know I'm just like everybody else. Hell, if you could have seen me fifteen minutes ago—"

"You're not like everybody else," Daisy said, misery in her voice. "You are Wonder Woman. You always have been."

"Daisy—"

"I want to be for Pepper what you were for me," Daisy said. "And if I go to college, if I get a job, a real job, not a movie job, with a real home for Pepper, no moving around, then she'll see—"

"We'll make it happen," Lucy said. "We'll do it together, just like we used to. Remember? Stuck like glue to each other."

"Not if I'm in *jail*," Daisy wailed.

"Okay." Lucy patted her hand. "You're not going to jail. I'll just find some good reason to cancel the shoot on Thursday. That way, whatever it is won't happen."

"They won't *let you*," Daisy said, her voice sobby. "Connor will do it anyway. And I think Finnegan would do anything he had to. They're driven, Lucy, it's big, big money. *Millions*."

"Uh huh," Lucy said, thinking fast. "Okay, we've still got all day tomorrow and most of the day Thursday to work this out. We don't shoot until after dark on Thursday. So I can still fix this."

"*How?*" Daisy began to cry. "If I go to jail, will you take care of Pepper?"

"No," Lucy said, "because the only way you're going to jail is over my dead body. But Gloom will take her. They can watch *High Noon* and sing 'Us Amazonians' together."

"It's *not a joke*, Lucy," Daisy said through her tears. "You can't fix it this time. These guys are pros, they have guns, you can't fight them."

"The hell I can't." Well, guns. That might be beyond her. "Okay, maybe I can't alone, but I have a secret weapon." Lucy tried to make her voice light. "He's a pain in the butt, but he's good with guns."

Daisy sat up, blinking tears away. "You can't tell Wilder. Connor is furious about him. He's afraid he'll snoop around and find out what's going on."

"I'll play it by ear," Lucy said.

"Lucy, *you can't*," Daisy said.

"Look, don't tell me how to save you, just trust me that I will, okay?" Lucy ducked her head down to look into her sister's face. "Have I ever failed you?"

Daisy shook her head as the tears started to roll down her cheeks again.

"Well, I'm not going to start now." Lucy got up and put her arms around her.

Daisy collapsed against her and cried, but it was different this time, a sort of worn-out relief spending itself in tears, not hysteria. "I just wanted to do it myself," she said, but all the fight had gone out of her.

"I will fix it," Lucy said into Daisy's ear. "I swear I will. I will. And then we will go back to New York and put Pepper in school and you can go to college and we will be a family again. I will fix everything."

"All right," Daisy said, exhausted, a dead weight against Lucy's side.

Lucy held on, patting her, and tried to make a plan.

For a start, she needed backup.

Definitely J. T. Wilder, she thought and closed her eyes.

9

It took Wilder eight minutes to make it to the diner, and when he entered, he saw Crawford in the same booth. Predictable, which was not good in covert operations. Hell, nobody was doing anything right.

"Move," he ordered.

Crawford looked up, startled. "Why?"

Better than "what," but not by much. Wilder pointed at the other side of the table, and Crawford reluctantly vacated the seat that had its back to the wall and took the one across from it. Wilder figured he'd get the why in about four or five years.

Wilder sat down. "Who have you got in the swamp?"

"What swamp?" Crawford said, looking genuinely confused.

"The swamp by the Talmadge Bridge, near the movie base camp. Who's in there?"

"Nobody," Crawford said. "Why would we have anybody in there?"

Wilder sat back as the waitress approached.

"Beer," Wilder said.

"Same," Crawford said without looking over his shoulder at the waitress. When she was gone he said, "We've got nobody in the swamp, but I have some intelligence for you," as if he was eager to please. "Lucy Armstrong. She's worked in film for over fourteen years, the last twelve on her own as a director of commercials. She specializes in animals, does pretty good, but this project is her first feature as director. The previous director, Matthew Lawton, died Friday. We checked: heart attack, no foul play. Neither one of them had a file."

Wilder understood that. Most normal, red-blooded, apple-pie-eating, tax-paying Americans did not have an FBI or a CIA file. You had to get on the radar to get a file. So Armstrong wasn't on the government's radar. And that jived for Wilder, except that she was on his damn radar. He shook that off. "If she didn't have a file, how'd you find out this stuff?"

Crawford blinked. "I googled for it."

Jesus. "Finnegan called Armstrong this morning and threatened to sue her if she didn't follow the schedule."

"Could you get the number off her cell phone?" Crawford asked.

"You think Finnegan would be stupid enough to call her on a traceable line? Or leave caller ID?" That *would* save everyone a lot of trouble, Wilder thought. But the odds of that were the same as Finnegan showing up on the set.

"You're right. Neither Armstrong or Lawton had any apparent contact with Finnegan before this movie-financing thing. We don't know if they've ever met face to face, and we still don't think Finnegan is even in the States. We've got no reason to believe that Lawton knew about Finnegan's background. We think he just took the money to finish the movie, keep some of it for himself."

The waitress came back with their beers, and Wilder waited until she was gone to ask, "And Connor Nash?"

Crawford frowned for a second as he searched his mind. "Nash— he's a foreign national, right?"

"Speaks Australian, which is just like English but different."

"What?"

Wilder took a deep breath, and waited.

Crawford pulled out a PDA. Wilder wondered where that had been at their first meeting. "Let me see. We did run a check for non-U.S. citizens on the set. I mean the FBI did. After 9/11 it's been standard—"

Wilder didn't need a speech on protocol and how 9/11 fucked the country up in more ways than people realized. "What do you have on Nash?"

"Here it is. Not much. Australian, like you said. Been in the States on and off for the past eight years."

"Where is he when he's off?"

"Um, we got three trips back to Australia. One to Germany." Crawford squinted at the PDA. "Hmm, this is odd. He's been in Iraq four times. Sixty-day stints working for a company called Blue River, whatever that is."

Wilder sat straighter. "Blue River is a security contractor." Wilder knew plenty of guys who'd worked for the security contractors in that true clusterfuck of a country. It was the one place that made the movie set look like a well-oiled machine. "Nash was gunslinging for them. What else?"

"Gunslinging?" Crawford asked, and Wilder thought, *He's never been out of the country if he doesn't know that. A real cherry.*

"A lot of new companies sprang up after the Second Gulf War, making easy money off all the contracts being let by the U.S. Most of the security work was done by private firms, guns for hire. Gunslingers."

"Oh." Crawford looked like he was carefully filing that away for later, and Wilder began to feel as if he were teaching CIA 101. Crawford continued tapping the screen with the stylus. "Nash was in the Australian army. Did seven years as an NCO."

That also made sense. Wilder had had no doubt from their first meeting that Nash had been military. "What was his specialty?"

"Something called SAS."

Wilder went cold. "Special Air Service. Who Dares Wins."

"What?"

"Who Dares Wins. That's the motto of the SAS. They're the Australian equivalent of U.S. Special Forces. They were founded as the Australian version of the British SAS. Bad guys to go up against, good guys to have on your side." He'd been glad to be on their side during the early days of the Second Gulf War. Not so glad now that he might be going up against one on the set. *Fuck,* he thought. *Connor Nash.*

"Does it list his specialty?"

"Weapons. Secondary of demolitions."

Damn. Figured. They didn't have dishwashers in the SAS. "Anything else?"

Crawford took a cautious sip of his beer, as if the liquid were going to attack him. "Nash has worked on fourteen movies in the past twelve years. This is his second one with Armstrong. Which means she could be in on something with him now."

"No." Wilder processed it. So Nash worked for Blue River in between movie gigs. That made sense. With his SAS background he'd earn top dollar. Enough in sixty days to live on for a year if he was reasonably frugal. Then he had his movie income, although Wilder had no idea what a stunt coordinator pulled in. They didn't seem to be living in the lap of luxury on this movie. "Did Nash do any time in Ireland where he might have run into Finnegan?"

"No record of it."

"How about Mexico? Was Nash down there when Finnegan got nabbed?"

"No."

There was a long silence while Wilder tried to figure out the connection between Nash and Finnegan, and then Crawford cleared his throat nervously. "Finnegan did some things in Iraq after the overthrow of Saddam. Smuggling."

Bingo, Wilder thought. "You should have told me that up front, damn it. What are we playing, hide the intelligence here?"

"I didn't put it together until right now," Crawford said. "I mean, I read the files, but there was so much information I didn't see the possibility of Finnegan and Nash meeting there."

Wilder shook his head. "Anything could have happened after Baghdad fell. The Army had planned on using six divisions, but the politicians screwed up the assault from the north and there were only two and a half. The place was wide open. A lot of vultures just like Finnegan flew in to pick over the leavings." He picked up his beer. "You have a picture of Finnegan?"

"Taken eighteen years ago." Crawford pulled it out of his coat pocket, flashing his revolver again, and handed it to Wilder, who checked his nemesis out: a burly, handsome man with white hair and piercing blue eyes in a truly bad Hawaiian shirt.

Wilder was impressed. The kid had done okay boiling it down and following up on the old director. Of course, he had to be smart; the CIA had probably recruited him out of some Ivy League school that would never have allowed Wilder to look at their catalog, never mind enroll.

Crawford leaned back so that his jacket fell open, again exposing his revolver. "You're probably wondering about my gun."

Nope.

"It's my dad's."

Oh, crap. Wilder ran his hand along the side of his empty mug and gestured for the waitress with two fingers. There was silence until she came and left.

"He was a cop," Crawford said, picking up his beer and taking a deep drink. "He'd been a cop but hurt his knee chasing down a bad guy. They retired him at quarter pay and he couldn't take care of a family on that. So he worked security at a supermarket."

Wilder wanted to leave. There was Armstrong with Nash dogging her, and Finnegan lurking in the background, making money for shithead terrorists, and the ghost in the swamp. . . . He cut off Crawford's life story: "Could Finnegan have somebody in the swamp?"

Crawford looked disappointed at having his story interrupted. "What makes you think someone is there?"

"I felt it today. I heard a strange noise."

Crawford made a face. "Probably just some fisherman or hunter."

"No," Wilder said. He figured telling Crawford about Pepper's ghost wouldn't go over well. "There's somebody bad in there. What are you not telling me?"

Crawford froze and then tried to shrug it off. "Nothing. I'm telling you nothing."

"Screw you," Wilder said, shoving his chair back. "Your man almost got a little kid killed—"

"No, no," Crawford said. "We really don't have anybody in the swamp."

"What then?"

Crawford hesitated, and Wilder stood up, leaning forward toward the CIA agent.

"Wait." Crawford swallowed. "When Finnegan was nailed in Mexico he was buying the art on consignment. For a Russian named Simon Letsky."

"That doesn't sound Russian."

"A Russian Jew. Known as the Smart Don."

Aw shit, Wilder thought and sat down. Why couldn't it be the Dumb Don?

"Letsky is reported to be the most powerful organized-crime boss in Russia. My source couldn't tell me much, but Letsky is considered by many insiders to be a very bad man. Finnegan stole the jade for him."

Wilder glanced at the white-haired smiling Irishman in the photo. *You asshole, you're in way over your head, aren't you?* "And Letsky probably wasn't very happy about his fifty-million-dollar Viagra shipment being taken."

"No."

Wilder tried to figure the angles, but hell, he was just a Special Forces guy, not a cop. "And you think Finnegan is laundering money through the movie for Letsky in order to pay him back?"

Crawford shrugged. "It's the logical deduction."

"No, it isn't. Four million isn't close to the fifty million Letsky paid."

"I can do the math," Crawford said, looking sullen. "But Letsky most likely didn't put the entire amount up front. Probably just enough to entice Finnegan to get the jade, with the balance paid on delivery. But that's it. That's all I know. I'm not keeping anything else from you, I swear."

Wilder gave up. He stood, sliding the picture into his pocket, shook his head, and walked out.

When he was on the sidewalk, he looked back into the diner. Crawford had switched seats and was facing the door, almost smiling.

Wilder paused. Why was Crawford smirking? He'd missed something. He could feel it. He shook his head again and went toward his Jeep. It was late and he just wanted to get some sleep before the next fuck-up happened.

With Crawford in charge, there was bound to be another one along pretty soon.

The next afternoon, Lucy met Daisy when she got off the shuttle at the Wildlife Refuge.

"How are you doing?" she asked. "You okay?"

Daisy nodded, still a little wobbly. "I think that cry did me good. Well, the cry and you. Thanks for rescuing me again."

Lucy waited for a smile and didn't get one. "Well, that's my job. Daize, about the pills—"

"I didn't take any today," Daisy said, tiredly. "I figure you're here, maybe I don't need them. Just hand everything over to you, no worries." She sounded brittle, almost angry, but then she finally smiled—weakly, but still a smile—and said, "So where's your secret weapon?"

Lucy nodded to the side of the road, where Wilder looked less delighted to be dressed just like Bryce, who looked less than delighted, especially with his copy of Bryce's knife strapped across his chest. Wilder was so much the real thing that he almost made the knife look right. "The swelling's gone down on Bryce's face so that's all right. We're good to shoot. How's Pepper?"

"Looking for craft services, of course." Daisy's smiled wavered. "Aunt Lucy needs her apples since Stephanie is falling down on the job."

"Stephanie is mad as hell about something," Lucy said, resigned to having an assistant who hated her. "She's stomping around sneering at people. But then, what else is new?" She looked around for Pepper and didn't see her. "Pepper didn't go—"

"Into the swamp? No." Daisy sounded sure. "And she never will again without J.T. She was really terrified in there until he rescued her. She says she's J.T.'s egg now, which I don't get, but if it keeps her out of the swamp, what the heck." She looked at Lucy. "You really hit the mark with her, buying that Wonder Woman outfit. The only reason she didn't wear it to bed last night was because I told her she couldn't wear it today if she did. She put it on the chair beside her bed and stared at it until she fell asleep. You did good, Aunt Lucy."

"Good." Lucy put her attention back on Wilder, looking lean and tough in camouflage, and Bryce in the same getup, looking like he was going out for Halloween.

"So they're still pals?" Daisy said, looking at them, too. "Even after Althea?"

Lucy shook her head at the mystery that was men. "I'm guessing Bryce doesn't know that Rambo did Bambi. Plus, Wilder did save Bryce's butt in that bar fight, so Bryce has to love him for that."

"J.T. saved a lot of people yesterday," Daisy said.

"Fucking hero," Lucy said, trying to keep the warmth out of her voice. Thank God, Gloom was too busy to hum Bonnie Tyler at her. *Change the subject.* She nodded toward the long straight road ahead of them leading into the Savannah Wildlife Refuge, now crowded with cast and crew, one of whom was reporting to Finnegan. "Great location. No trees to screw up the chopper and we don't have to pay to shut it down to traffic."

"Yep," Daisy said. "Great place for J.T. to fall out of a helicopter."

"Well, at least it's keeping him out of bars," Lucy said. "I don't like the way that fight happened."

Daisy shrugged. "Couple of good old boys trying to be tough, beat up the famous actor."

"Bryce isn't that famous. Plus, he's a comedian. It'd be like kicking a mime."

"Very tempting," Daisy said.

Lucy grinned at her. "You *are* feeling better."

"Yeah." Daisy sighed. "Listen, I probably overreacted last night with that crying fit—"

"Your kid lost in a swamp full of gators?" Lucy shook her head. "No, I'd say you were right on the money."

"I could not find Crafty," Pepper announced from behind them, and Lucy turned and saw her, looking frustrated in her blue-and-white-starred skivvies and blue cape, her binoculars around her neck. "I wanted to get you apples and then look for my ghost, but I cannot find Crafty."

"It's over there, honey." Lucy nodded toward the table full of junk food that was set up out of the way of the cameras.

"Great," Pepper said and started toward it.

"No candy," Daisy called after her. "Only fruit." She shook her head and started after her daughter, and Lucy was still smiling when she turned and found Connor in front of her.

"She okay?" he asked, nodding toward Pepper with real concern on his face. "I heard this morning—"

"Where were you last night?" Lucy said, wanting to smack him. He'd given Daisy drugs, damn him.

"Rehearsing with Karen," he said, looking taken aback. "You know, the helicopter pilot—"

"I know," Lucy said.

Nash frowned at her. "Damn, Lucy, if I'd had any idea Pepper was in trouble—"

"What were you rehearsing?"

"This stunt." He grinned at her. "Hey, you want to know what I'm doing, you need to stick closer."

He might have been with Karen, but he hadn't been rehearsing, she thought. That was why Stephanie was looking like murder. Lucy looked past him to Wilder, the antithesis of him in every way. "I don't want to know that much about you," she said and walked over to the monitors, leaving him stunned behind her.

Wilder had been having a trying afternoon. First there was Bryce's gun: It was a stunt gun, but Bryce held it in a way that made Wilder nervous. Then there was Wilder's outfit: He was dressed identically to Bryce in the stupid tiger-stripe fatigues and web gear with his copy of that damn knife strapped across his chest, looking like an idiot. And finally there was Armstrong across the road, distracting him, talking to Daisy, looking a lot like Wonder Woman except for that long dark braid down her back. If he ever got close enough, he was taking that braid down—"

"How do I hold this thing?" Bryce said, frowning at the gun.

Wilder sighed. "Here." He held out a hand for the submachine gun.

Bryce reluctantly parted with it, and Wilder took the MP-5 in his hands. It was a German-made gun, the weapon of choice among counterterrorist units around the world, the same as the one Wilder had cached close by, except that his would work for real. Out of the corner of his eye, Wilder could see Nash watching them.

He removed the magazine and then checked the chamber. The rounds were blanks and there was a blank adapter plugged into the barrel. He checked to see that the adapter was secure, since it could be lethal if it became a projectile fired by the blast from the blanks. Just to be safe, Wilder knelt down and quickly thumbed out the thirty rounds from the magazine onto a box, making sure every single one was a blank. Then he began reloading.

"What are you doing?" Bryce asked.

"Making sure no one gets hurt, particularly you."

Bryce nodded. "That's good. I remember that guy died making that movie. You know, Bruce Lee's kid."

Wilder remembered reading about that. The stunt gun had malfunctioned. "That won't happen here. Nash did a good job."

"Thanks a fucking lot, mate," Nash said from behind them. He looked at the gun in Wilder's hand. "Satisfied?"

"Just doing my job."

"So am I. And I've been doing it a hell of lot longer than you have. Don't mess with my gear after I've prepped it."

Wilder nodded and glanced over at Armstrong and caught her watching them. She turned her head, and he thought, *Go away, Nash. Far away. Iraq would be good. Afghanistan. Pluto.*

Nash looked pointedly at his watch. "You guys good to go? Or you got a bar fight you got to get to?"

"I want to be in the chopper," Bryce said, lifting his chin, and Wilder forgot Armstrong to focus on this next disaster.

"You will be in the chopper," Nash said. "For the ground shot once we land the bird after the air shots. It will look like you're in the air, so don't worry."

"No," Bryce said. "I want to be in it for the first part. Where it catches up to the car. The skid sequence before the jump."

Wilder thought, *Oh, fuck.*

"No." Nash said it as an order.

That's telling him, Wilder thought. *Not that it's going to work.* Bryce had that mule look on his face again.

Bryce drew himself up, his face blotchy with stress. "It's a daylight shot, so I should do it. People have to see me in action scenes to think I'm an action hero. I can do it. I held my own in the bar fight. Just ask J.T."

Nash looked at him, one eyebrow raised.

"Bryce didn't hesitate," Wilder said, truthfully. *He got in the way, but he didn't hesitate.*

"Lucy isn't going to—" Nash began, but Bryce cut him off.

"So don't tell her until it's over. I'm the star here."

Nash looked at Wilder, mad as hell but fighting to keep a lid on it. "Are you saying he can do this? That you will guarantee he won't get hurt?"

"Nope," Wilder said.

"I'm getting in that copter," Bryce said, "and I'm going to stand on that skid, just like a real action hero." He caught himself. "I am a real action hero."

"Uh, Bryce," Wilder said.

"And if I don't get to do the stunt"—Bryce drew himself up—"I might get so upset that I couldn't shoot for a while. Till maybe next week. That would cost you more than the insurance."

"*Fuck,*" Nash said, his voice savage now.

"It will save you time with the helicopter," Bryce said. "You won't have to keep it here to do my shots on the ground because they'll already be done."

"Listen, Bryce," Nash began in a totally new voice, almost begging. "We've storyboarded this and—"

"I'm in the helicopter on the skid or there's no more shooting this week."

"Lucy will go crazy," Nash said.

"I'm the star."

Wilder sighed. He'd seen behavior like this before. A three-star general had come to Afghanistan and demanded stupid things in exactly the same manner. Wilder had been tempted to toss a grenade his way.

Nash glared, looking like he wanted to chuck a grenade or two himself. "Fuck it. It's your ass." He stalked off, pulling his cell phone out.

"Let's get this done," Bryce said, his voice deeper now that he was feeling macho.

Wilder ignored him and cocked his head as a familiar sound reached his ears, sending a surge of adrenaline through his body. Inbound helicopter. *It's just a movie,* Wilder reminded himself, but it didn't matter. Going in on a mission or getting pulled out, that's what the sound of a helicopter meant to him.

"Let's *go*," Bryce said, channeling G.I. Joe, as a four-seater Bell Jet Ranger with the doors off touched down.

Wilder followed him to the helicopter. Once inside, he leaned forward to get the pilot's attention, easier to do because the doors were off. Her name was Karen Roeburn, Bryce had said when he'd pointed her out, the same tough-looking brunette in an Army flight suit that Armstrong had pointed out the day before. His second ex-wife used to come home dressed like that, smelling of jet fuel.

Wilder tapped the pilot on the shoulder, and she turned and lifted her visor.

"I'm Wilder," he yelled over the sound of the rotors.

"I know," she yelled back. "Captain. J.T. One each. Government issue."

"Bryce is going to be on the skid today in the air, so keep it low and give him a smooth ride."

The look on her face told him what she thought about that. "I take orders from Nash, not from you."

"Right." He sat back, noting that she was programming a handheld GPS, a global positioning system that she had attached to her knee-board. He found that odd; it wasn't like it was hard to find this place in the daylight.

"What are you doing?" Wilder shouted to be heard above the chopper noise.

She looked startled for a second. "Fixing waypoints."

"Why?"

She stared at him. "You a pilot?"

"No, but—"

"Let me do my job."

Boy, everyone was getting real touchy, Wilder thought. It wasn't like they were going into a hot LZ.

Bryce settled into the front right seat, trying to be nonchalant but looking pale, and Nash finally arrived and sat down in the back beside Wilder, his equipment bag at his feet. "Let's go, Karen," he said, patting her on the shoulder, and with a slight shudder the chopper lifted.

Bryce got paler as the ground receded beneath them.

Wilder leaned across and tapped him on the shoulder. "Buckle up."

The actor jerked at the tap and then nodded. He fumbled with the shoulder straps, his hands shaking, and finally managed to get the male end into the female end. Wilder hoped he was better with women than with seat belts.

"We're airborne," Nash announced into his headset, which Wilder had to assume was part of his standing operating procedure since any fool within miles would be able to see that.

He watched Nash get the gear ready for Bryce's big scene. He hoped there was a barf bag in it. Bryce looked like he was going to be needing one.

Nash hooked a thin metal cable to the locking snap link on the back of Bryce's hidden harness and played out its eight-foot length, making sure there were no kinks, routing it so it wouldn't catch on anything inside the bird, competent and professional. Wilder began to relax.

Then Nash untied the six-foot loop of climbing rope attached to the other end of the cable and clipped the cable directly to a tie-down point on the floor of the chopper, and Wilder tensed again.

That wasn't right. The rope was the cushioning for the steel cable, one-third stretch built into the nylon. Without the rope, the steel cable had no play at all. If Bryce fell out, the cable would keep him from splatting onto the road below, but the snap of the abrupt halt eight feet down could break his back. Wilder had seen the rig on the bridge and this was different. There was no need for different.

Nash was stuffing the loop of rope back into his kit bag. Wilder put his hand on the bag and his head next to Nash's and yelled over the sound of the rotors, "What are you doing?"

Nash glared at him. "Bryce is going to put his feet on the skids of the chopper," he yelled back. "He's going to have three points of contact with the aircraft at all times. The cable is just a safety."

Bryce looked over his shoulder. "What's going on?" His voice was almost drowned out by the sound of the blades, and he was definitely green now.

Wilder gave him a thumbs-up and turned back to Nash. "Why'd you take the rope off?"

"He doesn't need it."

"It's part of the gear, right?"

"Yeah, but we don't want it caught on film and it adds three extra feet of fall and we're going to be low and I don't want him scraping along if he does fall."

"What are you guys talking about?" Bryce yelled. "J.T.?"

He sounded scared. *Damn it,* Wilder thought. Why was Nash dicking with things? "Everything's fine," he yelled to Bryce. "We're almost set." He tried to pull the kit bag out of Nash's hands, but the stunt coordinator hung on.

"The slack rope goes back on," Wilder yelled.

"It's *my stunt.*"

Nash glared at him, and Wilder held his eyes. *Come on, don't make me take it away from you. Put the rope back on.*

Nash looked away, out at the horizon. "All right. All right." He took the rope loop out and hooked it up again. Then he leaned forward and tapped Bryce on the shoulder. "We can still put Wilder in your place," he yelled.

Bryce's face was pale and damp, but he shook his head.

Wilder stuck his head next to the other two. "Really. It's no sweat, Bryce. I've lost count of the number of aircraft I've hung out of or jumped from. Normal part of my workday."

Bryce swallowed as he glanced out the open door to the ground. He shook his head firmly. Wilder had seen that look before, when he'd been a jumpmaster for inexperienced jumpers. Bryce was scared but he had made up his mind to do it. Wilder glanced at Nash, who looked none too pleased.

"Seat belt off," Nash ordered.

Wilder watched Bryce fumble with the buckle and realized that the actor's hands were shaking badly now. Probably should have stuck with comedy.

Wilder checked the outside. They were already a half mile down the road and the car was less than ten feet in front of them. The camera truck was about fifty feet in front of that. The road was perfectly straight. It should be simple.

Nash yelled to Bryce, "Okay, mate, feet on the skids."

Bryce turned toward the open door and cautiously slid his feet out, searching for the skid by feel, trying to look down.

"Eyes on the horizon," Wilder yelled. He pointed over Bryce's shoulder. "Look at those towers." He kept his eyes on Bryce edging his way out the door and in his peripheral vision kept a lock on their relative position with the picture car. Althea was looking over her shoulder at them. Maybe she'd be impressed that was Bryce out on the skid and fall back into his bed.

Nash stuck his head out the back door to do a quick check on where Bryce's feet were. Wilder resisted the urge to give him a nudge out the door since he didn't have a safety cable.

"Okay, mate," Nash yelled to Bryce. "Put your weight on your feet. Don't worry, we've got the cable just in case. And the chopper will be steady. Right, Karen?"

"Roger that," the pilot said.

"Now point the gun at the car," Nash yelled.

Wilder watched as Bryce awkwardly tried to aim the gun, but it was obvious the actor's entire focus was on the hand holding on to the chopper's door frame, not the one holding the MP-5. Well, he'd still give him points for effort. Bryce might be an idiot, but he was a game idiot. "Looking good, Bryce," he yelled and then sat back.

It was going to be a very long afternoon.

. . .

Below them, Lucy had checked with the EMTs leaning against the ambulance at the end of the road, making sure they were the real deal and not some scam Connor had cooked up to cut costs. Reassured, she went back and sat down at the monitors beside Daisy and Pepper, who were squinting up at the sky.

"Is J.T. in that helicopter?" Pepper asked, handing her an apple.

"Yep," Lucy said, taking it. "Thank you. He's going to be okay, Pepper, he's probably jumped out of a hundred helicopters—"

"Nice day for a disaster," Gloom said, sitting down on the other side of her.

Daisy grinned at him, and Lucy felt better than she had since they'd pulled into the base camp lot two days ago. *Mission accomplished,* she thought as she bit into her apple. Or it would be as soon as she got Daisy out of there the day after tomorrow.

"Hello, Gloom," Pepper sang out.

"Hello, Peppermint. Taken any walks lately?"

"No," Pepper said. "I am staying right here, and watching J.T., and looking for my ghost."

"All right then." Lucy picked up her headphones. "How we doin' out there?" she said to Gloom.

"Ask me when the stunts are over," Gloom said.

Above them, Wilder edged his way out onto the skid, holding on for dear life as the wind beat at his tiger stripes.

"Funny," Gloom said, squinting up at him. "I thought he'd be more dashing than that."

"You try being dashing on a helicopter skid," Lucy said, but she was disappointed, too. From down here, Wilder's body language pretty much communicated "terrified." So much for her secret weapon.

Well, he was still impressive on the ground.

"He's probably just being extra careful," Daisy said, her voice doubtful.

"Ready when you are," Connor said over the headphones.

Gloom stood up. "Here we go," he called to the set. "Stand by."

"Roll sound," Lucy said, and listened to the set echo back, "Rolling."

"Take one," the guy with the clapper said, snapping it shut in front of the camera.

"Action," Lucy said and watched the copter in the monitor, Wilder standing stiffly on the skid. She put her apple down half eaten on the edge of the monitor cart. *It's not dangerous, he's cabled in—*

"Afternoon, ma'am," somebody said from behind her in a deep Cajun accent, and she jerked around to see a tall, handsome, weather-beaten man wearing aviator sunglasses and a worn leather flight jacket tipping his crumpled pilot's hat to her. She'd seen him before, she knew that, but at the moment it didn't come to her.

"*Cool* sunglasses!" Pepper said.

"Gloom." Lucy put her eyes back on the monitor, and Gloom turned toward them. "We got a gawker."

"Thank you very much, darlin'," the man was saying to Pepper. "And may I say, that's a very fetching outfit you have on today."

Pepper smoothed down her WonderWear and beamed, and then he nodded to Lucy as Gloom stood up to get rid of him. "I was just wondering if you could direct me toward Captain J. T. Wilder."

Gloom sat back down again.

"Or failing that," the Cajun said, "a friendly actress in need of companionship. You wouldn't be a friendly actress now, would you, chéri?"

"No, I'm the director and we're shooting a scene right now." Lucy stared at the monitor where Wilder looked positively wimpy on that skid. *He really should stay on the ground,* she thought. *He's so good on the ground.*

"Very pleased to meet you," the man said. "I'm Rene LaFavre, J. T. Wilder's comrade-in-arms."

"You're a friend of J.T.'s?" Pepper said, delighted. "So am I!"

"J.T. is a man of discernment in his friendships," LaFavre said, smiling at her.

"Yeah," Pepper said. "Do you want to come to my party tonight?"

LaFavre put his hand over his heart. "Tragically, I have a previous engagement."

"Mr. LaFavre," Lucy said, staring at the copter, where Wilder now looked rigid with terror.

"That's Major LaFavre, darlin', but you can call me Rene."

"Thank you, Rene. Captain Wilder is on that helicopter skid up there."

LaFavre looked up. "I don't think so."

Lucy squinted at the helicopter as it dropped closer and then looked at the monitor. "Gloom," she said, her voice rising. "That doesn't look like Wilder on the skid." She looked again as the helicopter dropped closer.

"That's *not Wilder*," Lucy said, standing up. "That's *Bryce. Connor*," she yelled into her headset. "What the *hell* is Bryce doing on that skid?"

10

Tyler saw the copter coming from the west, right on time.

Then he looked at his cell phone and read the order he'd gotten fifteen minutes earlier: *Mission canceled.*

What the hell did that mean? He was ready to go. Fuck, he was more than ready, he was primed.

"Fuck you," he said to the phone. "I say it's a go."

He tossed his empty beer can over his shoulder and got down to business. He was a half mile to the south, in one of the abandoned towers that dotted the old Weyerhaeuser paper mill factory on the Savannah River, using a regular scope as the sun was still a good two and a half hours from being gone. It was going to be a very difficult shot. Moving targets always were.

The slanting rays of the sun were warm on his skin. A great fucking day. Perfect for shooting.

He ran the sight over the bridge and brought it to rest on the Kid's mother. He could get her with one shot, so easy, let the Kid see what it was like to be alone, nobody fussing all the time. Right beside her was the Kid—

Staring straight at him through those binoculars.

He stepped back from the window and swore. She couldn't have seen him, the little bitch, but Jesus, she was freaky.

The sound of the rotors grew louder and he snapped into mission mode and raised the gun to see the helicopter in the scope. He thought of the vulnerable points he could shoot to make it drop like a rock. The transmission. The appropriately named Jesus bolt that held the blades on. And with the chopper flying perpendicular to his position, he could put a shot right through both people in the front seat. One bullet, two kills, every sniper's dream. Actually four kills, as the chopper would then be unpiloted and crash, taking out the two in the back.

That would be so cool, Tyler thought. Big points in a video game. Get him extra lives to move on to another level.

The sound of the rotors grew louder, and Tyler turned the gun back toward the low-flying helicopter and slowed his breathing.

Mission.

He focused on the gun, the sight picture, his breathing, his heartbeat. In between beats, he fired.

Wilder felt the aircraft shudder and dived to the floor for the nylon rope even as Bryce dropped from sight. His fingers closed on the rope as the safety cable snapped taut and he heard Nash swear as the snaking steel cable cut his hands. Then the rope broke free of the anchor point—*fuck, the rope broke*—and Wilder tightened his grasp on the nylon, Nash's skin-on-metal friction giving him the split second he needed to get a solid hold.

"Get him *down,*" Wilder yelled at Karen through the boom mike. "*Now.* The cable is not secured. It is *not* secure, and Nash and I are holding it."

She obeyed instantly, bringing the chopper to no forward speed as she descended, ever so carefully.

His arms were burning and he could see the blood flowing over Nash's hands, ripped by the cable. *Bad for traction,* he thought and braced himself as Karen brought the chopper in. Through the door he could see Armstrong running underneath—*Lucy*—and then Karen said, "He's down. He's safe. Lucy and some guy got him."

"Fuck." Wilder could feel the weight off the rope but still he didn't let go. He looked at Nash with sympathy. "I got it."

Nash nodded and slowly unwrapped his hands from the bloody steel, hissing in pain as he did so. Wilder let go of the rope and it disappeared over the side.

He spoke into the mike as he got a bandage from the first-aid kit on his web gear. "Put us down as soon as they're out from under, and tell them we need the EMTs." Then he tapped Nash on the shoulder, holding up the bandage. Nash sat back and closed his eyes as Wilder went to work. The cuts looked painful but not serious, and Wilder relaxed enough to let in the thought that he'd been ignoring.

Rope doesn't break, not like that.

Nash swallowed and said, "Thanks, mate."

"No worries," Wilder said, and worried.

When the skid had broken, Lucy had yelled, "No!" and shoved Daisy to one side to get to Bryce before his pedaling legs hit gravel. LaFavre was right by her side, moving very fast for someone who talked so slow. They grabbed Bryce just as his feet touched down and pulled him back, slowing him to a trot, LaFavre smoothly unhooking the cable from the back of Bryce's harness as they brought him to a stop. Then there were people everywhere, taking Bryce from her, asking a thousand questions, all variations of, "Are you all right?"

No, she wanted to say as she let them take him, the EMTs closing in. *He's not all right. He just fell off a goddamn helicopter.*

Lucy picked up her headset again. "Who's hurt?" she said, remembering Wilder's call for the EMTs.

"Nash cut his hands," Karen said, her voice almost lost in the rotor noise.

Lucy swallowed. "How's Wilder?"

"Fine," Karen said. "We're down in a minute. I can't see the skid. What happened?"

Lucy looked at the helicopter. The right skid was dangling almost straight down. "The skid broke, I think."

"Excuse me, ma'am," LaFavre said. "Are you talking to the pilot?"

Lucy nodded.

"Might I have a word with him?"

"Her." Lucy gave him the headset.

LaFavre smiled. "Her?" He held the headset between them so she could hear, and said, "Pilot, this is Major LaFavre, Task Force 160. You've got a bum right skid, detached in front, still attached the rear, but not able to sustain landing. Recommend you head to Hunter Airfield and swap that bad boy out. They can put a brace out for you. I could make a call for you and make sure you get special treatment." Lucy noticed that the accent came back stronger during the last sentence.

"Shit," Karen said. "Change in plans. I can hover and drop Nash off so the EMTs can check him. Then I have to go back to the airfield, I'll need Wilder for that."

"And me, darling," LaFavre said.

"Who the hell are you?" Karen snapped.

"Why, I introduced myself, my chéri. Major Rene LaFavre. And who do I have the pleasure of discourse with?"

"Lucy? Who the hell is this guy?" Karen sounded distracted.

Lucy reached out and took the headset back before LaFavre asked Karen out for dinner and a sleepover.

"He's a friend of Wilder's," she said into the headset to Karen. "A pilot. I want to talk to everybody in that copter when you're back."

"Roger that," Karen said.

When the chopper was hovering less than three feet off the ground, LaFavre and one of the EMTs grabbed Nash as Wilder passed him out on the side with the good skid. Despite his pain, Nash looked embarrassed about being passed from chopper to ground like a bag of potatoes. LaFavre tipped his cap at Lucy, then grabbed Wilder's offered hand, put a foot on the good skid, and jumped on board.

Beyond them was Bryce, still white as a sheet but now surrounded by about twenty people, including Mary Vanity, who was offering him anything he wanted. He'd be fine, Lucy knew. He'd go to dinner on this story for years.

She, on the other hand, was not fine. Something had gone very wrong up there and on this shoot, there was no chance it was an accident. "*Stephanie,*" Lucy said, not bothering to look behind her. "Go get that cable and bring it to me. Then go to the base and pick up Karen and Wilder, and while you're there find out what happened to that skid. *I want to know everything. Go.*"

Stephanie went.

Lucy surveyed the scene, looking for anything, anybody who was out of place. Bryce was already expanding under the attention. Nash had closed his eyes and was wincing as an EMT and Doc checked his torn hands. LaFavre was in the hovering helicopter, and as she watched, he bowed at the waist, touching the brim of his cap in salute.

Next to him, Wilder was braced in the door, looking straight at her.

Lucy picked up her apple and bit into it again, thinking, *It was supposed to have been you on that skid.* Whatever was going on, he was in the middle of it. And she was going to find out what it was before somebody killed him.

Then the helicopter lifted off again and she went to find out what the hell Bryce had been doing on that skid.

Wilder broke eye contact with Armstrong as Karen lifted the chopper and turned it toward the airfield. She'd looked mad as hell tearing into that apple, which couldn't be right; he'd just saved her star's butt. And LaFavre had given her his Cajun bow *and* a salute. What more could a woman want?

On the other hand, it was Armstrong. Not an easy woman.

LaFavre leaned close so he could be heard, the light reflecting off his aviator sunglasses. "J. T. Wilder. Always causing trouble."

"Swamp Rat LaFavre. Everything was fine until you showed up."

"Watch who you call Swamp Rat." LaFavre sat down in the seat and Wilder joined him, trying to avoid the splatter of Nash's blood. "Just came out to check on the actress you promised me."

"Did you see what happened?" Wilder asked.

"Yep."

"So what happened?"

LaFavre shrugged. "Don't know. Skid broke while your man was on it."

"You ever hear of a skid giving out?" Wilder asked.

"I've heard of everything that can go wrong with a chopper going wrong." LaFavre leaned over to inspect the right skid of the Jet Ranger. "We ripped a skid off one of the Little Birds in the 'Stan sort of like that. Hit the roof of a building during extraction of a team." He turned to Wilder. "You mean that wasn't planned?"

"Nope."

"Well, that sucks." A sly smile crossed LaFavre's face. "So how are those actresses?"

Wilder thought of Althea. "Dangerous."

"Right. I could use some of that danger. That little blonde in the car, woo-hoo. Hot, very hot."

"Yeah," Wilder said, trying to sound offhand. "Did she look familiar to you? Like maybe she was in some movie about the Navy?"

Blow Me Down," LaFavre said. "Ran a lot on late night Showtime. I have the DVD. Second ensign on the right in the shower scene. A truly fine piece of cinema." He nodded toward Karen. "What's the story there?"

"I tried that route," Wilder said. "You don't want to go there."

LaFavre laughed. "Ah, my friend, but you do not have my charm, wit, and good looks."

Wilder watched the land speed by below them, thinking that since he was now undercover, he should probably question Karen. Of course, he wasn't going to be good at it—his first ex had always said he had all the subtlety of a sledgehammer. Which he had considered kind of a compliment, because a sledgehammer could be a damn effective tool. Still, he could try charm. He grabbed a headset and spoke into the intercom. "Learn to fly in the military?"

"Nope," Karen said. "Took a correspondence course from an ad in the back of a comic book."

LaFavre snorted.

Great. A wise-ass pilot. He'd *lived* with one of those. "My ex-wife was a chopper pilot." He'd never used that line before with a woman, but it seemed the only thing he could say here to get some common ground; this wasn't exactly the bar at the officers' club.

"Lucky her."

So much for charm. Next to him, LaFavre was silently laughing his ass off.

"Yeah, real funny," Wilder said to him, pulling the mike away from his mouth. "Let's see you do better."

LaFavre looked out the door of the chopper, noting landmarks. "We're a minute out." He grabbed hold of the stanchion between the front and back doors and swung himself out and around from back seat to front, taking the copilot's seat. "You got clearance, my dear?"

"I'm not your dear, and I'm cleared," Karen said.

"I could take it in if you'd like," LaFavre said. "Tower knows me."

"I'm sure Tower does," Karen said. "But it's my aircraft."

"Whatever you say, my darling."

"I'm not your darling."

Better than TV, Wilder thought and listened while LaFavre got shot down over and over again until they were hovering about ten feet over the runway. A military Humvee drove slowly out toward them and halted, just on the other side of a red line painted around the contractor's area. A guard was manning the .50 machine gun in the Humvee's turret and there was no doubt he had live ammunition loaded in it. Wilder knew what that red line meant: Don't cross or get shot. Beyond the red line were the helicopters of Task Force 160, at least those that weren't deployed, and from the scant numbers it appeared that most were overseas. Wilder wondered how many of those Nighthawks and Little Birds parked there he'd flown in over the years. He could see a handful of people in flight suits working on the choppers. Several glanced his way, most likely wondering the same thing Wilder was: Why the hell was the right skid hanging like that?

A civilian mechanic from the contractor's hangar wheeled out a contraption that looked like a metal sawhorse. He put it on the tarmac and then he moved about twenty feet away from it and began making hand and arm signals, guiding the helicopter in. Karen positioned the chopper and then descended on the mechanic's signal. Wilder noted that the normally loquacious LaFavre was silent during the maneuver, which meant it had to be difficult. The sawhorse braced against the right side of the bird as the left skid touched down. The mechanic ran forward and used a couple of bolts to secure what remained of the right skid to the device. Done, he once more went to the front of the chopper and signaled to Karen with a finger across his throat, a signal Wilder had never been particularly thrilled with in any situation.

"Nice," LaFavre said to Karen, which amounted to an effusion of praise for him.

Karen was unimpressed. "You can get out now."

"Certainly, my sweet."

"I'm not your sweet."

LaFavre got out as Karen began hitting the switches, turning off the engine with much more vigor than was needed. Wilder hopped off and took a look at the right skid. The front skid extension from the body of the helicopter was broken, the metal twisted.

"Looks like the bolt blew out," the mechanic said.

"Happen often?" Wilder asked, having flown hundreds of hours in helicopters and never heard of it.

"Never seen it before."

LaFavre was on his knees, taking a closer look at the break point. "Anybody want to hurt your actor?"

"No," Wilder said. "Got some people might want to hurt me."

"That's a given based on your lack of charm and wit," LaFavre said. "But you weren't on the skid."

"I was supposed to be," Wilder said. "Last-minute change."

LaFavre whistled. He looked at the break point. "My friend, that is not good."

Wilder could see that Karen was not a happy camper as she joined them and stared at the twisted metal where the skid had parted from the chopper. She looked like hell without her helmet, her dark hair plastered by sweat to her head, her skin pale.

"You look quite delicious with your helmet off," LaFavre said to her.

"Can the bullshit," Karen said.

LaFavre put his hand over his heart. "I am deeply wounded. But willing to overlook, given the stress of the moment."

"Can we get another bird and finish the shoot?" Wilder asked her.

Karen gestured at the other two civilian aircraft parked in front of the contractor's hangar, both aging Hueys. "Different choppers. We need this one."

Wilder looked longingly across the field at the svelte new Nighthawks, the Special Operations version of the Blackhawk. All-weather capable, powerful, armored, and they had guns, which Wilder liked. Or even one of the four-seater Little Birds with their mini-gun pods on the right skid.

"Dream on," Karen said. "Unless the smooth talker here can get you one."

"The name is Rene LaFavre, my love." He held out his hand.

"I'm not your love."

"But you could be."

Karen rolled her eyes. "Where did you get this guy?" She turned to the mechanic. "How long to fix it?"

The mechanic let out a long spit of chew onto the tarmac. "Half an hour. Then my boss will have to test-fly it. FAA regulations, anytime a repair is done on an aircraft. Got to be test-flown and signed off."

Wilder glanced at the sky. Even with the delay, they'd still have some daylight.

"Can your boss fly it out to the film set?" Karen asked.

The mechanic nodded. "Sure. He can use that as the test flight. We'll just tack it on the bill."

Not my money. Wilder smiled. Hell, it was Finnegan's money.

"Come on in the office and fill out the paperwork," the mechanic said. Karen sighed and followed.

Wilder turned to LaFavre. "Could she put a chopper down on that bridge?"

"I don't think anybody could," LaFavre said, watching her go. "Flying between those cables or under those towers would be quite a feat. But she'd be one of the ones I'd let try. You know, she's not very friendly but I can warm her up."

"Some women just don't get your charm."

"I'll try harder."

Wilder rolled his eyes. "You said this wasn't good," he said, nodding toward the skid.

"Anytime something breaks on an aircraft, it isn't good, my friend." LaFavre put his hand where the bolt had given out. "Could be metal fatigue. Could be a heavy-caliber round punched through at just the right spot. Of course, I'm not a ballistics expert and we're not in a combat zone."

"That would be a hell of a shot," Wilder said, staring at the twisted metal.

"Yah," LaFavre agreed. "Or someone was shooting at your actor thinking it was you and made a bad shot."

The two men stood silent for several moments, staring at the skid.

"Fuck," Wilder finally said.

"Fuck indeed, my friend. Something going on that you're not talking about?"

Wilder considered letting LaFavre in on the CIA angle when someone yelled, "Major," from across the red line. LaFavre waved that he would be coming and slapped Wilder on the back. "I'll be around for a little while. You got my number. Give me a ring. I'll show you my latest investment."

"Will do," Wilder said, having no clue what LaFavre was referring to, but sure it was something off the wall and about a woman.

But LaFavre wasn't ready to go quite yet. "Who that?"

Wilder turned and saw a car pulling up, closely followed by a military police escort, and noted that Stephanie was driving. He had a feeling Ms. Lucy Armstrong wanted them back. The car stopped at the edge of the tarmac and Stephanie got out. She leaned against the car and stared at them, looking bored, her dark hair blowing back in the wind, and after a few seconds began to drum her fingers on the roof.

"Man, you just be knee deep in the good-looking women on this movie," LaFavre said.

More like neck deep, Wilder thought. He was more concerned about the possibility of a bullet hole in the chopper than LaFavre's testosterone.

An MP got out of the escort car and eyed Stephanie with interest, and Wilder remembered that she was beautiful in a deadly embrace kind of way. The man had no idea what he was dealing with, Wilder thought, and neither did LaFavre.

"She an actress?" LaFavre said.

"No, she's the Angel of Death," Wilder said.

"I've done one or two of those," LaFavre said, unfazed. "Got to use the dark swamp voodoo on them."

"Let's go," Karen said to Wilder as she came out of the hangar, catching the last of what LaFavre was saying. Then she looked over at

Stephanie and said, "Oh, God, *her*," and walked over to the car. She opened the back door and got in, leaving Wilder the front seat. So much for female bonding.

"That doesn't look good, boy," LaFavre said, shaking his head at the car. "Those are not happy women."

"So you're not coming with us?" Wilder said.

"My unit's just over there." LaFavre jerked his head toward the Nighthawks. "But if there's a cast party, you call me."

"You bet," Wilder said.

"Especially if that director's there. She's—"

"No," Wilder said, surprising himself.

LaFavre raised an eyebrow. "No?"

"No," Wilder said, sure this time.

"Well, good for you, boy." LaFavre slapped him on the back.

"No," Wilder said. "Not that."

"Not yet," LaFavre said. "You keep working, you'll get there. Just don't tell her about your ex-wife. Wives. I've heard some piss-poor pickup lines in my life, but that's about the worst." He tipped his hat to the two women fuming in the car. "Patience is always rewarded, my friend." Then he turned and jogged back to his unit and the real Army.

"Then I should be having a better time," Wilder said, and headed for the car.

Stephanie burned rubber leaving the airfield, not saying a word. *Friendly bitch,* Wilder thought as he buckled his seat belt. Maybe the MP escort did know what he was dealing with, because no blue lights came on and they made it to the gate without being stopped. Wilder waited for the two women to start talking about shoes or giving birth or whatever it was that women talked about, but both were silent as stones.

"How's Bryce?" Wilder finally asked Stephanie.

She shot him a look across the front seat. "All right. No thanks to you."

"What did I do?" Wilder was truly mystified.

"Bryce hired you to be his stunt double. It should have been you on the skid."

Karen spoke up from the backseat. "Give it a rest. It was an accident. They're fixing the chopper. We'll be able to do it again before nightfall."

Stephanie looked up in the rearview mirror at her, her eyes cold. "We shouldn't be doing it at all."

Oh-kay. So they wouldn't be talking about shoes. Wilder slid a little farther down in his seat.

Karen said, "I didn't write the damn movie," her voice as cold as Stephanie's.

"I didn't write the bullshit stunts," Stephanie snapped back.

"None of your business," Karen said. "The stunts are Nash and me."

She drew out "Nash and me," and Stephanie set her jaw and stepped on the gas, and Wilder realized there was a history here that he didn't particularly want to know about. But with the two women furious with each other, they might get careless and tell him something new. *Oh, hell,* he thought, and stepped into the minefield.

"So how's Nash?" he said to Stephanie.

"His hands are cut," Stephanie said, shortly. "The EMTs are taking care of him."

Wilder looked over his shoulder at Karen. "You meet Nash in the Army?"

"No," Karen said.

Stephanie pushed harder on the gas, and for the next twenty minutes they broke every posted speed limit until they raced over a turn bridge that spanned the Savannah River. Then she slammed on the brakes and took the turn onto the gravel road way too fast.

Mad or stupid? Wilder wondered, but then she stopped the car, spraying gravel, and glared over the wheel.

Straight ahead on the road, in the middle of the movie set, Armstrong was talking to Nash, her face determined, his stony. While they watched, she turned and saw the car and narrowed her eyes. Then she put her hands on her hips and waited.

She looked angry.

She looked really good angry.

LaFavre would have a heart attack.

"She wants to talk to you," Stephanie said to Wilder, sounding like a hall monitor about to turn him in for running with scissors.

"She wants to talk to me first," Karen said, and got out and slammed the door, the sound reverberating through the car.

Wilder watched as Nash said something to Armstrong and walked away staring at the bandages on his hands, ignoring Karen's approach even though she slowed as she passed him.

Stephanie looked through the windshield, her face drawn with dislike. "Well, don't keep her waiting," she said to Wilder with a knife in her voice. "She likes things done her way."

"Who doesn't?" Wilder said and got out of the car.

Next time the Angel of Death showed up as his driver, he was walking.

After the helicopter had gone, Lucy and Gloom had gotten the set back to a semblance of normal pretty much on grim determination alone. Fortunately, they were good at grim determination. Even Stephanie had obeyed orders. She'd found the cable and given it to Lucy, almost babbling, "It took me longer than I thought it would, somebody had unhooked it from Bryce and tossed it away, I had to hunt." She'd looked flustered for the first time since Lucy had known her.

"Thank you," Lucy had said, taking the cable from her. "Go get Karen and Wilder at the airfield," and she'd gone without argument, a good sign, Lucy had thought. And she needed a good sign because they were going to have to do the next stunt. The cameraman swore they'd gotten enough of Bryce before he fell to edit into the shot, but now Wilder was going to have to jump out of that helicopter on a cable. She went over to video village and sat down behind the monitors beside Daisy, not happy at all.

"That was ugly," Daisy said. She looked serious but not upset enough to reach for pills, still under control.

"Yeah," Lucy said. "I want to know what happened before I send anybody else up there."

"You don't have much time," Daisy said. "We're losing the light. You've got time for one, maybe two shots if they get back fast."

"Wilder does not go up there until I find out what happened and fix it." Lucy sat back in her chair. "He can be a pain in the ass, but I want him breathing and driving me crazy, not dead and making me feel guilty."

"Good for you," Connor said, and she jumped a little, surprised he was there. He was standing on the other side of the monitors, pale and quiet and, Lucy guessed, in pain.

"Are you okay?" she said.

He waved that away with one bandaged hand. "No big deal. But good for you for doing the stunt again. You are going to do it again, right?"

Lucy narrowed her eyes at him. "What the hell was Bryce doing on the skid?"

He flinched at her tone. "He insisted and Wilder agreed. I think Wilder put him up to it."

Lucy stared at him, dumbfounded. "The hell he did. As you keep reminding everyone, you're the stunt coordinator. Nobody does anything without your say-so."

"Yeah, but you keep overruling me. No wonder Bryce won't pay attention to me." Connor leaned forward. "Look, Luce, you have to get rid of Wilder. He's the one who talked Bryce into it. It was his fault—"

"No." Lucy drew back. "For God's sake, would you stop whining about Wilder?"

Connor jerked back. *"Whining?* Lucy—"

"Connor?" Pepper came up to the monitors and climbed up into her chair so she could see him. "Do your hands hurt?"

"I'm fine, honey." He looked down at his bandaged hands and shot a wounded look at Lucy, clearly going for noble suffering, and Lucy thought, *Sweet Jesus, and I married this guy.*

"What is your problem?" she said to him.

"Problem?" He straightened at the tone in her voice. "I don't have a problem. I'm just trying to help my girl." He smiled at her, one hundred percent all charm.

"I am not your girl," Lucy said, and watched his smile disappear.

"Lucy. Come on." He glanced over at Daisy and Pepper, who weren't even pretending not to listen. "We were going to talk today, remember?"

"No." Lucy shook her head once. "I'm sorry. No."

His face twisted again, and she had to stop herself from saying anything else and making it worse. Then he said, "Fuck," and she followed his eyes down to his hands, blood soaking the bandages.

"I know," Pepper said. "That's a bad word, don't use it."

He'd clenched his hands into fists and opened his wounds, Lucy realized. He looked at her, blame in his eyes.

"*You* did that," Lucy said. "Don't even think about blaming me because you made yourself bleed, or blaming Wilder either." She turned back to the set and yelled, "Doc!"

Doc came out of the crowd, his glasses gleaming, and came toward her.

"Grab that EMT and get Connor to the ER, please, he's bleeding again," she said, and he nodded and went toward Connor, who looked at her, rage in his eyes. Well, too damn bad. She heard tires squeal and turned as a car pulled up in a spray of gravel. Stephanie was behind the wheel, glowering at her, and beside her was Wilder, looking as blank as ever. *That must have been a fun ride,* Lucy thought, and then Karen got out of the backseat, looking tense, and came toward her.

Lucy grabbed the cable that Stephanie had found and waited for

Karen as she slowed to talk to Nash, who walked right past her as if she weren't there.

"Aunt Lucy?" Pepper said.

"What, Pepper?" Lucy said, watching Karen and thinking, *You know something, dammit.*

"I saw the ghost," Pepper said. "It was in that building over there."

"Okay, honey," Lucy said as Karen came toward her, and then she jerked her head to the trees on the side of the road and Karen followed her.

11

When they were out of earshot, Lucy held up the cable. "I've been over this cable twenty times since it came off Bryce. Aside from Nash's blood, there's nothing wrong with it. And yet, we almost lost Bryce."

Karen shook her head. "It wasn't the cable. The rope broke."

"The rope?" Lucy let the cable drop to her side, confused. "What rope?"

Karen tried to look bored and just looked tense. "There's a rope at the end of the cable, because rope gives and cable doesn't, so—"

"Where's the rope?" Lucy said, not giving a damn about stunt theory. She wrestled with the cable until she could hold up both ends. "No rope. Where is it?"

Karen looked surprised. "It should be tied on there," she said, pointing to the end that hadn't been hooked to Bryce. "Somebody probably threw it away or it fell out somewhere." She shrugged again. "It broke. It happens."

"Does it now?" Lucy crossed her arms. "You'd think if it happened, they'd find a better way. After they'd dropped, oh, say, half a dozen people like eggs on the pavement, you'd think they'd say, 'You know, the thing about this kind of rope is, it *breaks*.' And then they *wouldn't use it anymore*."

Karen watched her, stony-faced.

Lucy leaned forward. "Listen to me. I am not your enemy, but I am your boss. You are on my team, and you answer to me, and you are going to tell me right now what the hell happened up there."

Karen shrugged. "The bolt on the front of the right skid gave way when Bryce put his weight on it. Then the rope that holds the cable to the tie-down in the copter broke. Wilder grabbed it and Nash grabbed the cable and the two of them held Bryce off the ground until I could get him down."

Lucy narrowed her eyes. "Was Wilder responsible?"

Karen shrugged again. "I don't know. I just fly the bird."

"Why was Bryce on the skid?"

"He wanted it," Karen said bitterly. "He said he'd shut down the shoot for a week if he didn't get to do it. Wilder and Nash both tried to talk him out of it."

"Wilder did?"

Karen nodded.

"Hell," Lucy said, knowing they'd been stuck. But Connor should have stopped the stunt. Which meant that finishing the movie on Finnegan's schedule was more important than keeping Bryce safe. *Big money,* she thought. He'd sacrifice damn near anybody for a great payday. She looked around to see if he'd left and saw him talking to Doc, Stephanie standing close behind.

Karen watched them, too, her face flushed.

"I don't know what this is, Karen," Lucy said, and watched Karen flinch as she said her name, making it personal, "but whoever's behind it, he's not on your side. The sabotage shows you that. Who else is going to catch hell for a defective copter except the pilot who checked it out?"

Karen looked startled for a second, as if she hadn't thought of that, which rattled Lucy more than anything else. Karen was following Connor blindly.

"Whatever it is," Lucy said, "get out now."

Karen stared back at her, unblinking, and Lucy sighed. "Get ready to try it again. And double-check the skid bolts when the copter gets here. I do not want to see Captain Wilder do what Bryce just did."

Karen nodded and went back to the set, and Lucy followed her out into the sunlight, where Wilder waited, staring out at the swamp, his face as impassive as ever. Probably looking for Moot to wrestle.

He's a monosyllabic, deadpan, tight-assed military man, she thought. *But he did not sabotage that stunt. In fact, if he'd been the one on the skid . . .*

In her mind, she saw him falling from the copter, smashing onto the pavement, bones cracking, blood spattering—

And he was going up there again, to fall out of the damn thing on purpose.

"Jesus," she said and went toward him just as the sound of an inbound helicopter echoed over the set once more. Wilder looked up and then headed toward the landing spot near where the gravel road met the highway.

Lucy picked up speed to catch him, reaching him only when he slowed as the helicopter came in for a landing. She stepped in front of him to stop him before they got in earshot of the crew. "Listen, you don't have to do this. You don't have to be a hero. We—" She stopped when he grinned at her. "What? I'm serious here."

"Oh," he said. "Sorry. Thought it was a movie quote. That 'you don't have to be a hero' thing."

"Movie quote," Lucy said. "At a time like this, you're thinking movie quotes."

"Well, it's from *High Noon*."

"Wonderful. *High Noon.*" Lucy took a deep breath. "And now, returning to reality, we can do without this shot. We—"

"No, you can't." He looked up at the chopper, probably checking for loose bolts. "That part of the script I did read."

"Great." She swallowed. "Fine time you picked to get literate."

"I liked the action parts. The love stuff made me sleepy." He smiled at her, and her heart picked up speed.

"We can fake it," she told him. "Have them edit the stuff we've got so it looks okay. Or just cut the scene. The hell with Finnegan, this movie is not worth dying for."

"I never fake it," he said, looking into her eyes. "And nobody's going to die." Then he looked past her, his face blank again, and she turned and saw Connor waiting for him as the helicopter landed, heavy leather gloves on over his bandages and Doc standing beside him looking miserable.

"What the hell?" Lucy strode toward him. "What are you doing here?" She glared at Doc. "You were supposed to take him to the ER."

"They take too long." Connor put his arm around her, dangling a gloved hand by her chin, but his eyes were on Wilder, who had followed her over. "Don't get mad, Lucy, love, you know I hate hospitals."

Wilder looked at them both, his eyes impassive.

Great, she thought. *A macho stare-off.*

"Besides," Connor said, "I have a stunt to finish."

"Oh, no," Lucy said, louder than she'd meant to, and Connor pulled his arm away. "You're hurt. If something else happens up there, you'll rip your hands up again." *And you won't save Wilder.* She turned to Doc. "You're going up in the helicopter with Wilder."

"*Lucy—*" Connor said, holding the gloves up.

"You're not going up there," Lucy said to him. "That's final." He stared at her for a moment, fury in his eyes, and she said, "Don't clench your hands."

He turned and walked away, not looking back.

"Don't screw this up, Rambo," she said, not looking at Wilder.

"That was my plan. Not screwing up."

"Funny." Lucy headed for video village, catching Doc's arm as she went, pulling him backward with her. "I do not want anything bad to happen to Captain Wilder."

Doc trotted backward faster to keep up with her. "Okay, Lucy."

"And I am counting on you to make sure that it doesn't."

"Okay, Lucy."

"Because if it does . . ." Lucy stopped and he overshot her, stepping forward to meet her again, his round face full of dread behind his glasses. "Your ass is mine. Two things had to go wrong up there for that last stunt to fail. A third thing on this one, and I'm getting a new stunt team."

Doc looked wounded. "*Lucy, we—*"

"Know more than you're saying," Lucy said. "I don't know what's going on with you guys, but *nobody gets hurt again.* Understand?"

"*Yes,*" Doc said. "Nobody was supposed to get hurt."

Lucy grabbed his arm again. "*What do you mean?*"

"Nothing," Doc said, sheet white now. "I wouldn't hurt anybody, Lucy. You know that."

"What are you doing?"

"Nothing." Doc stopped and tried again. "What I meant was that, on a good stunt, nobody ever gets hurt."

Lucy narrowed her eyes. "Whatever you guys are doing, it's over. Do you understand?"

"Yes, Lucy," Doc said.

"Good," Lucy said, not believing him for a moment. "Tell the others. And make damn sure that Wilder lands in one piece and walks away when this is done."

"He will." Doc's face was sober with sincerity. "He will, Lucy, I swear."

Lucy nodded. "Okay." She jerked her head toward the helicopter. "Showtime."

Doc nodded and ran, and Lucy turned to see Wilder by the copter, watching them both.

If I were a decent human being, I wouldn't let either one of you go up there, she thought, and stared at him a moment too long, reading the look on his face as sympathy for her. He shook his head and gave her a thumbs-up and climbed into the copter, and she thought, *Oh, hell,* and cared too much, which was stupid, she didn't care at all. The macho asshole had a Rambo complex, testosterone poisoning, thought he was immortal, never say die . . .

Don't die, she thought and sat down behind the monitors, her throat tight.

Wilder watched Lucy go back to the monitors, trying not to think about the way she walked. He was on a mission and she was part of it. You did not think that the mission had a great ass. You also did not notice that the mission seemed to care a lot whether you lived or died. And you definitely didn't like it that she did.

The mission, he thought and looked away to see the maintenance pilot climb out of the copter and bend his head close to Karen's, the two of them doing pilot talk. The blades were whooping by overhead very slowly, on idle, the engine purring so deeply that he couldn't hear what they were saying. *Hurry up,* Wilder thought, looking at the sky. The light was going fast and Lucy needed the shot. Several takes of the shot unless he didn't use the cable. He headed for the helicopter. Wilder climbed into the right front seat, the better to hear Karen and the test pilot, but Bryce came up and leaned in.

"Hey, man. Thanks once more."

Wilder nodded, trying to overhear the conversation beside him. Then the maintenance pilot walked away and he gave up and concentrated on the stunt and what Lucy needed.

"I mean it, man," Bryce said.

"No problem. It's my job." The smart thing would be to do the stunt without the cable.

"That's twice you saved my butt," Bryce said. "I know it's your job, but that was really . . ."

Wilder looked up and thought he saw tears forming in Bryce's eyes.

Even taking into consideration that Bryce was an actor, it was disconcerting. "Hey, you're my wingman."

"Oh, man," Bryce said, really tearing up. "J.T., you're just—"

"Gotta get to work," Wilder said fast, and Bryce nodded and backed off, frowning like a man and giving him a thumbs-up.

"You bet," he said. "Roger that."

Oh, Christ, Wilder thought, and then Nash came up, blocking Bryce, and Wilder stiffened. Nash thrust the MP-5 stunt gun at him harder than necessary. "I checked it, but you can double-check if you want."

"I trust you," Wilder said, and Nash nodded, fury in his eyes, and walked off.

As soon as Nash's back was turned, Wilder checked the gun. It was all right, the cable would be okay this time, and if they were going to move as slowly as they'd moved before, go in as low . . .

He could do it without the cable, easy. Lucy had three cameras doing coverage. If he didn't use the cable, they could probably get it all in one shot. He looked at the sky again. They'd have to do it in one shot if they wanted the light. Plus, he wanted to spend as little time as possible in the air when there was potentially a person with a big gun somewhere around.

Doc climbed into the back, his face grim, carrying a kit bag. He pulled out the cable, a new rope, and a body harness.

Wilder shook his head. "Forget it."

Doc blinked in confusion. "Forget what?"

"No harness. No wire. We're doing this thing in one shot. I'll shoot from the skid and do the jump."

Doc's jaw dropped. "B-but Lucy—"

Wilder didn't give him a chance. "The cable didn't do Bryce much good. We don't have enough daylight to do this a couple of times. And I need a fucking beer. So, one shot. Roger that?"

Doc snapped his mouth shut. "Lucy's going to be pissed."

"Lucy is already pissed," Wilder said, liking the way "Lucy" sounded when he said it. "She'll get over it. And she'll get the shot she needs. Anything else?"

Doc looked at him for a moment and then reached into his pocket. He pulled out a large bronze coin, slightly bigger than a silver dollar. "Coin check."

Wilder nodded, knowing that was Doc's way of telling him that he had his back. He decided to leave his in his pocket. "Fuck you. I don't have mine. I owe you a drink."

"And me." Karen was in the pilot's seat. "Anyone in hand-grenade-burst radius, right?"

"And you," Wilder said. He hoped they were thirsty enough that they'd keep him alive so he could buy them the drinks. "What did the mechanic say about the bird?" Wilder asked as Doc put the coin back in his pocket.

Karen put her hands on the controls. "He said he had no clue why the skid broke, but it won't break again."

Not a smart-ass answer, but not the whole truth, either, he was pretty sure. With a slight shudder, the helicopter lifted. Wilder felt a tap on the shoulder. Doc was holding a headset, mouthing the word *Lucy*.

Fuck. He put the headset on.

"Everything all right?" Lucy asked.

"Roger."

"Skid okay?"

"It's still attached, right? You have a better view than me."

"Funny guy. How about the cable?"

"It's fine."

"The rope?"

"Good."

"The harness?"

"Lucy, everything's *fine*." He looked back at the kit bag on the floor next to Doc's feet where he assumed all the equipment was in top-notch condition. "It's all fine." She was still quiet, so he said, "Lucy?"

"Be careful," she said, and he wasn't sure what had happened but he knew she was rattled. When she spoke again, she was herself. "Listen, Rambo, if you splat on the road, our insurance premiums double."

That would serve Finnegan right, Wilder thought. "Look, I've done this a million times. Sometimes with people shooting real bullets at me. Now stop bothering me and direct the damn movie."

He didn't wait for her response, just took off the headset and tossed it over his shoulder to Doc.

The chopper was at a hover. The convertible was ahead and below, Althea in the front seat with Rick. Everything started moving, in slow motion just like before, and Wilder fought back a laugh. *They think this is dangerous?* Try coming in on a hot landing zone with green tracers punching through the night looking like they were headed right between your eyeballs, and the pilot pushing the bird to the max, full speed because he did not want to be in the area one second longer than he had to, and knowing you were going to jump right into the middle of some heavy, honest-to-God real shit while the door gunners were blazing away in the other direction, their red tracers screaming by the green ones.

Doc nodded to him, and Wilder stepped out onto the skid, finding it without looking down because it was where the goddamn skid was supposed to be. He tested it, keeping half his weight in the bird, then stood outside, one hand on the door frame, the other holding the MP-5. He flexed his legs and did a slight hop on the skid, earning a quick glance from Karen, who felt the chopper move. Wilder smiled at her. He figured she probably wanted to give him the finger but a helicopter pilot always had to keep two hands on the controls.

Down in the car, Rick turned and pointed a pistol at the chopper and for a moment Wilder felt a surge of adrenaline. Then Rick fired several times, blanks, and Wilder relaxed. He swung the MP-5 up and fired his own burst, knowing if the damn thing were loaded with real bullets, he'd just put a stitch of rounds in the bad guy from lower chest up through his head, but of course in the movie the good guy missed. Stupid good guy.

The villain fired a couple of more times and missed. Stupid bad guy.

Wilder leisurely returned the fire, figuring it must look good on film, but feeling really dumb since the car and helicopter were moving at about five miles an hour. Stupid everybody.

Karen brought them even closer. Wilder dropped the MP-5 to dangle on its sling as they closed in on the car, ever so slowly. When it was twelve feet below him, he gauged the distance to the back of the car.

Stupid me, he thought and threw himself out into the air.

Lucy sat behind the monitors, her eyes glued on Wilder standing on the skid. *He called me Lucy.*

It was no big deal. Except he looked really good on that skid. Nobody would believe he was Bryce, his body was different, stronger, relaxed. *He's not afraid,* she thought. Must jump out of helicopters all the time. His girlfriend must not sleep at night. Maybe he didn't have a girlfriend. Not that it mattered. She shook her head and thought, *Concentrate, you dummy,* and Daisy yelled over the rotor noise, "What's wrong?"

"Macho dumb-ass," she yelled back, keeping her eyes on Wilder.

He called me Lucy.

It was such a stupid little thing, that he'd called her Lucy on the headphones. Not Armstrong. Which should have made no difference, everybody called her Lucy, it was nothing—

He swung the gun and fired at the car with efficient grace and then as Karen brought the chopper lower, he dropped the gun and fell, just as planned except—

"*No cable.*" Lucy rose up as he hit the trunk of the car, as he slid down the old Cadillac's trunk and landed on the roadway, rolling as Rick fired more blanks at him with enthusiasm, and Lucy shoved past Daisy and Pepper and ran toward him.

"Cut," Gloom yelled from behind her, and the Cadillac stopped, and Wilder got to his feet, wincing a little as Althea screamed, "J.T.? Are you all right?"

"Where's the cable?" Lucy went breathless as she reached him. *"What happened? How—"*

"Stop yelling," he said as he brushed himself off and then waved to Althea. "Nothing went wrong. I didn't use the cable."

Lucy stopped, her heart racing. "What do you mean, you didn't use the cable?"

"We were losing the light," Wilder said, as if what he'd done was perfectly rational. "This way, we got it all in one take."

"You didn't use the cable," Lucy said.

"I saved you blade time." Wilder frowned at her. "What's the problem?"

Well, I thought somebody had tried to kill you, you dumb-ass, only it turns out your worst enemy is you.

"Besides," Wilder said, with a smile, "it's Miller time."

Lucy turned and walked back to the monitors so he wouldn't see her shake, but after a couple of steps she thought, *Oh, no,* and walked back to him and slugged him as hard as she could on the shoulder.

"Ouch," Wilder said, putting his hand up.

"You didn't use the fucking cable," Lucy yelled. "What are you, *a moron? You could have been killed!"*

"Oh, come on." Wilder looked insulted. "I know what I'm doing. We moved any slower, I'd have fallen asleep up there."

" 'I know what I'm doing,' " Lucy mimicked. "Somebody's tried to kill you twice, but you know what you're doing. *I don't think so."*

She walked away and then went back toward him. He stood his ground but he looked wary, hands out at his sides.

She kept going until she was in his face, but he didn't step back. "You scared the hell out of me," she said, her voice low. "I thought you were hurt. When I didn't see that cable, I thought—"

She broke off, torn between rage and relief, and she saw his face soften.

"Lucy, I was trying to *help—*"

"No," Lucy said, going for rage. "You were doing it your way. If you wanted to help me, you'd have asked me first."

"Well, hell, I'm sorry then," he said, sounding mad, and she got closer.

"When we were in the swamp looking for Pepper," she said, so furious she was almost spitting, "I thought it would be best to call for her, I really wanted to call for her, it *killed me* not to call for her, but I didn't because you were the one who knew best there. You knew the swamp, you were the expert. So, you think you know more about making movies than I do, hotshot?"

"I might know more about falling out of helicopters than you do," Wilder said, exasperated.

"This is a movie, not a mission. You the expert on that or am I? Or do you always have to be the boss, even when you don't know what the hell the consequences are?"

"No," he said, his face closing down. "But—"

"You did the same thing Bryce did," she said and watched him wince. "You were so sure you were right, so screw the experts. I've got a spy on this set, Wilder, and so far today he's seen my direction ignored completely *twice*. Bryce is an idiot, but you're not. So, thanks a lot."

She turned and walked off and he said, "I'm sorry," sounding like he meant it.

She stopped and went back, hearing Althea giggle behind her, too upset to care that she was making a fool of herself, that it was worse because he was still calling her Lucy. "Are you all right?" she said when she was close again. "Did you get hurt?"

"Only when you punched me." He felt his shoulder. "I didn't see that one coming."

"Oh, but you saw the ground coming," Lucy said, mad all over again. "So all you had to do was *brace yourself* and *bounce,* I suppose."

"It's hard to miss the ground," Wilder said. "As they used to say in Airborne School, you can always count on gravity."

"Rot and die," Lucy said and went back to the monitors.

On the way, Doc intercepted her. "Lucy, I swear to God, he refused the harness and safety cable."

"I know, Doc," Lucy said, not stopping.

Doc stopped and fell behind, and Lucy sat down behind the monitors, still wanting to kill somebody.

"So how was it for you?" Daisy asked, while Pepper looked at her, her eyes huge.

"Completely unsatisfactory." Lucy settled into her seat, trying not to look at Wilder, now talking to Doc without any visible concern.

"Are you mad at J.T.?" Pepper said.

"Oh, yeah."

"Don't fire him," Pepper said, looking stricken. "He has to come to my party."

"He'll be there." Lucy stood up and called to the set, "Okay, let's do it again."

The entire set froze, and Wilder looked up, startled.

Lucy let the seconds tick by, and then said, "Kidding. We got it."

The crew relaxed and laughed, and Wilder grinned at her, and she sat back, shaking her head at him. *Dumb-ass.*

Then she realized Stephanie was looking at her with a great deal of interest. "What?"

Stephanie smiled. "Nothing," she said, and walked away toward Nash.

"I don't like it when she looks like that," Daisy said, watching her saunter off.

"I don't care what she looks like." Lucy took a deep breath, trying to get her balance. It took a lot out of a woman to be furious, terrified, and sort of turned on at the same time. *I'm going to have to kill him. Because otherwise—*

Stephanie opened the car door for Nash, and Nash looked back once at Lucy, his face dark with pain. Then he got in, and Stephanie smiled over at her, triumphant.

Him, you can have, Lucy thought.

Then she looked at J.T., on the edge of the set with a jubilant Bryce, infuriating and patronizing and too damn dumb to use a cable.

Him, you can't, she thought, and went back to work.

Wilder walked away from Bryce and the people still sucking up to him and stood on the edge of the berm, staring out over the swamp in the fading light. Now that he had time to think, what he was thinking wasn't good. Lucy said somebody had tried to kill him twice. He wasn't sure he was buying that, but when he put the bar fight together with the broken skid and Finnegan and the Russian mob . . . He sighed and took out his cell phone.

Four rings, then: "Swamp Rat Airlines. You call, we haul."

"Hey, Swamp Rat. It's J.T."

"Shiiiiit, boy. How's it hanging? Any more helicopters break?"

"I want to talk to you. Not on the phone."

"Figured you would. Meet me at Maraschino's. I'll show you my investments."

"The strip club in the shopping mall?" Wilder asked, although he knew that was exactly the kind of place where LaFavre would want to meet. The place probably had a seat with LaFavre's name on it. "See you there in fifteen."

"Roger that."

Wilder waved to Lucy, who missed it, deep in conversation with Gloom at the monitors, and then went down the dirt road to his Jeep and cranked it. As he drove toward the strip club, he mulled over what he knew and came up with not much of anything.

There were a lot of cars parked in front of Maraschino's. Wilder drove around the lot and combat parked, front end facing out, underneath an old oak tree. He didn't see LaFavre's car so he went over to the front door. Glass, spray-painted black with little clear streaks, which Wilder assumed were fingernail marks made by guys getting dragged out by bouncers. Classy.

Wilder pulled open the door and almost walked right into a burly man who filled most of the narrow entranceway. "Ten bucks." The man's bare arms bulged with muscles festooned with tattoos.

Wilder pulled out the bill and handed it over, but the man didn't move. "You packing?" He held up a metal detector.

Not a good sign, Wilder thought. "Yeah."

Tattoo Man frowned. "What are you carrying? Let me see."

This was a major pain in the ass, Wilder thought as he drew out the Glock. Then he pulled off his belt with the garrote in it. Then the dagger strapped to his left calf. Tattoo Man eyed the growing pile of weaponry with a raised eyebrow. "Expecting trouble?"

"It seems to follow me around," Wilder said.

"Sure that's the way it works?"

Wilder had to smile at that.

"You can leave all that with me or take it back to your car, but you are not going inside with any of it."

Well, he'd already paid his ten bucks. Shit. "I'll put it in my car," Wilder said, gathering the weapons and reversing course. "I'll be back."

"I'm sure you will be."

Going out the glass door, he bumped into LaFavre, still wearing his aviator glasses even though the sun had set a while ago. Schtick. Every pilot Wilder had ever met had some sort of schtick.

"It's nighttime, Swamp Rat," Wilder said, indicating the sunglasses.

"Working on my night vision." LaFavre gestured at the collection of weapons. "Figure one of the girls will attack you for your body?"

Been known to happen, Wilder thought. "Putting it back in the Jeep. Wait for me here."

Wilder went to the Jeep and secured the gear in his footlocker, then he rejoined LaFavre, who was chatting with Tattoo Man, obviously on a first-name basis. Wilder was subjected to the wand and then they were nodded into the club, thumping music making the floor vibrate under their feet.

Wilder followed LaFavre, who wove a path through the tables, stopping every now and then to greet someone. A skimpily dressed waitress sashayed up to LaFavre and draped her free arm around his waist, the other one balancing a tray holding several bottles of beer.

LaFavre gave her a peck on the cheek. "Candy, meet J.T. J.T., Candy. She's sweet."

"I'm sure she is," Wilder said. "Pleased to meet you, Candy."

Candy was a hard-looking twenty-five, and she eyed him up and down, establishing his net worth and finding him wanting, one of the reasons Wilder was not a big fan of strip clubs: They weren't about sex and fun, they were about money. Candy slid her arm from LaFavre and went in search of better prey.

"Got to dress better, my friend, if you want some attention."

Wilder stared at LaFavre, astounded. The aviator wore his beat-up leather flight jacket, faded ripped jeans, and alligator-skin boots that had seen better years, and his head was topped with his battered World War II–era flight cap.

"The jacket," LaFavre said. "Means I get flight pay. The girls know that stuff. A lot more than jump pay."

Wilder nodded as they took a table next to the stage. LaFavre crooked two fingers and another waitress zoomed by, depositing two bottles of Bud without even a "Hey, how's it going."

"That be Chantelle. She doesn't like me," LaFavre said, nodding toward the waitress's back as she sped away.

"I can't imagine why." Wilder raised his bottle. "To those who didn't come back."

LaFavre clinked bottles. "Amen, brother."

Wilder shifted uncomfortably in his seat, his back to the club door.

"What do you want to talk about?" LaFavre asked as his sunglasses focused on a girl who came out from behind the curtain and shimmied up the gleaming stainless-steel pole twelve feet to the ceiling. Using only her thigh muscles. Wilder had to admit he was impressed.

"I'm doing temporary work for the Agency."

LaFavre stopped looking at the dancer, lowered his sunglasses, and shot Wilder a look of unabashed pity. "Fuck."

"You said it."

"Here? Stateside?"

Wilder nodded. "Yeah, I know. This is most definitely a cover-your-ass gig by the Agency. I—and the Army—take the fall if this blows up since the Agency technically can't operate stateside."

"Technically you and the Army can't operate stateside, either," LaFavre pointed out as he slid the glasses up and put his attention back on the stage, where the girl was now upside down on the pole, gravity having no effect on her attributes. "Can you tell me the gig?"

Technically I can't, Wilder knew, since LaFavre didn't have, as they said in the parlance, "a need to know," even though he did have a top-secret clearance. But they'd already gone through the ritual of agreeing that this operation was a clusterfuck of responsibility and deniability without coming right out and saying it. The kid, Crawford, was probably doing his best, but he was still just a kid.

Wilder nodded. "The CIA thinks some money is being laundered via the movie. The backer is some shady moneyman that a lot of the alphabet soups are interested in. Name's Finnegan. He owes some Russian mob guy named Letsky and—"

"Wait a sec." LaFavre shook his head, but he was still looking at the stage. "What was that name? A Russian?"

"Simon Letsky." Wilder had a feeling LaFavre didn't have much blood left in his brain at the moment and he wished they had met somewhere where his friend could focus on the problem more closely.

LaFavre whistled, either at the information or the girl, who was now slowly sliding down the pole while simultaneously removing her top. "That's some deep shit. Letsky's bad, real bad. I've seen his name more than once on the daily intel sheets. He's worth billions. Arms dealer. And he's got ties to bad people. People who've shot at you."

Wilder processed that. He'd been shot at by Taliban in Afghanistan, insurgents in Iraq, and Al-Qaeda operatives in other places he wasn't supposed to have been.

"How can I help you?" LaFavre asked, leaning forward in the seat to get a better angle on the girl.

"I might need backup."

The song thudded to a halt and LaFavre sighed and leaned back in his chair, finally sparing Wilder a glance. "Man. This is the United States. Not the 'Stan. Not that I don't appreciate you saving my butt there, but . . ."

"I know." Wilder waited, hoping LaFavre would give him an answer before the next dancer completely wiped his brain clean.

LaFavre rubbed his chin. "We keep a Little Bird gunship and a Nighthawk on ten-minute alert all the time now. Both armed. But the order to put those in the air over the good ole U-S of A has to come from someone more mighty than thou."

Wilder didn't say anything, letting LaFavre wrestle with his official duty and his sense of honor. The music cranked and a new girl began crawling across the stage, taking LaFavre's attention.

"Well, my friend, since Finnegan and Letsky are sort of terrorists, I guess it is part of this here global war on terrorism," LaFavre finally said. "But don't call me about a paper cut or anything. Better be some real shit, with real danger, to real people."

Wilder felt relieved. "Thanks."

"Anything else?" LaFavre asked, as he smiled at the girl and twirled a ten-dollar bill.

Wilder shook his head. "Nope. Got a party to get to."

"Ah, yes." LaFavre reached in his pocket and pulled out a small package, without taking his eyes off the girl. "Present this with my compliments to the young lady."

Wilder took it. "Okay," he said, confused.

"How do I get hold of you?" LaFavre said, and then the girl spun onto her back, legs spread wide, and clamped them down on LaFavre's head, just like the pole, as he slid the bill under the side of her G-string.

"Call one-eight-hundred-clusterfuck," Wilder said, not sure LaFavre could hear.

"That bad?" The voice was muffled.

"Could be worse," Wilder said as he remembered Lucy. "You got my Satphone number. Use that."

The girl unclamped and moved on to her next victim. "I got it," LaFavre said, looking a little dazed, his aviator glasses askew on his face.

A voice cut through the thumping music: "Hey, asshole."

Wilder twisted his head and blinked at the five-foot-tall, abnormally big-busted, red-haired fireball who was glaring at LaFavre, now straightening his sunglasses. *How the hell does she keep from tipping over?* Wilder wondered.

"Ahh, Ginny baby," LaFavre said in his deepest accent, matching it with a smile Wilder envied. Now *that* was a reassuring smile.

But it didn't work. "Don't 'Ginny baby' me, you shit," the tiny girl said, leaning forward, apparently not caring that her massive breasts fell out of her sheer robe. Post-Althea, Wilder was not impressed. He was more concerned that the tattooed bouncer was edging closer, trying to listen in.

LaFavre dug into his pocket and pulled out a roll of bills. "I got a dime here and—"

"You owe me *five* dimes," Ginny countered. "I told you not to come by if you didn't have it all."

"A down payment," LaFavre said.

Ginny went past Wilder as if he weren't there and shoved her breasts into LaFavre's face. "You wanted them, you pay for them. That was the deal."

Wilder was puzzled for a second, then the lightbulb went on as Ginny smashed LaFavre's face into her cleavage. "That's your last touch until you pay in full," Ginny said, relieving LaFavre of the roll of money.

She bounced off, Tattoo Man edged back, and Wilder stared at LaFavre, who seemed pretty happy about handing a thousand dollars to a woman who had just called him an asshole.

LaFavre smiled. "She's something, is she not?"

Althea would have had LaFavre's life savings in ten minutes, Wilder thought, as he nodded in what he hoped was lecherous agreement. He tried to find the right word. "Unbelievable." That seemed to cover it.

"Worth every cent," LaFavre went on. "I look on them as an investment in her future." He pointed. Ginny took the stage, and within a minute was doing things that made Wilder reconsider—perhaps Ginny could teach Althea a thing or two. The music pounded behind her and Wilder caught a snatch of the lyric: "In these shoes?" *Shoes.* He thought of Lucy in those red boots up there on stage. Wonder Woman. Now that he'd pay money to see.

LaFavre leaned over as Ginny writhed along the edge of the stage, gathering money in her G-string from the slack-jawed men lining it. When she got to LaFavre he slid a twenty among the sweat-soaked greenbacks already stuffed there. "Do the pole, baby," LaFavre begged.

Ginny gave LaFavre a look that reminded Wilder of some of the ones that had been directed at him lately. "There's no money on the pole, dumb shit."

Excellent logic, Wilder thought, and also time for him to be going. He stood up and shook LaFavre's hand. "Thanks. I owe you."

LaFavre's eyes were on Ginny and his investments, now moving away. "Well, we are all supposed to be on the same side, but if this blows up, I never talked to you, I don't know you, and I disavow that you were even born."

"Good to know you got my back," Wilder said, knowing LaFavre wasn't hearing anything anymore.

If the terrorists ever hired Ginny, the free world was screwed.

12

Lucy caught the last shuttle back to base camp, so tired she sat with her head on the back of the seat, letting it bounce as the shuttle went over the ruts. Too much tension last night, too much tension all day, and then making a fool of herself over Wilder in front of the whole cast and crew—

"I need sleep," she said as the bus pulled into base camp and then opened her eyes when she realized she'd said it out loud.

Nobody paid any attention.

Okay, she thought, as she got off the bus and headed for the camper. *Check on Daisy, find Gloom, drive the camper back to the hotel, take a shower to get the dust off, then a hot bath so you can sleep . . .*

She opened the camper door and Pepper said, "Hooray, Aunt Lucy is here! The party can start!" and beamed, her WonderWear a bright splotch against the white camper curtains.

"Party!" Lucy said, trying desperately to sound excited. "This is—" She stopped as she caught sight of Daisy, sitting in one of the swivel chairs beside Pepper, her generous figure making the most of her size-small WonderWear. "Wow," she said and started to laugh.

"Laugh while you can, Monkey Girl," Daisy said. "Your Wonder-Wear awaits." She tossed a gold-painted rope across to her. "Do not forget the Lasso of Truth. We are nothing without our lassos."

"Put it on, Aunt Lucy," Pepper said, and Lucy laughed again and climbed into the camper.

She dropped the rope on the table and stripped off her jeans, shirt, and tank top. Then she pulled on the blue-starred pants and red camisole with the double gold *W*s over her underwear. "What do you think?" she said to them as she went back to the dinette.

Daisy burst out laughing.

"You look *wonderful*," Pepper said. "We *all* look *wonderful*."

Lucy slid into the swivel chair next to her, trying to forget her dreams of a hot bath. "So we need cake, right?"

"Gloom is bringing it," Pepper said importantly. "With a surprise."

"Gloom's surprises are excellent," Lucy said.

"And J.T. is coming."

"Good for J.T.," Lucy said, feeling more cheerful. "So what happens at a Wonder Woman party?"

"Well, we can talk about Wonder Woman," Pepper said. "We can each say something we know about her."

"I know something," Daisy said, bringing up a paper bag from under the table. "Or at least Estelle in wardrobe knows something." She took three gold lamé headbands out of the bag, each with a big red star glued in the middle.

"*Crowns!*" Pepper said, achieving ecstasy on the spot. She spread them out and took the smallest one. "They go on like this," she said, shoving the crown over her head, the elastic strip in back so that the lamé went across her forehead.

"Like that." Lucy watched Daisy pull hers on. "You look very cute in that," she said with a straight face.

"Uh huh," Daisy said. "Put your crown on, Aunt Lucy."

"Take your braid down first," Pepper said.

Lucy pulled the tie from the end of her braid and shook her hair loose. Then she pulled the headband on.

"You know," Daisy said, "you actually kind of look like her."

"You *do,*" Pepper said. "Go see yourself."

Lucy got up and opened the door to the tiny bathroom. Her hair color was right, but the rest, not so much. "Nope. I don't think Wonder Woman is ever going to look like she's thirty-four." She turned back to Daisy. "You know, I used to think her uniform was sort of . . ." She shot a glance at Pepper, who waited to hear. "Not . . . fashionable."

Pepper frowned, as if she wasn't sure what that meant but she didn't like it.

"But I was wrong," Lucy said, keeping an eye on her. "This thing has immense possibilities." She put her hands on her hips. "I'm feeling very powerful. Shazaam!"

"No," Pepper said. "Wonder Woman says, 'Sufferin' Sappho.' "

"You're kidding," Lucy said, while Daisy tried to stifle a laugh.

"I can show you." Pepper pulled one of the comics out of the pile of loot on the table.

"It's okay." Lucy went back to the dinette and sat down, yanking her WonderWear down as she sat, wondering if Wonder Woman had the same problem with wedgies. "I believe you. Sufferin' Sappho! It has a ring to it."

"I'm certainly going to be using it from now on," Daisy said, her cheeks pink. She still looked tired, but she also looked ten years younger than she had the night before, and Lucy relaxed and thought, *The hell with a hot bath.*

"You need your boots back on," Pepper said. "See?" She stuck out her rain-booted foot.

Lucy looked at Daisy. "Your mama doesn't—"

Daisy stuck out her red rain-booted foot from the other side of the table. "Go put those boots on, Aunt Lucy."

"Right." Lucy went back to the bed to boot up.

"And music!" Pepper yelled, and Lucy leaned over to the iPod dock and punched up Kirsty MacColl again until "They Don't Know" began to play.

"Remember when we used to dance to this?" Lucy asked, not knowing if Pepper would, it had been so long.

"Yes!" Pepper said, and as Lucy sat on the bed to pull on her boots, she came into the little hallway and began to bop to the music in her red rubber rain boots and WonderWear, looking like a very strange, very happy little go-go dancer.

Lucy laughed, she couldn't help it, and the last of her tension went away. She shoved her foot into the second boot and got up to dance, too.

Pepper had her eyes closed, bouncing on her boots, belting out, "We've got nothin' to lose," while she rocked her shoulders back and forth. Lucy caught her hands and she opened her eyes and smiled up, delighted, and they danced in the cramped little hall, the way they hadn't since Pepper had been tiny. *God, I've missed her,* Lucy thought, holding Pepper's hand up so she could pirouette. *I can't let them go again.* She looked up and saw Daisy biting her lip, her eyes bright, as Pepper sang, *"Bay-bee!"* on the turn, and she smiled at her sister and got the old Daisy smile back. Then Pepper belted out the next line, and Lucy danced her down toward the bed and back to the table, laughing with her, completely in love with her niece again, wondering how she could ever have let her family go.

Kirsty had just finished when somebody knocked on the camper door.

"Maybe it's J.T.!" Pepper said breathlessly as she yanked down her camisole. "I invited him."

"That would be fun," Daisy said, looking at Lucy, her face split with a grin.

Oh, God, no, Lucy thought just as breathless, yanking down her own camisole. Arguably, she was dressed, but still—

Daisy got her big yellow straw hat and held it in front of her as she opened the door.

"Oh, it's Bryce," Pepper said, just one shade short of rude in her disappointment.

Bryce looked in at Daisy, stunned. Then he caught sight of Lucy and his jaw dropped.

"Hello, Bryce," Lucy said, not bothering to cover up. Even if she could have blocked his view of the camisole and pants, there'd still be the tiara and boots to explain.

Bryce let his eyes go from Lucy to Pepper to Daisy. "Is this some kind of club?"

"Yes," Pepper said. "It's a Wonder Woman club."

"Oh." Bryce nodded as if that made complete sense. Which it probably did. If there had been a Superman club, Bryce would have been the first one there in blue tights.

"It's for girls," Pepper said. "But you can come if you want."

"Nope," Bryce said. "I understand about girls only." He looked at Lucy. "Could I talk to you for just a second? Alone."

"Is that okay, Pepper?" Lucy said.

"Just for a second," Pepper said. "The cake isn't here yet anyway."

"Good point," Lucy said and reached back for her white shirt before she went out the camper door.

"Great outfit," Bryce said, when they were standing in the twilight outside the camper and she'd shrugged on her shirt.

"Thank you." Lucy pulled her shirt closed across her camisole. "So what can I do for you?"

"That thing today with J.T." Bryce shifted nervously. "Saving me when the rope broke."

Lucy nodded encouragingly, thinking, *Go away, Bryce*.

"That was really something."

"The man's good," Lucy agreed.

Bryce sighed in relief. "So you're not mad at him anymore."

"Mad at him?" Lucy frowned. "Oh, yesterday. The bar fight."

"That wasn't his fault," Bryce said, evidently alarmed by the look on her face.

Several people had slowed on their way across the dirt lot, and Lucy realized that the shirt might not have been a good idea since it left her bare-legged except for her red boots. And then there was the headband.

"I'm sure it wasn't his fault," Lucy said. "That was a really smart move you made, Bryce, hiring him. I didn't think so at first, but he's great. You were right." She considered piling on more compliments to reassure him, but his face brightened right away.

"I knew you'd see it my way," he said, going back to confident man-of-the-world.

Mary Vanity opened the door to the makeup trailer, caught sight of Lucy, and almost fell down the steps.

Lucy took a step backward, toward the camper. "So you go rest now." She shot a glance at Mary Vanity. "Really rest. In your room. By yourself. You have some stunts of your own tomorrow night, you should be rested."

The stunts pretty much consisted of Bryce running around yelling with a non-gun, but that was close enough for Bryce to nod, soberly.

"You're right," he said, "I have to protect my instrument," and it took Lucy a moment to realize that he meant his voice.

"Right. Protect your instrument." *Do not laugh, he will take it badly.*

He patted her awkwardly on the shoulder and then crossed the lot, stopping to talk briefly to Mary before he went on.

She looked disappointed.

At least you're not wearing blue pants with stars on them, Lucy thought and went back inside and closed the camper door.

"What's wrong?" Daisy said, her face drawn again.

"Nothing," Lucy said. "He just wanted to make sure I wasn't going to fire J.T."

Pepper looked up from her Wonder Woman sticker book, her face alarmed under her gold headband. "You're going to fire J.T.?"

"No," Lucy said. "I think J.T. is super." Daisy snickered, and Lucy ignored her. "He's not getting fired, Pepper, don't worry." She sat down at the dinette and shoved her tiara back into place. "So what else do we know about Wonder Woman?" She kicked Daisy gently under the table and Daisy crossed her eyes at her and stuck out her tongue.

"She's in love with Captain Steve Trevor," Pepper said.

"There's something about a man in uniform," Daisy said, her eyes on the ceiling.

"Especially if he has a really big knife," Lucy said and Daisy laughed again. *That's good,* Lucy thought. If dressing up like a dork and making dirty jokes made Daisy laugh, she'd do it nightly.

"You should take off that shirt," Pepper said. "People can't see your top."

"Right," Lucy said, and took it off.

Somebody knocked on the door of the camper and Pepper said, "J.T.!"

The door opened and Althea poked her head in. "Oh. You're busy."

"Wonder Woman party," Lucy said, as brightly as she had for Bryce. "What can I do for you, Al?"

"Well." Althea licked her lips. "I was wondering . . ." She looked at Daisy and Pepper.

"I'll come out," Lucy said and went down the steps. "What's wrong?" she asked, when she'd shut the camper door.

"Do you think Bryce knows about me and J.T.?" Althea asked, looking anxious, evidently not noticing the Wonder Woman gear. Well, she'd probably worn stranger things in her career.

"No, I don't think he knows," Lucy said. "And I wouldn't tell him if I were you."

"God, no." Althea swallowed. "Because I think I might want to marry Bryce after all. You know."

"Uh huh," Lucy said, not knowing.

"Listen." Althea shifted in the dim light. "I think Stephanie knows about me and J.T. And she might think there was something with Nash and me." Althea added hastily, "She's wrong, of course, but . . ."

When does Connor sleep? Lucy wondered.

"Could you tell her not to talk about me?" Althea said, sounding vulnerable.

"Absolutely," Lucy said.

Althea shifted again. "That thing J.T. did, jumping out of the helicopter without the cable."

"Uh huh," Lucy said, thinking, *Oh, hell, she thinks that was hot.* Well, it had been. Sort of. Aside from the terror-stricken part.

Althea was shaking her head. "That was crazy."

"Exactly," Lucy said, jumping on it. "Not your kind of guy at all."

"Suppose we'd been together," Althea said. "Suppose we'd gotten married and suppose he'd gotten killed? He wouldn't have been there to take care of me."

"No, he wouldn't have," Lucy agreed, trying to put some indignation in her voice.

"And I just don't look good in black."

"Jewel tones," Lucy agreed. "Those are your colors."

"Right," Althea said, relieved to be understood. "So Bryce doesn't know?"

"I'm almost positive. And you know, I just talked to him, and he was going back to his room. Maybe if you—"

"I should go," Althea said and walked off in the darkness to her waiting car.

"Yep," Lucy said and went back into the camper.

She sat down and said to Daisy, "Bryce still doesn't know that Althea . . ." she glanced at Pepper, now nose deep in a comic book, "uh, dated Rambo, right?"

"I don't think so," Daisy said.

"Good," Lucy said. "Now, Pepper, exactly why does Wonder Woman have white stars on her blue underwear?"

"Because she fights for America!" Pepper put her fist in the air, the camper lights glinting off her aluminum foil bracelets.

"Got it," Lucy said and then somebody knocked at the door. *J.T.*, she thought before Pepper could say it, and then the door opened and it was Gloom, his arms full of bags and boxes, saying, "I got cake."

"Yes!" Pepper exclaimed, and Gloom came into the camper and filled up all the remaining space.

He put the cake box on the table and opened it, and Pepper sucked in her breath in delight. The bakery had done a pretty good job on the Wonder Woman drawing, but they'd done it in icing so lurid it looked radioactive.

"It's *beautiful*!" Pepper said.

"Is it chocolate?" Lucy asked.

Gloom looked at her with disgust. "Of course it's chocolate. The ice cream is vanilla." He put the half gallon on the table next to the cake.

"Ice cream," Pepper said, and bounced a little.

"We were just discussing Wonder Woman." Lucy got up for plates. "When she's surprised, she says, 'Sufferin' Sappho.' So that's what we're going to say from now on. You can say it, too."

"How can I not?" Gloom passed a plastic bag over to Pepper. "This is for you, Swamp Thing."

"I'm not going back in the swamp again," Pepper said virtuously, and opened the bag. *"A Barbie! A Wonder Woman Barbie!"*

"You're going to heaven for that," Lucy said to Gloom, passing him the ice cream scoop.

"And it was not easy to find," Gloom said, prying open the ice cream. "Do you know how many Barbies there are? They had a Super-Girl. She was wearing white mittens."

Pepper looked up from her Barbie box. "I *know*. Isn't that the *weirdest*?"

Somebody knocked on the door and Lucy thought, *For the love of God,* and squeezed around Gloom to open it.

Stephanie was there, hugging herself in the dark. "Can I talk to you?"

"Just for a minute or the ice cream will melt," Lucy said and went down the steps.

"I've been thinking, and if you tell me that you're not going to use the stuff we shot today, I'll believe you." Stephanie looked at her sternly. "I've watched you. I know you're used to dog food commercials but you're taking this seriously. You know it's bad for the movie. Just tell me it'll never be part of the film, and I'll let it drop."

"It's not my call, Steph," Lucy said. "I'm not editing it."

"If you don't send them the film, they can't put it in."

"If I don't send them the film, I can get sued for four million dollars. And I've said that for the last time."

Stephanie looked at her in disgust. "That's it, then."

"That's been it from the beginning. Let it go. There will be other movies."

"Not like this one. If you won't protect this film, I'll have to. You leave me no choice." She lifted her chin and walked away, probably congratulating herself on a great exit.

Now what the hell does that *mean?* Lucy thought, and then Pepper called, "Aunt Lucy!" and she went back inside for cake and ice cream.

She'd just stuck her spoon in her cake when somebody knocked on the door. "Sufferin' Sappho," she said, and while Pepper giggled, she swiveled around in her chair and opened the door.

J.T. stood there, his mouth open to speak, but when he caught sight of her, no words came out.

"It's WonderWear," Lucy said, surrendering to the inevitable.

"I know," he said, staring helplessly. "I just wasn't ready for it."

"J.T.?" Pepper stood up to look around Lucy. "J.T.! We have cake!"

"Great," J.T. said, still looking at Lucy. "Cake."

"You'll get used to it," Lucy said.

"I hope not," J.T. said.

"Come on, kid, give me your chair," Gloom said, and Pepper stood up so he could slide into her seat and then pull her into his lap.

"Usually we have root beer and cheese sticks, but today we have *cake*," Pepper said to J.T. as Lucy slid into Gloom's chair so J.T. could have hers. "And Gloom got me a Wonder Woman Barbie!"

"Whoops," J.T. said, climbing into the camper. "Guess you don't want this then." He handed her a Jax Comix bag and Pepper ripped it open.

"It's a *different Wonder Woman Barbie*," Pepper said, overcome by her good fortune.

"A different one?" Lucy asked.

"Jax." J.T. settled into the chair she'd vacated. "I told him to find one so he turned up with some collector edition. He said it was still a Barbie." He grinned at her. "I am learning."

Lucy smiled back at him, helpless not to. "Well, it's good you can be trained."

"She has a *blue cape*," Pepper said, almost vibrating she was so happy.

"Oh, and this." J.T. unbuckled something from his left wrist.

Daisy was shaking her head. "You can't give her your watch."

"It's not a watch," J.T. said. "It's a compass."

Pepper took it in both hands. "Cool! Can I wear it over the bracelets?"

"Yes," Lucy said. *A Barbie and a compass. And he fell out of a helicopter for me. This is a good guy.*

"I'll show you how to use it," J.T. said to Pepper. "That way you can always find your way home."

Okay, I'm yours, Lucy thought and tried to look uninterested.

Across the table, Daisy was grinning at her.

"Oh, almost forgot." He patted his pocket. "Major LaFavre sent you this." He tossed a package across the table and Pepper tore it open.

"Oh, *cool,*" she said and put on the mirrored aviator sunglasses, which made her look like a very patriotic little alien. "Do they go with the WonderWear?"

"Yes," Lucy said.

"Definitely," Gloom said.

"You bet," J.T. said.

"Oh, God," Daisy said, and Lucy looked across to see her smiling at Pepper with tears in her eyes. "You look wonderful, baby."

J.T. leaned close to Lucy. "I like your hair loose like that."

"Oh," Lucy said and gave up trying to look uninterested.

"Cake?" Gloom said to J.T., and somebody knocked on the door of the camper.

"I'll get that." Lucy got out of her chair to slide behind J.T., trying hard not to brush against him and failing. "Sorry," she said as he slid over into her chair.

"This is so cool, J.T.," Pepper said and deserted Gloom to crawl into J.T.'s lap, much to his alarm. She turned the compass one way and the other, trying to find north, which was probably a lot harder through the sunglasses. "Do you know what Wonder Woman says when she's surprised?" Pepper looked up at him so that his reflection was mirrored in her sunglasses.

"Uh . . ." J.T. looked at Lucy, helpless.

Lucy smiled and opened the door.

"I need to talk to you," Connor said, his voice harsh, and her smile evaporated.

"I'll be right back," she told Pepper, not missing the grim look on J.T.'s face, and then she went down the steps into the darkness. "This is Pepper's party," she said to Connor. "Can't this wait until morning?"

"What is he doing?" Connor said, looking into the camper, and Lucy turned and saw what he saw, J.T. with Pepper on his lap in LaFavre's sunglasses, Gloom handing him a bowl of cake and ice cream, Daisy laughing across the table at him.

"Why is he in there?" Connor demanded.

"Because Pepper invited him," Lucy said. "Because he saved her in the swamp last night when you were *rehearsing,* and because he brought her a compass today. Because he's a good guy and she likes him."

Connor slammed the camper door shut, leaving them in darkness. "You get rid of him *now*. He's fucking up everything."

"*He* is?" Lucy felt her temper rise. "He's saving everything. You're the one who's screwing up. You know damn well J.T. didn't sabotage that rope, but I'm pretty damn sure that *you did*. Which is why he's going to be the one in the helicopter tomorrow night, not you."

Nash leaned closer. "*That stunt is mine. Tomorrow is mine.*"

"No." Lucy took a step toward the camper. "J.T.'s the only one I know for sure *didn't* sabotage that rope, so he—"

Nash slapped his hand on the camper beside her head, close enough to make her ears ring. She froze as he glared at her, breathing heavily, no shock of apology in his eyes. "He's not going to take this away from me. He's not going to take *you* away from me. I have *plans,* Lucy."

"I don't belong to you," Lucy said steadily. "I never did. Any thoughts I had of coming back to you were gone the moment I knew you put that look in Daisy's eyes." He flinched and she kept going. "She trusted you and you set her up, you're setting them all up, and I'm stopping it n—"

He grabbed her arm and yanked her to him, and she said, "Ouch!" as the camper door opened. She wrenched away and saw J.T. standing there, tense and still.

"You're ice cream's melting," he said to Lucy after a long moment, but his eyes were on Nash.

"Can't have that," Lucy said, trying to keep her voice light.

"I'm going to be there tomorrow," Nash said to Lucy. "We're not through with this."

Lucy ignored him and walked back up the steps into the camper, J.T. moving back to let her in.

"You're missing the cake, Aunt Lucy," Pepper said, then squinted at her. "What's wrong with your arm?"

Lucy looked down to see the red splotches where Nash's fingers had bitten into her. "Nothing. Did my ice cream melt?"

"Almost," Pepper said.

"That chair," J.T. said, pointing to the one he'd just left, and Lucy sat down in it, putting her arms around Pepper as the little girl slid into her lap.

J.T. took the chair by the door.

I shouldn't like that but I do, she thought, and then she ate her ice cream, relaxing in the warmth of the camper filled with the people she loved, trying really hard to pretend that tomorrow was just another day.

Wilder left the camper around ten, after Gloom but before Daisy and Pepper. It had been nice in there in an off-the-wall kind of way. He and Gloom had gotten into a discussion of the classic Western showdown in the street ("That never happened in real life," Wilder had told him, "the movies invented that, it's a really stupid way to fight."; Gloom had said, "I don't care, I like it.") and had agreed that *High Noon* was the greatest Western of all time, with Pepper chiming in that she thought so, too, although it appeared it was the only Western she'd ever seen. Daisy had told him that their expletive of choice was now "Sufferin' Sappho," and Pepper had told him that she was his egg, both of which confused the hell out of him. Then Pepper said she'd seen the ghost again, this time in a building, and he paid attention, but she didn't seem as sure as she had before, distracted by her Wonder Woman stuff, so he let it go. He could have her point out the building tomorrow, maybe take a trip over there, see if there was any evidence somebody had been there.

But it was hard to concentrate on anything but Lucy, laughing and calling him "J.T.," and he realized that he didn't give a damn about much of anything if he could watch Lucy laugh, all the tension lines gone from her face, her eyes lit up and smiling at him, her dark hair finally out of that braid, spilling over her shoulders onto that Wonder Woman WonderWear. Pretty damn good.

But when Gloom left and he was the only one not wearing the underwear, he thanked Pepper for the party and left, feeling both relieved and disappointed when he was alone out in the dark again. It was simpler alone in the darkness, but Lucy wasn't there. He thought of her in his Jeep, in the passenger seat with her shirt open, that Wonder Woman thing underneath, her hair free and blowing as they drove down some two-lane road in the Southwest heading due south toward Mexico where there were no satphones with alerts for war or the CIA. The desert. No one around. The sun warm on their faces. Listening to Jimmy Buffet. Beaches, bars, booze, and just one woman. Just—

His eyes adjusted to the light and he saw Nash over by the side of the lot, punching numbers into his cell phone, looking mad as hell. *Good,* Wilder thought, and settled in to wait until he left. He tried to decide if Nash approaching Lucy's trailer again was a killing offense. If he touched her, he was dead, but . . .

Perhaps a warning. The man was on edge, so Wilder was prepared for the worst when Nash saw him.

"What the fuck do *you* want?" Nash growled as Wilder approached.

Wilder couldn't see his hands, so he kept his own close to his sides. He could hear Nash's breathing. Damn, the man was pissed about something. "Heard you did a stint or two working for Blue River."

"Fuck you."

"Excellent vocabulary."

"Why are you here?"

"Same as everybody else. Make some money. Get laid." *Fuck you over.*

Nash took a step forward. "Leave."

Wilder grinned. "Right. That'll do it."

"You have no idea what you're messing with," Nash said.

"Oh, I have an idea," Wilder said, his left hand sliding around and getting close to the butt of the Glock. But he did not touch it, there was the rule, and he knew that Nash knew the rule, too. It was good to deal with another professional. Bryce would have tried to hug him by now.

Nash's hand was hovering near his quick-draw rig. And the Australian had a crooked grin on his face. "Your call," he said in a voice that was void of accent or emotion.

Wilder looked into his eyes and reevaluated his assessment of dealing with a professional.

Nash was bonkers.

He'd done a good job of passing for sane, but Wilder had seen eyes like his before and it was never good. Plus, Nash had probably spent thousands of hours drawing that damn howitzer, honing his fast draw. Wilder figured he needed to apologize to Gloom: there might never have been a showdown in the Old West but there was one here in the low country. Right now.

"Draw," Nash said in that same flat voice. "I'm waiting, hero."

"Whatever you're planning—" Wilder began, but he could see Nash's fingers beginning to twitch.

"Draw," Nash repeated, the twitching getting faster. Wilder saw his eyes shift ever so slightly and he knew that was it.

Then somebody moved behind them.

He drew the Glock, but Nash's gun was already out, the fastest draw Wilder had ever seen, aimed at Mary Vanity, who was crossing the parking lot, oblivious to them both, her shoulders hunched as she talked on her cell phone. Nash met his eyes for a moment, and then they both straightened and holstered their guns, Wilder thinking, *Well, that made us look fucking stupid.*

"Pretty good, huh?" Nash said, his voice thick with pride and accent again. "Ever see anybody faster than me?"

"Fast doesn't mean good," Wilder said. "Ask any woman."

Nash started to laugh. "That's what this is about? Lucy? Hell, I don't care about Lucy, you can have her." His eyes slid left, like a reptile's. "Listen, here's a deal you'll like. I'll give you fifty thousand if you take Lucy and split tonight. You and Luce could have a real good time on fifty thousand."

Wilder wanted to reach for the Glock again. Arrogant *asshole*—as if Lucy were something he owned and could keep or give away.

"It's a good deal, mate," Nash said.

"I'm not your mate."

"Screw you," Nash said, his face tensing again. "Go back to Bragg. You're not part of this."

"You're not part of anything," Wilder said. "What happened, the SAS throw you out for faking it? Got no use for the fastest gun in the West?"

"I'm real SAS," Nash spat.

"*Were* real. You aren't one of them anymore. No team. You're a gun for hire, *mate.*"

"Fuck you." Nash stepped forward and Wilder tensed just as the camper door opened and Lucy came out, jeans and a shirt over her Wonder Woman stuff.

"What the hell are you doing?" she said, and both men eased back. "Whatever it is, knock it off. Gloom just called and said Stephanie passed him on the highway, going hell-bent for leather away from the hotel. Driving your van, Connor. What's going on?"

"My van?" Nash asked, eyes sliding left again.

That's a tell, Wilder thought and saw Lucy press her lips together; she knew it, too.

"Don't lie to me; what's going on?"

Nash shrugged. "I don't know. The van was missing when I came to get it. I was going to get Doc and look for it but then Wilder here—"

"What's in the van?" Lucy said.

"Stunt equipment," Nash said. "Prop guns."

"Why do you have the prop guns?" Lucy said, coming closer.

"Because I'm the propmaster on this shoot," Nash said. "Jesus, Lucy, stop micromanaging."

"Then you start managing," Lucy snapped and turned to Wilder. "I have to find her. If she takes that stuff and dumps it, we don't shoot tomorrow."

Then why isn't Nash going nuts? Wilder thought, but he jerked his head toward his Jeep. "Come on, I'll drive."

"Wait a minute," Nash said, but Lucy was already heading for the Jeep. "Oh, relax," he called after them. "Just let her go, she'll bring it back."

Wilder got in the driver's side and started the engine, and Nash ran up and swung himself into the backseat at the last minute.

"You're overreacting," he said to them both.

"Where was she going?" Wilder asked Lucy.

"Gloom said she turned onto Route 17."

"Just let her *go,*" Nash said, and Wilder took off for Route 17.

Tyler was having a good night.

He'd gone into town and gotten some real food—fuck the Boss, he wasn't living on warm beer and stale Cheetos—ogled some waitresses, gotten the DVD with the Actress in it, and then come back in time to get new orders: STOP STUNT VAN—ROUTE 17.

He was humming Warren Zevon's "Roland the Headless Thompson Gunner"—a classic song and one his sniper unit in Iraq had favored before going out to blow some heads off—as he cut the wire leading to the warning lights on the drawbridge. He wrapped black electrical tape around both ends and connected them with a rubber band so he could find them later. Then he walked back toward the bridge along the two-lane road, breathing the cool night air blowing over the marsh, feeling the water soaking his wet suit.

He reached the bridge, unzipped the waterproof pack around his waist, pulled out a small GPS tracking unit, backlit it, and peered at the screen. It showed a small blinking dot moving along that road, about a mile away and approaching fast. The LoJack on the van. He looked to the north and saw the slightest tinge of glow.

Everything was set.

Tyler walked back to the northern end of the bridge onto dry land and then climbed over the guardrail and slithered into the muck until he found a solid perch where he could watch the road to the north. He could see the headlights clearly now. On high beam. Coming fast. He pulled out a small transmitter and pressed the red button. With a groan of metal gears grinding, the bridge began to turn on the center pedestal, opening without the warning lights alerting the driver.

Tyler's head went back and forth, as if he were at a tennis match, watching the progress of the bridge opening and then the van approaching. He was up and moving toward the road as the van smashed full speed into the right steel truss, moving so fast it actually slid up the truss about five feet before smashing back down and coming to a halt in the center of the bridge.

Tyler was still whistling as he hopped the railing and ran toward the van. Just before he reached the van, he glanced north and south, checking for lights. Nothing. He had thirty seconds, he estimated, in order to be safe. He hit the button and the bridge slowly began turning back to its normal position.

He reached the van and looked in the driver's window. The driver was wearing a seat belt, her body held upright in it. A woman. Dressed in black. Unconscious. Too bad that little snot with the binoculars was too young to drive. He'd snap her like a twig.

Tyler grabbed the woman's jaw, twisted her head, and checked the pulse in her neck. Faint but there. The distant sound of a car startled him. Glancing back, he saw headlights. He ran to the place where he had cut the wire and unpeeled the black tape, splicing the wires together and then wrapping the tape around them. He climbed over the railing and slid into the Savannah River. Then, as he heard a car pull up, brakes screaming, he began swimming with the current, away from the site of the wreck, toward the waiting warm beer and laptop with the DVD loaded in it.

It was a damn good night.

Wilder had tried to be businesslike as they sped down Route 17. He was helping the boss find some missing equipment, that was all.

He stole a look at Lucy in the moonlight. She was staring straight ahead through the windshield, her long hair blowing back, unbraided, just the way he'd imagined it, except that instead of the desert they were driving across the lowlands of South Carolina and they had that dipshit Nash in the backseat. *This fantasy needs work,* he thought.

"If you'd just let me handle this," Nash said.

"You're never handling anything of mine ever again," Lucy said.

All right, Wilder thought, and felt much better about Nash being in the backseat.

Then Lucy leaned forward and yelled, *"Stop,"* and Wilder saw it, too, Nash's van smashed in the middle of the bridge.

"What the *fuck?*" Nash said, finally sounding mad.

"Stephanie," Lucy said as Wilder braked at the last second, sliding the Jeep to a halt a few feet shy of the wreck.

"My *van,*" Nash said, and then Lucy was out of the Jeep—Wilder following—afraid of what she'd find.

13

Lucy saw Stephanie bloody behind the wheel, and said, "No!" She yanked open the door and then J.T. grabbed her.

"Don't touch her," he said, and Lucy stopped, knowing he was right.

He reached across Stephanie carefully, turned the engine off, and pulled out the keys, and Stephanie groaned and tried to straighten against the seat belt that held her.

"Stephanie, it's okay, we're here," Lucy said. "Where does it hurt? Can you move?"

J.T. was punching 911 into his cell phone, looking grim. *Don't let her be dying,* Lucy thought and put her hand gently on Stephanie's shoulder, barely touching her. "Stephanie?"

Stephanie turned her head, her face twisted, blood smeared on her mouth. "This is your fault," she said, her voice thick.

She coughed and then moaned, and Lucy said, "J.T.'s calling 911. Somebody will be here soon. Can I help—Is there anything—"

"Go *away.*" Stephanie coughed, her head drooping, and Lucy stepped back, afraid to upset her more. "Nash. Is he—"

"Connor, get over here," Lucy yelled, and he came around the back of the van. "She's hurt and she wants you."

"Yeah, and whose fault is that?" Nash came up to the window. "You okay?" he said to Stephanie.

"I'm sorry," Stephanie said, pain slurring her voice. "But I had to stop you—"

"Where's my keys?" Nash reached past her and felt the empty ignition.

"Please," Stephanie said, as J.T. held out Nash's keys.

Nash grabbed them and took them to the back of the van, and Stephanie coughed and began to cry, moving her hand to hold her ribs.

"Damn it." Lucy went to the back of the van and grabbed Nash's arm. "Get up there and talk to her. She's more important than your damn van."

Nash shook himself free, unlocked the back, and opened it, and Lucy saw the stunt gun inside, racked and ready, the harnesses neatly coiled and stacked in their cages, everything secure, hardly disturbed by the accident.

Nash sighed in obvious relief. "Nothing's hurt," he said and got out his cell phone.

"Are you out of your mind? *Stephanie is hurt.*"

"She's hurt because she stole my van." Nash began to punch numbers into his phone.

Lucy went cold. "What kind of a monster are you? My God, you were always a liar, but you had feelings. What happened to you?"

"You're being a little irrational, love," he told her as he listened to the phone ring.

"Irrational?" Lucy took a deep breath. "Expecting one human being to care about another is not irrational. Expecting you to be kind to a woman who loves you is not irrational. *Expecting you to put your fucking phone down when somebody needs you is not irrational.*"

He ignored her, and she ripped the phone out of his hand and slung it into the swamp, where it plopped and sank without a trace.

"What the fuck?" Nash said, rounding on her.

"*That* was irrational," Lucy said, and went back to J.T., who was talking softly to Stephanie.

"The rescue squad will be here any minute now," he was saying when Lucy reached him. "Can you move your legs?"

"They hurt," Stephanie sobbed.

"That's good," J.T. said. "You've got feeling in them. They might have been hurt when you hit the bridge, but broken bones heal. You—"

Lucy heard sirens, coming closer, coming faster, and J.T. smiled through the window at Stephanie.

"Just a minute, now. You're going to be fine. Just a minute."

Lucy leaned against the door, biting her lip, as Nash came around the van.

"Jesus, you're a crazy bitch," he said, and Lucy wasn't sure whether he meant her or Stephanie, but J.T. straightened. "I need your cell phone," Nash said to Lucy. *"Now."*

"Fuck you," Lucy said and walked back to the Jeep as the ambulance pulled up.

"Lucy, I'm not kidding," Nash said from behind her.

Lucy got into the Jeep and looked back. J.T. was standing between her and Nash, blocking his way.

"I can go around you or through you, mate," Nash said.

"No, you really can't," J.T. said, and then the EMTs pushed past them, and Nash ran to close the back of the van.

Lucy's cell phone rang, and when she answered it, Finnegan said "Lucy?"

"What do you want?" she said, in no mood for his Irish brogue.

"Would Connor be standing by?"

"No," Lucy lied. She was not playing secretary for two sociopaths.

"Can you tell me if he recovered his van?" Finnegan said.

"Yes. It's smashed into a bridge, along with the woman who was driving it." She was shaking, she realized. She could feel the cell phone move against her cheek. There was blood on Stephanie's mouth. Did that mean internal injuries?

"We've had an accident?"

"*We* haven't," Lucy snapped. "We're not bleeding all over the pavement right now." *Too many accidents, too much blood.* "This stops now. I'm shutting down your damn movie. Fuck you and your four million dollars."

"*Wait,*" Finnegan said. "Don't—"

"Forget it. Go play with your mole."

"*I'll meet you—*" Finnegan said, and Lucy clicked off the phone and watched the EMTs work on getting Stephanie from the van.

"I'll stay with her at the hospital," she told J.T. as he got into the driver's seat.

"No, you won't." He turned on the engine. "Fair or not, she's blaming you, and if she sees you, she'll get upset again."

He began to back the Jeep up, and Lucy said, "We should at least stay until—"

"Let Nash handle it." J.T. pulled back onto the road. "He's the one she wants, and if we're not there, he'll have to answer the questions. He's the one with answers anyway."

"What do you mean?"

"I mean that when I came out of the camper, I heard the noise of the van leaving, and he was mad but he wasn't chasing Stephanie, he was on the phone."

Lucy shook her head. "Still not following."

"Nash called somebody to stop her," J.T. said. "And that somebody caused the wreck."

Lucy swallowed. "He wouldn't do that. He wouldn't hurt . . ." *I don't know that,* she realized. *I don't know him at all. He's not Connor anymore, he's some crazed bastard.*

"You okay?" J.T. said.

"No," Lucy said. "Not even close."

Five minutes later, Wilder pulled up in front of Lucy's camper, not sure what to do for her. "Look, Stephanie's going to be all right. She was talking, her mind was clear, the EMTs were fast—"

"I know," Lucy said. "But there's something very wrong here and I don't know how to stop it."

"Hey," he said, feeling guilty about the CIA, and she turned and smiled at him, rueful in the base-camp lights.

"You, however, are very right. Thank you for everything, for being so good to Stephanie and for taking me there and for Pepper's gifts."

He shrugged, not sure what to say.

"Right. You're the strong, silent type." Lucy leaned forward and kissed him swiftly on the cheek. "You're the best, J. T. Wilder."

Then she got out of the Jeep and went into the camper before he could get organized enough to say, "Wait."

That was probably good. It was late. She'd had a tough night.

She thought he was the best.

Wilder started the Jeep and went down the dirt road that Pepper had taken into the swamp. He'd scouted the location earlier and found that the road ended a little farther past where he parked the Jeep, so he doubted anyone would be coming that way. Still, the woods were full of dangerous creatures.

Of which he was one. *Yea, though I walk through the valley of death, I will fear no evil, for I am one of the baddest in the valley.* He was tempted to go to the cache and recover his MP-5 submachine gun. When in doubt, bring in heavier firepower. And he had plenty of doubts because there were too many questions yet, starting with how the hell Finnegan thought investing four million dollars in a movie was going to get him fifty million in jade phallic symbols.

I'm chasing a guy for the CIA who's chasing stone dicks, he thought. *It'd be so much easier to just shoot somebody.*

Well, the hell with it for tonight. He had something better to think about.

Lucy Armstrong. In WonderWear.

He forgot about the MP-5 and grabbed his bedroll out of the back of the Jeep. He took a chem light and broke it, the green glow giving him a little bit of illumination as he headed into the forest. About twenty yards in was a one-foot-high earth-covered ring surrounding a twenty-foot-wide circle in the middle of the massive oak trees and palmettos. A shell circle where Native Americans had camped for centuries on end, depositing empty shells all around the site, which were eventually covered over with dirt and grass to form the ring.

Wilder hooked the chem light over a palmetto frond. Then he pulled off the bungee strap and unrolled the self-inflating sleeping pad. It was only a quarter-inch thick, but enough to get him off the ground, which was the point. He'd slept on that thing all around the world, from minus sixty in the mountains of Afghanistan to plus one-twenty in a wadi in Iraq.

Satisfied that it was full, he screwed shut the valve, then lay down on top of it on his back, grabbing the chem light and sticking it into a pocket, where its light was shuttered. He pulled the camouflage poncho liner over his body up to his chest and stared up at the sky. He kept his clothes and boots on. Just like on a mission. He pulled the Glock out and placed it on the pad near at hand. Just like on a mission. He thought of Lucy again. Not like on a mission.

Good vibes. That's what had drawn Wilder to the spot. Good things had happened here. People had been happy here. He could see the stars overhead through the interlocking oak tree limbs. The smell of the swamp, rich and vibrant, carried on the slight breeze. More good things could happen here. Maybe would later, once the danger was gone, the stunt was over, the movie was finished. He turned on his side.

He always slept well under the stars. But not tonight. Tonight there was Nash. Finnegan. Letsky.

Lucy.

Fuck the mission for a while. He focused on Lucy.

Wilder smiled and relaxed for the first time in days.

When Lucy stepped into the camper, Daisy was sitting at the table, the bottle of Glenlivet in front of her with a half-empty glass, listening to Susanna McCorkle sing "It Ain't Necessarily So" on Lucy's iPod.

"Hey," Lucy said.

"Hey yourself." Daisy topped up her glass and then pushed the bottle over to Lucy. "Did you get the van back?"

"Stephanie crashed it into a bridge. She's on her way to the hospital. The van . . ." Lucy realized what they'd done and started to laugh without much humor. "Nash is stuck on a back road with a crumpled-up van and no cell phone, explaining to the cops what happened. Now that's funny." She dropped into one of the chairs and picked up the bottle. "God, what a day. Hell, what a *night*."

"Why the hell did she take the van?" Daisy said, her voice harsh.

"Trying to stop the shoot," Lucy said, suddenly aware that Daisy was looking grim again. "Look, don't let this make you crazy—"

"Too late." Daisy took a drink. "She going to be all right?"

"I don't know. She was talking." Lucy bit her lip. "She didn't want me anywhere near her."

"Well, you are her chief rival for Connor. Not that she has a chance, but—"

"She can have him," Lucy said, remembering the way Nash had looked at her. "God, he was a bastard to her."

"Well, she has nobody to blame but herself." Daisy sat back, holding her glass to her chest. "He was sleeping with Karen when we started the shoot. Stephanie didn't give a damn about that."

"I think he's been with Althea, too," Lucy said, remembering the actress's nervous denial. "I'm amazed he never hit on you."

"I'm like his little sister," Daisy said flatly. "He takes care of me." She drank again and then sighed. "Well, he gave me fifty thousand. I don't think he realized he was screwing me over. When I couldn't sleep, he got me the pills. And when I asked for you, he told Finnegan and then called you himself." She shrugged. "He does take care of me. And I kept telling myself this would be good for you. I wanted this to be your big break."

"I've had my big break," Lucy said, exasperated. "That's why I'm in New York. It's the capital city of Big Breaks." She leaned forward. "Look, forget Nash. Let me take care of you. Bring Pepper and move in with me. I have a loft. There's plenty of room and—"

"Yes," Daisy said, her voice tired in surrender.

"Or not." Lucy put her glass down. "I mean, I want you there, but not if it makes you miserable."

Daisy shrugged again. "It's just, New York is your place."

"I really hate L.A.," Lucy said, feeling guilty. "And it's not like New York is a *small* town. Many people there do not know me."

"So maybe we compromise." Daisy leaned forward. "We could stay down here. Pepper loves it down here. It's warmer and everything moves slower. We could start over together. Brand-new place for both of us. Fresh starts for everybody and we're a family again."

Susanna sang softly behind them, as Lucy thought, *I don't need a fresh start.*

Daisy must have read it in her face. "Or maybe not." She sat back. "Look, I'm sorry if I jumped the gun, telling everybody this was your big break. I was just sort of hoping that you and Connor . . . He really has been good to us, Lucy, great to Pepper. And he really does love you."

Lucy sighed and drank some of her scotch. "I know. He was always so much of what I wanted, strong and tough and brave, but he's a liar and a cheat, too. Gloom was right. He hasn't changed, he's just gotten more subtle about being a selfish bastard." *And now he's out in the cold.*

She looked at Daisy. "I just screwed up your last fifty thousand, babe. I told Finnegan I was canceling the shoot."

Daisy's eyes widened. "And he's letting you?"

"He doesn't have any choice. I hung up on him. And threw Nash's phone in the swamp." She shook her head. "I don't know how much that's going to stop them, but at least I can slow them down long enough to send the crew home."

Daisy sighed. "That last fifty thousand was probably too good to be true anyway." She nodded. "Thanks for saving me again."

Lucy waved her away. "You know, I can't believe I ever thought Nash could be what I needed."

"You needed Will Kane," Daisy said, nodding sympathetically.

Lucy smacked her glass down. "Is there *anybody* who hasn't seen that damn movie?"

"Just you." Daisy smiled at her. "Even Pepper's seen it. Which reminds me, thank you for the best night of my daughter's life."

Lucy relaxed into the plush chair as Susanna sang on, her soft voice slowing Lucy's pulse. "She was really happy, wasn't she?"

"I owe you, Luce," Daisy said.

"No, you don't. She's my niece, I get to do stuff for her because I'm her aunt."

"And because I owe you, I'm going to give you some really good advice."

"Oh, good." Lucy lost her smile. "Okay. Why not?"

"I think you should go jump that Green Beret."

Lucy sat up. "Excuse me?"

Daisy nodded calmly. "I said—"

"I know what you said. You said I should go find a man who hasn't shown any interest in me and ask him for sex. Let me think. No."

"Oh, please." Daisy leaned back, more relaxed now. "He can't take his eyes off you."

"That would be the WonderWear."

"He fell out of a helicopter for you, Luce, what more do you want?"

"I don't know." Lucy drank some scotch while she thought about it. "A pass would be good. You know, some indication of interest." *He liked my hair down.*

"He didn't like it when you were outside with Nash during the party."

"*I* didn't like it when I was outside with Nash. Look, that's just J.T. He saves people."

"It's J.T. now, is it?" Daisy said, grinning. Behind her, Susanna began to sing "Someone To Watch Over Me," and her smile faded. "I love this song."

"It's a good one."

"That's what you always were." Daisy looked sadly into her drink. "For as long as I can remember, you were there, watching over me. You still are." She bit her lip. "Thank you for canceling the shoot."

"Well, you know, big sister," Lucy said.

"Who watches over you, Luce?" Daisy looked at her over her scotch. "All those years when we were growing up and you took care of me, who was watching over you?"

"Hey," Lucy said, sitting up.

"And then you married Nash, but he didn't do a very good job, did he? J.T. would watch over you."

"Listen—"

"And you could watch over him because he needs it, too, Luce. You'd be good for each other."

Lucy shook her head. "If you'd come back to New York with me, we could watch over each other." She leaned forward. "Really, Daize. There's work for you and schools for Pepper and colleges for you and I miss you both so much—"

"All those things are down here, too," Daisy said, and looked strained again. "Plus, you know, warmth."

"Alligators," Lucy said.

"The ocean."

"Hurricanes."

"J.T."

Lucy sucked in her breath. "Uh, big hurricanes."

Daisy shook her head. "You really happy in New York?"

"Well . . ." Lucy frowned into her drink. "I like what I do. And New York is the greatest city in the world. 'Happy' may be pushing it."

"Because J.T.'s down here permanently, not just for this shoot. He teaches at Fort Bragg."

"He teaches?" Lucy said, taken aback.

"Yeah. Bryce told me. He teaches at some Special Forces school. You could see him all the time. *Pepper* could see him all the time. She keeps saying she's his egg. She wants a family. She wants *him* in the family."

"That I can't deliver. I don't think he's a family kind of guy." Lucy tried to relax into the music, taking the edge off her lousy day. "This really is a great song." She closed her eyes and listened to the liquid notes. "Funny how the really great stuff has a few years on it. Eighteen-year-old scotch, seventy-year-old music—"

"Thirty-something Army captains," Daisy said.

"Daize—"

"I'm not teasing, Lucy," Daisy said. "I mean it. He's a good guy. Close your eyes and think about him. About him, not the shoot or whatever the mess is, just about him. Because you care a lot, Lucy. It shows."

Behind Daisy's voice, Susanna sang, "There's a somebody I'm long-ing to see," and Lucy remembered J.T. close to her in the swamp, catching her as she fell, his hands strong on her. J.T. coming to get her when Nash had been threatening, J.T. beside her in the Jeep, J.T. falling out of a helicopter for her, J.T. just standing there, every inch a hero. She gave up pretending to be responsible and memorized the planes of his face and the way his smile came slowly, and the light in his eyes . . .

Oh, God, she thought, *don't let me fall in love with him. Lust I can handle but—*

"Don't screw this up, Luce," Daisy said.

"You're not helping."

"Yes, I am." Daisy pushed her glass away. "I've had too much to drink to drive, and I'm so tired I'm going to fall off this chair. So I'm going to crawl in bed in the back with Pepper. If you decide to drive to the hotel, wake me up when we get there, and I'll go pack so we can leave. But I hope you don't. I hope you go find the guy who needs you like you need him."

"Such a romantic," Lucy said, trying to keep her voice light.

Daisy shook her head and started down the short passage to the bed where her daughter slept, dreaming of Wonder Woman.

"Wait," Lucy said, and Daisy stopped. "I want us to be together. I don't want to lose this again."

Daisy nodded. "Me either."

"So we'll work something out," Lucy said. "New York or here, we'll work something out. But we'll be together. Okay?"

Daisy's eyes filled with tears. "Okay," she said, her voice breaking.

"And we'll take care of each other," Lucy said, nodding.

Daisy nodded back, and sniffed.

"Good night," Lucy said, fighting her own tears.

Daisy came back and hugged her, strangling her just like Pepper had. "I love you, Luce," she whispered.

"I love you, too, babe," Lucy said, putting her cheek against Daisy's hair as she hugged her back. "So much. From now on, we're together."

Daisy nodded and then pulled away, sniffing. "But we need a man around, too, to like, hook up the stereo. Go get the Green Beret. He'd be good."

"I don't know if he does stereos," Lucy said, and Daisy gave a watery laugh and went back to bed.

Lucy wiped away her tears as Susanna sang on. A man in her life would be good. She rolled her eyes at herself. So antifeminist of her to sigh for a man to watch over her. "A woman needs a man like a fish needs a bicycle." Well, that was wrong. A woman needed a man the way a woman needed a man. Which in her case was badly. Susanna sang about need, and Lucy swallowed scotch and lost herself in the music until she realized there were tears in her eyes again. Then she straightened and thought, *Pathetic. Needy and pathetic. A little scotch and I liquefy. Well, that's wrong. I'm tough. I don't need no man to love me, no how. Nope. Sure don't.*

It didn't help. By the time Susanna started the next song, singing, "There were chills up my spine," Lucy was lost. *I want that,* she thought. *I want to look at somebody and feel that. I want to touch somebody and feel that.* Susanna sang on, smoothing out the refrain again, and Lucy thought, *Not somebody. Him.* She'd been focusing on Daisy, on Pepper, on the movie, but underneath all of it, he'd hummed in her blood, making her breathe faster when he was close, making her look for him when he wasn't.

Lust, she told herself. Perfectly understandable. Perfectly healthy.

And really a good deal for J.T., too, and not just for the sex. He was so reserved, it was probably hard for him to connect with people—real connection, not Althea connection. *I could give him real warmth. I could rescue him . . .* She let herself fantasize his mouth hard on hers, hot on her body, and everything faded away as the heat spread until Susanna finished her last slow verse. Then Lucy thought, *Enough waiting.* Nothing wrong with going after a good healthy boink with a good healthy guy after a very tough day. Get rid of some tension, share some warmth.

Make love with J.T. until her brain melted.

Okay, I want him, she thought, relieved to acknowledge it.

And I want him now.

Then she put down her scotch, turned off the iPod, found her flashlight, and went out into the woods to get him.

14

The thing about the woods at night, Lucy thought as she walked along the side of the road, was that it was dark. Really dark with the trees branching over the road, shutting out the moon, dark enough that the miniflashlight from her purse was fairly ridiculous. Gator dark, one might say. *Sufferin' Sappho, it's dark.* She thought about going back and then thought, *No,* and kept going, shining her flash on the ground ahead. She was not going to spend another night trying not to think about what she wanted when she could have him.

She was pretty sure she could have him.

She tripped over something in the grass and played the flash over it, remembering how J.T. had tracked down Pepper. Tire ruts, the dirt freshly cut. Had to be J.T. and his big-wheeled Jeep. She followed the ruts with her flash but they disappeared into the trees along what could barely be called a road, more an afterthought at the end of one. The woods got really dark, darkest where the ruts went, and she thought, *It didn't used to be this hard to get a guy to sleep with me,* and followed them in.

As soon as the real road disappeared behind her, she lost her sense

of direction and stuck with the ruts as her only hope, not only of finding J.T. but of ever getting out again. And when she found the Jeep
and he wasn't in it, she had a moment of panic. Going on would be
suicidally stupid, staying here would be unbearably frustrating, going
back would be worse than the other two combined.

"J.T.?" she called into the darkness and waited a moment. Nothing. *Oh, come on,* she thought. How far into the woods could he have
gone? "J.T.?" she called again, louder this time, and then jumped
when he said from behind her, "You know, it was nice and quiet here
until you showed up."

She turned around and played the flashlight in his face for a second
before he took it out of her hand and shut it off. She stepped closer.
"You know, you're damn hard to find."

"That was the point. It's easier to be alone if you're damn hard to
find."

Lucy stepped still closer and he didn't back up. "Yeah, but you
didn't want to be alone," she said, praying that was true, and then she
leaned in and kissed him, almost missing his mouth in the dark until
he corrected for her and kissed her back, his mouth hard on hers, his
hand cupping the back of her head. He tasted right, hot and sweet,
and she gave in to the kiss, letting it flood her. And when he pulled
back, she was dizzy from him, clutching him as she sucked in air, trying to get her breath back.

"Okay," he said, sounding as breathless as she was. "The way back
to the road—"

"You have *got* to be kidding me," Lucy said, and he said, "Right,"
and kissed her again and made her blood pound, and then he pulled
her away from the Jeep, a little deeper into the woods, as her heart
raced.

The light was better in the small clearing they came to but she still
stumbled over the foot-high ring that surrounded the clearing.

"What's that?"

"Shell ring."

"Huh?"

"A spiritual place. Very old and sacred."

Sacred, she thought, and wondered if she'd go to hell for thinking what she was thinking in a sacred place. But those old earth goddesses had thought that way, too. She'd seen the carvings. "Works for me," she said, and then she saw that the only thing in the circle was a thin mattress with some kind of camouflage cloth tossed over it. "This is it? Where's your tent, your sleeping bag, your Coleman lantern? Where's the S'mores, for Christ's sake?"

"S'mores?"

Lucy shook her head. Obviously he'd never been a Girl Scout. She'd just have to settle for him being a Green Beret.

On the other hand, she was about to get someone to hold in the forest at night. *Us Amazonians,* she thought, and started to laugh.

"The way back is over . . ." he began, and she pulled her shirt off over her head and tossed it to him, flashing her WonderWear at him.

He caught it and shut up.

She hopped on one leg to pull off her boot, thinking, *This can't be seductive,* and then dropped it and pulled off the other, while he stood there watching her with that unfathomable look on his face. Then she unzipped her jeans and shoved them off. "This would be working on you better if there were more light," she said and tossed them to him.

He caught them with his free hand. "It's working." But he reached into a pocket and pulled out a small, green glowing stick, which he hung on a palmetto frond. "Did you bring the rope?"

"Just me," she said and stripped off the red Wonder Woman camisole and tossed it to him, too. "I'm not seeing much enthusiasm," she said as she shoved off the blue-starred bottoms, and he caught those, too, and then she stopped, not ready to take off her underwear and be naked for him, not yet.

He dropped the bundle of her clothes he'd been holding and stepped over it to get to her, catching her arms when she tried to put them around him.

"There," he said, and gently pushed her toward the ground cloth.

"Romantic," she said, and knelt down on it, trying to figure out what the hell it was in the dim light. It was definitely camouflage, but that was pretty much J.T.'s signature color. He probably had the matching china. When she looked up, he was gone, and she felt a moment of panic again. "J.T.?"

"In a minute," he said from the shadows outside the dim glow of the stick, and from his outline it looked like he was stripping off his shirt. *Modest,* she thought. *Well, okay.* At least they were getting someplace.

She went back to exploring the bed situation. Just some kind of pad with the camouflage cloth over it and that was it. *You couldn't fall for a millionaire with a Swedish mattress,* she told herself as she crawled under the thin cover. *You had to want Nature Boy.* She heard something rip in the shadows that sounded like Velcro—*Velcro?*—and then a zipper, and then something snap like spandex, and she thought, *I really don't want to know,* and tried to settle in on the quarter inch of whatever it was underneath her. "You know—" she said, and then he was beside her, under the cover, and she shut up.

His body was long and hard against her as he pulled her close, his muscles tight from use, and she shivered a little because it was him, for real, not a fantasy, playing her fingers over his chest, smiling in the dark when he sucked in his breath. "You know," she began again, and he kissed her and she forgot what she was about to say as she lost herself in the weight and the heat of him. The simmer in her blood flared as she wrapped herself around him and felt hard muscle press into soft flesh. *This is good,* she thought, feeling a little dizzy, while he unfastened her bra and slid the straps off her shoulders, as efficient with that as he was with everything else. *Good, clean, American outdoor sex. Yep.* She pulled away to help him, feeling her breasts fall free, already tight and swollen for him so that when he touched her, she leaned into his hands to ease the pressure there, whispering, *"Oh"* against his neck because he felt so good.

He said something under his breath and kissed her again, his mouth hot, and while she was reeling from that, he dropped his head to her breast, and she shuddered, feeling the touch of his tongue, the tug of his mouth, all the way to her groin. She moaned as he moved up to bite her gently on the neck and slid his hand between her legs, and she arched to meet him without thinking.

God, you feel good, she thought, and then his hand stroked over her again, his fingers sliding carefully under the elastic of her pants, then smoothly inside her, and she lost her breath as she coalesced around him and made him the center of everything. He knew where to touch her, how to touch her, and she melted boneless against him as he drew in his breath and said, "God, Lucy." He kissed her then, and she fell into him, not giving a damn about anything except what he was doing to her and how impossibly good it felt. *I should be helping here,* she thought as he moved his hand away a few minutes later, but then he slipped her pants down her thighs, kissing and biting his way down the curve of her stomach—*Oh, God, yes*—and she opened to him, arching her hips to his mouth, shuddering under his tongue, and rocking with him as all the frustration and longing she'd felt for him rose and built and twisted inside her, multiplied a thousand times because it was him, and then she broke, shuddering under his mouth, breathless and shaking and helpless.

J.T., she thought, drowning in him, and then he moved up beside her and she rolled to press against him, but he said, "Wait," a little out of breath himself, and moved away from her.

"J.T.," she said, trying to pull him back, and he said, "Condom," and then a moment later rolled back to her, and she curved into his heat, warm and sated and wanting him closer, much closer, part of her, inside her.

"Thank you," she said into his ear, and he stopped and said, "For what?" calm and cool and suddenly annoying because he wasn't as destroyed as she was.

"The condom," she said, thinking, *So not romantic.* "The orgasm." She shifted on the pad he thought was a bed, trying to find a place for

her hipbone that wasn't on a rock or tree root. "The great accommo-
dations."

He shook his head in the dark. "You come your brains out in a sacred place and still you complain. You're a hard woman to please."

"Hey," Lucy said. "I'm pleased. I just said—" and he kissed her
again, pulling her hips into his this time, and she felt him hard against
her and shut up, curled herself around him as his fingers tightened on
her, and the heat flared again. *Stop trying to make this something it isn't,*
she told herself. *Especially since there's a pretty good chance the rest of the
sex is going to be just as good as the first part.* She rolled onto her back,
pulling him with her, wanting to feel his weight on her, and he put his
hands on each side of her, balancing over her, larger than she'd
thought.

"Touch me," she said and wrapped her legs around him, and he
laced one hand through her hair and brought her mouth up to his,
kissing her thoroughly as he bore down on her. She moved against
him, feeling him hard between her legs, wanting him inside her, but
he waited, touching her everywhere, making her breath come faster,
deeper, her body liquid, slippery with need, and just when she was
ready to scream, *Now, damn it,* he moved his hand down and stroked
her open, sure and insistent, and she felt him move into her.

She drew in her breath at the shock of him sliding hard and thick
inside her, and then she opened her eyes and looked at him looming
in the dark above her, rocking into her, and was amazed. *J.T. Wilder,*
she thought as her breath came raggedly, *inside me.* She held on to
him, trying to remember that it was just physical, that it didn't matter
that this was J.T., hot and real and holding her tight, making her
dizzy while he kept her safe. *It's just sex,* she told herself, and then he
moved deeper into her, careful not to hurt her, and she shuddered as
he hit something good. He bent down and said, "Shhhh," with so
much tenderness that she came undone, all her defenses gone, nothing
to keep her safe but him. He felt so right, not just good, but *right,*
nothing to guard against, nothing to fear, it was right that they should

be this way together, interlocked, *fused,* and she relaxed into him, stopped being just a body for him, stopped making him just a body for her, and loved him with everything she had.

She whispered, "J.T.," and he slowed and whispered, "It's all right," and she said, *"I know."* She kissed his cheek and then his mouth, gently, again and again, as she began to move against him, with him, taking him in deeper, rocking slowly so she could feel the slide of him inside, giving him all of her because it was him, because it was going to be him from now on, knowing what she'd known since she first saw him on the bridge, that this was the beginning.

"Lucy?" he said, and she slid her hands down his back, learning the territory of him, the way his muscles moved as she touched him, the secret places on him that made him hers, thinking, *Here,* as he drew in his breath, *Here,* as he shuddered against her, *Here,* as he moaned her name, feeling herself glow with the knowledge of him. *Mine,* she thought and tilted her hips, and he rolled with her, pulling her on top, and then she began to explore in earnest, fingertips and tongue, sliding down his body, feeling him slide out of her as she kissed her way down. He had round scars that she guessed were from bullets, thin scars that might have been knife cuts, muscles that tensed under her fingers, nerves that twitched under her mouth, and the more she learned him, the more she loved him, until she stripped the condom off and touched him with her tongue, heard the sharp intake of his breath in the night, felt his body tighten under her, and took him completely, making him her own.

She felt his hands stroke into her hair, felt him move to her rhythm this time as her fingers bit into his thighs, digging into the muscles there. And when, a few minutes later, he pulled hard on her hair, she moved up his body, breathing heavily in the dark, and sank down over him, taking him into her. He rose up, saying, "Lucy!" and she shoved him down, arching over him. "You're mine," she said, and kissed him deep and slow as she tightened herself around him. "Mine," she whispered against his mouth and began to move, and he slid his hands down her back and said, "Oh, God, Lucy," and surrendered to her, moving with her, pulling her close.

The woods closed in around them, dark and deep, and she thought, *This is the safest place I'll ever be,* we *are the safest place I'll ever be,* and lost herself in them, in the pulse they made together. They rocked each other closer, higher, hotter, the pressure building inexorably until she was tight everywhere, the sizzle bubbling beneath her skin, craving his touch, his hands, his mouth. Her breaths became sobs, and he rolled, pinning her beneath him, and the weight of him bearing down on her, pulsing deep inside her, made her clutch at him as he held her tighter. He whispered, "Let go, Lucy," and she gave herself up, felt the kick in her blood and then the surge, and she cried out and let him take her, over and over, shuddering safe beneath him, mindless with lust and love.

When J.T. moved away from her hours later, Lucy roused at the loss of his heat, then came awake completely as he stood. "What?"

"It's almost dawn," he said from the darkness, making rustling sounds as he got dressed.

Lucy yawned and peered into the darkness. "I can't see it." She lay back, still half asleep, and saw the stars overhead, a million pinpricks of light, a million possibilities ahead of her. And all of them with J.T.

She laced her fingers behind her head. "There are an awful lot of stars up there in a very dark sky. I don't think that's dawn."

"It's close," he said, and she decided that anybody who camped with gators probably knew when dawn came better than she did. "We call it BMNT in the Army," he added. "Beginning morning nautical twilight."

Oh, good. Military terms. That was what she wanted to hear. So much better than, *Last night was the best of my life, and I'll love you forever.* "Nautical. Are we at sea?"

"No. But this is when the bad guys always attack. So we always do stand to."

"'Stand to'?" Lucy stretched. "Sounds good to me. Can you stand to lying down?"

Wilder laughed and she liked the sound. "It means get ready for the Indians to come riding in. They always attack just before dawn in the movies, right?"

Guess that's a no. Just her luck, she'd fallen for the one man in the world who wasn't interested in morning sex but who was worried about Indians riding in. Low sex drive *and* politically incorrect. Probably because he watched too many damn Westerns. Well, they could work on that. She sat up and felt around for her clothes, finding her shirt first and putting that on, then her jeans, wondering how long it would take to convince him that they were soul mates. She'd probably have to bring him back to consciousness after she dropped the forever part on him, so the soul mate thing could be even trickier. *More sex,* she thought. *That might help. It would help me.* She stood up, still half asleep, wishing they were in a hotel room someplace so that she could close the curtains and drag him back to bed.

Dragging him back to swamp in the approaching daylight did not appeal as much. For one thing, she really did not want to see where she'd been sleeping. Not that there'd been much sleeping.

But tonight, definitely a bed, she thought. "You ever had room-service breakfast in bed?"

"Nope."

What a surprise. "We'll try that next time," she said, keeping her voice light. "But we have to be *in a room* first."

"Here." He handed over her bra, and she said, "Thank you," automatically and squinted at the ground to find her underpants. "This afternoon, before the shoot," she told him, when she had her underpants and bra rolled into a ball. "You and me. In a hotel room. Yours, mine, I don't care, but there's going to be a bed."

"What makes you think I'm that easy?" he said.

She stepped across the bedroll and pulled him to her, kissing him good, feeling herself shiver because it was him.

"Right," he said when he came up for air. "This afternoon. Hotel room."

"Damn straight," Lucy said, and kissed him again, loving the way he made her head reel. "You are definitely my Animal of the Month," she said, and kissed him one more time, and then she sighed and started off for the road until he caught her. "I have to get back," she said, tickled that she'd gotten him that easily, and he turned her in the opposite direction.

"That's back," he said, pointing through the woods in the other direction.

Okay, so you're not that easy. "I knew that," she said, fighting a grin. "I was just testing you."

"How'd I do?"

"You're adequate," she said, and he swatted her on the rear as she stepped across the bedroll and headed back for the camper.

By the time Lucy hit the edge of base camp, the sky was just beginning to show pink in the east and she was awake enough to realize that walking out of a swamp with some of her clothes in her hands could cause comment. And then there was the goofy smile she was pretty sure was still on her face from being swatted on the butt by a tight-assed military man.

Such a human thing for him to do. Much like the things he'd been doing for the rest of the night, she thought, and grinned again. She sidled around the back of the trucks and made it to the camper without seeing anybody, feeling stupid for sneaking, but too damn happy to really care. She'd had great sex with an epiphany in the middle. Let 'em comment.

Then she yanked open the door and saw Daisy sitting at the camper table, yawning.

"And where have you been, little girl?" Daisy said, grinning sleepily.

"In the woods with a wolf." Lucy climbed into the camper. "Why are you up before dawn?"

"I left my pills in the motel, so I couldn't sleep," Daisy said, and Lucy felt her giddy happiness slip away.

"But you were so tired and happy—"

"I was thinking about what you said," Daisy said. "About not shooting tonight. They'll never let you cancel, Lucy. I appreciate you trying, but they won't stop."

Oh hell. Lucy kicked herself. One night of lust in the woods and she forgot about everything but herself. Daisy was right, there was no way Nash was just going to roll over because she said so. Well, at least they had J.T. on their side. She was developing a touching faith in his ability to save people.

"But if we make it through this, we're going back to New York with you," Daisy said, and Lucy stared at her. Daisy shrugged. "I'll get a job or work with you, and we'll find a school for Pepper, and maybe I can go to school nights. But you're right, from now on we're together."

Lucy sat down in the chair across from her. "Daisy, I know you're not happy about New York." *So maybe I'll move down here and start over.* In the clear light of a satisfied morning, that option was looking better. Not practical, probably not even possible, but better.

"It isn't New York. I wanted to make it on my own," Daisy said.

"You have been." Lucy leaned across to take her hand. "That's what's been wrong. Nobody makes it on their own. God, I'd be nuts if it weren't for Gloom. You're *supposed* to have backup."

"You never did," Daisy said.

"Of course I did," Lucy said. "I had you."

Daisy blinked at her. "I was your backup?"

"Always. You were always there for me." She tightened her grip on Daisy's hand. "And I'm so glad you're going to be with me again. I know it's selfish but I so much want you with me."

"Oh." Daisy blinked and swallowed. "Oh, that's really good, that I was your backup. I know it's not true, but it sounds so good."

"It's true," Lucy said, and thought, *I'm just not sure I want to go back to New York now*. How wimpy was she if one night of great sex could make her move next door to alligators? "About New York—"

Somebody knocked on the door of the camper and opened it.

"You left—" J.T. said, and stopped as he saw Daisy. He was holding Lucy's WonderWear, which Lucy took from him smoothly.

"Thank you," she said.

"Why does he have your WonderWear?" Daisy asked Lucy, grinning at her.

"Because we had hot animal sex in the woods last night," Lucy said.

J.T. swallowed. "So. Well. I have to go now."

"Chicken," Lucy said. "But go ahead." Her smiled faded. "I have to call the hospital to check on Stephanie, and go talk to Gloom, and then Finnegan will probably call again—"

"Again?" J.T. said, stopping with the door half closed. "When did he call?"

"Yesterday at the accident, after I threw Nash's phone in the swamp," Lucy said. "He wanted to know if the van was all right and I said no. . . ." Her voice trailed off at the look on his face.

"How did he know the van was missing?" J.T. said.

"Nash probably called him," Daisy said.

"No," J.T. said. "I heard the van go when I saw Nash on the phone, he called whoever it was who stopped the van. I thought it was Finnegan, but if Finnegan called looking for Nash, it was somebody else." He frowned at Lucy, all business. "Why'd he call you?"

"I threw Nash's cell phone in the swamp before Finnegan could answer," Lucy said, feeling a little chilled by his focus on work. "So who called Finnegan?"

"The mole," Daisy said, "whoever that is," and Lucy watched J.T.'s face clear.

"I know who that is," he said and left.

Lucy got up to follow him. "Go back to bed," she said to Daisy. "I'll take you and Pepper to the hotel when we get back."

"Okay," Daisy said. "But when you come back I want to know who the mole is." She raised her voice as Lucy went out the door. "And *everything* you did last night!"

Lucy picked up speed to get to the Jeep before he left without her, telling herself that being disappointed because he was back in mission mode was ridiculous. J.T. would find the mole, she knew that, because he would always come through for her.

And that really is something, she thought, and began to run to catch him.

Lucy got to him just as he was heading down the road to his Jeep. "Wait a minute."

He slowed for her.

"Where are we going? Who's the mole?"

"Mary Vanity."

Lucy gaped at him. "You're kidding."

"Nash and I saw her crossing the lot with her cell phone, and then you came out. The only other person around to see Stephanie take the van was Daisy—"

"It's not Daisy."

"So it has to be Mary Vanity," J.T. said.

Lucy shook her head, flummoxed. That gormless, wet makeup girl had been keeping watch for Finnegan. And Nash had called someone to stop Stephanie. There were traitors everywhere, she couldn't trust anybody, and tonight people actually thought they were going to bring in the helicopter and shoot a stunt? Fat chance.

"Finnegan say anything else?" J.T. asked, interrupting her train of thought.

"He wanted to meet me."

J.T. froze in his tracks. "He's close by?"

"Well, I would assume so if he wanted to meet." She saw the look on J.T.'s face. "Why? What's wrong?"

"I was told he wasn't in the country."

"Told by whom?"

J.T. headed for the Jeep again.

"Hey," Lucy said, trying to catch up. "Look, there's no hurry, I told him I'm canceling tonight's shoot, so it's all over anyway. Except for him suing me for four million dollars. Do you think he's really going to do that?" Her head started to throb.

"I don't think canceling is an option," J.T. said as they reached the Jeep. "Get in, we'll talk about it."

"It's an option because I'm doing it." She stopped beside the Jeep, wary now. He couldn't possibly be trying to talk her into shooting those stunts, not with everything that had happened. "This is over. No more accidents, no more sabotage, no more people in danger."

J.T. got into the driver's seat. "Honey, you have to keep the shoot going. Take as many people off as you can, but you have to keep it going. It's important."

The "honey" sounded good, but the gravity in his voice chilled her. "Tell me you're not part of this."

"I'm not part of Nash's plan. Get in the Jeep, Lucy, we have to go get Finnegan's number from Mary."

"What *are* you part of?"

He shook his head. "Just trust me—"

"No." She stepped back from the Jeep, the cold feeling settling in her bones. "You know, it's awfully convenient that you showed up right about the time everything went bad on this shoot."

"Lucy," he said, looking at her soberly. "You have to trust me."

"The hell I do." Lucy stepped back again. "I am through being everybody's patsy. You tell me who you're working for, or I walk away and shut down this movie now. I *will* do it, I will send everybody home and leave Nash alone with his fucking helicopter. *I will do it.*"

He met her eyes for a long moment and then said, "I'm working for the CIA."

"Oh, *Christ.*" Lucy looked away from him. *Boy, you sure can pick 'em, Armstrong.* "You are the fucking CIA. Literally the fucking CIA."

"I am not the CIA," J.T. said, looking grim.

"No, you just *work* for them. And I trusted you."

"No, you didn't," J.T. said. "You slept with me. It's not the same thing."

"I thought it was," Lucy said and started back toward base camp.

"Oh, come on, Lucy," J.T. said. "Get in the Jeep."

She turned around. "I was actually thinking about spending the rest of my life with you."

"What?" He looked so startled that she wanted to throw something at him.

"Hey," she said, clamping down on her hurt. "Last night meant something to me, okay?"

He frowned at her. "It meant something to me, too, but I usually don't propose after one night. Slow down a little."

"Really?" Lucy said. "How long does it usually take you to propose?" She read the look on his face and said, "You've been married before?" trying not to sound outraged. So much for saving him from a lifetime of loneliness. *God, you're stupid, Lucy.*

"See, this is why it's a good idea to know somebody longer than three days before you start planning a future," J.T. said. "It would have given me time to mention them."

"Them?" Lucy said, straightening. "There was more than one?"

"Two," J.T. said. "If you hadn't rushed me, I'd have told you about them."

"I'll keep that in mind with the next guy I sleep with," Lucy said and turned back toward base camp. *Yeah, you really rescued him.*

"Come *on,* Lucy," J.T. called after her.

I am an idiot, Lucy thought as she stepped over the ruts.

Somehow, the thought didn't make her feel any better.

15

By the time Wilder had the Jeep started and had caught up with Lucy, she was a hundred yards down the road and moving fast. "Come on, Lucy," he said again, as he pulled up beside her with the Jeep in first gear, his foot working the clutch to keep pace with her stride. "Get in here."

She didn't look at him at all, just kept striding along.

Okay, so he worked for the CIA and he'd been married. Technically, the CIA were the good guys here, and hell, he was divorced. She should be happy. Wilder could never figure women out. He guessed that was why he had exes. Thinking of that reminded him of his next move.

"I'm sorry."

Lucy's head swiveled, and he was appalled to see her blinking back tears.

"Lucy!"

She kept walking, her face stony. "Sorry about what?"

Crap. Lying to her? Getting married twice before he met her? Getting sucked into this mess by the CIA? Being born?

"Anything I did to hurt you." That should cover it. "Don't cry."

Lucy came to a halt and turned and faced him, so he shifted into neutral and the Jeep rolled to a stop.

"I'm not crying," she said, and her voice was steady. She stood there for a minute, digesting his words, turning them over, probably deep-frying them. Women. There was a reason he was in the Special Forces with other manly men. Then she said, "Okay. I'm upset."

No shit. He nodded, wary.

"I know I'm overreacting but . . ." She shook her head. "No but. I'm overreacting, period. You're right, last night was just last night, nothing to get upset about."

She looked at him narrowly, like she was waiting for him to say something, and he nodded again, not sure what to say but pretty sure whatever he said would be wrong.

Lucy cast her eyes to the sky in exasperation. "Oh, stop looking like that. I know you don't have a clue what I'm upset about." She looked at him, straight on. "Do not lie to me again."

Wilder's shoulders relaxed. "Never."

"Because in spite of your ex-wives . . ." She took a deep breath. "I really do trust you, you bastard."

Wilder nodded. "You can."

She swallowed. "This movie. These people. My family. I'm respon-sible for them. It's like . . ." She hesitated. "It's my mission."

Wilder nodded again.

"Which is why I'm not going to let the CIA hijack my set and en-danger my team. The team is more important than the mission. I'm shutting down the movie, J.T."

Crap. "Get in the Jeep, Lucy," he said, keeping his voice gentle.

"No more lying."

"I didn't lie," he said. "I just didn't tell you the whole truth."

"That counts," she said and got in.

He shot her a glance. "Then you lied to me too."

She snapped to look at him, scowling. "I never—"

"Daisy's not your sister," he said, knowing she couldn't be. They were just too different.

"She's my sister in every way that matters," Lucy said coldly.

"Adopted?"

Lucy swallowed. "Same foster home."

Shit. "I'm sorry."

"Don't be." Lucy faced forward again. "It was a good home. Nobody hurt us. We were fine. And she's my sister. She is absolutely my sister."

Yeah, Wilder thought. *Foster kids always have a good time. Boy, does this explain a lot.* "Look—"

"Daisy and I have been sisters since she was one year old and I was five. That's twenty-nine years and that's good enough for me."

Okay, then. "Fasten your seat belt," he said gently.

"J.T., we were fine," Lucy said, but she buckled herself in just as a black car came from the direction of base camp and swerved, screeching to a halt in front of them and blocking their way. Wilder recognized Crawford behind the wheel, dressed in a suit and looking older than the kid he'd been in the diner. Crawford stared at him, a cold look, different from any expression he'd shown before.

"Who the hell is he?" Lucy asked.

"I don't—" Wilder caught himself. "My CIA contact. Name is Crawford."

"What's he doing here?"

"I don't know." *Okay, this truth thing is working okay so far.* Two for two. "Listen, I wasn't lying when I came on the set. Bryce did hire me. Everything was aboveboard as far as I knew. But the CIA set it all up. That guy"—he jerked his head at Crawford, now coming toward them—"called me out of the blue to meet me after the first day. That was the appointment I went to that day, the day I got Pepper the Wonder Woman doll. He told me about Finnegan."

Lucy tensed. "What about Finnegan?"

Hell, where to start with that? Wilder opened his mouth to answer, but then Crawford was there at his door. He flashed an ID, and Wilder squinted at it. It said Crawford was a Special Agent with the FBI. What the fuck?

"Sir, may I speak to you?"

Wilder couldn't resist. "What?"

"Please step out of the vehicle," Crawford said with a straight face. Either he was very good or he didn't get it. Wilder wasn't so sure anymore.

Wilder opened the door and got out. Crawford put a hand on his arm and directed him away from the Jeep.

"What the hell happened?" Crawford demanded once they were out of earshot. "There's a police report on an accident with a van from the movie shoot."

"The assistant to the director of the film, Stephanie—" Wilder realized he didn't even know her last name. "She took the stunt van to stop the picture from shooting tomorrow because she thought the stunts didn't belong in the movie. Nash has the stuff from the van back."

"Good," Crawford said.

" 'Good'?" Wilder echoed.

"The movie goes as scheduled."

"Why?"

Crawford ignored the question and nodded toward the Jeep. "Who's she?"

Wilder looked back at Lucy, watching them with her arms folded and her eyes narrowed. "That's Lucy Armstrong, the director."

Crawford nodded and dismissed her. "So you ran this Stephanie into the bridge?"

Yeah, and then we waited for the EMTs. "No. It happened before we got there. We called 911 and then waited for them to show."

Crawford nodded. "Just checking. The cops say it looks like she lost control."

Wilder didn't say anything.

"There's no sign of foul play," Crawford continued, filling the silence. He stared at Wilder. "Do you have any reason to suspect otherwise?"

"Other than the situation?" Wilder shook his head. "Armstrong's going to cancel the shoot."

"No. I told you. Everything goes as scheduled."

"And I asked you why, and you ignored it, so I'm ignoring you," Wilder said even as his brain supplied the answer: *Because you know Finnegan is close, you asshole.*

Crawford fixed Wilder with a stare that added ten years to his personality. "That's an order."

"You can order me," Wilder allowed, "but you can't order her."

"I can order you to persuade her."

"How?"

"Use your imagination," Crawford said. "If you haven't already."

Wilder didn't take the bait, and Crawford backed up slightly. "Listen, this is very important." He nodded toward the Jeep. "You get her back to wherever she belongs. Meet me at the diner in two hours. I'll explain it to you. For now, you need to maintain your cover."

Cover's blown, kid. Wilder shook his head and walked back to the Jeep.

"What did he want?" Lucy asked when he was sitting beside her again.

"He wants to meet me in two hours." He looked over at her. "That gives us plenty of time to roust Mary Vanity."

"Only if you tell me about Finnegan. I want to know everything."

Wilder put the Jeep in gear and drove north. "Finnegan was IRA—"

"Oh, hell." Lucy took a deep breath. "Sorry. Go on."

"Then he went freelance and now the CIA thinks he's laundering money through the film."

Lucy frowned. "So why don't they arrest him?"

"They don't have any proof, and they don't know where he is."

"Oh, just hell."

"They told me Finnegan wasn't even in the country. So either that's wrong or they lied to me, and right now I'm kind of evenly split on which it is." Wilder shook his head. "But there's something wrong with their theory because Finnegan needs fifty million, which he's not going to get from the movie."

"God, no. Nobody's going to get fifty million from this mess. What does he need it for?"

"He owes it to the Russian mob. Or at least part of it."

"The Russian mob?" Lucy said faintly.

"Finnegan stole fifty million dollars worth of Pre-Columbian jade phallic symbols for a Russian mob boss named Letsky who thinks they cure impotence. Then he lost them. And somehow what Finnegan's doing with this movie is going to help him make amends with Letsky."

Lucy looked over at him, dumbfounded. "We're going through this hell because some Russian mob guy can't get it up?"

Wilder thought about it. "Yeah."

Lucy still seemed dazed. "Pre-Columbian what again?"

"Jade phallic symbols. Basically, jade penises."

"Oh." Lucy nodded. "This is probably not the time to ask this, *but what the fuck is wrong with you men?*"

"Uh . . ."

"Nash is screwing everything that moves, Bryce is screwing everything that moves and asks for his autograph, LaFavre is screwing everything whether it moves or not, and now the Russian mob has hired Finnegan to make sure that—" She shook her head. "Even the Pre-Columbians had a dick fixation. What's next? Mother-of-pearl boobs?"

Damn good thing she doesn't know about Ginnie, Wilder thought.

"I just don't understand how you guys got control of the world," Lucy said. "Half the time there's no blood in your brains, and you're still in charge of most of the governments in the world, most of the companies, and all of the military." She blinked. "Which actually explains a lot, now that I think of it."

Wilder glanced over. She was staring through the windshield. He decided to go the opposite of the sledgehammer and remain silent.

They were passing the strip clubs that lined the road just before they hit the bridge and Georgia. The signs were old and worn, boasting totally nude entertainment, which was redundant to Wilder. He was sure LaFavre knew the interiors of all of them.

Probably not the time to mention that to Lucy.

Also, a good time to drop the CIA, Finnegan, and the Russians.

No discussions about foster care, either.

Nor anything about ex-wives.

Fuck, Wilder thought. *This is not good.*

They hit the ramp for the Talmadge and began climbing. To the left, coming upriver, was a cargo ship, the deck stacked with containers, a couple of tugs keeping it in the channel as it made its way to the port, to the right. That would be a good job. A simple job. Just keep a ship going in a straight line. No dealing with the CIA and Finnegan and whoever else was behind the scenes; he could do without all of them.

He glanced over at the passenger seat.

But not without Lucy.

It was a strange thought, the idea that he could see a future with her, maybe not as clearly as she could, but a definite possibility once they'd had some time together. That's what he should have said. Crap. He was just no good with women.

The two ex-wives were kind of a tip-off there, he supposed.

They crossed over the bridge in silence and pulled into the crew hotel parking lot before she spoke again.

"I think Stephanie took the rope."

"From Bryce's cable rig?"

Lucy nodded. "I think Nash sabotaged the rope and she took it to protect him or blackmail him or something. I sent her after the cable and when she brought it back the rope was gone, and I think she took it to use it to control him to save the movie. I think that's why he wrote her off. He wouldn't tolerate that." She shook her head. "We're not any brighter than you guys, when you get right down to it. Sex makes us all stupid. Love's even worse."

That sunk in. "I'm sorry."

"About what?"

He shifted in his seat. "Nash and Stephanie."

"That they were sleeping together?" She shook her head. "She could have him with my blessing. They deserve each other. But she didn't deserve this, and she didn't deserve to have him walk away from her like that." She looked over at Wilder. "I really want to bring him down. Him and Finnegan."

"I'm working on it." Wilder got out of the Jeep.

"How do you want to handle this?" Lucy asked.

"What?" Damn, he was sounding like Crawford now.

"Mary. What do we do?"

Wilder paused. His experience in interrogation had been in places where people shot at each other and the bad guys didn't wear uniforms. Probably not the best tactics to use on Mary. "Uh, Good Cop, Bad Cop?"

Lucy nodded. "Okay. Listen, I'm still really mad at you so I'll be the Bad Cop."

Wilder opened his mouth to say something, but Lucy was already heading for the door.

"Okay, then," he said and followed her in.

The first person Lucy saw in the lobby of the crew hotel was Bryce, trying to sneak out.

"I don't believe it," she told J.T. "I'm pretty sure he started the evening with Althea."

"Well, at least we know Mary Vanity is here," J.T. said.

"Bryce," Lucy called, and the actor jerked back so hard he almost levitated. Then he smiled weakly and waved at her. When she didn't wave back, he came over to join them.

"Lucy," he said, trying to fake delight.

"So how's Mary?" Lucy said, thinking, *Is there any guy left in my life with blood in his brain?*

"Aw, Lucy," Bryce said. "You know—"

"What I know," Lucy said severely, "is that Althea cares for you, that she's ready to settle down with somebody she loves, and that you're cheating on her. Now, what do you know?"

Bryce blinked. "Settle down?"

Lucy sighed. "Bryce, you could have the wedding America dreams about. Stop screwing around and think about Althea." When he still looked confused, she added, "Think about your career. Pick a magazine to do the exclusive on the wedding."

"Oh." Bryce looked thoughtful. "I hadn't thought about the PR. I was just thinking about the effect on the box office. Could be bad."

"So could discussion as to why you're thirty-seven and not married," Lucy said.

"Oh," Bryce said, looking even more thoughtful, which was obviously a strain.

"Stick with Althea," Lucy said.

Bryce nodded without so much as a backward glance in the direction of Mary Vanity's room. "Thanks, Lucy. I'll—"

"There's something else," Lucy said, and Bryce drew himself up, probably prepared to play the outraged star if she went too far. "Stephanie's been hurt," she said and watched him deflate. "She's in the hospital. She had an accident in Nash's van."

"My God," he said, but she could see the wheels turning even while he looked shocked, concerned, and saddened, all appropriate emotions he could project at the drop of a hat. He took her hand. "You know, Stephanie loves this movie. She would want us to keep filming."

Right, Lucy thought and took her hand back. "Do me a favor. Go back to the cast hotel and tell Althea and Rick when they wake up. You're the star, they'll want to hear it from you."

She watched him expand again.

"We're still shooting tonight, right?" he said. "I can tell them that?"

"Yes," J.T. said.

"I don't think so," Lucy said, ignoring him. "I'll know more later."

"Well," Bryce said. "We should keep shooting." He stopped, as if not sure what to say next, and then collected himself and said, "I'm glad you're here, Lucy. You're doing a great job, handling everything for us like a real pro. We know we can depend on you. I think I can speak for the rest of the cast when I say we all appreciate what you've done for us, and we know you'll be there for us tonight."

"Uh huh," Lucy said, not particularly gratified to know she existed to serve. "Thank you very much." She nodded toward the door. "Best get back to the cast hotel before anybody wakes up."

"Right," Bryce said and then stopped. "How did I find out about Stephanie?"

"I called you," Lucy said. "Because—"

"—I'm the star!" Bryce said, nodding. "Thanks, Lucy."

"You bet," Lucy said and watched him go. She thought about what his face would have looked like if she'd started rattling off the night-mares that had their fingers in his movie. "The CIA is not SAG, Bryce," she could have said. "The Russian mob is not looking for a piece of the back end."

And the Teamsters had not taken out Stephanie.

Lucy took a deep breath.

"Now we go squeeze Mary Vanity," J.T. said.

"I'm pretty sure Bryce just did that," Lucy said and followed him across the lobby.

When Mary Vanity answered the door in her robe, she was beaming. Then she realized they weren't Bryce.

"Hi," Lucy said, feeling guilty about sending Bryce off to Althea until she remembered who Mary had been talking to. The hell with her, the little mole. "We have a few questions."

Mary's face had fallen when she'd recognized them, but now it hit the floor. "I have a right to my private life," she said, chin down.

"Of course you do." Lucy pushed past her into the room, where the bed showed every sign of having been slept in by one person. No romping. Poor Mary. "It's your phone life we're objecting to," she said, turning in time to see J.T. look at her in warning. *Yeah, yeah, okay, partnership, but I'm the Bad Cop.* "Captain Wilder has some questions."

He looked startled and then recovered enough to smile at Mary. He looked about as comfortable smiling at Mary as Mary did having them in her room. "We know you've been talking to Mr. Finnegan, Mary."

Mary flushed and ducked her head lower. "Have not."

This should be good, Lucy thought, folding her arms. *Rambo meets Jessica Simpson.*

"I realize you thought it was harmless," J.T. went on, his voice gentle. "But Mr. Finnegan is not a movie backer, he's a terrorist."

Mary jerked her head up. "No. No, he's *Irish.*"

This is going to take a while, Lucy thought and sat down.

J.T. nodded. "Yes, he was with the IRA and now he's with the Russian mob. They're laundering money through the movie."

Mary swallowed. "I don't even know what that means. I don't know anything about this."

J.T. nodded again. "What he's really doing is using the movie as a front for the Russian mob."

Mary blinked. "I don't know any Russians."

"You do now," Lucy said grimly. "And these aren't fun-loving, vodka-toasting Russians. These guys kill people." She leaned forward. "And you're helping them."

"No." Mary moved closer to J.T., shaking her head. "No, no. I didn't do anything."

J.T. smiled, which Lucy supposed was intended as reassurance. He really had to work on that.

"Mary, we know you called Finnegan when Stephanie took the van," he said, his voice full of understanding.

"And you told him when Captain Wilder came on the set." Lucy made her voice as sharp as possible. "Bryce told you he was here, didn't he? And you told Finnegan, and then the next day somebody pulled *a knife* on them in a bar." She saw Mary's eyes flicker. "You almost got Bryce *killed,* Mary."

"No," Mary moaned.

"And yesterday when Bryce fell off the helicopter . . ." Lucy shook her head. "I don't know how he's going to take it when he finds out you're responsible for him getting hurt *twice.*"

"No, *wait.*" Mary stood up. Her robe fell open and Lucy expected J.T. to look politely at the ceiling but instead he looked into her eyes.

"We know you'd never hurt Bryce," he said, and Mary nodded like a bobble-head, stepping closer to him as she pulled her robe together.

That robe falling open was no accident, Lucy thought, and then remembered she was the Bad Cop. "How do we know that?" she said to J.T. "It's because of *her* that Bryce's been hurt twice. I think it's our duty to tell him about her. She's with *the mob.* She could be setting up an ambush in her room." *Although why the Russian mob would want to take out Bryce is a mystery.*

Lucy straightened, trying for indignation. "She could be part of a plot to ruin the movie by *killing Bryce.*"

"No, no, *no,*" Mary said, blinking her false eyelashes as she moved another step closer to J.T.

Does she sleep in those? Lucy thought and then decided she probably did, in case Bryce stopped by.

"I'm sure Mary meant no harm," J.T. said, going for noble understanding. He was going to have to work on that, too. "Right, Mary?"

"Mr. Finnegan gave me ten thousand to tell him what was happening on the set," Mary said. "He didn't ask me to do anything except tell him what was going on, if anything new happened, what Nash was doing."

Hello, Lucy thought. *Doesn't trust Nash. Smart Irishman.*

"And I really needed the money," Mary was saying to J.T. "Bryce likes big boobs and I'm only a B cup, but he doesn't like the cheap ones so I needed enough money for the expensive ones."

J.T. blinked. "There are different kinds?"

Hey, Lucy thought. *Off topic here.*

"It's really the surgery," Mary Vanity said, confiding in him. "In the cheap ones, they just cut open your boob and put the implant in so you can see the scar."

"And the expensive ones?" Lucy asked, not wanting to ask but helpless not to.

"They go in, like, through your stomach," Mary said. "No scar. Much better."

Lucy put her hand on her stomach. "Right." She looked at J.T. "I am never getting implants."

He looked confused. "Why would you?"

"Well, she's only a C cup," Mary said. "I mean, right?"

"Right." Lucy crossed her arms over her chest.

"Bryce likes Ds," Mary said, helpfully.

"Uh huh." J.T. was clearly sorry about the turn the conversation had taken. "I don't think there's any need to tell Bryce any of this."

"Oh, *thank you!*" Mary Vanity said, clutching his arm.

"As long as you give us Finnegan's phone number," J.T. said.

"Sure." Mary pushed past him to grab her bag, a pink leather number with the initial M on it, the hot trend in purses from 2003. "Here it is." She shoved a piece of paper at J.T.

"It would be better if you didn't tell Mr. Finnegan we talked to you," J.T. said. "In fact, it would be better if you didn't call him again at all."

"Oh no," Mary said and swallowed. "Never again. Ever. You won't tell Bryce?"

"No," J.T. said.

"What about you?" Mary said to Lucy.

"My lips are sealed as long as yours are," Lucy said. "But if you call Finnegan again, Bryce gets the whole thing, storyboarded with sound effects."

"I won't, I *won't*." Mary's face crumpled. "Except I think he's going to marry Althea anyway. If I'd just gotten the money sooner, if I'd just had the *boobs* . . ."

"Maybe yours will be better," Lucy said. "Does she have the expensive ones?"

"Yes," Mary and J.T. said together.

Lucy looked at J.T. with what she sincerely hoped was contempt.

J.T. said, "We have to go now."

"We certainly do," Lucy said, glaring at him.

"Should I be on the set tonight?" Mary said, pitifully.

"No," Lucy said as J.T. said, "Yes," and Lucy glared at him again.

"We're probably not going to shoot tonight," Lucy said. "Stay by the phone and Gloom will call you if we need you."

"We're shooting," J.T. said.

"Stay by the phone," Lucy said and all but shoved J.T. out the door.

"I say we're not shooting," she told him when they were alone in the hall. "So stop undermining me."

"Lucy, you're going to have to," J.T. said. "Call Finnegan and set up a meet."

"What?"

"The people I work for would like to know where Finnegan is," J.T. said patiently. "Set up a meet for this afternoon."

"I am also the people you work for," Lucy said.

"Tell him if he doesn't meet, you won't shoot tonight," J.T. said. "You'll like that."

Lucy leaned against the flocked wallpaper. "You really think we really have to film tonight?"

"Not if we nab Finnegan beforehand."

Lucy took out her cell phone and held out her hand for the paper with Finnegan's number. "I refuse to do anything that might mean somebody is going to get hurt."

"Nobody's going to get hurt," J.T. began.

"I thought you weren't going to lie to me anymore," Lucy said and punched in the numbers.

"I hope," J.T. finished.

"Yeah, me too," Lucy said, and then Finnegan answered and she went to work.

Wilder dropped Lucy off at the camper so she could call the hospital to check on Stephanie and take Daisy and Pepper back to the crew hotel. Then he went to the diner to meet Crawford. He took the seat across from the agent and said, "So which alphabet soup are you?"

"What?"

Some things never changed. "Your ID this morning was FBI. You told me you were CIA. Or is it NSA? DEA? NRA? ASPCA?"

"Oh, I'm CIA," Crawford said. "I pulled the FBI ID because I didn't know who I'd be talking to. I'd just come from the accident scene and needed cover. People tend to get nervous when they see CIA."

Especially since the CIA wasn't legally allowed to act inside the borders. And if Crawford was carrying FBI ID, he was a leg up on the usual CIA clown. It meant he had official cover for action. "Was it an accident?"

"Yes."

"You sound very sure."

"The police forensics people went over the car and the accident scene. She hit the side of the bridge. Must have dozed off."

A rope breaks. A skid snaps. A driver dozes off. Three accidents. Three strikes. And now Finnegan was looming, which he imagined was the CIA's plan all along. Wilder tried to relax his back, resisting the desire to look over his shoulder. "Finnegan is coming this afternoon."

Crawford's eyes widened and Wilder glanced to his rear. Nobody with guns barging in.

"No shit?"

"Lucy—" He stopped. "Armstrong called him and told him she was shutting down the film. He insisted on meeting her. Today."

"Where? When?"

"We don't know yet. He'll call her back with that."

Crawford leaned back in his seat. Wilder watched his eyes. They were scanning the room even as he was thinking.

He didn't just learn that, Wilder thought. *Fuck-head's been playing me so I'd be off guard.*

"Okay," Crawford finally said. "Would she be willing to wear a wire and plant a bug?"

"You don't need to wire her."

"Why not?"

"Because I'm going to the meeting with her. And you're not wiring me either. Because you're arresting Finnegan, right?"

"Wrong."

"Why not?"

"Finnegan is just a piece of the puzzle." Crawford began to look less self-possessed. "We have bigger fish to fry."

Fuck. "You want Letsky. This whole circus is about Letsky."

"Right."

Lucy was going to be pissed. Wilder shook his head. "I don't see how—"

Crawford leaned forward. "Letsky has set up a meeting with Finnegan for midnight. We want that meeting."

Double fuck—Lucy was going to be really pissed. Not that she wasn't furious already. "Letsky's close by?"

"Given the timing of the meeting, yes. We suspect he's offshore, in international waters."

"So why don't you just go to the meeting place and take Letsky down?"

"We don't know where it is. We know when. Finnegan knows where. Could be anywhere within a couple hours' flying time. That's a big damn circle to cover."

"Why are they meeting?"

Crawford drummed his fingers on the table for several moments. "Finnegan owes Letsky and he's going to repay him."

"Fifty million?" Wilder asked. "Where'd he get that kind of money?"

"Not money," Crawford said. "Finnegan's giving Letsky the art he originally bought."

Wilder rubbed his forehead where a headache was beginning to pulse. "How?"

"Using the chopper in the movie stunt."

That's why they need the cargo net. But it still made no sense. "I thought the art was seized in Mexico. Where's it at right now?"

Crawford smiled. "You don't need to worry about that."

"What do I need to worry about other than you lying to me?"

"I didn't lie. I just didn't tell you the truth. You didn't have a need to know."

Wilder wondered how much more was going on that Crawford had determined he didn't have a need to know. Of course there was no point in asking that, because he didn't have a need to know. Spooks and their games.

Crawford reached under the table and Wilder tensed, but the CIA man pulled out a small metal case and placed it on the worn surface. He paused as the waitress came by and refilled their coffees. Then he opened the lid, revealing several objects set in foam padding.

"Tracking transmitter," Crawford said, tapping a dime-sized device. He touched the cigarette-pack-size unit. "Tracking receiver." He pointed at two smaller white pieces. "Extra batteries for the tracker. You shouldn't need them. This will all be over within twenty-four hours." He shut the lid and slid it across the table to Wilder.

"What or who do you want me to bug?" Wilder asked.

"Finnegan, of course, since you're going to the meeting and you won't let us wire you. I was going to have you put it on Nash, but we only needed him to lead us to Finnegan. Now that you've got Finnegan . . ." Crawford shrugged.

Wilder felt three steps behind and he didn't like it. "What's Nash's role in this?"

"He's getting Finnegan to the meeting with Letsky."

Wilder shook his head. "This is a pretty elaborate setup just for a helicopter ride. He could hire anybody for that."

"Oh, Finnegan is indeed laundering money through the film," Crawford said. "Two birds with one stone. He still has to make a living. He's been paying Letsky enough to keep him off his ass long enough to make restitution. Finnegan needs the helicopter scene for that. Law enforcement tends to get curious about helicopters buzzing bridges and the swamp, but not if it's a movie shoot."

"So during the last stunt tonight, Nash and Finnegan are going to take the chopper and fly to meet Letsky somewhere?"

"Right."

"Why does he need Nash?"

"It's complicated."

No shit. "Why don't you just take down Finnegan this afternoon and squeeze him for the location of the meeting?"

"Because Letsky will disappear if word of the takedown gets to him. You know how dangerous those kinds of ops are. And what if the squeeze doesn't work?"

Everyone talks if you apply the right amount of pressure. "I don't—"

"I don't care what you don't, Wilder," Crawford said. "I've already told you more than you need to know. The rest is none of your business."

Wilder resisted the urge to punch him. Probably get him another check in the column marked PROBLEMS DEALING WITH AUTHORITY FIGURES. Although if he showed them Crawford, they'd understand.

"Do you understand me, Captain Wilder?"

"None of this is my business," Wilder told him and walked out.

16

"So you're going to make nice when we go to the meet," Wilder said to Lucy when he'd met her back at the camper and explained it all to her.

"Why?" Lucy had that stubborn look again. "Why can't I just tell Finnegan it's over? He's not going to be suing me if he's got the Russian mob on his butt. I think it's definitely past time to cut our losses. Stephanie's going to be okay, Bryce didn't get hurt, you didn't get knifed, so I'm thinking we're pushing our luck here if we keep going. Let Finnegan have his stupid helicopter without my people on the bridge. We can put up the lights so the cops think we're shooting and then just leave—"

Wilder shook his head. "No good. We can't spook them with the change in plans. The stunt has to go off, and then Nash will take Finnegan to Letsky, probably with the jade in the cargo net. Letksy is a bad guy and he needs to go down, Luce. We have to do this."

Lucy took a deep breath. "I'm having a bad day."

Wilder nodded. "I need you to play nice when he calls with the meet location. Follow my lead. Do not tell him you're shutting down the movie unless I say that's what you're going to do. Let me handle this." He saw her face flush and added, "It's my mission, Lucy. To-night it's your movie, but today it's my mission."

"No," Lucy said. "Tonight it's my movie, but today it's my crew, my cast, my family, my people. I am not sacrificing anybody for the fucking CIA."

She shifted away from him, and he slid his arm around her and pulled her close, needing her warmth next to him.

"I'm not the CIA," he said, looking into her eyes. "I'm on your side. You have to trust me."

"Right," she said. "So about these two ex-wives—"

Her cell phone rang.

"That's Finnegan," Wilder said, and let her go. "Answer it."

Lucy took a deep breath and answered the phone.

Wilder drove up to the entrance to the Savannah Wildlife Refuge, fol-lowing the directions Finnegan had given Lucy, and stopped the Jeep.

"What's wrong?" Lucy asked.

What's right? Swamp mixed with forest lay all around. Indian country, his team sergeant would have said—perfect for an ambush. A metal bar was slid off to one side and a sign warned that the refuge closed at dark. Another sign indicated the road through the refuge was one-way. They had passed the exit about a half mile north of here. Bad omens, both of them.

"J.T.?"

Wilder tried to give Lucy his "no problem" smile but it was one he couldn't remember using before so he wasn't sure how it went over. "Everything's cool." He wondered if that qualified as lying as he drove down the gravel road that was set on top of a berm with swamp on either side. He slammed on the brakes as the metal bar rattled shut behind them. An even worse omen.

"Uh, still cool?" Lucy asked, her voice a little higher than usual.

A trap or somebody just making sure no one else joined the meet-ing? And who had shut it? Someone who had surveillance on them.

He did not like that at all. He slowly looked about. The cranes in the port to the south. The paper-mill towers. Hell, someone could be in the swamp itself with an angle on the road. Could even be Moot, lying out there licking her chops for her next meal to come down the road. Of all the possibilities, Wilder liked the idea of facing Moot the best. At least he knew what to expect with a gator, having been fully briefed by Pepper at lunch after she'd run out of Wonder Woman facts. Wilder smiled grimly. Pepper was better than Crawford at intelligence.

"J.T.?" Lucy's voice cut through the stillness.

This was why they'd used hand and arm signals on his old team and nobody had spoken when they were tactical. "It's all right." He opened the metal box between the seats and took out a Beretta 9-mm pistol in a well-worn leather holster. He pulled the gun out of the holster, checked the magazine, chambered a round, then flipped the gun and held it by the barrel, the grip toward Lucy. "Here."

She looked at him as if he were nuts. "This is your version of 'It's all right'?"

"Just in case," he said, extending the gun farther.

She took it reluctantly. "I thought you weren't going to give up your gun to anyone else again?"

Women and their memories. Never cut a guy any slack about the past. "It's my backup gun. You can have my primary if you want. Anything for you."

"That's really sweet, J.T." Lucy looked at the gun as if it were going to bite her. "Next time, try jewelry."

"Safety is on," Wilder said, pointing. "Flip it and then pull the trigger. There is a round in the chamber, so be careful. You have fifteen bullets."

"And double-tap, right?"

So she had been listening. "Yep." He took the gun back, slid it into the holster, then gave it back to her. "Loop your belt through this. Strong hand side."

As Lucy armed herself with no enthusiasm, he put the Jeep in gear and drove. He felt like he was back in Iraq, waiting for a roadside bomb to go off. But Finnegan wouldn't do that. He needed Lucy. He wanted this meeting to convince her to go with the stunt and they had already decided to go with the stunt, so everything was going to be fine. *Right,* Wilder thought to himself. Lucy lifted her shirt over the holster, hiding it from sight, but there was a distinctive bulge. "Don't take the gun out unless you mean to shoot and don't shoot unless you mean to kill."

"That will be never."

Her face was tense and he felt bad. The only sound was the tires' crunch on the gravel. The road went into a patch of trees, and Wilder used one hand to pull out his Glock and place it between his legs, at the ready.

Lucy drew back a little. "Should I do that? I am not going to shoot anybody but should—"

Wilder shook his head. "You're the backup. Finnegan will expect me to be packing. You, he'll wonder about."

"I'm wondering about me too," Lucy said. "Two days ago I was making a movie, then I hooked up with you, and now I'm carrying a gun to meet an international thief."

"Yeah, sorry," Wilder said but she kept going.

"You know, when I thought about us together, I figured I'd probably have to jump out of a plane for our anniversary or something, but I never thought the first thing you gave me would have a safety."

That's good, Wilder thought. *She's making jokes.* He stole a glance at her. He thought they were jokes. "My life has never been dull."

Lucy gave him a look. "How about we compromise from now on and go for 'not facing death daily'?"

They cleared the patch of trees and saw two hundred yards of straight road through the swamp before the next stand of foliage. The old oak trees they were approaching were so large that the gravel road was a pathway into a green tunnel. They entered and Wilder rolled the Jeep to a stop because there was Finnegan, sitting on the hood of a maroon Jaguar, wearing a loud blue Hawaiian shirt under an expensive-looking jacket and smoking a large cigar. A cane with a silver tip and a silver handle shaped like a stallion's head was within his reach. He looked like a rich, badly dressed Jolly St. Nick. An asshole, Wilder instinctively felt.

The sign behind Finnegan's car where the forest met the swamp read, IT IS A VIOLATION OF STATE & FEDERAL LAW TO FEED OR HARASS ALLIGATORS. Too bad. Finnegan looked big enough to keep a couple of them stocked for the winter.

Lucy got out of the car and went toward him.

"You're even more beautiful than your picture," Finnegan said to her, grabbing his cane in his left hand and leaning on it as he slid off the hood of his car. He switched his cigar to his cane hand and extended his right hand toward her, but Wilder noticed that the Irishman's clear blue eyes were on him.

Lucy did not take his hand. "You wanted to meet me?"

"Ah, Lucy, my darlin'," Finnegan said with a heavy brogue, which Wilder also figured was bullshit.

"You've been threatening me for two days," Lucy said. "Don't call me darling."

Wilder scanned the area, but there was no obvious security, even though he was sure Finnegan was not out here on his own. He slid his Glock back into the holster and got out of the Jeep.

"Oh, darlin', that's how business is." Finnegan shifted the cigar to his right hand again and gestured toward Wilder. "And who might this strapping lad be?"

"My friend," Lucy said. "Captain Wilder."

"Captain Wilder." Finnegan didn't bother to extend his hand toward Wilder. "I've heard of you." He drew hard on his cigar and looked back at Lucy. "And why do we need a captain of the Army here at a nice civilized meeting?"

"This isn't civilized," Lucy said, her eyes steady on him.

"Your 'friend,' eh?" Finnegan put just the right spin on the word to let them know he knew what their relationship was. "And poor Connor? Is he not your 'friend'?"

"No." Lucy looked annoyed, which was better than afraid, but not by much, Wilder thought. "Mr. Finnegan, people on my movie are getting hurt."

"Unfortunate," Finnegan said affably. "But accidents will happen. Nothing to do with me."

Lucy drew in her breath, and Wilder knew she was going to blow. He walked past Finnegan and checked out the car. "Nice wheels."

"You admire a fine automobile, Captain Wilder?" Finnegan said, turning away from Lucy as if she didn't matter.

"No. But since you want to talk bullshit, I thought I'd join in."

Finnegan nodded. "Ah, a man who likes to get to business quickly." He turned back to Lucy. "This really isn't negotiable, Lucy. We have a contract."

Lucy shook her head. "Oh, no. You—"

Wilder moved next to her, trying to draw Finnegan's attention. "Why are you so concerned about this movie being finished?"

"I want to see my name on a movie screen." Finnegan shrugged, tapping cigar ash on the ground. "Glory, if you will. An old man's whimsy."

"No," Lucy said.

Women. Wilder kept his face impassive.

"Lass—"

Lucy rolled over him. "The last time we did a stunt, we had injuries. We almost lost our lead actor. And now somebody's in the hospital."

Finnegan smiled at her over his cigar. "Lucy darling, I cannot be held accountable for someone falling asleep at the wheel. That happens every day."

"Not to people on my crew. Not like this. Nor do I have meetings in swamps every day." She shook her head, furious. "This is ridiculous. I—"

"We'd like a guarantee," Wilder said, his hand in his pocket, palming the bug Crawford had given him. "Nobody else gets hurt. Whatever it is that you're doing, you do away from the cast and crew."

He smiled, which made Finnegan pull back a little. Now all he had to do was figure out how to plant it on Finnegan. It didn't look like they were going to be hugging when they split, and pointing at the sky and saying, *Look, Halley's Comet!* didn't appear to be a good move, either.

Finnegan nodded, leaning forward, one hand on the silver handle of his cane. "Just finish the movie and all will be well. I'll throw in a one-hundred-thousand-dollar bonus for you, deposited right after you finish filming tonight."

While you're flying away? Wilder glanced at Lucy, hoping she kept her cool.

She looked enraged. "You think I'll risk my people for *money?*"

She was practically spitting, so Wilder figured it was time for a little interference for his wingwoman. "You keep the action away from the civilians, and the movie will be done tonight."

"The hell it will," Lucy said, turning on him. "I decide—"

Finnegan's eyes narrowed as he pointed his cigar at her. "I decide. It's my movie, lass. My money. *My* movie."

Wilder noticed that the brogue faded with the rise in anger.

"Then *you* film it tonight," Lucy said.

Finnegan swung his cane up and shoved the tip at Lucy. "You do what I tell you—"

Thank you. Wilder snatched the cane, palmed the end of it, and then twirled it and put the point on Finnegan's throat. "Talk nice to the lady. Or else."

Finnegan froze, his eyes small and hard. "Are you threatening me? Boyo, you have no idea who you are messing with."

Wilder nodded. Then he reversed the cane and offered the handle to Finnegan. "Sorry. Just concerned for the lady's welfare."

"I'm still here," Lucy said, her eyes flat on Finnegan. "And I can take care of myself. This is ridiculous."

Then do what we talked about and agree to finish the damn movie, Wilder thought as Finnegan took his cane back.

"The movie will be done tonight," Wilder said once more, with a glance at Lucy. Her face was flushed with anger.

Lucy looked furious. "I do n—"

Wilder put his arm around her and squeezed her shoulder. "Lucy knows I'll be keeping an eye on everybody's safety, and now with your guarantee, she'll finish the shoot. *Right, Lucy?*"

The silence stretched out, and then she nodded once, sharply.

"So there is no problem," Wilder said. *Except that I have to face this woman alone in a minute.*

Finnegan looked back and forth between the two of them, then he slowly nodded also. "Very good."

Wilder stepped away from Lucy. "Time to go."

When she didn't move, he tapped her arm, and she pivoted and stalked back to the Jeep. Fortunately, it didn't have a door for her to slam. Wilder nodded at Finnegan before getting into the driver's seat. He carefully drove around the Jaguar and then accelerated away, looping around toward the exit gate.

"What part of 'follow my lead' didn't you get?" Wilder asked Lucy.

Lucy turned eyes like razors on him. "The part where you suck up to the bad guy, boss me around, and put my team in danger." She was so mad, she practically bounced in the seat. "You saw him, J.T. He doesn't give a damn about anybody; he'd blow up the whole set if it'd get him what he wanted. That son of a bitch is a lying, thieving bastard, and you're flipping his cane around like a majorette on speed and then giving it back to him like—"

"Hey." Wilder held up the small tracker Crawford had given him. "What's that?"

"A tracker. Homes in on a small transmitter—a bug. That I just planted on Finnegan."

Lucy blinked. "When did you do that?"

"Just now. On his cane. Under the horse's head."

"Oh." Lucy's face eased. "Oh. That was pretty good." She looked over at him. "You think he's going to keep his word?"

"I think so," Wilder said. "It gets him nowhere to hurt people on the movie, Lucy. He just wants his helicopter so he can do what he needs to do."

"Which is?" Lucy said.

"Meet Letsky somewhere with the damn art."

Lucy took a deep breath. "All right. All right then."

"Plus, LaFavre will back me up if I need him."

"That hound?"

"He's the best at what he does," Wilder said. "We've been in some rough places together and we're both still breathing and have all our working parts because we have each other's backs."

Lucy considered that. "Okay. So now you tell me what the plan is for tonight. You do have a plan, right?"

"Right," Wilder lied.

"Good," Lucy said. "I'm waiting."

"Give me a minute." *A plan,* Wilder thought, and concentrated on that all the way back to the hotel.

Wilder was in Lucy's hotel room, checking his gun and trying to fig-ure out all the places the plan he'd come up with could go wrong, when she came out of the bathroom wearing a thick, fluffy white robe, looking delicious with no makeup, her long, dark hair wet from her shower.

Different plan, he thought, but the look she gave him was cool.

"What are you doing?" she said, dropping her eyes to the Glock.

"I called room service," he said, trying not to think about how naked she was under the robe.

"Oh." Lucy nodded at the gun. "Usually you don't shoot them. Tipping is good, though."

Somebody knocked on the door, and Wilder got up and hovered near Lucy's shoulder as she checked the peephole.

"It's the waiter," she said, patiently.

"All right, all right." Wilder put the gun back in the holster as he went back toward the window. Lucy signed the check and thanked the waiter, and when Wilder fumbled for his wallet, she said, "I tipped him on the check."

Damn. He'd have to learn how to do room service. Lucy tied the sash on her robe tighter and smiled at him. It wasn't the warmest smile she'd ever given him, but it was a smile.

Lots of room service, he thought.

As the door shut, Lucy turned over two cups on the tray and poured them each some coffee from the large white carafe. "You're better with your gun than your wallet."

"I told you, I never had room service before."

"Where have you been staying? Under a rock?"

"Almost. Afghanistan. Iraq. Kuwait. Thailand. Other places. No room service." The coffee was good, Wilder thought as he drained the tiny cup in one gulp.

"I can just give you the pot and you can drink from there." This time her smile was better.

"So we okay?" he asked, and her smile faded.

"Yeah."

Damn. He sat down on the edge of the bed. "Look, I'm sorry I didn't tell you about my two ex-wives, but you have to trust me."

"I do," she said, not meeting his eyes as she picked up her cup.

"No, you don't," he said. "And that's going to be a problem."

"Tonight?" She shook her head. "I'm not stupid, I'll do what you tell me."

"Not just tonight. After tonight."

"There is no after tonight." She sipped her coffee, staring out the window. "I think you made that pretty clear."

"No, I didn't," he said, exasperated. "I said we had to take it slow."

"Well, I'm leaving tomorrow." She turned back to him, her brows snapping together. "You take it slow, and I'll wave to you from New York."

Fuck. "Lucy—"

"I'm sorry," she said, putting down the cup. "I know we don't have time for this. Look, I'm mad, and I know that's dumb. I trust you not to lie to me. I'll do what you tell me to. But I know that if it comes down to me or the mission, it'll be the mission. That's just who you are. This is a professional relationship, not—"

"No," Wilder said and meant it.

"It was out there with Finnegan. You were all business out there."

He shook his head. "I honestly believe you and everybody else will be safe tonight. It would work against Finnegan to hurt anybody. He doesn't want cops and medics and firefighters on that bridge. He just wants his helicopter in the air with the movie shooting so he can fly over the swamp without anybody getting suspicious."

"The swamp." Lucy nodded. "That's where Nash is picking up Finnegan?"

"I'm guessing in the Wildlife Refuge. That's why we shot those helicopter scenes there." *And why Karen was programming her GPS with waypoints.*

"So that's it? Nash gets on the helicopter and flies off with Karen to pick up Finnegan?"

"With Karen and Doc. To pick up Finnegan and his goons and the art. Yeah. And then to wherever Letsky is. And the rest of us go home. They have no reason to hurt anybody, Lucy, and lots of reasons not to."

She nodded, and then came over and sat down beside him on the bed, which pretty much wrecked that train of thought. A strand of her hair slipped over her shoulder and caught on the terrycloth of the robe. He wanted to reach out and stroke it back, but he wasn't sure. *Wait.*

"That makes sense," she said. "But if something goes wrong—"

"Then it's over. We evacuate the bridge and everybody goes home." He felt a chill. She'd go back to New York, just like she'd said. That was something they'd have to work out. He wasn't sure what his future held, but with her sitting close, he was suddenly damn sure it held Lucy.

"Okay." She smiled at him weakly. "I trust you." She lifted her chin and kissed him, and he closed his eyes and thought, *No, you don't.* "I'm sorry I was so bitchy about the ex-wives," she said softly. "You're right, I moved too fast and didn't give you any time. Hell, I stalked you in the swamp. So I'm sorry about that—"

"I'm not," Wilder said, alarmed.

"—And about moving too fast and thinking this is more than it is, which is two healthy people enjoying a quick fling."

"Lucy," he said, "that's not—"

"And now here we are," she said brightly, "all alone in a hotel room with a perfectly good bed and a couple of hours to kill. And I have to tell you, last night was good. So I don't think we should waste this, do you? Nothing beyond right now, no future, just this for right now."

"Lucy—"

"Do you want me?"

"God, yes," Wilder said.

"Well, then." Lucy began to untie the belt to her robe.

He stopped her. "Wait a minute."

Her strained smile evaporated. "Don't tell me. No sex before the big game." She retied her belt. "Fine."

"You don't trust me," he said. "And you're not the kind of woman who's going to be happy having sex with somebody she doesn't trust."

Lucy looked exasperated. "I told you—"

"Prove it," he said.

"What?"

He got up and went to her duffel bag and looked through it until he found her WonderWear and under that her gold-painted Lasso of Truth.

"Uh, J.T.?" she said. "You're not going to be one of those guys who can only get it up if I'm in costume, are you?"

He dropped the WonderWear back in her bag and picked up the rope. Then he crooked his finger at her.

"Oh." She cleared her throat. "Well, it's not that I'm not, you know, interested." She looked at the rope in his hand with grave doubt. "Well, actually, I'm not."

"Do you trust me?" he said.

"Yes. But . . ."

He held out his hand and after a moment she stood and took it, and he pulled her to him, closing his eyes as she sank against him, soft and warm. "I said we should take it slow, Lucy. I never said it was a one-night stand or that we didn't have a future. We have a future."

"Oh." She swallowed. "So where does the rope come in our future?"

He gently pressed her toward the window, drawing shut the heavy curtain with one hand as he did so. "I do my best work in the dark."

"Well," she said, her voice going higher, "that was certainly true last night, but—"

"Shh." Wilder kissed her again, biting her lip softly as he felt her relax against him. "Do you trust me?"

"Yes," she whispered. "I really do. But this—"

He dropped the lasso on the table beside them, and she relaxed a little. Then he pulled a long piece of mesh camouflage out of his pocket and doubled, then tripled it, and she tensed again.

"Uh, J.T.—"

"You trust me?"

Lucy looked at the camouflage, uncertain. "Yes, but—"

Wilder placed the cloth across her eyes.

"Um—"

"No buts," he said. "You either trust me or you don't." He wrapped the cloth around to the back of her head and tied a simple knot. "I got this cloth in Denmark. Combat Swim School. We used it to cover our faces when we—"

"Tell me this is not your idea of talking dirty," she said, and he smiled.

With one hand he pulled her wrists over her head and with the other retrieved the rope from the table. "The Lasso of Truth, babe," he whispered in her ear and made her shiver as he looped it around her wrists.

"Well," Lucy said, but she didn't resist, biting her lip instead. He tied a loose knot, then tossed the other end over the curtain rod, looping it over the tie-back by the window frame.

Lucy said, "You know, there is a bed and it's—"

He tugged on the lasso ever so slightly, and Lucy sucked in her breath as her arms were drawn tighter. He lowered his head, still holding one end of the lasso, and kissed her in the hollow of her throat.

"Oh, God," she said and grabbed on to the curtain, bunching it above her head where the rope held her hands.

"You can trust me," he said. "I will never hurt you, I will never betray you, and I will always get you where you need to go."

He tied off the rope on the curtain tie-back and then loosened her belt, and her robe parted as he slid his tongue lower, tracing the inner curve of her right breast. Her body tightened under his hands as he lightly nibbled and kissed her nipple, and he felt her tremble against him, making little noises in the back of her throat. Then he went down to his knees and lowered his head and made her gasp again, and she tasted fresh and clean as he went between her legs, his hands sliding around her hips to grasp her ass tightly, not allowing her to move.

He tuned in to her breathing, soft and rapid, his tongue tasting her, moving inside her as her breaths changed to shallow sobs. After several minutes, she breathed, "Oh, God, *stop,*" and he ignored her, focusing on what he felt from her, not what he heard, the rhythm of her gasps, the quiver of her muscles. Then he felt her tense and shudder, crying out as she jerked hard against him, and the rod broke, and the curtain tumbled down, covering both of them as she collapsed and he caught her.

He laughed, her body hot on top of his, the thick curtain covering both of them. She was breathing hard, and he rolled her to one side and held her in his arms, resting his head against her long, powerful thighs, catching his breath, too.

"Wow," Lucy said and he laughed again.

Then he threw the curtain off and the late afternoon light cast a glow over her, magic, as she pulled the blindfold off and smiled at him, drowsy with satisfaction. He got to his feet, pulling her up warm into his arms. He tugged her toward the bed and tripped over the Lasso of Truth so that they tumbled onto the mattress in a heap with him on top.

Wilder began laughing again and pulled the lasso from her wrists, leaving traces of gold paint there, markings he'd put on her, but she caught it before he could toss it away, propping herself up on her elbows under him, her mouth almost on his, her eyes half closed and dark.

"Lasso of Truth, Captain Wilder?" she said, her voice soft with heat. "Do you trust me?"

"Yes," Wilder said with a smile.

"We'll see about that," she said and rolled so that he was under her, reaching for his wrists.

And then he forgot the CIA, Finnegan, the Russian mob, and everything else on earth but Lucy.

17

Three hours later, Wilder woke up, tangled in warm bedclothes and a warmer Lucy. He didn't want to move. Ever. If he could just stay there forever, he'd give anything. He looked down at Lucy, her head resting on his chest, her breathing slow and steady, with the slightest hint of a snore now and then, which made him smile.

This trust thing. It was good. And the distant future, that was looking pretty good, too.

But the clock on the side of the bed was ticking. The sun was going down and shooting would begin soon—film shooting only, hopefully. He thought about rousing Lucy, but he didn't want to. She was so sweet when she was asleep. So soft.

So not busting his chops for making her risk the lives of people she cared about to shill for the CIA.

Well, hell, that was his duty. That's what he did, he answered the call of duty.

Lucy stirred next to him, nestling closer.

Maybe it was time for duty to shut the fuck up.

Of course, Crawford hadn't ordered him to do anything. He'd

planted the bug. That should be enough. But Wilder did not trust Finnegan and Nash. Or Crawford, for that matter. And the duty that was calling now was to the woman he had his arms wrapped around, whose head rested on his chest. He had to cover her, protect her from Murphy, that little fucking Irish gremlin that was going to screw things up because Finnegan and Nash were shifty, double-crossing bastards, both of them.

Her cell phone rang, breaking the warm silence with its ugly sound.

Lucy stirred and then sat up as the phone rang again, yawning, the covers falling off so that she was naked to the waist. Exquisite.

"What?" she said, still groggy.

God, you're beautiful.

She frowned at him, still half asleep, and fumbled for her phone. "Hello?" Then she pulled it away from her ear. "Stop shouting." She listened again, frowning harder, waking up. "No. I did not cancel the cargo net."

Wilder froze.

"Nash, the only thing I want to cancel is the shoot. I did not call the rental place and cancel your damn net. Now leave me alone." She punched the button to turn the phone off and then dropped it on the bedside table. "He's just getting crazier and crazier."

"What happened?"

Lucy shrugged, which was nice of her since she was topless. "Some woman called and canceled the cargo net. He thought it was me."

"Karen." Wilder got out of bed and went over to his pile of clothes and weapons and began to gear up, knowing that Murphy had just shown up, all flags flying.

Lucy looked bereft. "Where are you going?"

Wilder was strapping on his protective vest, securing the Velcro fasteners. "Finnegan. I've got to shake him. Squeeze him."

"What are you talking about?"

"Karen canceled the cargo net because she isn't going to need it. She should have just left it on the rental, but pilots are anal like that."

"What does that have to do with Finnegan?"

"The only reason she wouldn't need the cargo net is because she's going to have room in the helicopter for whatever she's bringing in. And the only reason she'd have room in the helicopter is because she's not going to have people in it."

Lucy blinked, still not getting it. "She's going alone?"

"She's going with Finnegan and cutting the rest of them out. Doc, Nash, God knows who else."

Lucy swallowed. "That's why Nash is so furious. He's being double-crossed."

"Yep." He finished securing the Velcro. "So I've got to find Finnegan and squeeze him before Nash does."

" 'Squeeze him'?"

"Put the fear in him."

Lucy was frowning. " 'The fear'? What fear?"

Wilder finished securing the Velcro. "That it's one thing to double-cross Nash, but if he messes with you, he messes with me. And then he is done."

"Oh." She nodded, a little wide-eyed. "So you've done this before."

Wilder considered the question. "Yes. But only for my team."

She nodded again and then tried to look unconcerned. "So I'm on your team now?"

"It's our team now, Lucy. You and me." He put the Glock in place. The ankle knife. His belt. He had to go to the cache and get the MP-5. He picked the tracker off the table and turned it on and then looked at her.

She was sitting frozen on the bed, cross-legged and half naked like some goddess, and she was looking at him with her heart in her eyes. "Our team," she said, her voice strange, and swallowed again. "Good." She swung her fist in front of her. "Go us." Then she bit her lip. "So where are you going without me?"

She still hadn't moved. Wilder wished she would put some clothes on. She was just too damn distracting sitting there like that. He held up the tracker. "From what this tells me, downtown Savannah. Wherever Finnegan is. Probably in some Irish pub."

He reached into a pocket, pulled out the coin he'd shown LaFavre, and tossed it to her.

She caught it, her breasts moving as she grabbed it. "What's this?"

Wilder felt dizzy for a minute. *Get out of the kill zone, you're on a mission.* "Your coin. We'll inscribe your name on it tomorrow."

Lucy turned the bronze piece over in her hands. "Does this mean we're going steady?" she said, and her voice was flippant but her eyes were serious.

"Better than that," Wilder said. Then he was out the door.

Lucy sank back against the pillows, every inch of her satisfied, and looked at the coin. No matter how long she looked at it, it still wasn't a diamond ring, but she had a feeling it might be something better. There was a beret and a crest on one side and a scroll with his name on the other. It was just like J.T. to give her something cryptic but good. Maybe she could have a hole drilled in it, wear it around her neck. Unless that would be bad karma for the entire Army or something. The Army was probably anti-jewelry. She'd have to ask J.T.

J.T. *Damn,* she thought. *I had him right here and didn't ask him his first name.* And there had been that one moment when she was pretty sure she could have gotten his name, his rank, his serial number, his sun sign, his baseball card collection, and his Jeep if she'd just asked.

Of course, at that point she'd have given him anything he'd asked for, too. Actually, she *had* given him everything he'd asked for. She grinned to herself against the pillows and then started when somebody knocked on the door.

Oh goody, he'd changed his mind and come back.

She grabbed her shirt from the floor and buttoned it up as she went to the door. No sense in looking easy. No sense in putting underwear or pants on either, but definitely the shirt. To show that he was going to have to work at least five seconds to get her.

She threw open the door and said, "Okay, what's your—"

"Swear to me you didn't cancel that net," Nash said, his face pale.

Lucy backed up a step. "I didn't cancel the net. I have no reason to cancel the net. Whatever you're doing, just do it and get out of my life without hurting anybody."

"You—" He broke off, looking at her for the first time. "Where's Wilder?"

"He's not here." Lucy tried to close the door but he blocked it with his shoulder.

"He was here, though," Nash said, meeting her eyes. "I know you, Luce. I know what it takes to make you look like this."

"Just *go*," Lucy said.

"I don't get it," he said, and there was real hurt in his eyes. "That guy, he's just like me. You want that, why not come back to me? I'll give you everything you've ever wanted, Lucy. After tonight . . ."

"He's not you," Lucy said, so sure now that she wondered how she could ever have thought they were the same. "He's not a liar. He's not a cheat. He cares about people. He's a real hero, not a Hollywood fast-draw fake."

Nash shoved the door open and came in, slamming it behind him. "Of course he's a fake. Jesus, Lucy, you think he just happened to get this movie gig? He's working for somebody. He's conning you just—"

"I know who he's working for," Lucy said, backing up. "Now get out."

"Oh, no, I don't give up that easy." He came toward her and she scrambled to put the bed between them, ending up on the opposite side, facing him down.

"Get *out*," she said.

"Come on, Luce," he said, detouring around the bed. "Cut the crap. This is me. This is *us*. You know . . ."

She yanked her bag open and took out the Beretta J.T. had given her, fumbling it out of the holster to point it at him. "I'll shoot you," she said, gripping the gun with both hands to keep it from shaking.

Adrenaline was making her dizzy. "I will shoot you where you stand if you try to touch me."

"No, you won't," he said, and she knew he was right, she couldn't shoot anybody. "But I love your spirit, babe. I always have." He sounded almost sad, and she relaxed a little. "God, Lucy, I wish it didn't have to be like this. If things were different—"

"Things are like this because of you," she said, tensing again. "You're the one who set this all up, you're the one who talked Daisy into this and sabotaged that rope, you're the one who sent somebody after Stephanie, so don't even pretend this is some really sad twist of fate. You're getting exactly what you deserve."

He drew back. "Okay, then. So who's your hero working for?"

"Get out." She held the gun in one hand and reached for the phone. "Get out or I call security and have you arrested. You can't be on the bridge tonight if you're in jail, Nash."

"Nash?" he said, trying to smile. "Hey, what happened to 'Connor'?"

"I think he died," she said, phone in hand. "I think something awful happened to him because all that's left is you, and you're nothing."

He flinched.

"Just get out," she said, and let the gun drop. "Please, just go. Do whatever it is you have to do and don't ever come near me or Daisy or Pepper again."

Nash looked at her, his eyes bleak. "Okay, then," he said, sounding defeated. "Stay out of my way tonight and tell your hero to do the same. Especially him. Tell him to keep his distance or he'll be a dead man."

"Just go," Lucy said, suddenly tired.

He went out, closing the door behind him, and she put the gun on the bedside table.

I'm a mess in an emergency, she thought. *Thank God J.T. knows how to do this stuff.*

She went to throw the deadbolt and then she went back to the phone.

She trusted J.T., but it was time to call in her backup.

. . .

Fast exits were good, Wilder thought as he checked the GPS tracker. If he'd hung around in Lucy's room much longer, he'd never have left. And meanwhile, Finnegan was moving north, about three miles ahead of Wilder's position on Route 17. Wilder glanced at the MP-5 submachine gun resting on the passenger seat. He'd taken valuable time to recover it from the cache under the bridge. It was most definitely time for heavier firepower.

The sun was about down, hanging just above the low-country vista. Wilder took his eyes from the road to absorb the beauty, wondering, not for the first time, if this would be his last sunset. He wasn't fatalistic, just realistic. He had loaded weapons in the Jeep, he was following a rogue moneyman, a Russian mobster with a very bad reputation was lurking around somewhere, and the CIA was trying to play the whole mess from the outside. Wilder's experiences were that the CIA wasn't good at playing anything. But if this was his last sunset, it was a great one, made all the better because of the past twenty-four hours with Lucy Armstrong.

Lucy. If something happened to him . . . He pulled out his cell phone and punched in a number.

LaFavre answered on the second ring. "Swamp Rat Air—"

"Rene," Wilder said.

LaFavre stopped cold. "Yeah?"

"Need a favor if things don't go well tonight."

"What are you talkin' about, boy?"

"Lucy Armstrong. If something happens to me, you look out for her."

"Right," LaFavre said. "Maybe better if I come join you, make sure nothing happens to you."

"Nope," Wilder said. "Just take care of Lucy if I can't."

"You got it."

Wilder clicked off the phone and then snapped his eyes back to the road as an eighteen-wheeler roared toward him along the narrow two-lane highway and passed with a blast of wind. He glanced at the tracker. Finnegan's dot was curving around, which meant that once more, Wilder was driving along the route they had taken this morning looping back toward east Savannah and the airport. It seemed as if everything bad had happened in this area: the stunt going wrong, Stephanie's accident, the Finnegan meeting.

"Fuck," Wilder said as he saw the dot turn left into the Wildlife Refuge. Who was Finnegan meeting? He pulled the Jeep over to the narrow strip of grass on the side of the road. It was getting dark now, night falling fast. He twisted in the seat and spun the combination on the lock securing the footlocker in the back of the Jeep, then reached in and pulled out a set of night-vision goggles. He put the NVGs on his head, but kept them resting on his forehead, not covering his eyes. Not yet.

He watched the small screen and saw Finnegan's dot come to a halt. Looking at the terrain features on the map, Wilder realized Finnegan was in the exact same spot where he and Lucy had met him earlier in the day. He smiled grimly. First mistake. Violating one of Rogers' Rules of Rangering, formulated in 1759: Don't ever go back over the same trail.

Wilder pulled back onto the road and headed south. Checking the GPS one last time, he pulled the goggles down over his eyes when he was about a half mile from the exit gate and turned them on at the same time he turned off the headlights of the Jeep.

His world went green as the device amplified the ambient light. He drove to the exit gate at moderate speed. It was shut. Wilder went slightly past it, then pulled to the other side of the road. He parked the Jeep, grabbed the MP-5, and got out. Looking left and right, he didn't see the glow of oncoming headlights. He loped across the road, hopped the metal bar, and continued down the gravel road at a steady jog for a bit. Then he lay down on his stomach, peering to the south. The grove trees where Finnegan was hidden was directly across the swamp from him.

According to Rogers' Rules of Rangering, coming up on the site along the road was not a good idea. Wilder gave a small sigh, knowing he could not disappoint the long-departed Rogers, then slithered down the embankment into the black water. The cool water penetrated his clothes and he shivered. He untied the camouflage scarf that he had used to blindfold Lucy from around his neck—he was never going to look at that scarf the same way again—and dipped it in the water, then draped it over his head. It would diffuse the apparent outline of his head, a trick he'd learned from the Navy SEALs. Wilder moved forward, keeping his head and the goggles and the MP-5 above the water's surface as he pressed forward, watching everything through the open mesh of the scarf.

Tyler could see through his thermal scope that the Irishman's two security people, the ones he thought of as Football Player and Weight Lifter, were in the exact same places they had been for the afternoon meeting. Obviously they had never had a gunnery sergeant screaming at them for months on end that you never, never, never, occupied the same position twice. Never. The Corps had been big on repetition.

Weight Lifter was just inside the bar gate giving access to the refuge. He had it open, and if he followed form, he would shut it when the Irishman's visitor arrived. Football Player was forty feet down the road from the Irishman's position, sitting uncomfortably—based on his constant shifting—in a clump of palmetto bushes with a submachine gun across his knees. The Irishman was sitting on the front hood of his car. All three of them were waiting for a meeting that wasn't going to happen. Well, not with who they wanted to meet or in a way that was going to make any of them very happy.

Tyler reconsidered that as he centered the thermal sight on Weight Lifter's head. The man seemed uncomfortable and Tyler wanted to help with that.

Tyler breathed out very slowly and, when his lungs were empty, waited for that pause between heartbeats and the blood surge in his veins. He pulled the trigger back, a lover's caress, and the subsonic round raced down the barrel, out the suppressor, and hit Weight Lifter in the head less than a second later.

Two heartbeats after his first shot, he fired the second. Football Player's head slammed forward, chin bouncing off his chest, and then hung limply.

Time to get up close and personal.

Tyler put the rifle down and went into the water, sliding down his night-vision goggles as he headed toward the Irishman.

"So what's up?" Gloom said when he met Lucy on the bridge, keeping an eye out for traffic as the wind picked up.

"The jig," Lucy said.

"What jig?" Pepper said, and they both looked down at the little girl, shielded from the wind by Lucy's body, decked out in newly laundered WonderWear topped with a white cardigan and her jeans, plus LaFavre's mirrored sunglasses.

"It means we're almost finished," Lucy said, looking down at her double reflection. Then she looked at Gloom, dropping her voice so that Pepper couldn't hear. "Tonight, Nash is going to take the helicopter during the stunt and go pick up an Irish crook who is going to meet a Russian mobster to give him fifty million dollars worth of Pre-Columbian porn."

Gloom was silent for a moment and then he said, "Okay."

"The theory is that no one will get hurt since the last thing they want is cops on takeoff."

"It's a theory," Gloom said.

"But I don't like it, so I want as many people off this bridge as possible." Lucy nodded down the almost deserted span. "We don't need to actually film it, so we don't need makeup, we don't need sound. Just enough so that to the uneducated eye, it looks like we're filming a movie."

"Okay," Gloom said.

"How many people is that?"

Gloom thought about it. "The lighting guys can set up the lights and go back to base camp. We'll put the camera on a truck bed. I'll handle the camera and the clapper. You direct."

"What about me?" Pepper said. "Aunt Lucy needs me to bring apples and water."

"Thank you very much," Lucy said. "But tonight, there's no eating on the set. Not during stunts. It's too dangerous."

"Okay," Pepper said, looking unconvinced.

"And I suppose we need stunt crew," Gloom said.

"Count on it," Lucy said. "Nash, Doc, Karen, they're all in—"

"Hey, look," Pepper said, peering around Lucy's legs.

"Evenin', ma'am," somebody said from behind her, and she turned to see LaFavre, tipping his hat to her.

"Major LaFavre," she said, not sure what the hell he was doing there.

"They said down in base camp that y'all were up here," he said, and then he looked down to where Pepper was tugging on his pants leg.

"Thank you for my sunglasses," she said. "They're very cool."

"You look quite fetching in them, my dear," he said to her and then smiled at Lucy, but his voice was level and serious, not flirting at all. "You wouldn't happen to know where my buddy J. T. Wilder is now, would you?"

"Not exactly," Lucy said, feeling a flare of alarm. "He was going to meet someone."

"He appears to be concerned for your safety," LaFavre said.

"I'm concerned for my safety, too." Lucy relaxed a little. "Hell, I'm concerned for everybody's safety."

LaFavre looked down again at Pepper, who was yanking on his pants leg again.

"I cannot see," she said, hemmed in by six adult legs.

LaFavre reached down and picked her up effortlessly and set her on his shoulders.

"Cool," she said and wrapped her arms around his head, knocking his pilot's cap askew.

"Is this where the trouble's going to be?" LaFavre said, squinting up at the bridge.

"That's our guess." Lucy took a deep breath. "They're going to bring a helicopter in with a cargo net . . ." She stopped when he shook his head, making Pepper giggle.

"Too much wind. Damn near impossible to do it in no wind. With this . . ." He shook his head again. "Never gonna happen."

"Then where?" Lucy looked around. "We're shooting here. This is where they wanted it set up. This bridge, right here."

"I don't know." LaFavre looked around again. "Hard place to get off of. Block both ends, you got yourself a trap. Only way off is up in chopper—which I doubt your stunt pilot can do—or over the rail with a rope."

Lucy looked at Gloom.

"No idea," Gloom said. "Okay, you directing, me on camera, Nash, Karen, and Doc on stunts."

"And J.T.," Lucy said.

"Plus Bryce."

"No," Lucy said.

"That'll be the giveaway," Gloom said. "Unless you're going to tell Bryce that we're not really shooting the last stunts, he's going to throw a fit. And then if he knows you're not shooting the stunts, he's gonna throw a fit. So basically, he throws a fit—"

"Oh, hell," Lucy said.

"—And everybody will know in five minutes."

"Bryce then, but not Althea."

"Would Althea be the young lady in *Blow Me Down*?" LaFavre said.

"Uh," Lucy said, not sure what he was talking about.

"Yes," Gloom said.

"Very talented." LaFavre reached into his jacket and pulled out a card, which he gave to Lucy. "Should anything untoward happen this evening, you can reach me at that number."

"Thank you," she said, even more confused.

"And should you need assistance at any time afterward," he said, his voice kind, "I will be at your service."

"Thank you," she said, really confused now but even more touched. "Uh, Major LaFavre, do you know something I don't know?"

"We take care of our own, my dear." He looked up at Pepper, who was still hanging on to his cap. "Would you like to return to base camp, young lady?"

"Yes, please," Pepper said. "It's very windy."

"Yes, it is," Lucy said, looking out over the river.

"I'll tell everybody else to stay in base camp tonight," Gloom said, as LaFavre tipped his hat and started down the bridge with Pepper on his shoulders. "Pack up now so we can get out of here early tomorrow."

"That's good," Lucy said and thought, *Where is J. T.?* And what had happened that he'd sent his best friend to watch out for her?

"You okay?" Gloom said.

"Nope," Lucy said and followed LaFavre off the bridge.

Wilder saw a light glow directly ahead, which went out after a few seconds. Finnegan and his damn cigar. Stupid. As he moved through the chilly water, watching out for gators and other nasty critters, he hoped the asshole was enjoying his smoke.

Then he froze.

There was someone or something else out here. He couldn't say how he knew that, but he for damn sure knew it. The last time he'd felt this, he'd been on his way to Baghdad International when he'd ordered the driver of his Up-Armor Humvee to slam on the brakes. Fifty feet short of an improvised explosive device waiting to blow them to hell.

Wilder's nostrils flared as he slowly looked left, then right, searching. He caught a faint whiff of Finnegan's cigar.

Darkness was for predators. That had been true of every place around the globe Wilder had ever gone. But was this predator human or animal?

Movement to his right. Wilder had the stock of the MP-5 tight into his shoulder, the weapon just above the black mirror of the water's surface. A ripple, a wake, something moving. Wilder slowly let the air out of his lungs as he spotted the small dark spots of the alligator's snout and eyes. Not far away and moving south, just like him. Finnegan was drawing the predators in.

Wilder continued forward, the submachine gun at the ready.

He had halved the distance to Finnegan, but the going was slow. He could clearly see the red glow of the tip of Finnegan's cigar. Who was he waiting for? Nash?

He glanced right. The damn gator was keeping pace.

But so was something else. Wilder blinked as he swiveled his head back to the front and then went a quarter turn back right. What the hell? A dark blob was farther away than the gator, also in the water, moving in a line toward Finnegan. Wilder strained to see through the goggles. Not another gator.

Shit. A man, head covered just like his was. Nash? Pepper's ghost? Whoever it was, he was much closer to the damn Irishman than Wilder was. He pressed forward as his mind churned. Was Nash making his own move on Finnegan? Or was it the CIA? Had Crawford lied and the Agency was going to bring in Finnegan and squeeze him?

That didn't make sense. Fuck, nothing had made sense since that first night on the bridge except for the all-too-brief interludes with Lucy. That and Pepper; she made sense, too, in her own way, more than all the adults around her.

Mission focus. Or else there wouldn't be another interlude with Lucy or conversation with Pepper.

The fucking gator was still keeping pace. Wilder knew he wouldn't make it to Finnegan before the other person did. Hell, it was going to be a close race beating the gator there.

He almost felt sorry for Finnegan. But he never slowed for a moment.

Tyler glanced to his left rear. Gator. He smiled, wondering if it was his one-eyed buddy. He could feed the fat Irishman to her. There'd be enough food there for all her babies.

The glow of the cigar was like a beacon. *Dumb fuck.* The ground was sloping up now and Tyler could move faster. He wasn't worried about the old man spotting him—without night-vision goggles there was no chance.

Tyler reached the embankment, less than five feet from the Irishman, and paused. He drew the High Standard .22 pistol and quietly drew back the slide, chambering a round.

Then he paused and looked back to the north. He could see the V in the water from the gator's wake, coming this way. But beyond it was something else. Someone else. Close to the gator and closing. Which meant he had less than two minutes.

Tyler sprinted up the embankment, weapon at the ready, and drew a bead on the Irishman, who must have heard something because he spun about, sliding his fat ass off the hood of the car.

"Who goes there? That you, Connor? I don't know why you needed to meet—"

Tyler fired, the small round hitting the old man in the kneecap. The Irishman made a surprised sound and the leg went out, sending him sprawling to the ground.

"Johnnie-boy!" the Irishman screamed. "Peter!"

This was not a time for subtlety. Smash and grab.

Tyler ran up to the writhing figure and aimed. He put a round through the man's other kneecap and the Irishman screamed again.

"Who the fuck are you?" he gasped through clenched teeth.

"Your security's dead. Scream all you want. No one's coming."

Tyler realized that wasn't quite true, but he figured whoever else was coming through the water wasn't there to help the Irishman, either.

Tyler holstered the pistol and drew his knife. He put his knee on the Irishman's chest. He placed the tip of the knife against the man's left eyeball. "Lie and lose it. And that's just the start, old man, so make it easy." With his right hand, he reached into the old man's coat and retrieved his cell phone.

"Listen," the Irishman gasped. Tyler noted that there was no longer a hint of brogue. Just a heavy dose of fear. "Listen, we can deal. We can—"

"Two things. The container number and the coordinates where you're supposed to meet Letsky."

"I'll cut you in." The Irishman's face was gray with pain and terror. "I'll make you a partner—"

"You want to be my partner?" Tyler asked with a chuckle. "You want to cut me in, but you and that bitch pilot are cutting everybody out. How's that gonna work?"

"You need me," the Irishman argued desperately. "Without me, the deal doesn't—"

"There's been a change," Tyler said and slapped him on the side of the face with the flat side of the knife, getting his attention, as he put the point less than a quarter inch from the old man's eye. "Coordinates and container number."

"Fuck you."

"Wrong answer," Tyler said and pressed down with the knife.

Wilder stopped when he heard the second scream. Every damn thing in the swamp for a long way around had to have heard that scream. There was no brogue to it, but he had no doubt from whose throat it had emanated. And he knew the other stalker knew he was coming. He'd seen that pause at the base of the embankment. He'd also heard the cry for Johnnie-boy and Peter. With no response.

And the fucking gator was moving even faster, enticed by the scream.

Wilder knew it was too late for Finnegan, but he pressed forward anyway. Another scream. Wilder could have moved faster, but there was no way he was taking the MP-5 out of the ready position. Because someone was causing those screams and someone who could do that was not someone to be underestimated. Wilder was pretty sure old Rogers would be with him on this one, even though being in a swamp with a screaming Irishman and a gator had not been covered in the Rangering Rules.

Another scream. Wilder was close to the road.

Silence.

Wilder froze. His eyes swept back and forth, searching through the goggles, the muzzle of the submachine gun following his gaze. Nothing moving. But whatever had happened was over. And now it was time to watch one's own ass.

Because whoever had made Finnegan scream was close. Damn close. Waiting for him to do something stupid. And the silence from Johnnie-boy and Peter meant they, too, were probably not among the living.

It was the hardest lesson he had learned in combat: Do nothing.

He stood perfectly still, chest-deep in the swamp. Finger on the trigger. Listening. Watching. Sniffing.

A body came tumbling down the berm and splashed into the water and Wilder swung the muzzle to the left as it was met by the alligator, which snatched it up in its massive jaws.

Wilder knew the 9-mm bullets in the submachine gun would only piss off such a large alligator, and besides, he really had nothing against the critter. It was just doing what came naturally to it. Wilder dropped the MP-5 into the water where it came to rest on its sling and reached to his back where the Glock with the hot loads was holstered. He knew those rounds could punch through most body armor, so he hoped it would penetrate the gator's hide if need be. Shooting gators had not been taught at Bragg during Special Forces training, a serious oversight, Wilder was beginning to believe. If Pepper had had any say, it would have been.

Wilder drew the pistol out, water pouring out of the barrel, and fired a warning shot. The gator began to thrash, but he shifted up and fired several rounds toward the berm, trying to ensure that whoever had thrown the man in would have to take cover. If he went up there in chase, there was a very good chance he'd take a round right between the eyes, if the other person had also learned the same hard lesson of being able to wait. Wilder was willing to wager good money that the other person had indeed.

Wilder shifted back to the thrashing in the water. Then suddenly there was silence. He took an involuntary step backward, realizing the gator had gone under with its prey. He remained still, cognizant of predators all about. Finally, after five minutes, he waded forward toward the berm.

That's when he saw the flicker of movement to his left, along the road, flitting between the trees. A ghostly figure moving away at a sprint. Nash? Wilder aimed the Glock but he couldn't get a solid sight picture. It was gone as quickly as it had appeared and for a moment Wilder wondered if he'd been mistaken.

No.

Wilder considered pursuit, then decided he'd really like to see Lucy again before he died—which he was now hoping would happen when he was very old and in bed with her—and deep-sixed that idea.

There was something floating in the water. A piece of cloth. Wilder scooped it up. Part of a Hawaiian shirt soaked with blood and swamp water.

Finnegan was sleeping with the gators.

18

Lucy had taken Pepper back to Daisy, listening with half an ear to Pepper's enthusiastic recount of her time spent with Major LaFavre.

"He is a *very* good person," she told Lucy.

"I'm sure he is," she said and knocked on Daisy's door.

Daisy opened it, looking bleary-eyed. "Hey, pumpkin," she said to Pepper. Then she looked at Lucy and her smile faded. "What?"

"Don't come to the bridge tonight," Lucy said, as Daisy stepped back to let them in the room. "Pack your things and I'll pick you up as soon as filming is over. We're leaving right away."

"To go to New York?"

"Maybe. I don't know." Lucy sat down on the bed and almost knocked over Daisy's pill bottle. There were only four left. Good. "For right now, just away from here."

"What do you mean, 'maybe'?"

Lucy took a deep breath. "I mean, maybe we'll stay here. Maybe we'll start over here."

Daisy sat down beside her. "Really?"

Lucy looked at her. "J.T. knows we were in a foster home."

"So?"

"I've never told anybody that."

Daisy blinked. "Why?"

"Nobody's business."

"I agree. Why did you tell J.T.?"

"I didn't. He guessed. Well, he guessed we weren't sisters and then the rest . . . just came out."

Daisy nodded. "And what does this have to do with us staying in the South?"

Lucy swallowed. "I think J.T. is the rest of my life. I know I move too fast, but I really think he is. And that's a new life. And you want a new life. And I want to be with you, I want to play Barbies with Pepper until she's too old to play Barbies and then I want to talk about boys with her."

"Cool," Pepper said.

"So I think tonight after the shoot is over, we get in the camper and we drive to Charleston or Atlanta or someplace, I don't know, and we find a nice hotel and we sit and we figure out what we both want, and we pick a place and we start over. Together. Both of us. Partners."

Daisy drew a deep breath. "I'd like that very much."

Lucy nodded. "Yeah. So would I."

"What about your career?"

Good question. "Well, Atlanta's a big advertising town," Lucy said, trying to sound more positive than she felt. "And I'm sure they have many talented dogs there. Gloom can run the business part from New York. He loves my loft, he can move in." Actually, the more she talked about it, the more it all made sense. Something new. Brand-new start. Brand-new day. Brand-new love. "This is what I want to do, it's what you want to do, it's good. We'll have to figure things out together—"

"We can do that," Daisy said eagerly, and Lucy saw tears in her eyes. "We can *so* do that."

Lucy felt her own tears start. "You sound like Pepper."

Daisy swallowed. "I feel like Pepper. It'll be the three of us."

"And J.T.," Pepper said, watching them wide-eyed, as if waiting to find out if the crying part was good or not.

"And J.T.," Lucy said firmly.

"And Rene," Pepper said.

"Who?" Daisy said.

"Rene," Pepper said. "He's J.T.'s best friend. So we will cook dinner and they will come."

"Cook dinner?" Lucy said, not sure.

"I'll show you how," Daisy said and then grinned. "Yeah. *I'll* show *you* how to do something."

"Cool," Pepper said.

Lucy nodded. "Cool."

Daisy took a deep breath. "And we will have *such* a good time."

Lucy started to laugh. "Okay, so you pack and I'll go finish up this . . . movie . . ." *Oh, hell. The CIA and the Russian mob.* "And then we'll have a new life."

"O*kay*," Pepper said and went to drag her pink Barbie rolling carry-on out of the corner.

Lucy stood up. "I'll call you after the shoot."

"We'll be ready." Daisy stood up. "We will be so ready. Lucy, *thank you.*"

"Hey." Lucy slung her arm around her and kissed her cheek. "This is good for me too. Everybody wins."

I hope.

Lucy had finished packing her duffel and put it next to J.T.'s case when someone knocked on the door.

Nash, she thought. *He's found out we're stripping the crew off the bridge.* "Who is it?"

"It's me," J.T. said. "Who were you expecting?"

She unlocked the door and threw her arms around him so that he had to drag her with him as he came in. He kicked the door shut behind him and kissed her, and she hung on tight, so relieved to see him, she was speechless. Damn LaFavre, making her worry.

"I could get used to coming home to this," he said into her neck.

"Never leave me again," she said, and he pulled back.

"What's wrong?"

"Nothing," she said. "Well, I was worried. And Nash came by after you left."

His face turned to stone and she said, "No, nothing happened. Hey, you'd have been proud of me." She gestured at the Beretta on the nightstand. "I pulled a gun on him."

He shuddered and then wrapped his arms around her again. "He's not a good person to pull a gun on, Lucy. Don't do it again unless you're going to kill him. If you hesitate, he'll take it away from you. And then . . ." He held her tighter.

"Well," Lucy said, trying to breathe, "if he'd come any closer I would have killed him."

"Lucy, you didn't even take the safety off. I can see it from here. So could he."

Hell. "I forgot."

"Yeah." He kissed her cheek. "Don't pull a gun on him. On anybody, but especially not him. You only point a gun—"

"If you're going to kill somebody. I know, I know." Now that she was calm, she noticed he was soaking wet. And smelled like swamp. She pulled back. "Where have you been?"

"In the swamp," he said, letting her go. "Finnegan is dead."

Lucy felt sick. "You killed him?"

He looked insulted. "No. Jeez, Lucy."

"Sorry." She sat down on the edge of the bed. *I'm sleeping with a man I know could kill people.* She should have found that disturbing, not comforting, but there it was.

He kept talking as he unbuttoned his wet shirt. "I thought Nash did it, but if he was here with you . . ."

"He was here with me part of the time." Lucy crossed her arms. She was going to have to change her shirt, too. It smelled of swamp, thanks to her taste in men.

Well, J.T. was worth a little swamp stink.

"He wouldn't have had time to see you and get to the swamp," J.T. said as he stripped off the body armor. "You okay?"

Am I okay? Lucy considered the situation. "We still shooting tonight?"

"No," he said, and the way he said it made her pay attention.

"What happened?"

"I'm pretty sure Finnegan was tortured."

"Oh, God." Lucy swallowed. "I don't believe Nash would torture. He's crazy but he's not an animal."

"I think it was the ghost."

"Who?"

"The guy who Pepper's been seeing in the swamp. She was right. He's been there all along. He was there that night with Pepper and the gator."

"The ghost." Lucy swallowed.

J.T. pulled off his wet pants and got a fresh shirt out of the case. "But if he's moved up from shooting out helicopter skids and crashing a van to torture and murder, then anything could happen. You're getting out of here."

"Me?" Lucy straightened. "What about you?"

His cell phone rang before he could answer. He clicked it on and said, "Wilder," and then he sat down next to her on the bed, turning the phone so she could hear, too.

"What the fuck is going on?" Crawford's voice crackled.

J.T. looked unimpressed. "Reference?"

"Two bodies in the Savannah Wildlife Refuge and a missing Irishman."

Two bodies and *a missing Irishman?* Lucy looked at J.T.

"Two bodies?" he said.

"Some fat guy and another guy with tattoos, looks like a weight lifter."

J.T. relaxed a little.

He knows who they are, Lucy thought. *Jesus.*

J.T. said, "Finnegan is dead, not missing."

"How the hell do you know that?"

"Uh—" J.T. looked at her and Lucy thought, *Something else he didn't tell me.* "Well, I found part of his shirt. An alligator got the rest of him."

Not Moot, Lucy thought, and felt ill.

"Why the fuck were you out there?" Crawford said.

"Checking on things."

"Did I tell you to check on things?" Crawford didn't wait for an answer. "So much for the bug that was going to lead us to Letsky."

Oh, you're a real humanitarian, Lucy thought, and the look on J.T.'s face said he was thinking the same thing.

J.T. said, "Did you have him killed?"

"Oh, yeah, sure," Crawford snarled. "I killed the one link I had to my priority target. We noticed the bug wasn't moving for a while and went in to check. Found it on his cane. But no Finnegan."

"Why would Letsky take him out?"

"Letsky wouldn't take him out," Crawford said, clearly fed up. "Letsky wants his fucking Viagra art. And Finnegan was going to get it for him."

J.T. straightened. "I thought Finnegan already had the art. He just needed to deliver it."

"I do the thinking here."

"Then think," J.T. snapped, and Lucy thought, *That's my boy.* "Who do *you* think took out Finnegan?"

"Nash."

"Nash was here at the hotel when Finnegan was getting chomped up."

"How do you know that? You just told me you were in the swamp."

"Take my word for it," J.T. said. "I've got no reason to protect Nash. So who took out Finnegan if it wasn't Letsky or Nash?"

"Fuck."

The look on J.T.'s face told Lucy that wasn't the answer he wanted. The CIA had no idea who'd murdered Finnegan. *We're definitely not filming tonight,* Lucy thought.

"Okay." By his tone, Crawford was making a big attempt to regroup. "Here's the new plan. You bug Nash. If he makes the meeting with Letsky, we've got them."

"Does Nash have the art?"

"Uh. No."

"Then why would Nash make the meeting?"

"You just do as ordered. Bug Nash. Let this thing play out. If he gets the art, we'll let him make the meeting."

"Where is the art?"

"Just finish your goddamn movie. Do you understand, Captain?"

"How were the other two killed?"

"One shot each, in the head."

"Close range?"

"No. Looks like seven-point-six-two. Rifle."

J.T. looked at Lucy and smiled what he probably hoped was a reassuring smile. *Pathetic,* she thought and loved him more for trying.

"Captain Wilder?"

"Yes."

"Bug Nash. Leave him alone. Let him do his thing."

"Nash may be having problems."

Crawford breathed heavily into the phone. "What kind of problems?"

"His pilot canceled the cargo net that was supposed to hold the jade. I think that's what it was supposed to hold."

"So where are they going to put it?"

"In the chopper. Which makes me think there won't be as many people in there as Nash had planned."

"Double cross and Nash figured it out," Crawford said. "Fuck." He was silent for a moment. "They got the coordinates from Finnegan. They cut him out. Nash is delivering the art without him. *Bug Nash.*"

"Crawford—"

"Just *do* it, damn it."

The phone clicked off.

"Well, I would but you didn't give me a second bug," J.T. said to the dial tone.

"Oh, great," Lucy said. "Who else was killed?"

"Two of the guys who attacked Bryce and me in the bar. They worked for Finnegan, his muscle. The fight wasn't an accident. Finnegan wanted to take me out early in the game."

"There were three guys," Lucy said, her heart pounding. "Do you think the third guy is the killer?"

J.T. shook his head immediately. "No. Thin Man is the one whose knee I took out. I think he probably crawled away to hide until things clear up. Like Judgment Day, maybe."

"Thin Man?" Lucy said. "*Thin Man.* You named them, too?"

"Got to identify the targets," J.T. said, but Lucy could tell his mind was elsewhere.

"What was the seven-point-sixty-two thing?"

"Seven-point-six-two," he corrected. "Caliber of the bullet."

"Is that important?"

"Everything is important," J.T. said. "Means the ghost probably used a sniper rifle to take the security guys out. Then came in close with a smaller caliber suppressed weapon to finish Finnegan. Which means he wanted something from Finnegan." J.T. shook his head. "This is over. It's too damn dangerous now. These people will do anything."

Lucy sighed her relief. "Thank you. I told Daisy to pack because we were getting out of here right after the shoot. But we can tell everybody to go now. I don't care where we go, just so it's out of here, away from this damn bridge and that helicopter."

"LaFavre's quarters at Hunter Army Airfield," Wilder said. "You'll be safe there for the next twenty-four hours."

"Good." Lucy picked up the phone to punch in Daisy's room number. "Pepper will be thrilled to be on the road with you. She'll probably want to ride in the Jeep with her WonderWear and LaFavre's sunglasses."

"Works for me," J.T. said.

"And when she finds out she's staying with her buddy *Rene,*" Lucy said and then frowned at the phone as it rang again. "Come on, Daisy, pick up." It rang again and again, and Lucy began to feel cold.

"What's wrong?"

"She's not answering." Lucy swallowed. "J.T., *she's not answering.*"

"She's probably in the bathroom," he told her, but five minutes later, Lucy made him open Daisy's door with a credit card and they found her on the bed, unconscious, a glass overturned on the bedside table.

"Daisy," Lucy said and then saw the empty pill bottle next to a glass. A second glass.

"She had a drink with somebody," she said, but J.T. was already calling the front desk, telling them to send a doctor fast.

Lucy turned to him, shaking. "She's breathing, but she's out cold. I can't rouse her."

"Pepper?" J.T. called out. "Come out, honey, it's okay. *Pepper?*"

Lucy lost her breath. "Where is she? *Pepper?*"

"I don't know." J.T. looked ill. "Fuck, I should have listened to you and got you all out of here."

"Oh, God, they didn't take her, tell me—"

Her phone rang and Lucy started.

"Answer that," J.T. said grimly. "He's going to tell us what we have to do to get Pepper back."

Wilder watched Lucy pull the phone from her bag, her hand shaking. He wasn't sure if it was fear or anger or both, but he was sure she wasn't going to be able to handle the call. He held out his hand and Lucy passed the phone over as it rang again.

"Talk," he snapped into it.

There was a short burst of laughter. "This my man from the swamp? I've got the girl. You and your woman, the Director, you do the stunt tonight. You stay out of the way, and the little girl's back to you. Unhurt. If not . . .Well, there was Finnegan. And his two guards."

Wilder reined in his anger. "Prove you have her."

The laughter again, an edge of craziness to it that Wilder had heard before, but only in combat. "Sure. She never shuts up anyway. Hold on."

There was a pause and Wilder looked up to see Lucy staring at him with desperate eyes. He tried to give his reassuring smile, gave up on that, and just mouthed, *It will be all right.*

Lucy's expression didn't change.

"J.T.?"

Wilder recognized Pepper's voice. She sounded a lot saner than the man who had her and more calm than the two people in the room here terrified for her.

"Hey, sweetie," Wilder said. Lucy was holding her hand out for the phone, but Wilder knew that was not a good move. "Are you okay?"

"I do not like this babysitter," Pepper said.

"I don't like him, either," Wilder said. "But for right now, be nice to him. Then we'll come and get you."

"I know," Pepper said. "He said mean things, and I told him you are very dangerous when you are protecting me."

"Very dangerous," Wilder said and thought, *I'm going to kill the son of a bitch.* "Be brave and we will come and get you."

"Soon?" Pepper said, her voice going higher.

"It's going to be a while, Pepper," Wilder said. "We have to shoot the last movie scene before the babysitter will bring you to us. But we will hurry."

"Okay," Pepper said, not sounding okay.

"Pepper, I will get you as soon as I can," Wilder said, wanting to crawl through the phone to her. "I swear to you—"

"I know," Pepper said. "I'm your egg."

"Damn right," Wilder said, his throat closing, and then the ghost took the phone back.

"She's alive. Do everything I say, and she stays that way."

"You hurt her, and I will spend the rest of my life tracking you down."

"Oooohhhh. I'm scared." He laughed. "I'm too fast and too good. You were slow in the swamp. You'll be too slow again."

"What did you give Daisy?" Wilder demanded.

"Not a damn thing. Wasn't even there. Just do the stunt tonight and you get your egg back. Try anything funny, and hey, eggs crack."

"No," Wilder said. "They don't. I want you to answer with proof of life from this phone every time I call, or we stop filming."

"You stop filming and—"

"You hurt the kid, you're done. You keep her safe and happy, we do the stunt exactly as planned."

The phone went dead. Wilder hated turning the phone off.

"Who the hell was that?" Lucy demanded.

Wilder looked at Lucy. "The ghost." He saw the look on Lucy's face and realized he'd used the sledgehammer without meaning to. "We do the stunt, we get her back."

Lucy swallowed. "He's the guy who tortured Finnegan." She looked ill.

"We will get her back," Wilder said as somebody knocked on the door. "I swear it."

Then he went to let the doctor in.

Tyler stood on edge of the roof of the abandoned grain tower, the highest place around other than the bridge and the hotel, and stared across the river at the bright lights of Savannah. The sniper rifle rested on the concrete to his left, complete with bipod and thermal sight. Ready and waiting.

He pivoted right and looked at the bridge. The film crew was beginning to set up lights and cameras and put out cones, closing off the side of the bridge heading from Georgia into South Carolina. *Damn right.*

"So you should have games and stuff."

"What?" He turned to see the Kid sitting on the roof behind him, her back against a smokestack. She'd gotten dirt on her hands and then wiped them on her cheeks and she looked like hell.

She glared at him. "Babysitters have games and stuff. Connor said you were my babysitter. Where are the games?"

"Here's a game: You shut up." He looked back at the bridge.

"That's not a good game."

Here's a good game. I throw you off this fuckin' tower. He could probably get a shot in before she hit ground. But proof of life, that's what that bastard Stranger had said.

"I'm hungry."

"Shut up, Kid."

His cell phone buzzed. Not the Stranger for proof of life. He knew who it was and he knew what she wanted. What he had drawn out of Finnegan with the knife. The phone buzzed again.

"You should answer your phone."

Tyler barely noticed the third buzz. When it sounded a fourth time, he took it and canceled the incoming call. Then he punched in the coordinates that Finnegan had whispered to him through his agony. He hit Send, thinking, *This is the dumb bitch who tried to cut us out. Women.* He'd wanted to kill her but Nash had said no, she was the only pilot they had and they had to have the helicopter.

Well, when this was over, she had to land sometime.

Tyler heard a rustling behind him and turned to look.

The Kid was eating his Cheetos.

"These are not very good," she said, frowning at him. "They're not crunchy."

"They've been in the swamp," he said, wounded. "You try to keep anything crunchy in a swamp."

"If you had closed them up better, they would be crunchy," she said, her snotty little chin in the air.

"Not in a fucking *swamp*," he said, really wishing he could kill her.

"Bad word," she said.

He ignored her. It was either that or kill her, and there was that damn proof of life—

"Did you see Moot in the swamp?" she said.

"What?"

"Moot. The alligator with one eye. Did you see her?"

"Yeah, I saw her." Tyler checked the time. They should be heading for the bridge soon.

Behind him, the bag rustled again.

Fuck, he wasn't going to have any Cheetos left.

"You smell," the girl said.

Tyler thought, *You die,* and put his eye to the scope.

Lucy met J.T. and Gloom on the bridge. Three days before, she'd been new on the bridge, watching a helicopter land and J.T. get off. It seemed like a thousand years ago now.

"What did the doctor say?" J.T. asked her as she joined them.

"Daisy will be out for a while but she'll be fine. Estelle is sitting with her. The doctor's on call. She's going to be all right." Lucy swallowed. "We should get Pepper back before she wakes up, though."

"Jesus," Gloom said.

"Gloom just got here," J.T. said. "I called him—"

"Good," Lucy said. "Because that was my next move. We need a plan." She set her jaw. "This is out of control. We have to take back control. We can't just wait for them—"

"We're not going to," J.T. said. "What's the fewest people you can film the stunt with?"

Lucy stopped, forcing her mind away from Pepper. "We're way ahead of you. We have the crew set everything up and then they leave, except for me to direct, Gloom on clapper and camera, and you as

Bryce's double. The stunt team because the assholes want to be here for their damn plan. And then Bryce, unless we can convince him to leave the bridge during their big scenes."

"That's it, then," J.T. said. "We keep everybody else down in base camp."

Gloom nodded. "Okay, but here's what I don't get. J.T. just told me that all Nash and his cronies are doing is taking the helicopter and flying out to meet this Latsky—"

"Letsky," J.T. said.

"—But why a helicopter? It's not like there are mountains around here they have to fly up to. Why not a car or a boat? It'd be a lot less hassle and a lot less noticeable. Hell, with a boat and all these islands . . ."

"The weight?" Lucy guessed. "Jade penises have to weigh a lot. What difference does it—" She stopped because J.T. was frowning.

"Cargo net," he said. "They needed the cargo net for the art. But when they picked up Finnegan and the art, they could have just loaded it in a boat . . ." He closed his eyes. "Jesus, of course, that's it. They don't have the art."

"What are you talking about?" Lucy said.

J.T. pressed his hands against his temples. "I asked Crawford this morning where the art was and he told me not to worry about it. I got the feeling that Nash didn't have the art yet, that Finnegan had it. But—yeah, okay, this makes sense now—I bet you anything that Finnegan didn't have the art either, and the stunt is a cover for them getting it. They swoop down in the helicopter to wherever it is, load it in the net, and take off to go to Letsky. Nobody follows."

"Who's Crawford?" Gloom said.

"The CIA," Lucy said, frowning at J.T. "Well, why haven't they already done that? What's so important about tonight? Because they took Pepper to make sure we'd shoot *tonight*." She swallowed, thinking about Pepper alone out there with a madman. "I'm going to kill them all. That stuff I said about not shooting the gun? I can shoot the gun."

"The CIA is involved?" Gloom said, appalled.

"Actually, the CIA would be J.T.," Lucy said. "Can we—"

Gloom drew back. "I thought he was a Green Beret."

"He's that, too," Lucy said, feeling her temper rise. "Later, he's gonna open for Aerosmith. *Can we get Pepper back now?*"

"The art has to be close," J.T. said to Gloom. "That's why Nash picked the Talmadge for the stunt."

Gloom leaned back. "It's in a truck coming across the bridge? We'll only have the two lanes on one side shut down. The other half of the bridge will still be open to traffic."

J.T. shook his head. "I wouldn't take down a truck on the bridge. Too conspicuous, too hard." He looked out over the choppy river. "And in this wind, impossible. But Lucy's got a good point, the timing seems to be critical. The schedule is the thing that Finnegan and Nash have been insisting on."

"I don't care," Lucy said, ready to scream. "I don't care, *I don't care. How do we get Pepper back?*"

"We follow them," J.T. said, calm as ever. "I would like to know exactly what they're doing so I know where they're going, but bottom line is, we follow them. When whatever it is goes down, we each take one of the team. I follow Nash, you follow Doc," he said to Lucy. "As for Karen . . ."

"I'll do anything," Gloom said. "But it's only fair to warn you, I don't think I can take Karen. She's a black belt in karate. I'm a Ralph Lauren cowhide with brass grommets."

"You're going to run base camp," J.T. said, taking out his phone.

"Who's got Karen, then?" Lucy said.

"LaFavre."

"Poor Karen," Gloom said, brightening. "She's toast."

"Fuck Karen," Lucy said. "She's part of the team that took my Pepper. LaFavre can toss Karen out of the helicopter for all I care. So we wait for one of them to lead us to Pepper? That asshole could have killed her by then." Her voice caught. "God, J.T.—"

"She's not going to die," J.T. said. "They're going to need her alive to get what they need."

"The jade?" Gloom said.

"No. The helicopter," J.T. said. "We're going to make a trade." He checked his watch, pulled out his cell phone, and punched in a number. "Don't make me wait," he snapped when it was answered after the fifth ring. He listened for a minute and then his voice changed, soft and light. "Hey, P.L., how's it going?" He smiled as he listened to what she said next. "We'll get you crunchy Cheetos when we get you home. Aunt Lucy wants to say hi." He handed the phone to Lucy and nodded.

"Pepper?" she said, trying to keep her voice light.

"Aunt Lucy?"

"Yes, baby." Lucy felt her throat swell. "How are you?"

"I am hungry and the Cheetos are bad," Pepper said. "Can you come get me?"

"Soon, baby," Lucy said. "We just have to shoot the stunt and then that man will tell us where you are."

"We're up high in this building," Pepper said. "We can see the brid—" And then Lucy heard her say, *"Hey."*

The asshole came back on. "Not playing fair, there, buddy-boy."

"You hurt her, I'll kill you," Lucy said, trying to be matter-of-fact.

"Whoo-ee. This the mother? No, no, wait a minute, she's out cold. This is Aunt Lucy. Aunt Lucy with the great ass."

"If you hurt her—" Lucy felt her temper rise to the breaking point. *Steady.*

"Honey, you can come get me anytime you want."

"I will fucking castrate you, you limp-dicked—"

J.T. grabbed the phone from her. "I'll call again," he said and hung up. He looked at Lucy. "If you can't stay calm, you can't talk to him."

Lucy blinked back tears as Gloom put his arm around her. "Okay, we trade her for a helicopter. How the hell are we going to get a helicopter?"

"We aren't. LaFavre is." J.T. punched in the numbers.

Lucy thought about LaFavre taking the helicopter away from Karen. "He's not going to be able to charm her out of it."

"He has other skills." J.T. spoke into the phone, leaving a message.

"I hope they're painful." Lucy took a deep breath. "Listen, Pepper said they were high up in a building. She said they could see the bridge."

Gloom turned to survey the landscape. "That could be anywhere."

"But close," J.T. said. "That's something."

"That's not enough," Lucy said. "I want to do something *now*."

"Good," J.T. said. "You can learn to fall off a bridge."

"What?" Lucy said, jarred out of her fear for Pepper. "What happened to 'the molecules won't part for you'?"

He handed her a harness. "A controlled fall. On a rope. If something goes wrong, you need to be able to go over the side of this bridge, and I'm going to show you how to do that."

"Will it help me get Pepper back?" Lucy said.

"Yes," he said.

"Then show me," she said.

19

Wilder stood on the Jeep's back bumper, dressed once again as Bryce's double. He was parked in the breakdown lane on the east side of the Talmadge Bridge, just short of where Lucy's crew had set up the fake shoot. The sun had set not long ago, and the lights of Savannah sparkled along the riverfront on the south side. Wilder ignored the sight and unpacked his gear from his footlocker, stuffing it all into his battered green rucksack.

A long black metal case lay at the bottom of the locker and he stared at it for several moments, then pulled it out. He ran his fingers along the engraving on the top—his name, with the outline of the Special Forces patch below it. He thought of what Crawford had said about the two killed in the swamp. Sniper.

He put the case into a specially designed slot on the right side of the backpack.

He pulled out his keys to lock the Jeep and saw the Superman logo on the key chain Pepper had given him. It felt like a hole opened up in his chest and a cold wind blew through. He leaned forward and put his head on the support for the roll bar and heard Pepper saying, "Soon?"

"Ah, *fuck*." He tried to regain control of his breathing, of his heart, of his feelings.

It didn't work.

Not right away.

This is my fault, Wilder thought. *My responsibility. I told Lucy they'd all be safe.* His phone rang and he grabbed it. "Wilder."

"Hey, bud," LaFavre said. "Got your message. I was in a briefing. What the hell is going on? We got two gunships locked and loaded. Two lift birds ready to go get some Navy SEALs and kick ass. Waiting on some CIA dickhead's decision."

"Dickhead named Crawford?"

"Yep. Standing about twenty feet away with his buddies, acting important. You know him?"

"Yeah. Weaselly little bastard. Don't trust him. Where are the SEALs?"

"Close, based on the radio traffic and on the fact the lift birds are to pick them up if called. Within twenty miles."

SEALs, Wilder thought. Sea-Air-Land. Stud muffins whose brains sometimes turned to mush above the high-water mark, but no one better in the world on, or in, the water. He turned and looked down from the parking lot at the dark water of the Savannah River. Then he looked up from there toward the darkening horizon where the thousands of islands of the low country lay and beyond it the Atlantic. SEAL country. They'd even give Moot a run for the money in the swamp. He'd bet they taught alligator wrestling at Coronado.

"You there?" LaFavre sounded worried.

"Yeah."

"And where is there?"

"On the Talmadge Bridge getting ready to shoot our last scene with what I have a really bad feeling is live ammo."

There was a moment of silence. "What is going on?"

"You know that little girl you gave the sunglasses to?"

"Pepper." LaFavre's voice slowed. "What happened?"

"They took her to make sure we kept shooting the movie."

"Fuck. They planning on giving her back?"

"That's what they say."

"What do you say?"

"I say the bastard who has her just tortured a man and threw him to a gator."

"What do you need?"

"You remember that helicopter pilot you hit on?"

"Karen?"

"She's in on it. At the airfield now, probably right across the runway from you, getting ready to take the chopper to the bridge. They really need that chopper. Get it and we'll do a trade. Be careful. Karen has a black belt."

"I got a Glock."

"She has the coordinates for the pickup, or will shortly. We'll need those."

"I'll get 'em." LaFavre's voice was grim in a way Wilder hadn't heard since Afghanistan. "Don't worry, bud. We'll get your kid back."

"Yep." Wilder turned off the phone and nodded as he thought about having people you could count on. A SEAL platoon. LaFavre. Lucy.

And Pepper. She was five, but she was smart. He thought of her alone with the ghost and shivered in spite of himself.

Fucking ghost was gonna die for this one.

Lucy was standing by the bridge rail, scanning every tall building in sight, her muscles tense with worry, when J.T. came to stand beside her.

"How's it going?" he asked her.

"Althea's insisting on filming. She won't leave the bridge." *And Pepper's out there with a lunatic.*

"Great." J.T. took a deep breath. "Well, we'll set her up on a rope, too, then. Everything else okay?"

"Pepper's not." Lucy gripped the rail. "She's out there in the dark. With that crazy person. *And I can't do anything.*"

"I don't think he's crazy out of control," J.T. said, patting her on the shoulder clumsily. "I think he's the one who shot out the skid on the helicopter when Bryce fell. You're not out of control if you can do that. Damn good sniper."

"Oh, *Christ.*" Lucy shrugged his hand away. "He's the *bad guy.*"

"Yeah, but he's really good at it," J.T. said. "You gotta respect that and factor it in."

"You're crazier than Nash," Lucy said. "My next guy is going to be an accountant."

"There is no next guy." J.T. moved his hand to her waist and pulled her close. "I'm it."

Lucy leaned into him. "Oh, God, I hope so."

"Believe it. We're going to have some stuff to talk about when we get Pepper back."

Lucy smiled in spite of herself at his "when." Confidence. That's what she needed right now. "What about LaFavre?"

"I called him. He's in action." He straightened. "I'd rather stay here and pat you, but I have to go teach Bryce to be a hero now. I'll set up Althea's line, too."

"You got about ten minutes," Lucy said.

"That should do it." He grinned at her and walked off, and she watched him go and then looked back over the rail at the swamp, wondering if Moot was the gator who'd gotten Finnegan. Since Finnegan was dead at the time, it shouldn't matter, but hadn't Pepper said something about feeding alligators making them unafraid of humans? If you fed them humans, wouldn't that make them even less afraid? And Pepper was out there someplace. . . .

But someplace high, so no gators. One worry gone. Lucy squinted toward the grain elevators in the distance. They were high. But so was the hotel. So were the cranes in the port on the other side of the bridge. So were—

Gloom came up beside Lucy.

"We're good to go," he said, handing her a harness for Althea. "Depending on how loosely you define 'good.' "

"Thanks." Lucy took the rig and looked up at him, his long, cranky face trying to look sympathetic and just looking pained. *Confidence,* she thought. Time to stop thinking worst-case scenario, start planning for the future, for when Pepper was back. "Listen, when we get Pepper back, I'm staying down here with her and Daisy. Daisy and I are going to open a southern branch of the business, so you're going to have to run the New York office. From my loft."

"You sure about this?" Gloom said after a moment.

"I'm positive," Lucy said. "I need a new life. And they must need commercials with dogs down here, too, so I should be set." She lifted her chin. "That okay with you?"

"Under different circumstances, I'd be thrilled," Gloom said, looking depressed.

"We'll talk when we get her back," Lucy said. "We're going to get her back—"

"Lucy?" Althea said from behind her.

Lucy turned and saw the little blond actress, her face drawn and tense.

"J.T.'s talking to Bryce. He said you wanted to talk to me?"

"Yep." *Get to work, Armstrong.* Lucy held up the cable harness that Gloom had given her. "You're going to learn how to rappel off a bridge, babe."

"I'll go check on the camera," Gloom said and began to leave. Then he turned back. "Thanks. For the loft. And everything."

"You deserve it." Lucy turned to see Althea looking at the harness with no enthusiasm. "You don't have to do this," Lucy told her. "You don't have to be here at all. You can stay down in base camp."

"This is my big scene," Althea said, sounding very sure. "I'm going to be in it."

"Okay. Well, things may go . . . differently tonight." Lucy pasted a smile on. "So, while I know the storyboards call for you to wear this only as a safety, you might actually have to use it in case you have to rappel over the side."

Althea looked at her, eyes wide. "What's going on?"

"We're shooting a scene that could go wrong," Lucy said. "But Bryce will be there to take care of you."

Althea looked at her doubtfully.

"And J.T."

Althea still looked doubtful.

"You can trust them, Al. For tonight, there are two men you can trust." Lucy tapped her own chest. "See, even I'm wearing a harness. You and me in matching outfits. Except yours is a size two."

Althea thought about it. "Okay," she said and stripped off her camisole.

J.T. looked over and then looked away.

Nothing to see here, Lucy thought. That he hadn't already seen. Oh, screw that. All that mattered was getting Pepper back.

"Lucy?"

"Right." Lucy helped her get the harness on. "Okay," she said when Althea was rigged and clothed again. "Go over and have Nash check it and then have J.T. double-check that."

"What's wrong with Nash?" Althea asked.

"Nash is a bad guy," Lucy said. "We don't trust him."

"Oh." Althea blinked. "Is this the lying thing?"

Lucy hesitated and then thought, *Truth can't hurt.* "He kidnapped Pepper and he's holding her hostage until we finish this stunt."

Althea went white. "He *what?*"

"He's doing something crooked, and he needs to make sure the stunt goes off, so he had someone take Pepper into the swamp. And now we have to make sure the shoot goes off as planned so we can get her back. If you don't want to film—"

"That son of a bitch," Althea said, swinging around to stare at Nash, and Lucy drew back.

"Yeah, we think so, too." She looked at Althea closely. "You okay?"

"*Yeah,*" Althea said, recovering. "I was just really happy because Bryce and I are getting married, and this is just *ruining* my mood."

"Wonderful," Lucy said, not so sure. "Well, Bryce and J.T. are right over there, so if you want—"

"I think *Us* is going to want the pictures," Althea said.

"Good," Lucy said again, wondering at Althea's lousy pronoun use and then recognizing the name of the weekly. "*Us* is a great magazine." *Did you just hear me say Pepper's been kidnapped?*

"Cutting edge," Althea said. "I was really happy. And now *this*." She looked furious.

"The guys are over there," Lucy said, and thought, *I'm worried about Pepper and she's upset because the news is a buzz kill.*

Althea headed for Nash, looking grim, and Lucy took a deep breath. Getting close to showtime. She looked back out at the grain towers and then the port cranes. Pepper could be there. Pepper could be anywhere.

Hang in there, honey, she thought. *We're coming for you.*

Wilder had looked over at Lucy helping Althea in time to see Althea strip to the waist. *Oh, Christ,* he thought, and turned to Bryce to finish explaining Rappelling 101. When he was done, he said, "So you got it?"

Bryce swallowed hard and nodded, taking a quick glance over the edge of the bridge at the dark water below.

Wilder continued. "I've already prepped two ropes on the outside of the railing, double-secured with snap links. My own ropes, not Nash's. This is only just in case. You most likely won't have to do it."

"Right," Bryce said, trying to project confidence and failing miserably.

"You always have to have an emergency escape plan," Wilder said. "Remember, we talked about that at Bragg when we trained together."

"Right."

"Althea's counting on you," Wilder said, trying not to feel guilty. It seemed like a thousand years since he'd gone back to his hotel room to find Althea in his bed. He looked over and saw her with Nash now, getting her harness checked and also evidently bitching him out. She looked furious, and he looked stone-faced. Well, anything that fucked up Nash's day was good by him. He looked back at Bryce. "I think she's tense. You know. She's going to depend on you."

"Right," Bryce said soberly.

"Okay, then." Wilder took out his cell phone. "I've got to make a call."

"Right," Bryce said.

Wilder peered at him. "You all right?"

"I'm not a hero," Bryce said. "I'm an actor."

"Tonight you're both," Wilder said.

"Yeah?" Bryce began to look hopeful.

"Yeah. Remember the bar fight? You were right in there, you were my wingman."

"Right," Bryce said, hope fading. "Except I screwed up."

"You won't screw this up. Althea is counting on you. Lucy is counting on you. *I'm* counting on you."

Bryce nodded.

"Anything else?"

"It's okay about you and Althea," Bryce said.

Fuck.

"It was my fault, screwing around on her. You didn't know about us."

Oh, crap. "Bryce—"

"We're getting married," Bryce said.

Wilder clapped him on the shoulder. "That's great." *You poor son of a bitch.*

"*People* and *InStyle* are interested in the wedding."

"Uh huh," Wilder said, not a clue what he was talking about. What people?

"I thought you could be my best man," Bryce said. "I mean, if you wanted to be."

Not really. "You bet, buddy. Now you remember the drill here, right?"

"Right," Bryce said. "Maybe after the wedding, Althea and I could rappel off a bridge onto our honeymoon yacht."

"Good idea," Wilder said. "Mention it to her." *Before you shove her off the bridge when and if the shooting starts.* "Now, I really have to make this call."

"Not a girlfriend, is it?" Bryce said.

"What?"

"The last time, you said it was your girlfriend, but it wasn't. You're on a mission, aren't you?"

"Yes," Wilder said, surprised Bryce was that acute.

"Army stuff?"

"No," Wilder said, and thought, *What the hell.* "CIA."

"Whoa." Bryce nodded. "Is that who you're calling? The CIA?"

"Yes," Wilder said. "Anything else you need before I go?"

"No." Bryce squared his shoulders. "Anything I can do for you?"

Wilder looked across the bridge to where Nash was punching numbers into his cell phone, his anger back under control. "Just follow orders and don't go near Nash."

"Right." Bryce looked over the rail at the ropes again.

"Hi, baby," Althea said, coming to stand beside him. She looked mad as hell.

"I'm going to take care of you, Althea," Bryce said in his best leading-man voice.

"I know, baby," Althea said and looked past him, fury in her eyes.

Wilder turned and saw Nash talking to Lucy.

"Could you check my harness, J.T.?" Althea asked.

"Uh, yeah." Wilder did the fastest check he'd ever done, essentially making sure it was securely attached to her body and she wouldn't slide through it. Her breasts would help in that matter: good anchor points. "You guys are good to go, then," he said and headed for Lucy, phone in hand.

"Lucy, you have to get Wilder off the damn bridge," Nash said, and Lucy turned around from watching Wilder talking to Bryce and Althea and said, "No."

It was amazing how normal Nash looked standing there, a little tense, but he was always tense before a stunt, that's why his stunts always went well. He didn't look like a soulless, babynapping bastard at all. *God, I hate you.*

"This is crazy, Lucy," he said, leaning in closer. "This guy, he's got you so paranoid, you're working with no crew. This is no way to make a movie, you can't possibly get—"

"Don't tell me about making movies," Lucy snapped. "It's never been about making movies for you, it's always been about you, you showing off, you getting the girl, you being the fastest gun in the West. I'm sick of it and I'm sick of you." She leaned closer to him. "And I will do whatever is necessary to get Pepper back. If that includes sending you to hell, I will do it with a song in my heart."

His eyes shifted left, and he said, "What are you talking about?"

"I am never going to forgive you for taking Pepper. If you don't stop this stupid plan, and give her back, you're *dead*. I will see to it. Now *get off my set*."

"Not a chance," he said, and then J.T. came up behind him and deliberately shoved him out of the way.

Nash wheeled around, and J.T. said, "Back off."

"Fuck you," Nash said and walked off.

"That was immature," Lucy said. "I liked it. Next time knock him off the damn bridge."

Wilder punched buttons on the phone, listened, and then said, "It's me. Did you get the coordinates?" He nodded. "She give you any trouble?" He nodded again. "Bring it on in close." He clicked off and then dialed another number.

"What's going on?" Lucy said.

"LaFavre got the coordinates from Karen. Someone text messaged them to her on his phone."

"Karen just gave him her phone?"

"No." He put his attention back on the phone. "This is Wilder." He held it out so Lucy could hear. *Crawford,* he mouthed.

"What?" Crawford said.

"We got a lot of shit going on here," Wilder said.

"Just stay out of the way and—"

"Got a five-year-old girl kidnapped."

There was a long silence. "There's nothing that can be done about that right now."

"Letsky is more important than the life of a five-year-old?" Wilder asked, but Lucy could tell he already knew the answer.

"What did you call for?"

"I know where the meet is. Got the coordinates. I'll give them to you, if you do something for me."

"What?"

"You're missing a Major LaFavre. Supposed to be there in one of your birds."

"Yeah?"

"He's not AWOL. You assigned him to me."

"Hell, I don't care. The coordinates?"

"*You assigned him to me.* If he gets any backlash from this, people are going to find out how bad you fucked this up."

"Okay, hell, fine, I assigned him to you. Give me the coordinates."

"Tango-Alpha, Six, Four, Four, Seven, One, Eight."

"We'll check them out," Crawford said. "But—"

"Take guns when you check it out," Wilder said. "Take real Army guys who know how to shoot and stuff. Or even SEALs."

Crawford hung up and Wilder said, "Asshole," and turned the phone off.

"Will he do it?" Lucy asked.

Wilder nodded. "Yeah, but getting Pepper back is up to us." He started punching numbers into his phone again. "Okay, now we do leverage." He waited, holding out the phone so Lucy could hear.

"She's still breathing and talking," the voice came.

"I'm not as slow as you think, Ghost Boy," Wilder said. "You have something I want back, and I have something you want back."

"What the hell are you talking about?"

"I've got your helicopter."

There was a long silence. "Bullshit."

"Karen was picking it up at Hunter when she ran into some trouble." Wilder spoke slowly and clearly. "The trouble's a friend of mine named LaFavre and he has your bird. Thus, I have your helicopter. You want it back, you give me Pepper."

"I don't fuckin' believe you."

"Do you need the chopper to pick up the art or just for the rendezvous?" Wilder asked.

Again there was a long silence.

"Answer me," Wilder demanded. "Time's-a-wasting."

"Just the rendezvous."

"Good. You guys do whatever it is you're doing on the bridge. We'll stay out of your way. Bring Pepper to the rendezvous, I'll call in the chopper. Then we trade and you can get the hell out of our lives."

This time Wilder waited.

"Fuck you. All right."

The phone went dead, and Lucy let out her breath. "Is this going to work?" she asked, her heart pounding.

"Hell, yes," Wilder said. "Sufferin' Sappho, woman, have some faith."

"Okay then," Lucy said, really wanting to believe him. "It's show-time."

20

Wilder moved to his position near the railing. A container ship pushed by two tugboats came around the bend in the Savannah River, approaching the city's riverfront, about a mile from the bridge. It was much larger than the one they had seen the other day, a real mother of a—

Screw me, he thought and punched in Crawford's number on his satellite phone even as he looked to the right and saw Nash standing at the edge, also staring at the cargo ship, weapon slung over his shoulder, fast-rope tied off to the railing next to him.

Crawford didn't sound happy. "What do you want?" The sound of a helicopter thudded in the background and Wilder knew Crawford was flying toward the meeting location.

"Letsky's art is on the damn cargo ship, isn't it?"

"No."

Liar, Wilder thought angrily. "Don't—"

Crawford cut him off. "Letsky *thinks* his art is on the ship. Finnegan thought it was. Nash thinks it is. Because we let it leak that it was. There's a container holding cases that look like the cases the art was in on board the ship."

"Why didn't you tell me?"

"What difference would it have made?" Crawford was speaking fast, trying to explain his way out of the shit hole he'd dug. "We never thought it would go this far. It was a setup from the very beginning to draw Letsky out to where we could get him. We thought that Finnegan and Letsky would try to steal the art off the ship on the high seas, where we could take them down with no civilians involved. The whole movie thing caught us off guard. That's why we had to scramble and put you on that set."

"The SEAL platoon?"

"They're with me. And they're not going to do a damn thing to stop Nash from taking the stuff. Their job is to take out Letsky."

"You're an asshole," Wilder said and hung up.

He looked at Nash, who seemed mesmerized by the approaching cargo ship. Three minutes, tops. *Think fast,* he told himself. If Nash looked in the containers to check them and found out the jade wasn't there . . . No leverage.

No Pepper.

Damn it, he thought and headed for the rail.

Tyler scanned the container ship through his thermal scope. It was almost abreast of his location, less than a hundred feet away, so large it was blocking off the view of the Savannah riverfront completely. There was a cluster of warm bodies on the bridge, but as far as he could tell, there was no one forward of midship.

He went back and leaned the sniper rifle against the metal door leading to the staircase and picked up another gun with a regular sight on it. There was enough light coming off the bridge, the town, and the spotlights on the ship itself, that he could check the containers stacked up on the deck. The source in Mexico had said the one they wanted would be on the top layer, starboard side, so it could be one of the first off.

"What are you doing?"

Tyler gritted his teeth and ignored her. He read letters and numbers, starting from the very front. Bingo. Fifth one back from the bow, on top, starboard. Tyler adjusted for distance and wind, then pulled the trigger. The specially loaded paintball arced through the air and splatted against the side of the container, marking it with a splotch of glowing chemical mixture.

"Cool. What'd you do that for?"

Tyler tossed the paintball gun away. He saw that the Kid was right next to the sniper rifle. "Get away from that."

The Kid started and hit the gun, which slid toward the roof.

"Damn it!" Tyler grabbed for it, but the rifle hit the ground. He picked it up, checking for damage, but there didn't appear to be any. He hissed at the Kid, doing his best gator imitation, and went back to looking at the ship.

"What are you doing?"

"Nothing."

"Are you gonna shoot somebody?"

"Yeah. You."

There was a long silence and then he turned around.

She was sitting with her back against the wall, big tears rolling down her fat little filthy cheeks.

"Crybaby."

She sniffed and swallowed, smearing the tears off her cheeks with dirty palms. "Am not. You got any more Cheetos?"

"No." He turned back to the scope in time to see somebody move on the bridge, and his smile widened.

"Payday," he said to himself.

"I *said* do you got any more Cheetos?"

The Kid just *never* shut up. He took his drive-on rag, a strip of green cloth, grabbed her head, and wrapped it around her mouth.

"Should have done that a long time ago," he said as he gathered his gear.

She tried to claw it off, but he'd tied it good and tight. She began to gag, and then cry, and Tyler became worried that she'd choke on the rag. He'd never get his chopper if the little snot choked to death.

He ripped the cloth off. "Take it easy. Breathe." He put his hand under her chin and she sank her teeth into the fleshy part of his hand, and he reacted instinctively, his other hand hitting her on the side of the head. She dropped in slow motion, the momentum of the blow sending her rolling toward the roof edge.

Tyler grabbed her a split second before she went airborne.

Fuck. If she had gone, no chopper.

He threw her over his shoulder and headed for the stairs.

His fucking phone rang again. Fucking proof of life.

Tyler ignored it and hit the stairs.

Wilder felt the weight of the pack on his back, especially the pull of the long black case on the right side. He was tempted to take the case out, but it was too soon. He had to play this as long and as tight as he could because Pepper was out there. And the goddamn ghost wasn't answering his phone.

He could hear the chopper in the distance and looking to the east he could see its lights as it went in a holding pattern about a thousand feet away over the river. He glanced over at Lucy at the monitors, her face grim as she listened to the phone ring. Still no answer.

Wilder went over to where Althea was handcuffed to the back door of the truck.

"How you doing, kid?" he said.

"Okay." She looked paler than usual, but she tried to smile.

"It's okay," he told her. "We're all watching out for you."

"I know," she said. "But, J.T.?"

"Yeah?"

"Remember that gun you showed me? The Glock?"

"I've got it right here," he told her to reassure her.

"Could I have it?"

"What?"

"You know, to give to Bryce? So he can save me." She smiled at him wanly.

"Uh, no," Wilder said, trying not to shudder at the idea of Bryce with live ammunition. "But he won't need it. He knows everything he has to without the gun. And he's got that big knife."

"Oh." Althea nodded. "Okay."

"Great." Wilder surveyed the bridge. Just the stunt people, Lucy, Gloom, and Bryce. Everybody else was gone, ordered off the bridge by Lucy half an hour earlier.

High Noon. The townspeople were clearing out.

"J.T.?" Althea said from behind him.

"Yeah?"

"Bryce can't see me if you're standing there."

"Right," Wilder said and moved out of the line of sight.

Lucy gestured to him and he turned on the small FM radio in his combat vest.

"There's no answer," he heard her say through the speaker, her voice tight. "I called, there's no answer."

Wilder looked out at the ship, getting closer. "He's on the move," he told her. "Give him five minutes and try it again."

"You sure—"

"Yes," he said, "start the stunt," and a minute later he heard her say, *"Rolling."*

There was no echo on the set. Nobody there to echo. Ghost town.

Then she said, "Action," and Wilder watched as Nash, dressed as Rip, reached up to the bulky block of fake explosives he had attached to the back door next to Althea and pressed a button while she screamed and struggled. A glowing red display began a countdown as Nash ran toward the fast-rope he had waiting.

Such a cliché, Wilder thought. *Just get off the fucking bridge and out of Lucy's life.*

Nash grabbed the thick fast-rope, wrapped his arm around it, and disappeared off the bridge, sliding down toward the deck of the ship as the bow passed underneath. Bryce came dashing forward, trying to be the hero, looking wildly back and forth. The bad guys had disappeared and his girl was trapped with a bomb. What should a hero do?

Save the girl, of course.

Wilder glanced over his shoulder, gave Lucy his best reassuring smile, then ran forward to the fast-rope and grabbed hold to go after the bad guy.

His girl knew how to save herself.

Lucy checked the monitor. No film in the camera but still a nice shot of the armored car. If she had an apple in her hand and Pepper beside her, it would be a good night.

Get her back, get her back—

She looked at it closer.

The detonator looked wrong. Any other day, she'd have said, "What do I know from detonators?" but today was not that kind of day. "J.T.?" she said into her headpiece.

"What?" he said, sounding distracted, which he probably was, since he was somewhere between the bridge and the ship, descending fast.

"I don't think the detonator's right. It's smaller and it—"

"Tell Althea to get away from the truck." She heard a thump and Wilder's sharp intake of breath. "I'm on the ship."

"Well, get back here."

"Doesn't work that way—one-way rope. Gravity rules."

Lucy stood up. "Althea," she called. "We're going to go a different way with this shot. You can leave."

Althea nodded and tried to help Bryce unsnap the cuff. "It's stuck," she called back.

"The cuff is stuck," Lucy told J.T. over the radio as she started to run toward Althea. "What do I do?"

"Stuck?" J.T. swore, but his voice was low, almost a whisper. "It's not stuck, the asshole used real cuffs, which probably means real explosives. You—"

Lucy dropped the headset and ran for Althea. When she reached the car, there were sixty seconds on the detonator.

Lucy pulled the gun out of the holster under her shirt. "Hi, Al, how's it going?"

"Lucy?" Althea said, and then Lucy put the barrel on the chain and fired. Althea screamed and Lucy spun her around and yelled, *"Run,"* and Althea and Bryce ran for the rail while Lucy went flat out for the monitors, yelling, *"Get behind the truck,"* to Gloom, diving behind it with him just as the armored car exploded, catching a piece of hot metal on her cheek and something else on the back of her head.

Then she was on the ground behind the truck, hands over her head as metal rained down all around them.

Wilder was in the middle of the ship, crouched down on a container, MP-5 at the ready, when he heard the explosion from above. Hot metal went everywhere, sharp edges slicing through the air, heavy chunks thudding onto the river, steaming, and somewhere up there . . .

"Lucy?" Wilder whispered into the radio, more afraid than he'd ever been in his life.

Silence.

He swallowed. *"Lucy?"*

Maybe she was just concussed. Maybe . . .

"Lucy," he said, his voice sharp. *"Answer me, damn it."*

"Hey," her voice came over the headset, shaky. "I just got blown up. Give me a minute."

"Are you hurt?"

"No," she said, her voice unsteady.

"Are you all right?"

"Yes," she said, but she wasn't. He could tell.

"Where are you bleeding?"

"I'm not—"

"Don't screw with me, Lucy, *where did you get hit?*"

"My cheek," she said. "I'll probably have a nice scar."

"Scars add character. Where else?"

"Thumped the back of my head."

Wilder swore. "Double vision? Dizziness—"

"J.T., a fucking car just blew up behind me. Dizzy, hell, I'm mad. What did that asshole think he was doing? He was going to kill *Althea.*"

"He was creating a diversion," Wilder said, relieved that she was mad. "Probably supposed to keep me busy to give him time to get on the ship without me. I moved too soon."

"The ship's pretty much under the bridge."

"I know," Wilder said. "I'm on it." He looked to the right as his section of the ship cleared the bridge and saw two people dangling on ropes above the waiting speedboat. "Bryce and Althea got off the bridge." *They're just not getting off the ropes.*

"Are they okay?"

Wilder watched Bryce swing closer to Althea and fumble with her rigging. "Kind of."

"Kind of?"

Use the knife to cut her free, Wilder thought, and still Bryce fumbled.

Wilder went to the side of the ship, trying to keep an eye out for Nash and anything else that would kill him. He waved to get Bryce's attention, and by some miracle, after the fourth or fifth wave, Bryce looked over and stopped, stunned.

Wilder pulled out his knife and waved it at Bryce.

Bryce looked at his own knife.

That's good, Wilder thought, *make the connection.*

Bryce drew his knife and reached for Althea, and Wilder said a prayer to whoever protected fools and actors, put the sword back in the sheath, and went to look for Nash.

· · ·

Hell, Lucy thought, as her head throbbed. *Pepper. Damn it, I can't have a concussion, I have to get Pepper.*

"You okay?" Gloom asked.

"Great," Lucy said and looked over the top of the truck bed.

The armored car was in burning pieces all over the bridge, its glow lighting up the center span.

"Get off the bridge," she said to Gloom. "Get everybody packed up and out of base camp. Get them away from this hellhole."

"I'll wait for you in the camper," Gloom said and started down the bridge, giving the burning car a wide berth.

Lucy headed for the rail. The ship was almost completely out from under the bridge now and J.T. was on it. Althea and Bryce were hanging by ropes over the side above the dark water, Bryce waving his knife at Althea in the shadows. *No, really, trust Bryce,* she thought and then sighed. Below them, Doc waited in the boat, as planned in the stunt as a safety, only the running lights on.

I hate you, too, she thought. Kidnapping bastard.

She straddled the railing and watched as Bryce cut the rope and he and Althea did the short drop into the water.

Don't look down, she thought. *God, I hate irony.* She clipped the rope to her vest and looked out into the darkness at the skyline as instructed. Then she took a deep breath, threw her other leg over the rail so she was on the river side, and pushed off, extending her brake arm as J.T. had taught her so that she descended a good fifty feet before bringing it in tight and coming to a halt, swinging on the rope.

Then she heard powerful engines rev below, thought, *What the hell?* and looked down.

No speedboat anymore, just a body in the water.

"*No,*" she said and let go of her brake hand to slide off the rope into the water, hitting hard and shuddering at the cold as she went in. She swam toward the body—*Doc*—and rolled him over, relieved when he coughed and then worried again when he went limp as she supported him with her arm. It didn't make sense, Doc was one of the bad guys. Who—

She heard the helicopter coming in, which was a damn good thing since she was never going make it to shore with him. Her clothes were soaked and dragging her down, but she couldn't get them off without letting go of him, and if she did that, he'd go under. Even if he was part of the gang that had kidnapped Pepper, she couldn't let him go under.

Water splashed in her face from the blast of the blades overhead and she squinted, looking up. The helicopter was hovering just above them, slowly getting closer and closer.

The skid. It was right there, less than six inches above the water and two feet away. Lucy could see LaFavre in the darkness in the pilot's seat, grinning at her. He wasn't wearing his dark glasses this time but it made no difference as his eyes were covered by night-vision goggles bolted to his flight helmet.

She looped Doc's arm over the metal and then smacked him hard on the cheek. He came to and clutched the skid, more out of instinct than conscious thought, and Lucy grabbed hold of the skid with both hands and pulled herself up onto it. She reached down and grabbed Doc, pulling them both into the chopper to sprawl on the metal floor, where Doc promptly threw up half the river.

Lucy got to her knees as the helicopter lifted and looked at Karen in the back, her wrists handcuffed to a piece of chain, looking like hell.

"I swear, Lucy," she said over the rotor noise. "I didn't know he'd kidnap Pepper."

"Fuck you," Lucy said and took the handcuffs LaFavre indicated on the seat next to him. She cuffed Doc's hands behind his back and then let him fall forward again.

"No one was supposed to get hurt," Karen said, leaning forward, her face earnest. "No one was supposed to even *know*. That's what Nash told us."

"Well, he lied. And so did you. And then you tried to cut him out and it made him crazy." She leaned forward. "I warned you about this when the skid broke. I *told you* he'd take you down. *You stupid bitch, you could have stopped this and now he's got Pepper!*"

Karen pulled back, and Lucy rolled Doc over with her foot so he wouldn't fall out if LaFavre banked. Then she climbed between the seats and sat beside LaFavre, who was already gaining altitude. "Did you see Bryce and Althea? Doc was supposed to pick them up but . . ."

LaFavre shook his head. "Probably on the speedboat. It's by the big ship."

"That's where we're going. We head for the ship and we get J.T. Go."

"Not the plan," LaFavre said.

"Fuck the plan."

He shook his head. "Trust J.T. We stand off, watch and wait for the call. This is about the little sweetie."

Lucy swallowed. "But he's out there alone."

"No, he's not," LaFavre said. "We're here." He nodded to a pair of binoculars hanging between them. "Take those. See if you can find him. It's light enough on that ship."

Lucy picked them up and trained them on the brightly lit ship. "I don't see him."

"Keep looking," LaFavre said, and Lucy leaned forward, her heart pounding as she searched.

Wilder wished he had his night-vision goggles but the ship had its lights on and there was a lot of glow from the bridge overhead, thanks to the burning car. He was pissed. On top of kidnapping Pepper, Nash had been more than willing to blow up Althea, Bryce, and Lucy. What the hell was worth that?

He moved across the top of the stacks of containers, finger on the trigger, wishing the goddamn SEALs would get there, knowing they wouldn't because they had goddamn orders and goddamn Crawford had them winging out toward goddamn Letsky while things were going to shit here.

Over the throb of the ship's engines, he heard a splash off the starboard side and knew he was very close to Nash's position. Another splash. Nash was offloading the cargo, probably for pickup by Doc in the speedboat. Then the boat would go to the rendezvous with the chopper. As long as Nash kept moving and didn't stop to check that the jade was in the boxes, it would work out. Wilder realized the whole cargo-net-on-the-bridge thing had been bullshit. Misdirection by Nash. He wouldn't need the net until the rendezvous. No wonder he was pissed that LaFavre had pointed that out.

Wilder gave a nervous glance to his rear, knowing the ghost might be keeping watch, ready to pick off anybody who interfered. He'd yet to play his hand, which was good since it upped the odds he was actually going to bring Pepper to the rendezvous. And somewhere ahead was Nash with his back pressed so hard against the wall, he was probably through it to the other side. And the other side was pure desperation. And desperate people were the most dangerous of all.

Wilder heard a speedboat cut through the water and thought, *Nash's pickup*. He worked his way around the last container to see the boat, hearing its engine cut before he got a good look.

It was a cigarette boat, the one favored by drug runners, sleek and fast, stopped now, and Bryce was on the fantail, picking up one of the boxes Nash had dropped. *What the hell?* Two more boxes were already in the boat, and while Wilder watched, Bryce reached for another one, working fast, faster than Wilder had ever seen him do anything.

Bryce is working with Nash? Wilder thought, dumbfounded.

The world really was screwed up. So much for wingmen.

Then his sat phone vibrated in his pocket, making him jump. *God damn.* Wilder kept the MP-5 in one hand and pulled it out with the other.

"Wilder," he hissed.

"We got him."

Wilder blinked. Despite the static, it had to be Crawford because no one else would send such a vague message. "Who?"

"Letsky. He put up a fight and we blew his yacht right out of the water. Mission accomplished."

"That's great but—" And then he heard the slightest of sounds behind him and he swung around, dropping the phone and bringing the MP-5 to bear on Nash and pulling the trigger.

Nothing happened.

He automatically began to clear and recock the gun but Nash slammed the stock of his own MP-5 against the side of Wilder's head, dropping him semiconscious to the deck.

"Removed the firing pin the first night you were in the hotel," Nash said. "Before Althea distracted you for me. So busy checking *her* gear, you never checked your own." He kicked the sat phone overboard.

Wilder blinked, trying to clear the fog, and looked up into Nash's crazed eyes. He could hear a helicopter coming close. *Gotta move,* he thought, but his body wouldn't obey.

"Got a vest, don't you, mate?" Nash said it almost matter-of-factly, dropping his submachine gun to the end of its sling and drawing his big-ass pistol with one smooth motion, faster than he had in the parking lot. And Wilder knew that Nash was just like him—had hot loads that would cut right through his body armor like going through butter.

"We've got your chopper," Wilder managed to croak out.

"You're a damn liar," Nash said and pulled the trigger.

"I've got Wilder," Lucy said, seeing him on the deck. "He's—" Then her glasses moved to take in Nash, who lifted his gun and fired a single shot, straight into J.T.'s chest. *"NO!"*

"What?" LaFavre asked.

"He shot him," Lucy screamed. "Get *down there.*"

LaFavre swore beside her. "Who shot him? He has a vest, what—"

"Put me down on that ship."

They were two minutes out, two minutes that lasted a lifetime for Lucy, who kept her glasses trained on J.T. sprawled unmoving on the deck and fucking Nash, who jumped over the side of the ship and clambered on board the speedboat, which roared away.

LaFavre brought the chopper in just above J.T., and Lucy jumped out, stumbling, her heart in her mouth. She ran to J.T., dropping down beside him when she reached him. *"Damn it, you're not dead, you have your vest on."* She tried to pull him upright and his head lolled back, but he was breathing, that was something, he was breathing. "Oh, God, don't die, I love you," she said, and held on to him, dragging him toward the chopper, not sure she was doing the right thing.

He coughed, and she thought, *If he's got internal injuries, I'm killing him,* but then he coughed again and grabbed on to her.

"Are you shot?" she said, supporting his weight. "Are you hurt?" *Of course he's shot, you idiot, you saw it.* "Can you make it to the chopper?"

She supported him as they lurched together toward it. Way upriver, she could see the disappearing wake of the speedboat heading for the swamp, Nash and his damn jade aboard. Well, he could have it as long as J.T. was all right and they got Pepper back. That was all that mattered, J.T. and Pepper.

She pulled J.T. over to the chopper and all but shoved him on, her adrenaline surging.

"Where's he hit?" LaFavre yelled over the rotors.

"He had his vest on," Lucy yelled back.

LaFavre shook his head. "Nash had a pistol. Those were hot loads. He's hit."

Lucy ripped off J.T.'s shirt and checked his vest as he tried to sit up. There was no sign of a bullet wound.

"What the hell?" LaFavre said to him. "Why aren't you dead?"

J.T. winced and tapped Bryce's knife. The leather sheath was split and the blade was bent to hell.

"Bet that hurt," LaFavre said, grinning.

"Bryce's stupid knife saved you?" Lucy said and swallowed back tears.

J.T. blinked at her. "No crying in Special Ops, Lucy," he said, his breath coming better now. He patted her on the back.

She nodded and swallowed again. *Fucking Army asshole, you scared the hell out of me.* "Nash got away." She blinked. "But we've got Doc and Karen."

"Throw 'em off," J.T. said, sitting up with great care.

"Into the water?" Lucy said, more than ready to.

"Onto the ship," J.T. said. "By the time they get out of the cuffs and find their way back to land, it'll be over."

LaFavre nodded and rolled a now semiconscious Doc out of the helicopter onto the deck of the ship. Doc hit the deck hard and swore, and Lucy thought, *Good.*

Karen looked up at LaFavre and smiled. "You thought I was pretty sweet once."

"That was before your buddies kidnapped a friend of mine." LaFavre dragged her to her feet and pushed her out, too, watching her stumble onto the deck, mad as hell. He turned to J.T. "I got the RV coordinates. I can drop you nearby, wait for your call for the trade."

J.T. nodded. "Do it."

Lucy strapped herself in beside him. "What's going on? I found Doc in the water. Who's driving the speedboat?"

"You are not going to believe that," J.T. said and put a headset on as LaFavre lifted off. "Where's the boat?"

"Out of sight," LaFavre said. "I'll head for the RV."

The helicopter gained altitude and Lucy looked down at Doc and Karen on the container ship. Good riddance.

Beside her, J.T. reached into her pocket and pulled out her cell phone. "Proof of life," he told her.

Just get her back, Lucy thought and stared across the water as the swamp rushed toward them.

Tyler held the unconscious Kid in his lap as he revved the three-wheel ATV's engine and raced down the dirt track he'd scouted out through the swamp. He loved it when a plan came together. Even the improvising shit like snatching the Kid had worked out.

"Out-fucking-standing," Tyler screamed, the sound mixed with the sound of the engine echoing through the swamp. "I am *The Man*."

The cell phone vibrated in his pocket and he reluctantly brought the vehicle to a halt. "What now?" he demanded.

"Proof of life," the Stranger said.

"She's breathing," Tyler said. "All her fingers and toes. Still got her head."

"Proof of life."

"Proof of helicopter," Tyler said, and then the Kid began to stir. "Hold on." He shook her a little to wake her up, her head wobbling back and forth. "Hey, Kid. Your pal's on the phone." He put the phone up next to her ear. "Talk."

"J.T.?" the Kid said, all her sass gone. *"J.T.!"* she said and began to sob. She listened to him, gulping back tears. "Okay," she said and cried again.

Tyler took the phone back. "Helicopter. On the road where the first stunt was fucked up. By me. Great shot to that skid, eh?" He clicked off the phone before the Stranger could say anything. He'd been bitched at enough today. "You hang on," he told the Kid. "You fall off, the gators can have you."

Then he revved the engine, racing along the berm that paralleled the Savannah River, heading for the RV point, with the Kid clutching him and crying.

Finally, it was all coming together. There was going to be money, lots of it. And women, lots of them.

Everybody's gonna want a piece of me, he thought and leaned forward, triumphant.

Wilder shut off Lucy's phone and looked over at her, trying to look calm instead of insane with fury. "Pepper's all right." He turned to LaFavre, who had the chopper in a hover about fifty feet above the river and to the east of the Talmadge while he checked the glowing screen of the GPS.

"Got the bridge as a waypoint, naturally," LaFavre said. "Also got a spot upriver. Near the old bridge."

Wilder nodded, putting Pepper's misery out of his mind. This was why they had done the fall-out-of-the-helicopter stunt there and why Karen had been punching in the waypoint. It had been a rehearsal for their linkup after the heist. A boat could pull up right to that berm at the spot where the chopper would land. "That's the rendezvous point. Let's go." He glanced at Lucy and gave her a smile, trying not to think about Pepper's sobs.

"Roger that," LaFavre said. He banked the chopper and they flew under the bridge, heading upstream.

"Okay," Wilder said. "Here's the plan."

21

Five minutes later, Lucy stepped out onto the helicopter's right skid, and thought, *This isn't good,* and mentally apologized to Bryce for ever thinking he was a wimp.

"On our next date," she yelled across to J.T. on the opposite skid, "we are not going anyplace that has a swamp or guns."

He yelled back, "I'm partial to room service now."

LaFavre laughed. "I find this strangely romantic."

"You would," Lucy yelled. *Don't look down,* she thought. *Ground very far below, moving very fast, do* not *look down.*

"Ten seconds!" LaFavre said.

J.T. looked down into the swamp. "Ready?"

Lucy swallowed. There was a low bridge ahead, and she blinked as she realized it was the one where Stephanie had had her accident. The chopper banked slightly right. She took a deep breath and looked down and tried not to throw up. Directly below them, moving fast, was a gravel road—the same road on which Bryce had almost splatted just two days earlier. *Oh, God.*

"Five!" LaFavre called.

I hate this.

"Four!"

"You can do this," J.T. called.

"Three!"

They were less than ten feet above the road, still descending way too fast in her opinion. The helicopter shuddered and the nose began to lift.

"Two!"

"Follow me," J.T. yelled and disappeared from the other side.

"Now!"

"Oh, just hell," Lucy said and stepped off the skid.

She dropped less than six inches from skid to gravel, stumbling into a crouch as the rotors whipped overhead, then the engine whined in protest as LaFavre powered it to max and the chopper roared back into the night sky. J.T. grabbed her and pulled her down in the grass on the side of the berm so they were hidden, and she huddled against him gratefully.

"I miss my night-vision goggles," he whispered.

"I miss the dogs," Lucy whispered back.

"I didn't think we'd be in the swamp," he went on. "Bridge with lights, yes. Ship with lights, yes. Swamp, no."

"Okay," Lucy whispered. "Next time, I'll pack the night goggles."

"Next time," he said and laughed quietly. "God, I love you."

"What?" Lucy said.

He was quiet for a minute, and then he said, "I love you," and kissed the bridge of her nose. Then he pointed right, while Lucy was still breathless. "The speedboat is that way. I saw it coming in. Less than—"

"Wait a minute," Lucy said. "Do you mean—"

"Fuck you!" Nash's voice echoed through the air, and Lucy forgot everything else as J.T. froze and then pointed toward the other side of the berm and down about ten yards.

"The happy people are over there," he whispered. But then he nodded the other way, left along the road, back toward the Talmadge. "The crazy person and Pepper are probably coming from that way if they're not already here." He reached in her pocket and pulled out her cell phone, but before he could punch in the ghost's number, Lucy saw something move in the darkness and hissed a warning. J.T. looked right and nodded as he saw what she did: a figure staggering up onto the road, dropping one of the heavy plastic cases onto the gravel.

The figure straightened, and Lucy recognized Bryce. The actor turned and disappeared back down the other side of the berm. *"Bryce?"* she whispered, dumbfounded.

"Yeah, I was surprised, too," J.T. whispered back and finished punching the quick dial.

"Yep?" the ghost said, loud enough that Lucy could hear just from being close to the phone.

"We're at the RV," J.T. said, talking low. "Where's the girl?"

"Where's the chopper? You were supposed to land it, not do a touch-and-go."

"It's nearby. I'll tell you where it is when we have the girl."

Pepper, Lucy thought. *When we have Pepper.* She shivered. So close. So many things to go wrong.

"The girl's nearby. I tell you where when I get the chopper. And I don't see you at the RV. I saw three people at the boat. But not you and your lady friend. So let me see you." The phone went dead.

J.T. took the black case off the side of his pack and opened it, revealing the pieces of a sniper rifle set into the foam. He pulled out the stock.

"Where's Pepper?" Lucy asked.

"Close."

"Close, which way?"

"Since he's probably got this under cover with a long rifle, that way." J.T. nodded to the left. "I think we need to split up. I go after the ghost and Pepper, you stay here and watch if anything happens with our friends in the boat."

"No," Lucy said. "We're a team. We're not splitting up."

Wilder was silent for several moments. There was a distinct click as he slid the barrel into the receiver and locked it down. "All right. Got your gun?"

She fumbled with the holster and pulled out the Beretta, feeling about as stupid as she had the last time she'd held it. "Yes."

"Round in the chamber?"

"How can I tell? It's dark." *Jesus.* It's not like she did this every day. Only when she needed Pepper back. *Hold on, honey,* she thought.

"Here." J.T. took the gun, did something, and then handed it back. "You got a round in the chamber and the safety is off. So it's hot."

"Right."

"Put it back in the holster, carefully, and take this." J.T. held out his little machine gun. "It's also got a round in the chamber, safety off, set on automatic. You're going to spray a lot of bullets if you pull the trigger, so make sure there's a lot of people you want to shoot in the direction you aim."

"Thank you," Lucy whispered, thinking, *I'm gonna trip and take out half the swamp.* "But won't you need—"

"I've got this." J.T. held up the long rifle he'd just bolted together.

"Oh, good, yours is bigger." Lucy hefted the submachine gun. "You know, it's damn dark out here." She could hear the voices of Nash and Bryce and Althea, but she couldn't make out what they were saying, except that Nash was furious and Althea was bitching. They must have taken her hostage. *Should have thought that one through, boys.* She was pretty sure the swamp was not up to Althea's standards.

And the ghost, the fucking ghost had Pepper in this hellhole, all alone in the dark. "Pepper—"

"Ghost wants us over at the boat."

"With Nash?"

"Yep." J.T. got slowly to his feet, the long rifle in his hands. Lucy stood, too, trying desperately not to jar either gun and kill him. The submachine gun, in particular, felt wrong in her hands. Hell, nothing felt right at the moment, except for J.T. at her side.

"Let's go get our girl," J.T. said to her, and Lucy bit back tears.

"I love you, too," she said.

J.T. nodded. "Yeah, I know. Come on." Then he walked up onto the road.

Tyler slowed the ATV, cutting the engine noise, then finally killing it and letting the three-wheeled vehicle roll to a stop. He knew from his recon that he was about a hundred yards short of the rendezvous point.

He slung the Kid over one shoulder and with the other grabbed a bag of gear out of the cargo rack along with his sniper rifle. Then she kicked him, wriggling to get away, and he realized she'd been faking unconsciousness for a while. *Fucking stupid kid.*

He ran forward in the darkness with her over his shoulder. He could hear the helicopter behind him, in the distance and coming closer, but ahead he could hear voices raised in argument.

Fuck-ups. He halted less than fifty yards from the voices and knelt on the edge of the gravel road and dropped the Kid on the ground. The gag was tight around her mouth and her wide eyes were staring at him. He pulled out a long bayonet from his pack, held it high over his head as the Kid's eyes got even wider, and plunged it down.

Wilder paused as they got to a point just before the boat. He heard a voice raised high in a whine and recognized it immediately from four days of filming: Bryce was complaining about something. There was a glow ahead, but it was still damn dark.

Lucy bumped into him from behind.

"Careful," he whispered.

"Yeah, well, where's BMNT when you need it?"

"About six hours away."

Wilder nudged her and they drew closer to the boat. The glow was from a lantern of some sort, set next to Althea, who was sitting on the engine compartment, swinging her legs and looking into the cockpit. Nash was nowhere in sight, which wasn't good.

Bryce was pulling another of the plastic cases out of the water and onto the berm, floundering in the canal, struggling to hoist the case up. Physical labor. Wilder shook his head as they silently moved closer. That was hostage work. Bryce should have kidnapped somebody without a manicure.

They were less than ten feet away when Wilder called out, "Hey, Bryce."

Althea spun around on the fantail, shifting her attention from the cockpit. "J.T.? Is that you?"

"J.T.? J.T.'s here?" Bryce sounded delighted. He was waist deep in swamp water, and his face was turned up, searching the darkness blindly, while he slapped at mosquitoes.

"J.T., have you come to save me?" Althea called.

"Save *you*?" Bryce said, his whine turned up to eleven. "You're the one with the gun."

Oh, crap, Wilder thought. "Where's Nash?"

Both Althea and Bryce looked into the cockpit of the boat.

"Come on out, Nash," Wilder called. "We're working a trade here."

"Fuck you." Nash's head appeared above the windscreen. "I can't come out because the fucking bitch has got a gun on me."

"Althea?" Lucy said from beside him.

Well, it made more sense than Bryce, Wilder thought. Althea smiled innocently and Wilder could now see her right hand, a pistol in it pointed right at Nash.

"Can we go now?" Bryce asked.

"Poor puppy," Lucy said softly from behind Wilder. "Mary Vanity must be looking really good right about now."

"All we want is Pepper," Wilder called. "Although we'll take Bryce with us while you two work out your . . . problems."

Lucy's cell phone rang in Wilder's pocket, and he sensed Lucy's jump.

"It's okay," he said, trying not to remember all the firepower she had with the safeties off. He answered the phone. "Where is she?"

"East," the ghost said. "On the road."

Wilder turned and the beam of a flashlight suddenly appeared, shooting up from the swamp to a small figure on the edge of the road: Pepper, crying, her hands cuffed in front of her, a rope going from the cuffs to something pinned in the ground.

"*Son of a bitch,*" Lucy hissed and started forward but Wilder grabbed the back of her shirt and stopped her.

"*Wait.*"

"She's *crying.*" The rage ripped through Lucy's voice and Wilder felt the same, but he knew now was the time to be careful, very careful.

"Trust me," Wilder said, holding the phone tight against his chest so the ghost couldn't hear.

"I trust you," Lucy said, still staring at Pepper. "Now let me go get my kid."

Wilder put the phone to his head. "Let her go, and I'll order the chopper in."

"We had this conversation," the ghost said.

"You know I'm not giving you the chopper before I get the girl," Wilder countered. "Do you have a plan?"

"You're going to—"

Bryce yelped and there was a loud crash as he dropped the box.

Wilder turned to see Bryce, smeared with mud, lying on the top of the berm, the case he had been hauling up split open underneath him, its contents spilled out across the road, packing material and something bright green, which Wilder expected, and bright orange, which he did not.

"That orange thing does not look like jade," Althea said, moving along the edge of the boat to the berm, forgetting Nash behind her.

"Oh, crap," Wilder said, and even Lucy was still.

Althea had the gun in one hand, the lantern in the other. She reached Bryce and held the lantern up, looking down into the broken box.

She became very still. "What the hell is that?"

Bryce licked his lips, then clambered to his feet, picked up one of the shiny green things, and frowned at it. "I think it's a cucumber salt shaker. With a smiley face. See?" He turned it toward her, and when she didn't smile, he bent over and picked up one of the orange things. "Look. Carrots, too."

We're done, Wilder thought.

Althea let her gun hand drop. "Want to hear something funny about your jade, Nash?" she called back, her voice savage. "The fucking jade that was going to make all our fortunes? The jade you *tried to kill me over?*"

Wilder lifted his rifle and touched Lucy's shoulder. "Go get Pepper."

She nodded and was gone, and he was left to cover her, praying that the ghost wouldn't do anything stupid, and that Nash wouldn't take them all out when he realized he'd risked everything for comic cucumbers.

"I think the carrot's the girl," Bryce said, looking down at the pair in his hands, and then Nash made his move.

Lucy ran toward Pepper and the little girl saw her and said, *"Aunt Lucy!"* as Lucy stumbled and grabbed her, curling around her to shield her. "Almost there, honey."

She tugged on the rope and then began to move the bayonet it was tied to back and forth, trying to work it out of the ground.

"Aunt Lucy," Pepper said again, sobbing, leaning against her, "I'm scared," and Lucy thought, *Fucking bastards,* and kicked the bayonet with everything she had, and it came out of the dirt, wickedly sharp.

And then all hell broke loose.

. . .

As soon as Lucy was moving, Wilder had taken a quick glance over his shoulder, trying to locate Nash, but the stuntman had disappeared. *Bad development,* Wilder thought.

Althea was still staring at the broken box, but it was clear from her face that she was thinking fast. She took a deep breath. "Okay. I give up." She threw the gun down and held up her hands. "Call the police. I surrender."

"Doesn't work that way, you dumb bitch," Nash said, and Wilder saw him on the roadway behind her, a tall, lean silhouette with that goddamn fast-draw rig on his hip. "I *don't* give up."

Althea put her hands down. "Well, I do. I'm not going to jail. I'll deal. I know where Letsky is. I got the coordinates from—"

"Letsky's dead," Wilder said, not liking his current position with Nash in front and the ghost somewhere behind him, covering Nash. He looked east. Lucy had reached Pepper and was trying to work her free. He turned back. "It's over, Nash. The CIA blew Letsky and his boat up about twenty minutes ago."

Wilder saw Bryce straighten up holding Althea's gun pointed at Nash, and yelled, *"Get down."*

Althea hit the dirt and Bryce jerked in surprise and fell over backward as Wilder spun away from the clusterfuck by the boat to face the swamp and the ghost, snapping his sniper rifle up as he saw a muzzle flash in the blackness fifty yards away, past Lucy and Pepper. He fired on instinct, sending his own round directly into the flash. A second muzzle flash split the darkness, but this one was long and upright, firing into the air, and Wilder knew he'd hit the ghost, who'd tumbled backward as he'd fired a second time. Wilder fired two more quick rounds for insurance, then he spun about once more, going to one knee, in Nash's direction.

Lucy pushed herself off Pepper and pulled the little girl to her feet as she sprinted down the road, away from J.T., which was just so wrong, not knowing who had shot who, only knowing she had to get Pepper out of there. Then the helicopter was landing, LaFavre setting it down on firm ground, and she ran under the blades, not even thinking about it this time, desperate to get Pepper inside.

"What happened?" LaFavre yelled.

"Take her," Lucy said and shoved Pepper up into the copter.

"No, *Aunt Lucy,*" Pepper sobbed, holding out her arms to her, and Lucy yelled, "Be brave, be Wonder Woman, I have to get J.T.," and ran back down the berm, hell-bent for leather with her submachine gun in her hand, heading for the lantern glow where J.T. was facing down the bad guys alone.

She ran straight into Althea, who was crouching while running along the berm. Althea grabbed her and said, "They kidnapped me, Lucy, it wasn't my fault," as Lucy asked, *"Where's J.T.?"*

"I don't know. I ran when everyone started shooting." Althea looked around. "I don't even know where *we* are."

"Road's right there." Lucy pointed up the berm. "Follow it back the way I came and you'll see a helicopter. You can hear it, right? Get in. The pilot likes big boobs." *And you're one of the biggest boobs I know.* She tried to get around Althea to get to J.T. but the actress held on.

"You know," Althea said. "I really think you're a great director, and I'd love to work with you again—"

Lucy shoved her in the direction of the helicopter and took off running, hoping that nobody was bleeding into the dirt up ahead since there hadn't been any more gunfire—

She ran full into Bryce, who wasn't even pretending to crouch.

"Lucy!" he said, grabbing on to her. "I almost got shot."

"Helicopter," she said, shoving him past her. "That way."

Then she ran on to the end of the road.

Wilder could feel insanity radiating off Nash, who was now alone on the gravel road, slowly walking toward him, closing the gap. Nash's gun was still in its holster, and Wilder realized Nash hadn't drawn while his back was turned because he wanted a goddamn showdown. Wilder let the sniper rifle drop in the dirt to gain Lucy and Pepper time to escape as he faced Nash.

High Noon, Wilder thought, feeling the weight of the Glock in his thigh holster.

The townsfolk had cleared out, the flunkies were done in, and it was man on man. *I'm the good guy. Will Kane wins.*

Except Nash believed in this shit and had prepared for it. Wilder knew there was no way he could get the Glock out of its thigh rig before Nash had his gun clear of the quick-draw rig.

Shouldn't have made fun of that. "You already shot me once," he called. "Wasn't that enough?"

"But you didn't die," Nash said. "The minute you stepped on that fucking bridge that first day, I should have shot you down. You ruined everything."

"You were never going to get the jade, Nash," Wilder said. "The CIA was watching from the beginning, trying to get Letsky. That's where those cucumbers came from. Cut your losses—"

"I don't lose," Nash said, his voice dead. He stopped fifteen feet away and lowered his head. "Draw, asshole."

Fuck, Wilder thought, *I'm dead,* and then Lucy stumbled onto the berm and brought up the submachine gun, and Nash turned just a fraction of a fraction toward her as she sprayed bullets into the dirt at his feet and Wilder went for his Glock.

Nash corrected, his hand a flash for the butt of his revolver, and Wilder squeezed off two shots as he brought the Glock up, the first too soon but hitting Nash in the leg as the stuntman fired, knocking his shot off by a fraction, the second right beside it, kicking Nash's entire body backward.

Wilder held the Glock level, staring at Nash's body, his finger tense on the trigger, waiting for any sign of life. Nothing.

He removed his finger from the trigger and walked forward.

His hot load had gone right through Nash's vest and into his heart.

"Oh, God." Lucy dropped her gun, and then she was in his arms. "Are you all right?" she said, as he held on to her. "I couldn't leave you. Not alone, you said we were a team, I couldn't—"

He kissed her hard and she kissed him back and he thought, *That was too damn close,* and held her tight.

"I couldn't leave you," she said again into his neck. "Ever, I couldn't leave you."

He drew a deep breath. "I know."

She looked back at Nash's body. "So it's over, right?"

"It's over," Wilder said.

"I should feel sorry for him," she said. "I was *married* to him, but he took my Pepper and I can't. I'm just glad he's dead."

"I know."

She turned back to him. "What about the ghost? Is he—"

"I hit him," Wilder said. "He's either dead or gone. I'm betting dead." He pulled her along the road toward the helicopter. "Let's call Crawford in to clean up this mess and then go home."

"We don't have a home," Lucy said, sounding exhausted. "I gave my loft to Gloom. All we have is a helicopter and a camper."

"Well then, let's go make a home," Wilder said and pushed her ahead of him down the road, away from what was left of Nash.

LaFavre lifted the chopper off the ground, and Lucy held Pepper close, rocking her a little as they cleared the swamp. Pepper had stopped crying, LaFavre working his magic on her, and then Althea cuddling her until Lucy got back but then she'd climbed into Lucy's lap so fast she'd almost fallen off the other side. J.T. was next to them, and Pepper was holding on to his camouflage shirt with one hand even as she curled herself closer to Lucy. Bryce was seated cross-legged on the floor, somewhere between relieved and aggrieved, and Althea was in front, in the copilot's seat, leaning toward LaFavre.

"I was very scared," Pepper said, close to sobbing.

"I know," Lucy said, "but you were very brave."

"Yes, you were," J.T. said, and put his arms around them both. "You were like Wonder Woman."

"I even got tied up," Pepper said, straightening a little as her almost-sobs turned to sniffs.

"*Just* like Wonder Woman," Lucy said.

"Yeah," Pepper said, dragging a dirty hand across her dirtier cheek, keeping J.T.'s shirt clutched in the other. She sniffed again, but she seemed distracted, and when J.T. patted her back, she let her head rest on his arm, much calmer.

"You know," Bryce said, from his seat on the floor, with a glance up front, "I never told *People who* I was marrying. I just *hinted*."

Lucy took her eyes off Pepper long enough to feel sorry for him, dirty and mosquito-chewed while his ex-fiancée flirted with the guy in the great flight jacket. "Mary Vanity is saving up for new boobs just for you."

"Boobs?" Pepper said.

Bryce looked touched. "She's a great girl."

"Gonna be greater," J.T. said, and started to laugh.

Lucy put her cheek on Pepper's hair and hugged her closer. She was going to laugh again, too. As soon as she could do it without crying. There was no crying in Special Forces.

In the front seat, Althea leaned farther toward LaFavre, her camisole pulled even lower than usual. "Do you carry a weapon?"

For crying out loud, he's flying the helicopter, Lucy thought, but LaFavre just grinned at her, his eyes hidden behind the night-vision goggles.

"I sure do, darlin'," he said. "Want to see it?"

Lucy nudged J.T. "Aren't you going to warn him?"

"Yeah," J.T. said. "I'm gonna tell him if he's not careful, she's going to show up naked in his bed and touch his gun."

Lucy started to laugh and felt the tears start instead. "Oh, God."

"Hey," J.T. said, his voice soft. He tugged gently on her braid and then kissed her cheek. "It's okay."

"I should get lots of Wonder Woman stuff for this," Pepper said from between them, her voice still a little quivery. "I was very brave."

"Yes, you were," Lucy said, forcing back the tears. "So was I. I should get lots of stuff, too."

"Plan on it," J.T. said.

She looked at him, so close in the dark, the same grim, monosyllabic guy who'd walked onto her bridge four days ago, and thought, *Will Kane. And he loves me. Who knew?* and began to smile.

"Hold on, my friends," LaFavre called out and banked the chopper toward the roadway of the Eugene Talmadge Memorial Bridge. They flew over all the flashing police and fire-truck lights and the still burning armored car, right between the lines of cables, underneath the two towers.

"Wow!" Pepper said, straightening, and J.T. grinned at her.

"Do you use hot loads?" Althea asked LaFavre.

"Me marrying a makeup girl," Bryce said. "It's like *Pretty Woman*. Without the hooker."

"I deserve a *lot* of Wonder Woman stuff," Pepper said.

"Me too," J.T. said.

Lucy started to laugh.

"Hey," J.T. said, trying to look wounded and grinning instead.

"Not you," Lucy said. "It's just that I can hear them playing my song." She leaned toward him and kissed him hard.

"Lots of good stuff," Pepper said, and snuggled down between them.

It was weird being shot. Tyler wasn't used to it. It slowed him down considerably, especially with the swamp full of people, probably looking for him. Maybe he shouldn't have shot at the Actor, but it had been instinct, just like he'd been trained.

He slogged on through the swamp, moving slower now, finally stopping to lean against a mudbank. He just couldn't figure how he'd missed. He'd never missed before. Ever. Put the crosshairs on them and they died, and he'd had the crosshairs on the Actor, the dumb shit who'd picked up that gun—

Then he remembered the Kid knocking over the rifle, the scope hitting the ground. The scope. Knocked out of alignment by that fucking Kid.

Luck's running out, he thought, and slumped against the dirt mound, watching his blood seep into the water. Lots of blood. He couldn't stop it anymore. And he was so cold. Cold as Moot. No, colder. Cold as Finnegan.

He heard a splash and saw the V in the water, one eye coming toward him.

Women, he thought as the swamp grew dark before his eyes.

Always wanting a piece of you.